BLACKWELL'S PARADISE

BLACKWELL'S PARADISE

by

V.E. Ulett

Old Salt Press

www.OldSaltPress.com

Blackwell's Paradise - Copyright © 2014 by Eva Ulett

Published by Old Salt Press
Old Salt Press, LLC is based in Jersey City, New Jersey
with an affiliate in New Zealand

978-0-9882360-5-9

National Library of New Zealand Cataloguing-in-Publication Data

Ulett, V. E., 1962-
Blackwell's paradise / V.E. Ulett.
(Blackwell's adventures ; 2)
ISBN 978-0-9882360-5-9 (pbk.) —ISBN 978-0-9922636-6-9 (PDF)
I. Title. II. Series: Ulett, V. E. 1962-. Blackwell's adventures ; bk. 2.
813.6—dc 23

Cover design by Julie K. Rose & Broos Campbell
Natives and Captain Cook (1728-79) by Angus McBride, and Polynesian clubs and insignia of rank, from 'The History of Mankind', Vol. 1, by Prof. Friedrich Ratzel reproduced by arrangement with Bridgeman Art Library.
Interior design elements by Sabrina Frontiero

Publisher's Note:

This is a work of historical fiction. Certain characters and their actions may have been inspired by historical individuals and events. The characters in the novel, however, represent the work of the author's imagination. Any resemblance to actual persons, living or dead, is entirely coincidental.

CHAPTER ONE

Captain Blackwell had tried to love her but she was an awkward griping beast, and he found he could not. It was Sunday and the humiliation of the day's inspection of the men at divisions and the ship before Vice-Admiral Lord Nelson was still fresh in his consciousness, though it approached the mid point of the first watch. Captain Blackwell swayed on his quarterdeck with the motion of *Assurance*, 44, the unweatherly, aged fifth rate he'd once considered a plum when appointed to command her, at the behest and through the influence of his wife's father.

A plum was not what Captain Blackwell and Lord Nelson had found in that day's inspection, unless it was a rotten one. Captain Blackwell had known for some time of course, since first taking her out that *Assurance* was suffering very much in her knees, and he suspected her planking and timbers were three parts decayed. She made tremendous leeway and had to be pumped constantly, wearing the men down and leaving them with less will and spirit for sail handling and gunnery exercises. Captain Blackwell knew it all and abhorred it, yet to have the whole confirmed by a seaman of Lord Nelson's stature made him exceedingly glum.

A long conversation had followed the inspection, when Lord Nelson advised a survey of *Assurance* before taking her into the Pacific. "You cannot possibly take her far foreign, Captain Blackwell. The brute will kill you."

Captain Blackwell could not disagree. But a survey might, and probably would, kill other matters close to his heart. The commission to take *Assurance* into the Pacific for surveying and protection of trade, the leave he had in his orders to carry his wife on the cruise, were likely to disappear should he raise the hue and cry. He was near to certain *Assurance* would be condemned and then there should be no guarantee he'd be given another ship in a peacetime Navy, or a mission that so exactly suited his interests.

Yet it wouldn't be in his interests, nor those of his new wife Mercedes, to say nothing of *Assurance's* officers and crew, to die in an aged and used up man-of-war rounding Cape Horn. Captain Blackwell had been miserable for many days thinking over the issue of his ship, and his discomfort had been trebled when he was assigned to carry Lord Nelson to England. Before starting his cruise he was to bring the hero home, along with Lord and Lady Hamilton and their suite.

He tried to suffer with his current state of conflicted feelings privately; he'd even conceived the notion Admiral Gambier knowingly assigned him an un-seaworthy command as a means of ridding himself of Mercedes. A natural child was an inconvenient thing for an evangelical admiral. But to have to do the civil with his important guests, and act as though his professional life were not unraveling, was almost more than Captain Blackwell could manage.

He might have been at a stand but for Mercedes supporting him. She was very dear to Captain Blackwell, she'd never once repelled him when he'd tried to board. It was she had taken the tiller of this peculiar social barge with Lord Nelson, Nelson's dolly — as Captain Blackwell thought of Lady Hamilton — and Lady Hamilton's diplomat husband. He wouldn't have known how to proceed, but Mercedes arranged their sleeping quarters with neither fuss nor outcry. They moved to the Master's cabin and gave over to Lord Nelson the captain's sleeping quarters with its fixed berth large enough for two, and the exclusive use of the great cabin. Lady Hamilton ostensibly occupied Mercedes' little sleeping space, and her husband had the coach.

One of the longest evenings of his life had been lived in company of his guests, and had Mercedes not been beside him setting an example of good breeding he didn't know how he would have come through. It was their fifth evening out of Gibraltar and Captain and Mrs. Blackwell were invited to supper in the great cabin. After supper Lady Hamilton was to treat them to her famous Attitudes, a pantomime performance wherein she struck poses in various costumes.

The whole affair made Captain Blackwell frankly apprehensive. He was extremely concerned Mercedes not be slighted by his guests, and more particularly not by Lady Hamilton. Mercedes' mother might have been a lady of easy virtue but Captain Blackwell's wife had never been one, which could not be truthfully said of Nelson's dolly.

In the event Captain Blackwell hardly knew where to direct his gaze before the sight of Emma Hamilton as the plumpest Diana The Huntress and Circe he had ever seen. He wondered a man of sense like Lord Nelson could countenance such mummery. But the Vice-Admiral sat by with a smile that seemed to suggest he could not imagine any man despising Emma's charms. Captain Blackwell sympathized with Lord Hamilton. The old diplomat rose halfway through the performance and in his courtly way claimed age's prerogative of retiring early.

The rest of them had been obliged to flog through the remainder of Emma's Attitudes. The entire experience reminded Captain Blackwell of nothing so much as the performance he'd seen in Ceuta, when the Dey of Oran's harem danced at a feast celebrating Ramadan. He'd been supremely uncomfortable then as well, unsure where to look, struggling to keep a neutral countenance. At last it was over, Lady Hamilton concluded in the costume of a dancing girl. She tripped over to them as though coming off a grand stage instead of taking the few steps separating them in the great cabin.

Captain Blackwell couldn't utter a word; but Mercedes, in the gentlest tone, complimented Lady Hamilton on how lifelike her Attitudes were.

"Do you think so, indeed?" Emma cried. "This costume is 'The Favorite of the Harem'. I understand you were in a seraglio, Mrs. Blackwell, so I would make sure you should know."

Captain Blackwell would have been on his feet next moment had Mercedes not answered straightaway, "Yes, that's true Lady Hamilton, the Dey of Oran's harem. And I do assure

3

you, your portrayal is so very like. It is indeed, even more like than the Dey's ladies themselves."

They all stared at Mercedes, and she returned them a frank level gaze. Captain Blackwell thought she'd gone too far making sport of an aging English matron; the entire evening had gone on too long and ought to end. But Nelson's dolly clapped her hands and exclaimed over Mercedes' great compliment. She insisted on frequently repeating that she was more like than the Dey's ladies themselves. Captain Blackwell had never been more relieved to get away from a social engagement, even if it were to retire to the cramped Master's cabin. Two cots awaited them there, one lower than the other. Sailors conceived it easier for a lady to climb into a cot low slung.

On the quarterdeck Captain Blackwell felt ready to retire to his cot. He was worn out with contemplation of the problems of ship and survey, but he'd been unwilling to quit the deck. There was an ugly cross-grained sea running, and *Assurance* was shipping even more than her usual load of sea. Captain Blackwell could hear the pumps clanging only when he searched for the sound, so accustomed had his ear become to their constant operation. A dense haze lay over the water, obscuring visibility in all directions. He kept the deck another glass and then decided to go below.

"The deck is yours, Mr. Verson. Keep her very well thus."

He would have been ashamed to admit he longed for his berth in the captain's sleeping quarters. His double berth with bedclothes made by Mercedes of fine soft Egyptian cotton, a wedding gift from those same ladies of the Dey's harem. He'd undoubtedly gone a little soft since his marriage. Where before he'd been accustomed to long, wet nights on the quarterdeck and retiring to a few hours rest in a solitary cot, he now missed lying in fine sheets with a willing woman. That was Lord Nelson's privilege to enjoy at the moment. Captain Blackwell made his way below to the Master's cabin in the gunroom, and separate cots with purser's blankets for him and his lady.

He stepped carefully into the cabin, passing his sentry outside the flimsy door — he still was the ship's captain — and entered as quietly as his near sixteen stone allowed. But he found

Mercedes lying awake in her cot, with a cat curled on her mid-section, and the cabin lit by a dark lantern. She'd been unwell the last few days, since the morning following the appalling dinner party with Lord Nelson. It was unusual for Mercedes; she'd been strong enough to survive cholera in Ceuta, and in Captain Blackwell's experience she'd always been a healthful companion. Yet he shouldn't wonder that evening with their guests had made her ill.

He came and bent over her in the cot. "How do you do, sweetheart?"

"Very much better. Would you put Queenie down?"

Queenie was Mercedes' cat, a tawny-coated miniature wild beast that Captain Blackwell had named after he'd beheld her domineering ways. He obliged Mercedes, lifting Queenie off her, setting the cat gently on her neat feet and even opening the door for her when she departed, tail up, to do her nightly round of the ship.

"Thank you for your kindness to me these last days." Mercedes held her hand out to him.

"What, sweetheart? In sickness and in health, you know." He took her hand, loosening his stock with the other.

"I am in health now, and truly I should like to show you my gratitude." Mercedes tossed aside the bedclothes, revealing her lovely naked body.

"Oh, Mercy." They had only been intimate once since moving into the Master's cabin with its canvas walls, and that had been standing up. "These timbers are three parts rotten, and I'm afraid we shall both end up on the deck if I add my weight to yours."

Mercedes sat up in the cot and pulled him close. "Pretend you are a midshipman again. Surely you took a girl or two into your cot?"

He might not have been persuaded even then; he was no longer a stripling midshipman, he was a heavy, close to middle aged post captain; but when Mercedes bent her knees and brought her shapely legs on either edge of the cot, Captain Blackwell could no longer hold back.

It was not easy to keep the bulk of his weight off her in the canvas bed. Lovemaking in a cot was a challenge, but Captain Blackwell was determined to see it through. As always when shipboard they were quiet. He was bringing Mercedes to that state he delighted to see her in — her hair disarrayed on the bolster, her cheeks flushed, her parted lips about to whisper his name, a gaze of love and passion that surprised him still — when there was a report like the sound of a 32-pounder and the ship was brought violently aback.

The cleat holding one end of the cot tore out of the beam overhead and in the tremendous lee lurch Captain Blackwell and Mercedes were thrown to the deck.

He landed uppermost. "Dear God, Mercedes!"

Captain Blackwell was on his feet and dressing. So ingrained was his training in the Navy that he was preparing himself to go on deck even before kneeling to see to his wife.

"What is it, Jim, what's happened?"

Captain Blackwell helped her to her feet. Naked and shaking, she looked at him with unfocused eyes.

"Have I crushed you?"

"Captain Blackwell, sir," a midshipman's voice called through the canvas. "Mr. Verson's duty, sir, and we've struck — "

"Yes, yes, Mr. Hogan, I shall be on deck directly. Don't come in here, youngster, as you value your life!" The latch had turned under the midshipman's anxious hand.

"Mercedes, we must get you dressed."

"Yes." She'd found her shift and put it on, but she was unable to manage the laces of her corset and turned to Captain Blackwell. "Help me, if you please."

"Why do you wear the bloody thing? You have the trimmest waist I've ever seen." He did up the laces in an instant; he was after all a seaman, used to cordage and complex knots.

"I don't think you should like it were my breasts around my waist when I reach forty. You must go, I can manage."

"Can you, sweetheart?" Captain Blackwell looked earnestly into her face. "Listen to me now. The sentry will bring you to me when you are ready. Lord Nelson may offer you a place in his launch, you must not accept. That dolly of his might panic, and cause merry hell in an open boat."

Captain Blackwell bent and put his cheek against hers, and then he took up his sword and jacket and went out the door.

CHAPTER TWO

Mercedes heard Captain Blackwell speak to the sentry outside the Master's cabin and then his retreating steps as he rushed to the quarterdeck. She believed he was mistaken about Emma Hamilton, she was a lady prepared to cling to life if ever there was one, but Mercedes' thoughts were strangely disordered. She was having trouble dressing herself in the attire best suited to the present crisis, though she'd really no idea the nature of the emergency. When they'd crashed to the deck Captain Blackwell's weight atop her had been bad enough, worse was the tremendous knock of her head against the planks, and then a second rebounding concussion.

She managed to pull on the clothes at last, breeches, shirt, stockings, boots, jacket and waistcoat, greatcoat over all. Mercedes' facilities must have been far more disordered were she to forget the sash into which were sewn her mother's jewels, and Captain Blackwell's purse; she tied these round her waist beneath her shirt.

She opened the door to the cabin and stepped out into the naval world. Mr. Hoffinger of His Majesty's Marines saluted. The entire crew saluted her, but the marines were particularly smart about the courtesy. "Captain Blackwell is forward on the gun deck, Ma'am, this way."

The marine lieutenant led Mercedes forward, past crowds of men hurrying up on deck and more running down below. There was a minute gun firing a signal of distress. Told to follow, she trailed dumb and confused behind Captain Blackwell on the starboard side and Mr. Bransford, second lieutenant, on the larboard as they led parties of men down the row of guns, drawing the charges.

They drew the remaining charges of the main deck guns, and then moved on deck to the bow chasers and the quarterdeck carronades. No one spoke to her, and Mercedes remained ignorant of what had caused this controlled chaos. Midshipmen and *Assurance's* lieutenants ran up and conferred with Captain Blackwell at intervals. She heard him give orders for the provisioning of the boats.

"Four and half foot of water in the well, sir, and three on the lower deck." *Assurance's* carpenter reported to Captain Blackwell.

Mercedes heard the carpenter's words at the same time the first cramp doubled her over. She clung to a stanchion on the quarterdeck, the sensation like a hand inside her squeezing her innards. The pain was not where it had been when she suffered from the cholera; this was lower down and resembled the cramps of adolescent girlhood, increased twenty fold.

"What is it, Missus, did you eat something?"

Mercedes straightened with an effort. "I must have done." She stared at young Jack Verson, the first lieutenant's son. "What's happened to the ship, Jack?"

"Why, she's struck. Tore out her rudder, though Captain's shipped another, but she's hulled. A terrible great hole, Missus, and she's taking on water like a...like a ..." the boy stopped short.

"But struck what? Were we not at sea, what could we have struck?" Mercedes felt she could question six-year-old Jack Verson without breach of naval etiquette.

"No one knows, Madame." Lord Nelson stepped over from the taffrail. "But struck she has, and there is indeed a terrible great hole. I saw it myself." The Vice-Admiral nodded to young Goodman Jack, who bowed in return. "Your husband is steering for Cork and we shall lower away the boats in a moment. God send they swim in this sea."

"Amen, sir." Mercedes and Jack chimed together.

"May I offer you a seat in my launch, Mrs. Blackwell?"

"You are very kind sir. But I cannot accept. No, thank you, sir."

"You are under other orders, I apprehend." Lord Nelson gave her his penetrating stare.

"Yes, sir, that would be the way of it."

"Then you are unique, Mrs. Blackwell. For I have never met a woman able to follow orders, they always will do as they please. Orders are not for them — at least I never yet knew one who obeyed."

Lord Nelson paused as though awaiting Mercedes' response, but what reply could she make to such a speech. She studied Lord Nelson in the gloom of the night. He was very different from Captain Blackwell; small, frail, crippled and half blind; yet that was merely the outside of the man. In character, in the inward man, Mercedes sensed similarities between the Vice-Admiral and the Captain. Virility, the air of command, an authority that had nothing to do with height or build, but was founded on experience, discipline, and natural boldness. When it was clear Mercedes did not wish to comment; her silence must have struck the Vice-Admiral as singular, given the company he was used to keep; Lord Nelson spoke again.

"Captain Blackwell will run her ashore on the coast of Ireland, if ever he can. He has not sufficient boats. The jolly boat was dashed against the ship half a glass since when some over eager landsmen — "

"Grass coaming lubbers," Jack Verson muttered.

"Just so," the Vice-Admiral said. "They tried to launch her ahead of orders. Now, you will not reconsider, Mrs. Blackwell?"

"No, sir, thank you." Mercedes curtsied. "Godspeed to you and Lord and Lady Hamilton."

"I shall tell Captain Blackwell, he is not to stay with the ship." Lord Nelson gave her a significant glare.

"Yes, sir. Thank you, sir. Thank you very much indeed."

Her relief was great, at the same moment she could hardly credit her husband might be required to stay on a sinking ship. Lord Nelson took Captain Blackwell aside on the quarterdeck, with *Assurance's* officers at one remove, and where she and all the other supernumeraries attending on the quarterdeck might see.

Their conference concluded, and Lord Nelson made for the great cabin to bring up his companions. Captain Blackwell moved to the larboard main chains where the important guests would leave his ship. He roared for marines, sideboys, and the bosun and his mates to attend the Vice-Admiral's departure.

Mercedes was near the mainmast when the next spasm came on. She was standing behind Captain Blackwell and Narhilla, who had been assisting Lord Nelson and his party over the side into the Vice-Admiral's launch. When the pain ebbed Mercedes crept over and peered at the launch and her people. How they'd managed to get Lord and Lady Hamilton into the boat with the sea heaving to such a degree she didn't know, but there they sat with nearly identical pale frightened faces. Mercedes supposed it could only have been done by the skill of the British seamen.

Narhilla, Captain Blackwell's coxswain and one of his followers, turned round. "Never a care, sir. Tom Allen will see them through." He spoke of Lord Nelson's coxswain, the best type of seaman.

"Amen to that." Captain Blackwell came and gently took Mercedes' arm, as she'd been longing he should do.

"Sir! Captain Blackwell, sir!" Mr. Bowles, midshipman, came panting up from below. "Some of the hands have broken into the spirit room."

Captain Blackwell dropped Mercedes' arm and drew his sword. "Marines there! Follow me."

The next hour was a blur of pain and anxiety for Mercedes. Captain Blackwell left the deck, and then reappeared as one emergency succeeded another. When he was not on deck Mercedes was in the charge of Mr. Verson, she stood side by side with young Jack for much of the time. The little boy was the only one aware of Mercedes' suffering. He held her hand to comfort her, not because he was afraid of sinking in a ship at sea.

The same could not be said for one part of *Assurance's* crew, who'd overwhelmed the marines at the spirit room door, determined to die drunk as Davey's sow. The majority of the men attacking the marine guard had never shipped under Captain Blackwell before. These raw hands were positively shocked at his ferocity when he leapt into the midst of their revel and began knocking heads together. His sword was in his hand, but he used only the flat of it and the hilt, dealing out sharp blows. The marines, formerly lined up seated against the bulkhead, rose and returned to their duty, and soon the malefactors were overcome. The disconsolate men were marched away either to the main deck to await the order to board the boats, or to the forepeak where the ship's surgeon, Doctor VanArsdel, would patch up their broken heads.

On deck the fog had lifted and they were able to make out the coastline at about three miles distance. Captain Blackwell immediately ordered the ship's boats launched. The lieutenants and young gentlemen having been assigned to specific boats with their divisions, Captain Blackwell distributed the awkward sods that had broken into the spirit room into the boats, each with its complement of marines. Earlier he'd asked Mr. Verson to call for volunteers to stay with the ship and run her on shore.

It was a laborious, dangerous task launching *Assurance's* four remaining boats. But the barge, launch, and the two cutters were far more seaworthy than the crippled frigate, once the danger of dashing against *Assurance* was past. Captain Blackwell, Mercedes, and the remaining Assurances, watched the boats ship their oars and pull for their lives in the heaving sea.

Under main and mizzen staysails, making astonishing leeway, Captain Blackwell conned the ship. He attempted to follow in the wake of his boats heading for shore. When they were within a mile of land they encountered a sand bank running parallel with the shore. *Assurance*, wallowing along, was well in back of her boats.

Breakers were exploding against the sand bank with a continuous roar. The boats had to wait a chance, lying on their oars, for a break in the succession of waves in order to pull to calmer waters. The launch, in the lead, took an opportunity and rowing with a mad zeal made it to the other side of the bank. The red and blue cutters likewise ran through intact. The barge, however, jibed at the last second and was instantly capsized. Men, oars, boat, buckets, provisions were tossed into the sea like a handful of pebbles on a pond.

Captain Blackwell saw the wreckage as *Assurance* passed. He was searching for a gap in the breakers that might denote a broader channel, a deepening of the water. He found none. Afraid to run clear of the beach Captain Blackwell called, "Helm hard a-port."

Assurance was brought violently aback, fast on the sandbank. The lurch of the ship was not as wrenching as when they'd first struck, she'd been making only a few knots. The wind blowing right on shore and the following sea pushed *Assurance* into the bay beyond the sand bank. But *Assurance's* rotten bottom was beat in, her back broke, and she would soon go to pieces.

For the second time that evening Captain Blackwell assisted Mercedes to her feet. She looked dreadfully shaken and it was in his mind, as he stood on the canting deck with his broken ship beneath him, that he should have compelled her to go into the launch with Mr. Verson. He'd nearly done so, but Mercedes was at his side as the launch was manned, and sensing what was in his mind she'd said, "Don't make me part from you, Jim." It was probably her calling him that name, which she never did except during their intimacy, caused him to relent.

Now his concern was to get Mercedes safely ashore and yet be the last to leave the ship. He and Mercedes could swim but the water would be mortal cold, and the greater number of his men could not.

"All hands!" he called. "Shipmates, we are going to build a raft."

He set men to collecting empty water casks, several had floated to the main deck where inches of water covered the gun carriages. They hunted for carpentry tools, and began taking down bulkheads for planking. In the event the raft was not needed, the red cutter with Mr. Bowles commanding came alongside *Assurance*. But the activity had kept the men in spirits, and from thoughts of drowning in the surf within sight of safety and the beach.

Captain Blackwell and Narhilla handed Mercedes into the cutter, one on either side of her, just as they'd done for the Vice-Admiral.

"God bless you, Mr. Bowles," Mercedes said.

"And you too, ma'am." Mr. Bowles, ever gallant, made a bow from the waist with a smile lighting his exhausted face.

Mercedes sat down in the stern, one arm clutching her waist. Captain Blackwell walked the length of *Assurance's* deck one last time, with his commission to take her into the Pacific in his jacket pocket, and the ship's log and books under his arm. He stepped off *Assurance,* the last to leave her deck, now almost on a level with the cutter's.

"Oh!" Mercedes cried, after the order had been given to pull away.

Captain Blackwell leaned down to her. "What is it?"

"Queenie! We did not take Queenie off."

Captain Blackwell's face went blank.

"Begging your honor's pardon, and Missus," McMurtry said. "But I seen Queenie go aboard the Vice-Admiral's launch."

"Aye, sir. Me too, sir," piped up stern oar.

"Well, there you have it," Captain Blackwell said. "And ain't it just like her."

The men responded with a low chuckle, a bit freer with their captain under the circumstances.

"Pull away."

CHAPTER THREE

Even in the dark of night Mercedes could see there was nothing like two hundred eighty men on the beach. Those closest did give a ragged cheer as their captain came ashore. Forty men were presumed dead in the capsizing of the barge, and it appeared many more had simply walked off inland when they came ashore. To prevent further desertions the marines had set up a perimeter of the encampment. Captain Blackwell left Mercedes with the red cutter in the company of two Marine privates and a corporal, and walked off with Mr. Bowles to inspect the camp.

Mr. Bowles returned a half hour later. Mercedes was sitting in the cutter with both arms wrapped around her body. There was no longer any mystery over what ailed her, she'd felt the first warm blood sliding out of her in the boat, when she'd had the scare about Queenie.

"Captain sends his compliments, ma'am, and I am to inform you Mr. Verson has taken a party inland for relief," Mr. Bowles said. "All remaining officers and petty officers are ashore excepting those lost in the barge, and he shall return to you directly."

"Thank you, Mr. Bowles." Mercedes gasped, turning her face from the young man. "Won't you sit down? Forgive me for saying so, but you have the look of a foundered horse."

The young gentleman Mr. Bowles, seventeen years old, thanked her kindly and collapsed in the bow of the cutter, going instantly to sleep. Mercedes longed for her cot aboard *Assurance,* for the little sleeping cabin Captain Blackwell had built for her, similar to the one she'd had aboard *Inconstant*, the 28 gun frigate he'd commanded when they'd first met. More particularly she wished for the quarter gallery, the captain's private toilet in the stern of the ship. Soon she would have to lie down in the bottom of the boat, alongside Mr. Bowles, and let the miscarriage happen.

She was still sitting in the boat, bowed over, when Captain Blackwell returned. He went to Mr. Bowles and shook him awake.

"Sir!" Mr. Bowles sat up.

"I'm taking my gig's crew inland to find a house where Mrs. Blackwell can lie. You are to remain here with Mr. Bransford and Mr. Wilson." Captain Blackwell paused. "You should stand for lieutenant while we are on the beach, Mr. Bowles, I shall give you a certificate. If I had a ship to command, you should be acting third lieutenant."

"Thank you, sir," Mr. Bowles said, hastening to add, "aye, aye, sir."

"Give you joy, Mr. Bowles." Mercedes voice came faint from the stern.

She almost wished to stay on the beach, to be left alone and to get on with what was coming. But it was unthinkable to argue with Captain Blackwell, and she stood without a word and leaned on the arm he offered.

It was a quarter mile to the nearest homestead. Though not far in distance the way was over rocky, uneven ground and when they were at last on a level track Captain Blackwell moved to head the party. Later he returned to her, where she'd fallen back in the column. Normally she could match the pace of the men, and Mercedes was sorry to be a drag upon him.

She remained at the end of the file until they stopped before a cottage, almost a hut, with a lean-to alongside sheltering the animals. Captain Blackwell came to her and led her up to the cottage door. He gave the door a few resounding raps.

Mercedes stood with the men listening to the immediate stirring and shuffling inside the dwelling. A baby began to cry, and at once Mercedes felt an increase in the flow from her body. The blood would be soaking her breeches by now. She closed her eyes for a moment, before the door was opened and lantern light shone out.

"Forgive the intrusion. I'm Captain Blackwell of His Majesty's Ship *Assurance*. There's been a wreck. Did you not hear the gun?"

Captain Blackwell spoke to a grave faced, square jawed man holding up a lantern in one thick fist. Beside the man in the doorway was a sandy haired boy of eleven or twelve.

"What if I did?" the man replied. "You British want no interference from us."

Behind Captain Blackwell his men shifted uneasily. A woman's urgent whisper came from inside the cottage.

"I seek your charity, sir. I have my wife with me. Might she lie at your hearth out of the weather? My men and I will take shelter in your barn, with your leave. In the morning we depart for the nearest village."

"Caleb!" A stout woman pushed the man aside and addressed Captain Blackwell. "Where is your good wife, sir? She must certainly come in, there is room by the hearth with the little ones."

"Thank you, Ma'am, this is Mrs. Blackwell." Captain Blackwell turned to Mercedes. The cottagers and the boy looked startled, they'd no doubt taken Mercedes for the captain's aide-de-camp.

"I am very much obliged to you," Mercedes said.

The Irish cottagers smiled at the sound of a soft feminine voice, as did many of the men standing behind Captain Blackwell.

While the men were settling in straw in the lean to, Mercedes took Captain Blackwell aside. "James, take this." She lifted her shirt and unwound the sash of jewels and pressed it into Captain Blackwell's hand, along with his purse.

"Why, bless you sweetheart. I did not think of it. How fortunate you did. Else where should we be?" Captain Blackwell nearly smiled.

Mercedes reached a hand up and stroked his face. Captain Blackwell captured her hand and kissed it. Then he leaned down and kissed her, clasping her very tightly for a moment.

Several of the men and the cottagers cast furtive glances at them, prompting McMurtry to say to one of the raw hands, "Turn away your glims, cully, it's more respectful like."

When they parted Captain Blackwell came away with a bloodstain on his breeches that he did not in the least remark.

Inside the cottage Mercedes counted five small children by the hearth under a single blanket. A child of no more than one and a half or two held the baby. The woman showed Mercedes where she might stretch out next the children. Mercedes made the children's acquaintance, asking the mother to name each one.

"I shall be very happy to share your bed for the night." Mercedes smiled at them. "But first, may I ask for the privy ma'am?"

The woman led Mercedes to a shack at the back of the property.

"Thank you again, Mrs. ..."

"Cohen, ma'am," the woman said.

"Thank you, Mrs. Cohen. I shall be a while and I beg you will not wait. I can find my way back to the children. I would be obliged if you would send your boy to tell the men, the Captain's men, they must find another place of ease."

Mercedes went into the privy. In the cold, damp, stinking dark she spent one of the most miserable nights of her life. She'd been wretched before and that not long since. In North Africa she'd considered herself abandoned and been ill unto death. The miscarriage was a different kind of affliction. Her body felt like it was collapsing as it expelled the nascent baby; her and James' child; coming out of her in gouts and gobbets of blood and tissue.

Just after dawn lit the sky with its' gentle hopeful rays, it was over. Mercedes did the best she could, on shaking legs, with a bucket of water she found inside the privy to clean herself and her surroundings. Nothing could be done with the stained breeches and she shuddered pulling them on wet and sticky against her skin. At the back door of the cottage Mercedes met Mrs. Cohen coming out with her eldest son.

"Why Missus, have you not been abed all night?" the woman exclaimed. "Jesus, Joseph and Mary, that is never blood on them breeches! Joe, run for the blanket!"

"But, Ma — "

"Run!"

Captain Blackwell was sitting in the lean to, his bulk overflowing a three-legged stool. Some of his men were awake while others snored on. Captain Blackwell had not slept. Twice he'd walked back to the beach to stare at the wreck of his ship by starlight and moonshine. He'd watched the sun come up and illuminate the stranded *Assurance* and his men, camped in a straggling crescent on the rocky beach. He'd just returned and seated himself when the boy from the cottage came pelting up.

"Sir! Captain, sir, Ma says come now. Oh, the woe! Your missus has thrown off the bairn."

Captain Blackwell did not quite grasp his meaning, but the boy's urgent tone communicated much. He sprang up and followed.

McMurtry called out to him, "Permission to return to the cutter, sir?"

"Granted," he said over his shoulder. McMurtry hurried away with Narhilla. Captain Blackwell scowled; apparently his steward had understood more than he.

Inside the cottage, on the floor beside the hearth, Captain Blackwell found Mercedes. She looked small and vulnerable beneath a disreputable blanket. He knelt beside her with a pain in his chest. The evening just past he'd believed himself sunk to the farthest depth of misery, but looking at Mercedes' pallid face, her nearly blue lips, those lovely lips, he was perfectly convinced he could be far more miserable were he ever to lose her.

"Mercedes, sweetheart. What is it? What's happened?"

"A miscarriage," she said. "I am sorry."

"Oh! Oh." Captain Blackwell was confounded. He thought of crushing her on *Assurance* between his bulk and the deck, and of the long night following. This was the life he led her. "I did not know you was with child."

"Neither did I!" Mercedes gulped back a sob.

He took her hand and leaned over her, as though he would shield her. He tried to embrace her, but it was awkward while he knelt and Mercedes lay on the earthen floor. He could find nothing to say and he blamed himself for having no words of comfort to give her. Mercedes' white face frightened him, and she must have lost a mort of blood. Her tears nearly unmanned him. He didn't wish to shed any in front of the cottagers and his men, and so he remained hard and silent.

For some moments they mourned together, clasped by the hands. Captain Blackwell finally stood and addressed the master of the house. "Do you have a gig, or a dogcart?"

"None at all."

"Nor do any of your neighbors?"

"No. I have a barrow, if you want it."

"A barrow, sir! A barrow! Do you expect me to put my wife in a barrow like a common, drunken — "

"James, please." Mercedes tried to interpose.

No one heeded her. Captain Blackwell and the cottager had come toe to toe. Caleb Cohen matched him in poundage and height, but Captain Blackwell's recent losses gave him an odd moral force, and he seemed to tower over the other man.

"Sir! Captain Blackwell, sir," McMurtry called from the doorway, "we brought up a stretcher."

Narhilla and McMurtry came in with one of the wide plank thwarts from the red cutter swaddled in canvas sailcloth. Captain Blackwell lifted Mercedes into the stretcher; she was light, insubstantial. He could have carried her for miles.

"Where is the nearest village?" Captain Blackwell asked. "How far, if you please."

"Just under three mile. I'll send the boy with you."

Captain Blackwell took the first spell carrying Mercedes' stretcher at the head, but he soon became aware he could not bear much weight with his left hand: the wrist was swollen and purple. He gave the order to set her gently down and Narhilla took his place. Walking beside the stretcher, Captain Blackwell tried to remember when in the long sequence of the night he'd received the wound. It came to him when he glanced down at Mercedes. He recalled the impact on *Assurance's* deck when he put out his hand to try to break his fall, lest he do her some terrible injury.

"Such a fool," Mercedes murmured just then.

Captain Blackwell straightened from leaning over her and stared straight ahead over the brilliant green countryside. The professional mask came down over his features, concealing his troubles beneath.

CHAPTER FOUR

At first Mercedes was wakeful during the trek to the village of Burne, chastising herself for ignorance. She'd been unwell for three days. She should have known she was with child; she prided herself on being responsible when it came to her intimate health; she should have taken more care. Gazing up into his unshaven face when she gave him the news, and seeing that fierce expression run across it, Mercedes wondered if Captain Blackwell blamed her. She accused herself: "Such a fool," she'd murmured right before the steady rhythm of the men's steps lulled her, and blessed sleep overtook her.

She woke in an upstairs bedchamber. Captain Blackwell's voice had awakened her; she was lying in the stretcher on the floor of the room.

"Bring that water hot and hot, do you hear me there?" He was giving orders to the publican and his wife, while a chambermaid scurried about the room. "And I'll have clean linen on this bed, if you please."

He helped her up when the bath was filled in the dressing room, and the bustling people of the inn had gone. The nasty stained blanket they left in the stretcher. Mercedes handed her breeches out to Captain Blackwell to dispose of, after peeling them off in the screened bathing space.

"Shall I help you, sweetheart? Do you need help?"

Mercedes eyes filled with tears. She was pouring water into a basin so she could sponge off the worst of the bloody remains before stepping into the bath.

"I can manage, James, darling. Will you do me a very great favor?"

There was a long pause and at last Captain Blackwell replied, "Of course, Mercedes."

"I need clothes and...please purchase several blankets and have them sent to the Cohens. That blanket was their only one, the children will be cold." Mercedes bent over, gripping the wash handstand, and trying to command her voice. "You have much to do and I know you must attend to your men. I'm sorry to ask more of you."

"No, sweetheart, no." Captain Blackwell's voice held a note of misery.

"I'll be very well alone for the time, you need not fear leaving me." She stopped short of telling him she wanted to be alone so she could cry unreservedly, a thing she feared he would not like.

Captain Blackwell promised to send up clothing and a meal in an hour or so, to give her time for the bath, but he begged she would keep her bed that day. Once she'd eased herself into the water Mercedes called to him to walk into the dressing room, where he could wash and shave before returning to his duties. He stooped and kissed her wet cheek and clasped her hand in parting. Immediately after Captain Blackwell left the room, Mercedes face crumpled and she abandoned her composure.

She took Captain Blackwell's advise and slept between fresh sheets in a nightgown offered by the kind landlady of the inn, who'd also brought her the means to deal with the flow of blood. Before suppertime she rose and fingered the gown and small clothes the Captain had purchased for her. Mercedes considered changing into the clothes in case Captain Blackwell returned. She imagined eating a quiet meal together the way they'd done in the Master's cramped cabin, where she'd last been happy with him. Captain Blackwell did not come in and Mercedes ate supper in her nightgown, sitting up in bed.

She awoke some hours later. The bedchamber was dark, but a sliver of moonlight slanting through the window struck a line between her and Captain Blackwell on the bed. He was propped up on top of the bedclothes, with one arm behind his head, wearing breeches and shirt. His eyes glinted as he stared straight ahead.

"Why do you not take off your clothes and get in with me? You must be quite done up."

"I didn't want to disturb you, sweetheart."

"Pray get in bed. " She rose and went into the dressing room to use the close-stool.

When she was returning Mercedes stumbled in the dark and Captain Blackwell was instantly up and holding her under the elbows. He supported her back to the bed. After settling in, Mercedes caught his hand before he could rise from his seat beside her.

"I'm sorry about our child. Can you forgive me?"

"Forgive you? Have I ever been unkind to you?" Captain Blackwell might have remembered when they'd first met, and he'd allowed Mercedes to believe there would be consequences if she didn't yield to his carnal desires, for he added, "Since we've been man and wife, I mean to say."

"Of course not."

"Then how can you think I would blame you for something you could not control. Was it my fault, indeed? Smashing you in that dreadful manner I shouldn't wonder."

Even in the gloom Mercedes could see Captain Blackwell's anguished expression. "No, James." She reached up and stroked his haggard face. "I don't know what caused the miscarriage. Maybe it wasn't meant to be, from the start when I was unwell. It often happens like that with first..." Mercedes fell silent. She knew Captain Blackwell was uncomfortable with certain aspects of sex; he wanted to do it, not talk about it. "If it is not the loss of the child, what it is? Do not tell me you are not vexed to the very soul."

Captain Blackwell gave her a half smile that instantly faded; he dropped her hand and stood up. Stiffly, almost self consciously, he took off his shirt and breeches, lifted the bedclothes on his side of the bed and got in naked beside her. But he propped himself up with an arm behind his head and stared straight ahead as before. He remained so long in a black study Mercedes decided he wasn't going to share his trouble.

At last he said, "I did not like to burden you after what you've suffered, and what you've lost. I shall have to stand a court-martial, for the loss of my ship."

"But she was three parts rotten. Lord Nelson will say so, won't he?"

"That's as may be. But I was her commander and I'm responsible for her loss. All my officers are also answerable."

"I'm sorry." Mercedes extended her hand to clasp his arm. "I don't think he did it wittingly, James, gave you that ship. Admiral Gambier, I mean."

Captain Blackwell looked at her, startled.

"They would never have put Lord Nelson aboard her had they known," she said. "You and I would not be missed. But he is the hero of England."

"Hard to argue with that, sweetheart." Captain Blackwell took her hand from his arm, lifted it to his lips and kissed it. "God send the Vice-Admiral and his people got safely ashore. If not I dare say I shall suffer the same fate as Byng."

"Who is Byng?"

"An admiral in the last war, in the last to last war. Never mind, it don't signify."

"I don't think there is the least chance you will be convicted, if that is the word. But should the Admiralty be so mistaken, so terribly misguided, would they allow me to go to prison with you?"

Captain Blackwell reached for her and took her in his arms. "You would do that, follow me even to prison?"

"Yes, yes." She kissed him once, twice.

"I doubt it will come to that, providing Lord Nelson survives. Sleep now, Mercy," he whispered to her. Mercedes turned in his arms so her back was to him. "Were I to be found guilty of negligence, mishandling, lubberly goddamn conduct, I should be dismissed the Service, the most likely event."

Mercedes shivered under his encircling arm. She could find no words of solace to give him, knowing how much of his honor, indeed his happiness, was tied to his profession.

"Sweetheart." Captain Blackwell mistook her shivering for real chill, or a consequence of her loss of blood and illness. He moved closer against her, to warm her. "You are not to mind my poking you, nor to think you need do anything about it. Do you hear me now, Miss? It is only I can't help it when I'm this close to you, and thinking of what I should like to do to you."

"What should you like to do to me?" Mercedes smiled, the only time she had that day.

Captain Blackwell swept her hair aside and kissed the back of her neck. "Everything. I should like to kiss you everywhere, and make you cry out with pleasure."

"I love you too, Jim. And I shall not let you forgot that promise."

He could not have said anything better calculated to reassure Mercedes of his love and devotion, it was the greatest comfort he could have given her.

The innkeeper at Burne served them a hearty English breakfast next morning; two kinds of sausages, bacon, a beefsteak, eggs, kippered trout, toasted bread and currant jam, and coffee. Mercedes ate more than she really wished to, to satisfy him she was mending.

They spoke of ordinary concerns, a pair of breeches and black coat were to be sent up by the tailor that day. Captain Blackwell was anxious not to appear in the uniform of the Royal Navy now he had no ship under his command, but all their possessions had been lost in the wreck.

"If you will purchase linen and needles and thread I will make you a pair of new shirts without loss of a moment, stockings too, if you will but get the wool."

"You are to rest." He rose to take his leave, tucking his number two scrapper under his arm; McMurtry had managed to preserve a small chest with his uniforms, epaulettes and cocked hats. "I do not care overmuch for this." He fingered Mercedes' nightgown, covering her from neckline to ankles. He had forbidden such articles of clothing in his cot. "We will run out in the boats to *Assurance* and take off what we can, she rides high on the bank. I misdoubt your clothes and things will be ruined with the sea water."

"Never mind clothes, I can make more. Another husband is not so easy to get. So I beg you will remember I married a man, not a uniform, or the Royal Navy, or a ship."

Captain Blackwell let her out of his embrace eventually, and went out to pursue the business of his day.

He returned to Mercedes surprisingly soon, stepping into the room just before dinnertime with a basket on his arm, beaming all over his face.

Mercedes was amazed. "What is it, James?"

"Astonishing good news! Lord and Lady Hamilton, Lord Nelson and his launch's crew all came ashore safe at Kinsale, and are posting to Cork to take ship to England. Thanks to Mr. Verson they knew where to find us, and they send their compliments and this, by the mail coach not a half glass since." Captain Blackwell lifted the lid of the basket and Queenie leapt out. The cat gave the pair of them a disdainful, injured look, and jumped on the bed where she began to lick her fur with her back turned purposefully toward them.

"Oh, oh, I am so glad. Give you joy."

"That is not all, sweetheart. Doctor VanArsdel is downstairs in the taproom."

"The Doctor! I thought he was in the barge."

"He was. Some of our people survived, swept onto the next beach. They caught up with the main encampment last evening. The good doctor has already found himself a fresh suit of clothes, and purchased a few instruments of one of his fellow medicos. I asked him to see you, Mercedes, I thought it would be best."

"I shall be delighted to see Doctor VanArsdel." Mercedes added, "Since you think it best."

When Captain Blackwell brought Doctor VanArsdel into their bedchamber Mercedes came forward, neat and trim and dressed in the new gown, and gave the doctor her hand. They were old friends and old shipmates. Doctor VanArsdel had been surgeon in the ship *Inconstant* where Mercedes had first been held a prisoner.

"How do you do, Doctor? I am so glad to see you. We feared the barge's people were all lost. You must give us your account."

"The Captain already knows my tale, Miss Mercedes. But I shall be happy to recount it, while I examine you, if you wish. How are you, ma'am? I am very sorry for your loss. Has the bleeding stopped?"

"Just today it has, Doctor."

"Should you like your husband to remain in the chamber while I examine you?"

Captain Blackwell stood before the door with his cocked hat under his arm, in a perfectly rigid attitude, that mask settled over his features he wore when he watched men flogged at the grating.

"Captain, perhaps you would like to take your dinner downstairs sir," Mercedes said. "Doctor VanArsdel will come to you when he's done."

A fraction of Captain Blackwell's relief was evident in the speed with which he bowed and took his leave.

Doctor VanArsdel finished his dinner in the public room of the inn with Captain Blackwell seated across from him. Captain Blackwell had already dined when Doctor VanArsdel sat down. They spoke of the wounded among the surviving crew of *Assurance*. As soon as the doctor had lain down knife and fork, Captain Blackwell said, "Shall we take a turn out of doors, Doctor?"

Captain Blackwell naturally did not wish to discuss his wife's intimate health in a public room. Outside it was a bright, crisp and lovely February day, as beautiful as could be wished for, for salvage work.

The doctor slowed when they'd progressed far down the lane. "I found no scarring in my examination, sir. Miss Mercedes should suffer no lasting effects. Miscarriages are quite common, you are to be aware. There should be no reason she cannot conceive and carry other children."

"You greatly relieve my mind, thank you Doctor."

"Medicine is an imprecise science, sir, and my prognosis is to the best of my knowledge. It is always possible a condition exists that I do not detect."

Captain Blackwell bowed. "How soon may she comfortably travel, sir?"

The doctor gave Captain Blackwell a sharp look, a hint of disapproval in his gaze. "Comfortably, I cannot say, sir. She might travel safely in another pair of days, three days let us say, and in a well-sprung carriage. What would benefit Miss Mercedes most is rest and quiet. It is almost fortunate we are not at sea with the constant bellowing out of the bosun and the endless hullabaloo."

Captain Blackwell's face set in a severe expression. His officers would never have made such a tactless comment. Petty officers were another breed; and surgeons, with their education in another science entirely, were foremost in lubberly behavior.

"I am taking her to my father's rectory at Deane. A mere day's ride from London."

"That should be ideal, sir." Doctor VanArsdel nodded. "I understand you shall have to be in London in the coming days, but I must caution you that the atmosphere of that town may not be the most conducive to Miss Mercedes' recovery. In fact, sir, I must also mention that she should be excused her conjugal duties for a time."

"How long, Doctor?" He wanted nothing more than to be clear about orders.

"It is somewhat as though she has had a lying in, when I would council a six week abstinence. A fortnight, sir. And it would be altogether better were you to allow her to come to you when she feels ready to resume her duty. It is no small thing, what she's suffered."

"I appreciate that. She shall have all the time she requires."

He had to work to keep a smug smile from stealing across his face. Doctor VanArsdel and the rest of the world saw in Mercedes a demure gentlewoman. Only he knew it was demureness fraught with passion, and she would come to him as soon as ever she was well. She should have her fortnight and more, if she needed it.

Captain Blackwell next brought out, "You are aware, Doctor, Mercedes has been trying to control her fertility. At my behest." He did not wish the doctor to think Mercedes refused to bear his children, when quite the opposite was the case. "She warned me the...methods she uses to prevent conception often fail. Is there anything a man can do, sir?"

"Yes, there is, sir." Doctor VanArsdel wrote out the direction of several apothecaries in London where prophylactic shields could be purchased. Captain Blackwell experienced a wretched bashfulness, tucking the scrap of paper in his pocket. The doctor said, "Any reputable, well stocked apothecary will have them, sir. And then there is another procedure by far the most effective. You must spend your seed outside her body."

Captain Blackwell blushed to the roots of his hair, and Doctor VanArsdel turned aside to hide a self-satisfied grin. A midshipman came hurrying up, announcing the arrival of the master attendant from Kinsale, and relieved Captain Blackwell of his discomfiture.

Discomfort they had aplenty in the five coach stages to Cork. The expense of a chaise and four weighed upon Captain Blackwell's mind, but he was unwilling Mercedes should be jostled in a public conveyance. He managed to get them aboard the *Amphion* frigate, Captain Sutton, returning to England to be new coppered. Captain Blackwell was gratified when Mercedes' health improved aboard ship. The color returned to her cheeks, and gaiety to her manner. Captain Blackwell couldn't help but wish Doctor VanArsdel should see his opinion of the detrimental effects of shipboard life put down. He fancied both he and Mercedes were happiest at sea.

But they had another two stages after arriving in Portsmouth to endure, and once again Captain Blackwell engaged a post-chaise and four. "My father shall think I'm topping it the nob before my new wife," he reflected, as they bowled along on the last stage of their journey to Deane.

"Should you like bread and butter?" Mercedes was seated across from him in the coach. She bent toward her basket on the floor.

"Certainly, sweetheart. Have you some in your basket? I hope Queenie has not been at the butter." And then glancing out the carriage window, he said, "Wet evening for a stroll."

He slid over on the bench to look at two ladies who stood to the side of the road as the carriage passed, rainwater dripping from the rims of their bonnets. One of the ladies looked up, directly into Captain Blackwell's face.

"Bless me, its Jane," Captain Blackwell cried. "Ahoy there, coachman, heave to! All aback! Do you hear me there?"

Captain Blackwell leaned out and slammed his hand against the carriage side. The vehicle was brought up and he leapt out, returning a few moments later to hand the two dripping ladies into the carriage. Settling himself on the bench beside Mercedes, and having given a different direction to the coachman, the awkwardness of the situation sunk in.

"Mercedes, may I present Jane Burney. Jane, my wife, Mercedes." Wife number two please to make the acquaintance of wife number one. It might have been better to leave them by the wayside, but it would've been a terribly churlish thing to do, especially as Jane had seen him gawping out the carriage window.

Yet neither Jane nor Mercedes acted the least discomposed, both too well breed to show it if they had been. Jane presented her sister Charlotte to Mercedes, and the ladies smiled on one another with real pleasure.

"Should you like a bit of bread and butter?" Mercedes asked.

The carriage ride shared with Jane and Charlotte Burney to their brother's rectory at Ibthorpe had been surprisingly comfortable, thanks to Mercedes' easy manners. He'd married Jane the previous year during a most unsettled time, when he thought Mercedes had perished in Africa. It was no excuse that he'd done so under pressure from the Reverend Blackwell and Jane's family, and to call the fourteen day marriage a disgraceful interlude was to put a kind slant on the matter. Jane had sought an annulment after finding the prospect of real relations, of lying with him, too heinous either to contemplate or attempt.

"I shall stop the allowance I make her if you wish, Mercedes," Captain Blackwell offered, once they had put Jane and Charlotte down at Ibthorpe. He had subscribed ten pounds per annum from his pay to Jane when he learned that a great reason for her agreement to marry him had been her poverty. Jane's other reason had been a mistaken, a horridly unfounded notion he was not interested in conjugal relations.

"I do not wish it," Mercedes said, from the darkness of her side of the coach. "I should not like to have to manage on ten pounds a year. It may be she counts it her only income. And after all, I have you."

"The prize bull," he said, feeling something between amusement and shame.

"Just so."

He heard the faintest of chuckles.

It was well after suppertime when Mercedes and Captain Blackwell at last reached the rectory at Deanne, their journey's end. Stopping at Ibthorpe had made them late. They were welcomed at the other rectory by Reverend Blackwell, his housekeeper Betsy and her husband Henry, a man who'd been old when Captain Blackwell was a boy.

Captain Blackwell observed while his father became more and more taken with Mercedes. She was an irresistible novelty, a woman who'd sailed from America to Europe to North Africa, and married the native son. Who could account for it? His father provided a collation for their supper, but he barely allowed Mercedes to partake of it with his constant questions and exclamations.

Mercedes took only soup and wine and Captain Blackwell did not like the tired look of her, a weak smile was fixed on her face. They'd been in the carriage more than ten hours and then there'd been that deuced unexpected meeting with Jane.

Captain Blackwell stood up. "We must retire now, sir, if you please. It has been a very long day."

"Of course, of course. Betsy will show you to your rooms and Henry shall bring up the baggage." The Reverend rose with a regretful look, but he brightened when Mercedes approached him with a "Goodnight, sir," and kissed his cheek.

"McMurtry brings a trunk in a day or two, when he comes up by the mail. This is all there is at present," Captain Blackwell said, in an aside to the manservant, taking up their portmanteau. "I can manage, if you will take the basket into the kitchen. Has the cat run off already?"

Mercedes gave Captain Blackwell's arm a grateful squeeze as she took it to go upstairs.

"What is this, Betsy?" He exclaimed, when Betsy stopped outside his mother's bedchamber and opened the door for Mercedes.

"The Reverend says Mrs. Blackwell is to have your mother's rooms, sir."

"Frank's room will do, it's next to mine." He took Mercedes' arm and led her down the passage.

"The Reverend says Master Francis's room is too small and cramped for a lady," Betsy called after him, "but the bedclothes are clean, sir."

"Too small and cramped, indeed." Captain Blackwell snorted, steering Mercedes into his bedchamber. It had a dressing room connecting it to his brother's room.

Mercedes had lived with him in the cabin of a 28-gun frigate, he very much doubted she would balk at lying in Francis's cramped little room, nor in Francis's childhood bed. If his father thought he would stand for Mercedes sleeping on the other side of the house from him, the Reverend was mistaken. His fortnight of abstinence was nearly over, or so Captain Blackwell hoped and trusted.

Captain Blackwell left next morning for London, to give up his sword at the Admiralty, and to inquire into the date of the court martial. It was the first of many such times when he flogged up and back to town. The Admiralty's standing order seemed to be, check again next Tuesday week, inquire in a fortnight.

On returning from that first trip to town Captain Blackwell brought Mercedes a dressing gown of the type she'd owned before. A charming garment that opened in the front by untying a sash, with the promise of smooth, warm naked skin lying just below. But Captain Blackwell was finding he could seldom be alone with his wife during the daylight hours. The neighborhood of Deanne, formerly so cold to him, the annulment of his marriage to Jane a subject of enthusiastic gossip, was now eager to receive him. The attraction was of course Mercedes.

The Reverend Blackwell was in the vanguard of those monopolizing Mercedes' time. He was a reading man and when he learned Mercedes liked books he glowed with the pleasure of having someone in the house again of similar tastes. He showed her his library, eagerly discovering which books she'd read. Captain Blackwell's brother Francis, a diplomat in Africa, was sorely missed at home. The Reverend longed to talk of books, and Captain Blackwell was of no use in that line.

For his part the Reverend began to conceive the notion Mercedes was an angel sent to make his latter years comfortable. If only James would be given a ship and go on an extended foreign cruise, leaving Mercedes and a grandchild to live with him. His son might have fulfilled the Reverend's hopes at a stroke.

Mercedes watched Captain Blackwell approach on a stout mare, his posture weary, his shoulders bowed. She gently withdrew her hand from the Reverend's arm; they were standing together in the neat parish cemetery before the grave of Emma Blackwell.

"She was never completely well again after her lying in with Frank. My belief is it was James took the vigor right out of her. The size of that boy's head, like a melon. An absolute melon. I do not say this to frighten you, for I make sure that, being of Latin origins, you shall be far more successful in child bearing. Emma was delicate, yet not all Englishwomen are so. Why, only look at Jane's mama, eight healthy children. Well, seven really, one must not count the half-wit son George."

"How I should have loved to know your dear wife. Excuse me, sir, here is Captain Blackwell."

"James?" said the Reverend, peering round in the twilight as though they had not been able to see Captain Blackwell, riding up the perfectly flat country lane, for the last half hour.

Mercedes met him in the lane and Captain Blackwell dismounted with a great heave of his bulk out of the saddle. He leaned down and brushed his cheek against hers.

"Good evening to you, sir. I want a private word with Mercedes, if you please."

Standing beside the wicket into the cemetery, Captain Blackwell announced the court-martial was set for one week from the day.

"You will take me with you, for the trial?"

She was sorry for her eager, pressing tone, but she'd been imagining the long delay that must attend news of the outcome of the trial making its way from London to Deanne. She didn't think she could bear it, not being there to support him in one event or the other. Little did she know of the Admiralty, but the close view she'd had of the justice of the Royal Navy did not make her mind easy. Mercedes feared he would be taken from her without farewell, in the case of conviction.

Captain Blackwell merely shook his head. She took the gesture for one of weariness rather than a firm negative. They ate a somber supper and Captain Blackwell retired immediately afterward. Mercedes longed to accompany him, but the Reverend expected to take his evening's leisure in her company. He pressed her like a child to one more game and then another of backgammon, chattering the while on one of his favorite topics — the grandchildren she was to give him.

"I have no hopes of Francis," the Reverend said. "Though he writes me he shall bring two grandchildren ready made to me, if his suit prospers with the Persian woman. My sons seem to prefer the exotic to the home-spun." The Reverend smiled at Mercedes in winning fashion. "I do not know that I shall be fond of step-grandchildren. How would you feel, were you to have to care for a brat of James's by another woman?"

"As to that, sir, I cannot say. But as to Zahraa's children, they are the loveliest mannered, most amiable boy and girl you can imagine."

She'd known them when they'd lived together in the Dey's harem. Their mother Zahraa, the woman Francis Blackwell was courting, had been one of the Dey's many wives. Mercedes missed her, they'd become much attached, though she did have the comfort of other lady friends in the neighborhood of Deanne.

Mercedes found most women agreeable companions, she was naturally inclined to trust them. Men were another matter. Mercedes couldn't forget as she gazed across the backgammon board at Reverend Blackwell, as she took her meals with him and went out walking and visiting at his side, the hint Francis had given her of the Reverend's character: his mishandling of Captain Blackwell's prize money. This had left James a poorer man than most post-captains of his seniority and service record. An injury done him was felt by her, however long ago it might have been. She was cautious in her conduct toward her new father. Had the

Reverend asked his son, Captain Blackwell would've told him Mercedes was capable of playing a deep game.

Faced with Captain Blackwell's dark unhappy mood, Mercedes maneuvered to clear the house. She finally convinced the Reverend he must return an overnight visit promised at Ibthorpe. Reverend Blackwell left in his gig after dinner, and then Mercedes sent Betsy and Henry to stay the night with their son, the curate of Chawton. It was bold, chasing them from their own home, but she did not care for nicety so much as giving James her best love and comfort.

They returned from a long after dinner ramble and with a sigh Blackwell sank into an armchair in the parlour. The Naval Chronicle was on a table near at hand. He did not reach for it; he'd already read the entire number; instead he sat contemplating how long it would be before his own fate was printed there. The idea stirred cold resentment in his heart.

Mercedes came in. She'd taken off her bonnet and cloak, and there was a glow on her cheeks from their walk. She looked fresh and lovely.

"James, you are aware we are alone in the house? You will not forget the promise you made me."

"Promise, Mercy?" He didn't stir from his comfortable chair. "I can't say as I recall."

He stared at her, a neutral look upon his face, with something of his stern quarterdeck gaze. Next moment Blackwell leapt to his feet and made a dash for her. Mercedes turned and ran laughing up the stairs. His heart lightened at once, and he bounded after her like a boy. He could have caught her and thrown her over his shoulder, taken her on the passageway floor, but he wouldn't have handled her roughly for the world. He allowed her to run into his bedchamber before him, laughing and breathless. She disappeared into the dressing room and Blackwell immediately began loosening his stock and unbuttoning his waistcoat.

"James, will you help me please?"

Blackwell heard the quaver in her voice and his hands froze in the act of undoing his clothing. His heart was suddenly gripped with cold once more. Mercedes had never made the least fuss about their intimate relations. She'd always just marched out and gotten into his cot. Blackwell was fearful of a change to what he was used, afraid she might grow timid as a consequence of the miscarriage. He flung his waistcoat on the bed, suddenly exasperated with himself for all his misfortunes, and stalked into the dressing room.

The sight of her made his heart beat hard. Mercedes looked round at him wearing white silk stockings to her thighs and satin pumps he'd bought her on one of his trips to London. Above her thighs, nothing, she was bare. Bare, lovely, creamy skin. Blackwell rushed up behind her, unclasping the hooks of his bulging breeches.

He reached an arm round her, brought her hard up against him, leaned over her and breathed in her ear. He kissed her neck, her back, finally pressing his lips against her bottom, while fondling all of her he could reach.

"You need to stand on something, sweetheart."

"Where is a gun carriage when you need one." She referred to how they'd done this maneuver shipboard.

Blackwell kicked over a trunk and stood her on it.

"How is it you always know what I want?"

He was covering her from behind, Mercedes' hands flat against the wall, his next to hers. Mercedes curled her arm behind him, as though trying to bring him closer. He could get no closer to her.

"Perhaps it's because...Oh, Jim!" She gasped, dropping her hand to his buttock and rocking her bottom back against his loins. "Because I want the same thing."

The Reverend Blackwell entered a dark and cold rectory. He'd insisted on being driven home, finding the Burneys, though amiable people, unable to offer him the attention and ease he was lately finding at home. On the cheerless return in the gig to Deanne, the Reverend comforted himself by picturing his own hearth, with Mercedes alongside the fire. She might give him supper made with her own hands, the way she'd done for James on his late arrivals from town. But Reverend Blackwell found neither fire, nor daughter, nor comfort of any kind.

The rectory was perfectly quiet and still and then the Reverend heard a thumping upstairs, and he smiled. They were taking supper in their rooms, Mercedes and James, and that must be James' heavy tread he heard. The Reverend began to ascend the stairs. How charming it would be to share their cozy meal, and how surprised and delighted they would be he had come.

The door was ajar to James's bedchamber and the Reverend walked into the darkened room, the low light of a single brace of candles shone through the dressing room from Francis's chamber. The Reverend moved quietly forward. He stood and gazed longer than he should have done, and then the Reverend bolted through James's bedchamber and out into the passage. A riot of emotions nearly made him stumble. He had a rock hard erection such as he'd not experienced for many a day, and his breast was a whirl of shame, jealousy, lust, and anger. He'd always suspected his eldest son of being a selfish brute. James was willfully denying him the grandchild that would tie Mercedes to hearth and home, to England, to him. The Reverend did the only thing he could under the circumstances; he took to his bed.

Betsy came along the passageway hesitantly, not liking to approach the captain and his wife while they were still in their bedchamber, but orders was orders as the captain's rude servant McMurtry would have said. The captain's strong voice could be heard even in the passage, and his lady's softer one, when Betsy knocked on the door.

"What is it, Betsy?" Blackwell answered the door in breeches, stockings, and with an open shirt. The top of the scar was visible that ran from his breast to his navel, one of his worst wounds.

"The Reverend is taken ill, sir," Betsy said. "He says will you come?"

"Of course I shall. Pass the word for McMurtry to saddle the cob."

"Oh no, sir, he's here. And he wants Mrs. Blackwell too."

Mercedes walked out of the dressing room just then, clad in a morning gown, with her hair neatly arranged atop her head. Blackwell scowled; he'd found the door to his chamber ajar the evening before, when he went in to fetch the wine. He could not recall if he'd properly closed it, so distracted had he been chasing Mercedes up the stairs.

"Your father is unwell?" Mercedes gaze was one of concern.

"My father is here."

"He wishes you to attend him, ma'am," Betsy said.

"Of course." Mercedes hesitated after looking at him.

"Let's all go," he said.

He could hardly object to Mercedes attending his father, had she been a man she would have been a surgeon's mate, she'd done the duty of one aboard *Inconstant*. Studying her straight back as he followed her down the passage Blackwell reconsidered; had she been a man she would have been an officer. She had the dash and the spirit.

He hung back with Betsy near the doorway while Mercedes went immediately and sat beside the Reverend, propped up in his bed, pallid and strained. Mercedes measured his pulse and spoke to him in a gentle voice, questioning him about what he'd eaten, when he'd first begun to feel unwell, where his felt pain. She palpated his neck and underneath his jaw, leant forward and put her cheek against his forehead for his temperature. When she asked his permission to put her hand beneath his nightshirt to touch his stomach for the same reason, the Reverend's eyes went heavenward. It put Blackwell in mind of Queenie when she was scratched in a welcome spot. Mercedes announced she did not think the Reverend's malady was anything that his own bed and the comfort of home would not soon set right.

"And you shall be here to attend me, my dear," the Reverend said.

Mercedes glanced over her shoulder at Blackwell. "That is not my place to decide."

"You will excuse us a moment, sir." Blackwell held his hand out to Mercedes.

He led her out into the passage and closed the bedchamber door, leaving Betsy with his father. Blackwell looked at Mercedes questioningly, the phrase "The butcher's bill?" was rising to his lips, but she took his meaning.

"I could not find anything physically wrong with him. His pulse is strong and regular and his temperature normal. He appears to have had a sleepless night. Perhaps it was returning so late last evening, and the disruption of his normal routine unsettled him. He seems to fancy he is unwell."

Blackwell was deeply vexed, and mortified. For a moment he could not trust himself to speak. He gave Mercedes a stern look. "Go downstairs, ma'am, if you please."

Mercedes opened her mouth as though she would remonstrate but then she nodded, officer-like, and gripped his arm briefly before turning for the stairs.

"Betsy, I want a word with m'father."

"Where is Mercedes?" the Reverend asked as soon as they were alone.

"I sent her downstairs."

"Ah, to fetch me a tray? How kind."

"She will fetch nothing, sir! You forget Mercedes has seen real wounds, serious illness, and suffering and death. Do you think she could not tell you are gammoning us, sir?"

"She never said such a thing!"

"No, no indeed, sir, she is altogether too kindhearted. But you may trust I will not stand for her kindness to be presumed upon, for you to make a servant of her, fetching and catering to you."

"I never intended such a thing, how dare you say so, James. I merely wanted to give her someone to care for, to spend her tender love upon. Women need that, to be mothers and caretakers. But it is clear this is something you do not comprehend or you should have got her in the way all ladies want to be who love their lords."

Blackwell's anger grew, and the recollection of the open bedchamber door was stirring unwanted speculations. He could not bear the thought of anyone, *anyone*, besides he seeing Mercedes in the condition she'd been in much of the previous evening. He became incautious; "She was with child, sir."

"And?" the Reverend said, sitting up eagerly in bed.

"She lost the child. The night of the wreck." Blackwell hung his head and cursed himself for a fool.

"Is it any wonder? Dragging her aboard a ship of war, exposing her to every danger. You are afraid your consequence with her will be reduced were you to give her a child. You have no idea what a woman needs, James." Color was back in the Reverend's face, and he sat straight in his bed.

Hardest to answer were accusations containing truth, but Blackwell was not to be outdone. "If you think I married for your comfort and convenience, sir, you may think again." He took no satisfaction from the wit of the rejoinder, but the slam he gave the bedchamber door as he stalked away relieved his feelings to a greater extent.

"McMurtry!" Blackwell called out from the stairs. "Skip over to the Dog and Feathers and order a carriage for noon. Noon, do you hear me there?"

He walked into the breakfast parlour and found Mercedes seated at the table, waiting for him. His face softened. "Pack you things, Mercy, sweetheart, we're leaving for London."

Captain Blackwell encouraged her to write their news to the Reverend once they were settled in London, in spite of the row, the regular set to they'd had. He was ashamed of the quarrel and of having no private house to take Mercedes to in London, no family home to offer her. Captain Blackwell had a standing invitation to stay at Lady Oxford's townhouse whenever he was in London, and had he been a bachelor he might have accepted. But it did not seem fitting to land in the middle of Lady Oxford's brood, labeled the Bourne Miscellany by the *ton* for the variety of fathers her children could claim. Captain Enoch Bourne was his particular friend and brother officer, but he'd only just wed himself, and he and his new wife were already swelling the number of Lady Oxford's household.

It was not that he did not wish to expose Mercedes to Captain Bourne's rakish brothers and foul mouthed sisters. Mercedes was neither timid nor a prude, and she'd certainly heard all manner of oaths shipboard. He took rooms at the Golden Ball, a respectable hotel frequented by Navy men, because he needed to be alone. He could no more have borne a social round than he could have fled before the enemy. His heart was in such an anguish of anxiety for the trial that he could hardly bear his own company.

He need not have concerned himself about their lodgings for Mercedes' sake, she was indifferent to where they lay, providing it was clean and secure. She learned the domestic economy of the hotel, and divided the remaining duties between herself and McMurtry. In the evenings she was content to sit with him quietly sewing or reading, just as when they were at sea in happier times.

Frequently he fell into black studies. A wish would arise his father were more like Lord Nelson's, who'd given Burnham Thorpe rectory over to Nelson and his wife Fanny, such was his desire they should make his home their own. Beneath all other thoughts and concerns was a fervent hope he might not be dismissed the service. When the loss of his livelihood, of the professional honor he'd worked for man and boy, overwhelmed him in his fireside ruminations, Captain Blackwell would look up at Mercedes. He hoped she might not have to make do with a jobbing, merchant captain for a husband.

His desire for solitude in the days before the court-martial did not mean Captain Blackwell behaved ill. He was a good-hearted generous man, and far too disciplined to make those around him feel his unhappiness. His wife and steward put meals before him that he ate with near his usual appetite, though with little relish; he escorted Mercedes in the afternoons to various parks and London attractions. Overall he did his best to carry on as though his life had not taken several ugly goddamn turns.

CHAPTER FIVE

Captain Blackwell had passed a restless night, one of many, when he would wake for the changing of the watch, often rising to pace in the sitting room. The morning of his court-martial he sat across from Mercedes looking somber, his face care worn. He could not address his breakfast with justice, and hardly attended to her remarks. At one moment she said, "How I hope Lord Nelson will attend, you and he are so much alike."

Captain Blackwell gave her a weak smile. "That is handsome in you to say, but I believe the resemblance ends with we are both the sons of parsons. He was made post when he was twenty-two. I was thirty, a veritable grey beard."

"No, not old yet, Jim. Nor anywhere near." Mercedes took his hand across the table.

When he embraced her in taking his leave his kisses and caresses were dutiful and absent, as they'd been during the entirety of their stay in London.

Mercedes returned to her seat at the breakfast table after Captain Blackwell went out. and stared at the uneaten sausages, bacon, eggs, smoked herring and soft tack. She'd watched him grieve his heart out during the last days. He would return to her either restored to happiness or more completely broken hearted. In the one case she would share his joy, in the other she must convince him to go to sea in a merchant command, and show him her respect for him was unchanged. Mercedes sliced the bread rolls and began to fill the opened buns with the meat from the table.

When McMurtry came in to clear the breakfast dishes Mercedes was waiting with a basket containing the sandwiches wrapped in handkerchiefs.

"A hackney coach and we are going to the Admiralty," she said.

McMurtry's ill favored mug screwed up in disapproval. But Mercedes put up her chin in an imitation of the captain's manner, and McMurtry knuckled his forehead. "Aye, aye, Missus. Hackney coach to the Admiralty."

Captain Blackwell sat in the court anti-chamber stiff, straight, and correct in his best dress uniform, in company with his lieutenants and midshipmen. The first and second lieutenants, Mr. Verson and Mr. Bransford, had both followed Captain Blackwell into *Assurance* from his last command. They were as silent as he. But the midshipmen; there were eight of them ranging in age from ten to the oldster, Mr. Bowles, at eighteen; were not capable of enduring the long tedious wait while the court put itself in order without beginning to shove and poke one another, and whisper in low voices. At last a Marine sergeant opened the anti-chamber door and called them into the court. The officers of *Assurance* filed in behind Captain Blackwell, who entered reaching down to steady a nonexistent sword.

The court sat behind a massive table, six post-captains, the President of the court, and the judge-advocate, and court clerks. Captain Blackwell made his bow to the court. The officers, observers, and witnesses were seated. Lord Nelson was not in attendance. The judge-advocate stood and read through a long document stating by what authority the court assembled, His Majesty's this, that, and the other; the part of meaning to Captain Blackwell was, "to enquire into the loss of His Majesty's frigate *Assurance* by her commander James Blackwell, and by the officers and company of said frigate."

Captain Blackwell was called upon to give his account. He stood before the court in the characteristic manner of sea-officers with his legs planted apart and his hands clasped behind his back, staring straight ahead as though facing execution, and boomed out in a voice not meant for a courtroom, "At nine-thirty in the evening of January 6 *Assurance* was steering north-northeast for Plymouth in a strong gale at eight knots, when the ship was brought hard aback. The encounter with an unknown obstruction stove her hull to a width of six foot and a breadth of four foot." His voice held a steady strong pitch as the ship approached Cape Clear, Lord Nelson and his party were sent away, and finally *Assurance's* boats dispatched. Captain Blackwell concluded, "I remained with *Assurance* and a crew of forty men, running the frigate on a sand bar a mile west of Burne Sand Cove on the morning of January 7, the time approximately 3 o'clock in the morning."

He was allowed to sit down, in a chair apart and at the front of the assemblage, while his officers were questioned and gave their evidence. There were no witnesses apart from *Assurance's* Sailing Master and the Master's mates, duly called by the court. Observers were plentiful, many having hoped for a glimpse of the famous trio — Lord Nelson and Lord and Lady Hamilton. The court was on the point of retiring for deliberation and sentencing when Sir Evan Nepean, the First Secretary, entered the room. He excused himself to the court and took the President aside. When the men's heads rose from their conference the court was ordered to be cleared.

Back in the anti-chamber once more the officers of *Assurance* waited in a slightly easier atmosphere. Each had had his say or been questioned, and to have that part behind them was a great relief. But there was still the question of the ruling and sentencing. They could hear the murmur of voices from the court, and the youngest midshipman, straining every nerve and fiber piped up, "Bless me, I believe that's Lady Hamilton."

When they were escorted back into the court forty minutes later it had been cleared once more, of all observers and witnesses. Captain Blackwell and his officers stood by rank before the court. The judge advocate read out, "Having maturely and deliberately weighed and considered the whole, the Court is of the opinion that the loss of His Majesty's late Ship *Assurance* was caused by her striking upon a submerged rock until then undocumented during a strong gale in approaching the English Channel. That Captain James Blackwell previous to the circumstance, appeared to have conducted himself in the most zealous and officer-like manner, and after the ship struck, his coolness, self collection, and exertions, were highly conspicuous and that everything was done by him and his Officers, within the power of man to execute, previous to the loss of the ship, and afterwards to preserve the lives of the honorable Vice-Admiral Lord Nelson and his suite, as well as those of the Ships Company and to save her stores on that occasion; and therefore adjudge the said Captain James Blackwell, his Officers and Men, to be most fully acquitted."

Captain Blackwell's vision swam before him but he stepped forward at the appropriate time to receive his sword from the President's hand. The President's worn and haggard face was all abeam. Captain Blackwell felt quite at sea; there was a blur of handshakes and smiles and half laughter. He collected himself at last and moved purposefully toward the passage outside the court, headed for the stairs and the porter at the door.

"Captain Blackwell, Captain Blackwell, if you please sir!" A clerk hurried up to him. "Sir William Rule requests a word with you, sir, if you please."

The request from the Joint Surveyor of the Navy made Captain Blackwell gape at the young man before him. "My compliments to Sir William and I shall wait upon him in half an hour. I must run downstairs and dash off a note to Mrs. Blackwell. Pray understand, the result of the court-martial."

"Of course, sir, I did not mean to...Yes, sir."

Captain Blackwell sprinted down the stairs feeling like he had at twenty, his heart beating hard, life was full of possibility again. "Tom, Tom Porter there, pen, paper and ink, if you please. I wish to send ..." He left off, noticing a woman walking on the other side of the street. A woman whose black gown and veil could not hide her shapely figure. Her stride somehow betraying her sensuality, at least to Captain Blackwell's eye.

The porter's one-eyed squint followed his gaze. "Aye, sir, that lovely young creature has been walking up and down t'other side of the lane this last half glass and more."

"That lovely young creature is Mrs. Captain Blackwell, Tom." His broad grin allowed he'd taken no offense at the porter's loose talk.

He was off next moment, taking his life in his hands and racing across the street choked with carriages, brewer's carts, hackney coaches, conveyances of every kind, even a cart pulled by a dog and driven by a boy of nine or ten. Captain Blackwell ran up on the other side of Parliament Street, hailing a passing hackney in his strong quarterdeck voice. The coach brought up and Captain Blackwell, catching up with Mercedes, took her arm and put her into the carriage.

"Where to governor?"

"Hold hard coachman. Give me a moment."

He jumped into the coach beside Mercedes, and taking her in his arms he gave her a resounding kiss.

"Acquitted, James?" Mercedes smiled when Captain Blackwell permitted her to breath again, as if she hadn't known the moment she saw him skipping across the street like a boy.

"Acquitted, Mrs. Blackwell. Honorably acquitted. And I fancy Lord Nelson and his honored friends may have had to do with that last part. I shall tell you all about it but at the moment I'm hard pressed. Sir William Rule, the surveyor of the Navy, has requested a meeting. I must dash."

"Take this." Mercedes put her hand into the basket beside her and handed Captain Blackwell two sandwiches.

"Bless you, sweetheart. I am fairly clemmed."

Finishing the first two sandwiches and starting on his third, Captain Blackwell paused long enough to ask, "You never came here alone, Mercedes?"

"Oh, no. McMurtry came with me. I sent him for a pint of beer."

"I hope he brings two."

"See here, governor," the coachman called, "this ain't no moveable supper house. Where's it to or out of my coach."

"Which it's to the Golden Ball in Pall Mall. Know it cully?" McMurtry said. "But just you hold hard for a trick or I'll know the reason why." He leaned in the coach window and passed two pints of ale to Captain Blackwell. "Give you joy, sir. Heard it at the Pig and Oaks just down the way, the place was all a hum and a twitter."

"Thank you, McMurtry. Escort Mrs. Blackwell back to the hotel, then you might consider yourself at liberty." McMurtry would want to enjoy the notoriety of being in the ship that had saved Lady Hamilton and Lord Nelson.

McMurtry climbed up on the box beside the disgruntled driver. Captain Blackwell embraced Mercedes. "Won't I just show you, tonight, how grateful I am for all your tender love and care of me."

Sir William Rule expounded on the great inconvenience which was constantly being felt by the officers of His Majesty's fleet, especially when ordered abroad, from the want of sufficient information respecting the navigation of those parts of the world to which their services might be directed. They were therefore to press ahead with the mission described in Captain Blackwell's last orders; the orders were to be new issued, of course, when another ship was assigned. Captain Blackwell's heart soared at those words.

"On the purely mercantile side, sir," Sir William said, "we shall also gratify our City men, the Canton and North West trade, to say nothing of the whale fisheries. They clamor every year like clockwork since Colnett's voyage for more surveys, identification of watering and refueling positions. The loss of *Assurance* trebled the hue and cry. 'If we cannot safely navigate home waters, but must run aground of unknown obstructions even on the coasts of England and Ireland, how can we expect to profit in the Great South Seas.'"

Captain Blackwell was opening his mouth to excuse himself for that ridiculous phrase 'unknown obstruction', but Sir William happily forestalled him.

"Your conduct after the wreck sealed the bargain, sir. The whaling fleet was in raptures over the vast amount of naval stores and provisions you were able to salvage from *Assurance*. The captain who will stay on sight near a week overseeing such work is the man for them. Positive raptures. I daresay you shall have another ship within the fortnight."

The same harried clerk stepped in after this welcome news was delivered, to announce that the Secretary of the Navy now wished for an interview with Captain Blackwell when he was at liberty.

He was hurried into the First Secretary's presence and after an exchange of civilities, Captain Blackwell took a seat across from Sir Evan.

"No doubt you are basking in the approbation of the technical and scientific ends of the Service, Captain Blackwell, and rightly so. You have my sincerest felicitations upon your acquittal. But I have asked you here to make you aware there are certain dismal factions that are crying out." Sir Evan gave Captain Blackwell a pointed stare upon pronouncing that word dismal; in the Service Mercedes' natural father, Admiral Gambier, was sometimes called Dismal Jemmy. "Certain individuals well placed among their Lordships are crying out against 'celebrated officers defending their favorites who ought better to be held to account for the loss of the Navy's valuable property. Striking unknown obstructions, indeed.' Those were the very words."

Captain Blackwell could do no more than gape in response. From the heights of feeling fully alive again, with the prospect of another ship and commission in the immediate future, he was brought to earth with a shrieking crash by his father-in-law's unaccountable ill will. What astonished him most was that through him, Admiral Gambier should wish to injure Mercedes.

"Thank you for telling me this, sir," Captain Blackwell said. "I had really no idea such a sentiment existed."

Sir Evan shook his head sadly, as the master at a not particularly gifted school boy. "There is not so much said against your professional character in this outcry, you must understand, as there is condemnation for being championed by that celebrated officer who spoke out so vehemently in your favor. He is given the morals of a dancing master by the dismal faction, his behavior toward his wife roundly hissed, and his success in action severely resented. And though the ill will of these god-fearing men extend more to him than to you, sir, it shall be you who will bear the brunt of their condemnation should any unsuccessful action ensue."

"The ship I have been promised."

"Just so. Were you to return from this voyage with the frigate and her crew in good order, a prodigious store of maps and commercial information under your arm, and perhaps trailing one or two enemy prizes in your wake, all will be as it should be. But the memories of the self-righteous are long. The court had it in contemplation at one point to demand you pay the value of the ship *Assurance* to Government, and I do not think I exaggerate when I tell you, your professional career and reputation rests upon the successful outcome of this Pacific mission."

When Captain Blackwell had expressed his gratitude for the First Secretary's indulgence; his astonishment was such that he could barely bring out the appropriate words; Sir Evan shook him by the hand and said kindly, "Quite apart from ships, Captain Blackwell, the Navy must retain her valuable officers. I have not so much done you a kindness by bringing you here today, as the Service itself. You might learn more of these dismal affairs from Captain Bourne, whose brother as you know sits upon the Board."

After an anxious week of wondering what the malice of another of their parents was to do to them, and hiding that fact from Mercedes, Captain Blackwell found Sir William to be correct in his conclusion; he was assigned command of a frigate. His delight and relief were unfeigned.

"*L'Unite*, 44," Captain Blackwell told Mercedes. Seeing her face cloud, he hastened to add, "She is nothing like *Assurance*, she carries all her long guns on the main deck, and she's a fine, weatherly sea boat. Fast too, according to a reliable source. I met *L'Unite's* sailing-master, Mr. Strong. He was along of Colnett, you know, in '93. A respectable, valuable man to have on this cruise."

"An English ship with a French name?"

"She is a French ship with an English name, sweetheart, French built. She was *Indomitable* when they had her, now she is our *L'Unite*."

"I wish you joy of her with all my heart, James. And I'm so glad you value her Master. Who is Mr. Colnett?"

"Captain Colnett was sent out on a mission similar to ours, to investigate for our whaling fleet in the islands and coasts of the Pacific. He wrote a book of the experience." Captain Blackwell knew Mercedes' love of reading. "Ah, and here, look at this. This part you shall most approve." He withdrew his orders from his jacket pocket and smoothed the parchment sheets before her, pointing with satisfaction to the phrase, 'The Lords High Commissioners for the Admiralty give leave Captain Blackwell may carry his wife, a native speaker of Spanish.'

"Ain't I the fortunate son?" He managed a broad grin, though in his heart he felt anything but.

Captain Blackwell had been unable to arrange a meeting with Enoch Bourne until their last evening in London before departing for Portsmouth and the hard labor of fitting out. He and Mercedes were to dine at Lady Oxford's house and afterwards attend the theatre with Enoch Bourne and his new bride.

"What kind of name is Missy?" Mercedes asked about Bourne's wife, as they were dressing for supper.

"It ain't no kind of name for a grown woman, but she isn't grown. She's barely nineteen. Margaret, perhaps, or...why I don't know. Missy! She is half his age. Some men like to finish raising their wives, do you see?"

"And others will take whoever they can board and carry?"

Captain Blackwell made a feint at Mercedes but he was not in earnest. He wanted to cut along to Lady Oxford's townhouse, and be done with this damnable business with Enoch Bourne. After which, for the sake of his sanity, he had determined to enjoy this last evening in London.

"Damnable is what it is," Enoch Bourne was saying, "A damn shame you should be caught up in it, Jim old cock. Admiral Gambier and his followers cannot say enough ill of his lordship. Adulterous, froward, ill-bred."

Captain Blackwell was looking conscious, thinking that Admiral Gambier ought not to cry out so against adulterers, yet sharing the same human failing did not seem to prevent him doing so.

"What neither me nor m'brother Phipps can comprehend is, why the outcry should extend to you. A man who had the mere misfortune to be carrying his lordship back to England."

"Unless I am to be blamed for delivering the Vice-Admiral in one piece."

Enoch Bourne raised his wine glass to him with a nod. They were together in one of Lady Oxford's upstairs sitting rooms while the rest of the party was assembling downstairs prior to going in to supper.

"So you did, and the honorable acquittal cannot be undone." Enoch shook his head. "Perhaps it is the fact that Dismal Jemmy and his cronies lost on those scores makes them bitter. Yet Phipps said the hue and cry against you and Lord Nelson smacked of something personal, at least on Gambier's part."

"He has never had a kindness for me," Captain Blackwell said quite truthfully, and then he felt compelled to dissemble before his friend. "What there can be in it of a personal nature, I can't make out. As you say, I have barely a passing acquaintance with his lordship."

"Well," said Enoch, with a little, knowing purse of his lips, "your stomach must be crying out. Shipboard hours and naval etiquette are not for this house, nor anything near. And you should probably like to rescue Mrs. Blackwell from, ah, questionable company."

Supper was a chaotic, sprawling affair with no discernible start or end. People came in and were heartily welcomed, and went out at random to hisses and calls. It was much like theatre, Mercedes believed, by which she meant no disrespect to the Bourne Miscellany. She liked them for their youthful gaiety and high spirits. At her end of the table they refrained from flinging food at one another's heads, and she was grateful. Mrs. Captain Bourne, Missy, fit in famously with her husbands' rake-hell brothers and with his sisters, who were given to breaking out in the language of the lower deck.

"Mrs. Captain, may I trouble you for the roast beef? Blackwell's plate stands empty." Enoch's sister, the one they all called Billingsgate, motioned down the table to Mercedes.

"I shall help him," Missy cried. "Here is the saddle of mutton to hand."

"I did not mean you, little Miss Missy. I would not call you Mrs. Captain until you've earned it as Mrs. Blackwell has done. Missy should like to serve up a big hunk of you, Blackwell, I'd wager a pony." Billingsgate's tone in this aside was none too subtle.

"Now Ma'am, there is no need to come it the hard horse," Captain Blackwell said. "Thank you, Mrs. Bourne, I could just do with another slice." He gazed with particular attention at Missy's bosom as she leaned over him with the serving dish.

Mercedes recognized that glitter in Captain Blackwell's eye as he surveyed Missy's white skin. With her flame red hair and her coltish good looks and spirits Missy was an exquisite young woman. London was full of them, from the demi-reps they would see in their numbers at the theatre, to the daughters of the upper ten thousand. Mercedes wondered how she would keep a man of Captain Blackwell's fierce animal spirits attached in the midst of such temptation. It was perhaps fortunate they were putting to sea.

She appreciated the truth of Lord Nelson's remark 'every man is a bachelor after Gibraltar.' She would not expect fidelity from him were he away on an extended cruise. But neither did Mercedes have any notion of being left with his reverend father, the way Lord Nelson had done to Lady Nelson.

"As I was saying, ma'am, one of the honorables must have a copy of Colnett's book. I will make inquires if you wish." Captain Bourne and Mercedes were seated next each other, across from Captain Blackwell and Missy.

"Oh, books! That is why I do not go to university," Captain Bourne's brother, Cripplegate said. "I would be obliged to read books. Why should I bother when I might go to the play. What are you seeing this evening, Mrs. Captain?"

"I should be very happy to accept of your kind offer regarding Colnett, Captain Bourne," Mercedes said. She turned with a smile and a nod to Cripplegate. "Hamlet, and then Bluebeard."

"Blackwell goes to Bluebeard! Ah ha ha!"

But Bluebeard was interrupted in a most interesting part when the green curtain came down in Drury Lane theatre at eleven-thirty, the Bishop of London having decreed performances should be over by twelve o'clock. It being short of the hour there was a great noise and outcry. Lord Oxford's rather bad box was up one flight of stairs, and surrounded by the boxes of London's finest courtesans. Mercedes saw one of these damsels faint away at the same time two separate fights broke out in the pit. Several young men jumped upon the stage and began to caper, tearing down the curtain and the scenery.

"Oh, look! Isn't that Cripplegate?" cried Missy, pointing. It was hard to mistake the young man with the club foot dancing on stage.

"That caps it." Captain Bourne stood up. The crowd in the pit started hurling chairs at the chandeliers. "Jim, let's go for a carriage."

Both captains quit the box. Mercedes wondered at them leaving their wives alone in the riot, but she supposed they would have left a midshipman to attend them if one were by. She and Missy watched the spectacle of destruction with a degree of fascination. Now the crowd waded into the orchestra and began attacking the instruments. So many chandeliers had been broken Missy said, in a thrilled voice, "In a moment we shall be left entirely in the dark!"

Into their box ambled two young men, London beaux, one with a collar starched so high he could scarcely turn his head, the other sporting a luxurious mane of hair.

"Why, look what we've found, Bertie," the beaux of the lion mane said. "Two prime bits of muslin."

Missy lifted her fine head. "We are captain's wives, sir. Captains of the Royal Navy."

"Hoot toot!" declared stiff neck Bertie. "I like a little play acting myself, honey, in the right setting."

Mercedes stood, clearly the beaux believed them women of easy virtue since they were seated unattended in an area of the theatre virtually given over to the damsels. She suspected they were drunk, and she was extremely concerned. Not so much for what the beaux might do; though she did long for a side arm — a sword, a rapier, a midshipman's dirk, a belaying pin — just in case she was forced to make an impression on these dim boys; but for the consequences if either of the captains were to make their appearance and find the scoundrels offering insult to their wives.

"She is quite in earnest, gentlemen. We are not that sort of women, I am Mrs. Captain — "

"Yes, yes, dear," said lion mane with a flourishing bow. "And you may call me Lord Byron, if you wish."

Missy gasped, and the other one, Bertie, took advantage of the distraction to try to pinch Mercedes. She easily evaded his clumsy paw and wished she could plant him a facer, but violence would never do. If Captain Blackwell were to walk in and find her grappling with this boar it might be murder. Mercedes had no desire to watch him stand another trial for man-slaughter.

She heard the handle turn and saw the door beyond the backs of the beaux begin to open. "You do not seem to credit a hint, gentlemen, so I shall show you what type of women we are." Mercedes grasped Missy in her arms and planted a kiss on her mouth, exactly the way Captain Blackwell had often and often done to her. She even pressed her tongue against Missy's lips until they parted, for authenticity's sake.

The mouths of the beaux, and that of Captain Blackwell behind them, dropped open.

"Oh, I say — " began the beaux impersonating Lord Byron.

"Get out, cully, before I knock your heads together." Captain Blackwell's voice came harsh out of the darkness.

"Good luck to you, big buck, these here are some strange skirts."

In the carriage ride away from the theatre the ladies might have taken Blackwell's silence for extreme irritation, but the truth was he'd had such a shock of pure lust he still reeled from it. When he'd walked in to Lord Oxford's box and seen Mercedes grasp Missy and kiss her, the sexual jolt he'd experienced had been like the roar of a full broadside. It had almost knocked him over. Since then his face had been rigid and set, and he'd never been so grateful for a darkened theatre, leading the ladies out with his breeches tenting before him.

"Should you like to come up for a glass of porter, Jim?" Captain Bourne offered, when the carriage was stopped before Lady Oxford's house.

"No, thank you, brother. We shall call in the morning to take leave of you, if we may. Good night, Mrs. Bourne."

He restrained himself for a moment as the carriage moved away, and then he turned to Mercedes seated beside him, seized her and dragged her onto his lap. Blackwell burned for her as fiercely as he had when she'd first walked the deck of his ship and he'd longed to take her to his bed. If anything his desire for her was stronger now he knew the glorious body underneath Mercedes' elegant gown, now he knew the strength of the limbs that would lovingly clasp him.

Blackwell was not aware how far he'd pressed the point until Mercedes gasped out, "Jim! Not here."

He removed his hand from where he'd plunged it up the bodice of her gown, and loosened his other arm from clutching her across her back and buttocks. It was a damn good thing they were quitting London and putting to sea, he would at once shield her from their misguided fathers and redeem his professional character. If they were to stay in England, he might be forced to fight more than one duel over his clever, passionate, unpredictable wife.

CHAPTER SIX

"L'Unite, off Portsmouth

Dearest Brother Frank,

It is my sincerest wish this letter might find you in Gibraltar returned from your sojourn in the East, with the wife and son and daughter you so much desire to call your own. Wherever this may find you, I had to share with you my joy at being allowed to continue in the glory line. I was acquitted in the loss of *Assurance*, honorably so. I fancy that last part had much to do with a certain chest I salvaged of Lady Hamilton's fripperies that she valued much. But I should not be glib, brother. Lady Hamilton said some handsome things at the trial when she need not have done. Among other things it pains me I was not able to save any of Mercedes' belongings, nor protect her from that graver loss I recounted to you in my last.

I have had the good fortune to be given *L'Unite*, 44, and my orders are to stand unaltered in all but the name of the ship. You will appreciate the happiness this gives me, knowing as you do it has always been my wish to keep Mercedes by me. I am very happy as well, and fortunate in my officers. Mr. Verson is my premier and young Jack sails too, in course. The refined Mr. Bransford is my second lieutenant, and Mr. Bowles, just passed for lieutenant, will stand my third. They are men I value exceedingly, and having served with me before they know my ways. We are to have Doctor VanArsdel as ship's surgeon, which seems to gratify and comfort

Mercedes to a greater degree than I would have supposed. *L'Unite's* Master is Mr. Strong, a man possessed of a prodigious store of maps and experience in the Pacific. You may imagine my satisfaction in this last.

I have a full compliment of eight midshipmen. One most unexpected, a young man you may remember from our brush with *La Trinidad*. Juan Luis Montelongo presented himself a week ago with a purse of money for fitting out, and a note from Mr. Martinez respectfully requesting the boy be taken on as volunteer and midshipman. Mr. Montelongo is fifteen, a bit old to begin training as a sea-officer. On the other hand he has been to sea as captain's servant in *La Trinidad*, and as I set the whole in motion with Mercedes' uncle months ago I could not in conscience turn the youngster off. I will tell you I was powerfully surprised Mr. Montelongo should wish to serve again after what happened to him."

Captain Blackwell paused in his letter writing, lifting his pen and gazing past where Mercedes sat knitting near the stern windows. He sincerely hoped he made no mistake in taking Juan Luis Montelongo into his ship. Experience had taught him the damage one unstable man could wreak upon a ship's company. But the exceedingly handsome, polished, Mr. Montelongo had something of a winning way about him. He stood up with manly fortitude to Captain Blackwell's lecture declaring he would brook no irregularity in his ship, and demand of Mr. Montelongo the same as of any young gentleman entering on the books. Captain Blackwell admitted him as a volunteer, first class, and even guided him, through Mercedes, in the purchasing of the necessaries for his sea chest. In truth Captain Blackwell was amazed, astonished that Mr. Montelongo should choose to ship with officers and men who remembered his having been sodomized when a prisoner aboard *Inconstant*.

Captain Blackwell dipped his pen.

"But it is not for me to judge. In consequence of being burdened with so many young gentlemen I am obliged to take on a school master, who comes in the form of a chaplain, Mr. St. James. As the young man is also a naturalist you will see the Royal Navy intends to wring every ounce of service from the poor fellow.

I find I have given you a more minute account of my affairs than will interest you. It is because I had rather not approach the next subject at all, and only do so after the most serious consideration. The case being this, Frank, I had a most prodigious row with my father before parting from him at Deane. This was before the court-martial. What passed between us has shaken my trust in him to a greater degree than his mere mismanagement of my money could ever have done. A matter that you set right in any case, brother. My father chose to interfere in my marriage and that I cannot abide.

I want to make it clear to you that should anything befall me, you who are forever lecturing me about seeking a less dangerous profession will not bring me up for speaking plain in this instance, should I be knocked on the head and Mercedes need support it is my expressed desire you support her, not my father. Pray be assured I will make all of this known to Mercedes exactly as I write it you. I cannot really imagine a circumstance in which she would need anyone's support, being as you are aware a woman of considerable parts. But you will find enclosed with the present a witnessed copy of my Power of Attorney. The original I give to Mercedes, and I leave a third copy with Coutts. This entire matter pains me a great deal, brother, but it gives me even greater pain to contemplate my father making a pet of Mercedes for my wish to the contrary not being made known.

I fear you may think me an undutiful, ungrateful scrub of a son to our father, but a stronger duty and love compels me to share with you what I have done. Mercedes desires her best love to you and to Zahraa and Miriam and Farrokh. She bids me tell you that Queenie the cat, Miriam's kind wedding gift, remains in England. It seems Queenie is in the increasing way and no one at the rectory will hear of her being moved. Dear Frank, I hope you will believe I remain,

> Your Affectionate Brother,
> Jma. Blackwell"

CHAPTER SEVEN

L'Unite was anchored in the harbor of Rio de Janeiro above Isle dos Cobras, in view of a monastery situated on a hill northwest of the town. A half dozen British merchant ships were scattered about the harbor that had been convoyed by the man-of-war to Brazil. The L'Unites, the right man-of-war's men, called the merchantmen 'those slab sided tubs' among other unkind sobriquets. The whalers among them were bound fishing from the coast of Peru to the Sandwich Islands. The season for sperm whale approached, from May to November in the Pacific waters.

This small portion of the merchant fleet had had a sad time of it, straining to keep company in the crossing from England. *L'Unite* was a fine swift sailer indeed, constantly firing guns to bring the masters' attention to a maneuver or encourage them to pack on more sail. In a strong gale of wind in latitude 21° 30', and longitude 36° west Captain Blackwell lost four of his flock. But when the gale abated he herded them together again. The merchant captains were heartily sick of him by the time Cape Frio was raised.

The storm had been the highlight of an otherwise tedious passage. Captain Blackwell had felt like a man with a thoroughbred charger between his legs that must keep to a Sunday walking pace. The gale offered an opportunity to observe the crew in heavy weather, and as nothing important carried away it wasn't a serious event. Captain Blackwell was in the main pleased with the efficiency of his officers and the ship's company.

There were the inevitable awkward sods among *L'Unite's* hands, as in any man-of-war's crew. The defaulters list he'd reviewed with the Master at Arms at eight o'clock that morning was on Captain Blackwell's mind.

"Mercedes, we are to punish this morning at five bells. No women allowed on deck." He'd finished breakfast and was working his way through a pot of coffee, watching Mercedes move about the great cabin bringing her sewing things in from the sleeping space. "I'm afraid we shall have a flogging today."

Mercedes came and sat with him at the table, a look of concern on her face.

"It's Saunders, foretopman," he said. "A prime reliable hand, soft-spoken, a West Indian. I cannot conceive what possessed him to raise his hand to Mr. Strong."

"Must you flog him indeed?"

"Oh, aye, he did this in front of witnesses. There is no help for it."

The bosun piped hands to witness punishment. Captain Blackwell heaved himself out of his seat, buckled on his sword, and reaching the deck he clapped his cocked hat on his head. At the same moment, he set his features in a hard expression for the duty ahead.

The marines were lined up with bayonets fixed. *L'Unite's* officers, sweating in their broadcloth uniforms, ranged the quarterdeck. They wore side arms and faced the men mustered to divisions. Every man toed a seam, many an imaginary one, on the ship's deck, attentive to the captain, their officers, and the day's miscreants. The ordinary cases of drunkenness and failure to jump sharp at the word were dealt with, and sentenced to the usual stoppage or reduction of grog.

The Master At Arms read out, "Able seaman Saunders, sir, did answer back and raise his hand to Mr. Strong, Sailing-Master."

Captain Blackwell gazed at Saunders standing before him with his head bowed. Saunders normally wore a knit cap, pulled low over his brow, but naturally before his captain he appeared with his head uncovered. The man's hair put Captain Blackwell in mind of snakes, or Medusa, with long, thick, coiled braids springing in every direction.

"Saunders, I've heard what Mr. Strong has to say on your conduct and the incident of Thursday last," Captain Blackwell said. "What have you to say?" His voice reached even to the men lined up on the forecastle.

Saunders raised his head slightly, but did not look him in the eye, and uttered something soft and low that Captain Blackwell could not hear.

"Come, Saunders, you are rated Able," Captain Blackwell said. "Speak up, man."

"I only pushed his hand away, sir," Saunders said in a low tone, but directly to Captain Blackwell.

Captain Blackwell heard Saunders' statement right enough but he was not at once sure what it meant. When it occurred to him Saunders might be saying he'd raised his hand only to fend off a blow, he felt a wave of distaste for the service. He would have to flog Saunders equally for raising his hand in his own defense, as for raising it to threaten an officer. The requirements of the service and of discipline demanded it. The hard and impassive face he turned to Saunders and the gathered crew belied his emotions.

"Mr. Bowles, Saunders is in your division. Have you anything to add?" Seeing Mr. Bowles begin to open his mouth, he hastened to add, "Relevant to this case, Mr. Bowles."

"No, sir."

"Very well. Saunders, I find you guilty of insubordination and raising your hand to an officer. I sentence you to a dozen lashes. Master at Arms, seize him up."

Captain Blackwell had barely finished those orders, to a stirring and writhing of the collected men before him, when a high pitched distinctly feminine shriek pierced the air. Every man on deck turned toward the great cabin. Captain Blackwell's face became more furiously set, and the only sound in the dead silence following the cry was the drawing of his sword.

"Mr. Verson, you have the deck. Carry on with punishment." Captain Blackwell turned and stalked toward his cabin.

"She's going to catch it something cruel without it's bloody murder below decks," McMurtry murmured to Narhilla, standing alongside of him. "Poor little Missus."

At the door of his cabin the sentry stood at attention, white faced.

"Open the goddamn door," Captain Blackwell called to him.

The sentry flung open the door and followed Captain Blackwell into the great cabin. Mercedes was mincing along the stern lockers with a tomahawk clutched in one hand.

"Hell and death, woman. What's the infernal screeching about?"

"Oh James!" Mercedes cried, running to him. She brought up short when the sentry stepped from behind him. "Captain, forgive me for crying out, I'm terribly concerned. It was a spider, a great hairy one the size of your fist."

On deck, amid the tension of the rituals of rigging the grating and the bosun's mate trying the cat out of the bag, the captain's roar of "A spider!" relieved the charged atmosphere for the space of several moments. Comments were exchanged in undertones; "Suppose it's the great bird eating spider of the Amazon," followed by, "This ain't the fucking Amazon, mate."

"She says it's hairy, a prodigious aggressive spider," piped up the youngest midshipman, Mr. Allen of the canine hearing.

"Strip!" ordered Mr. Verson.

The chaplain, Mr. St. James, standing near the condemned man to loan him divine support, heard Saunders say, "Could be a banana spider. Poisonous."

Mr. St. James immediately fled the deck, while Mr. Verson's eyes turned heavenward.

Captain Blackwell's heart had not been in the bellowing out he'd been obliged to do when he found the ship's routine had been interrupted by a spider. He'd really wanted to take Mercedes to his breast and press her in his arms after finding her prepared to wield a tomahawk against an insect. But Captain Blackwell had his duty and he'd been called from one extremely unpleasant one to another in this present of haranguing his wife. Mercedes and the sentry stood before him hanging their heads.

"Oh, there it goes, sir!" Mercedes cried, pointing at the starboard bulkhead.

Mr. St. James dashed into the cabin as Captain Blackwell stalked over to the spider, raising his hand to crush it against the bulkhead. "Sir! Captain Blackwell, sir, the spider is poisonous. I shall trap it, sir. And then I shall have it a specimen."

Captain Blackwell froze in mid stride and turned to the chaplain. "Is punishment concluded, Mr. St. James? Did Mr. Verson dismiss the company?"

"No, sir, I thought I must warn you — "

"You are one of the ship's company, are you not Mr. St. James? You have no business here unless and until Mr. Verson dismisses the ship's crew. No, hold a moment, sir." The young man, crestfallen, was moving toward the door. "Take away that wretched spider and show a leg. And do not get bitten, dead parsons don't look well with the Admiralty. What now?" This last was to ten-year-old midshipman Mr. Allen, who pelted full speed into the cabin.

"Mr. Verson's duty, sir, and you are wanted on deck." And then the fresh-faced boy, in what he imagined was a whisper, blurted out, "It's Saunders, sir, he's not a man at all."

Before he quit the cabin, Captain Blackwell heard Mercedes' murmur, *"Dios mio."*

On deck Captain Blackwell met a galvanized set of officers and men standing very still and silent. Doctor VanArsdel stood beside the prisoner, in front of a stony faced Mr. Verson.

"When Saunders was ordered to strip he...she demurred, sir," Mr. Verson reported. "And when the bosun and his mate went to assist, she resisted and then called out for the doctor."

"Doctor?" Captain Blackwell said, stepping up to the pair on whom all eyes were fixed.

"Saunders is female, sir, at least above the waist. I would have to examine — "

"Yes, yes, Doctor, thank you. Goddamn, hell and death," Captain Blackwell muttered under his breath. Louder, he said, "Mr. Verson, dismiss the ship's company. Mr. Morrow, all hands to splice the mainbrace. Doctor, if you please. Saunders, in my cabin."

Mercedes had been looking on, with the marine sentry standing beside her, at Mr. St. James's efforts to trap the spider when Captain Blackwell came back into the cabin. The sentry scurried out and Captain Blackwell desired her to accompany the doctor into the sleeping cabin for the examination of Saunders. It had taken only a brief humiliating moment with Saunders's trousers lowered to establish she was the same beneath her rough seaman's slops as Mercedes under her fine muslin gown.

"May I just have a word with Saunders, Doctor? Now we are no longer exactly in Royal Navy territory."

Doctor VanArsdel bowed and went out into the great cabin to confirm the matter to Captain Blackwell.

"How long have you served, Saunders?"

"Seven years, Missus. How else could I be rated able seaman?"

"Seven years living as a man! Pardon me, I would not intrude."

"I should be living so still but for that sad bugger Mr. Strong. He's one of those as fancies boys. He tried to put his hand between my legs and I push his hand away. Mr. Strong sets up a hue and cry so when men look round, there we are arm to arm. That's what done me, never was near a flogging offense before."

"I'm sorry for it." Mercedes' heart was already misgiving her, over whether she should be obliged to tell this to the Captain. "It is a life you cherish then, the seaman's life?"

She motioned Saunders to the sea chests and they both sat down.

"I don't know as who's to say cherish, it's better than what I had. I was one of the women the plantations loan out to the ships when they put into port, in Antigua. I hid in the cable tier of *Thetis*, 32, Captain Hotham, stole slops and when she put to sea I step forward, a runaway slave. Captain Hotham, he was short handed because of the yellow jack, he says 'We'll make a topman of him.'"

"And so he did, Saunders, for Captain Blackwell says you are a...a prime hand."

"I am obliged to him, Missus." Saunders knuckled her forehead. "It's a hard service, but it's better than the other, and I earned my rating."

Mercedes could not imagine the hardship of her previous life, nor how Saunders had hidden her sex and her cycles sharing a head with hundreds of men. Countless other questions of how she'd managed for seven years to pass as a man in a ship of war occurred to Mercedes, while she and Saunders sat regarding one another with astonishment on both sides.

"I take it you should prefer to stay with the ship?"

"Of all things. Or transfer into another ship at my old rating. Black folk are slaves here. I only know English and Creole. I don't have the Portuguese, and without I am on a ship...I will be good for only one thing."

As she stood up Mercedes felt dizzy, even nauseated in the warm, close cabin. "We had better join your officers."

The scene in the great cabin was a peculiar one. McMurtry had joined Mr. St. James in attempting to trap the spider, which was uncommon sprightly. When they approached very close it reared up and offered challenge. Captain Blackwell and Doctor VanArsdel stood back while various implements, a pewter mug, a coffee grinder, a wine glass, were tried and discarded as spider traps.

Everyone in the cabin turned to Mercedes and Saunders when they emerged from the sleeping space. Saunders strode purposefully to the bulkhead where the spider dashed and clapped her large woolen cap over it. "A piece of parchment, mate," she said over her shoulder to McMurtry. And when McMurtry supplied the sheet, Saunders slid it between the bulkhead and the rim of the cap and brought away the spider inside. She gathered the mouth of the cap in her fist and presented it to Mr. St. James. "A banana spider if you please, Reverend. You must smoke him as soon as ever may be. He is mortal poison."

Captain Blackwell caught McMurtry's eye and jerked his head at the cabin door. McMurtry followed the chaplain out.

"Doctor, ma'am, please be seated."

He and Saunders were left facing one another, just as on deck.

"How long have you been serving in the Royal Navy, Saunders?"

"Seven years, sir. Three years in *Thetis* in the West Indies, then paid off in England, and another four in *Lively*, 36, on the North

American station. And I had hopes of a good long cruise with *L'Unite*, your honor."

"A good long cruise." Captain Blackwell nodded at her, beginning to pace, a growing anger in his eyes. "How dare you, sir...ma'am. The Navy ain't no Tom Tiddler's Ground, no place for play acting as you well know." Captain Blackwell stopped speaking abruptly. The person looking back at him was a thorough going seaman. A man —a woman — who could hand, reef and steer, lay out on a yard in a gale of wind, stand a watch, and support a midshipman taking a prize into port. "What do you suggest I do with you, Saunders?"

"Permission to remain aboard, sir."

"The Navy's got no use for women." Captain Blackwell refused to look at Mercedes. In a remote part of his mind he wondered how much he'd wounded her that day.

"Sir, if I may," interjected Doctor VanArsdel. "I could do with another loblolly boy, if you prefer Saunders not work on deck."

"And where is she to berth, Doctor?" Captain Blackwell rounded on Doctor VanArsdel.

"She might sling a hammock in the pantry," Mercedes said. "Captain, in Portsmouth you offered me to ship a woman, a maid, do you recall?"

Captain Blackwell remembered his relief when Mercedes had refused that offer. He bowed to her.

"Saunders could be on the ship's books as my servant and attend to whatever duties you see fit."

Captain Blackwell paced up and down, his expression hard and abstracted. At last he called, "McMurtry!"

"Sir!" McMurtry stepped eagerly into the cabin.

"Pantry keys to Mrs. Blackwell. Saunders is to berth in there and you shall ask Mrs. Blackwell when you require the keys. Pass the word for Mr. Verson."

When Mr. Verson entered the cabin Captain Blackwell was still pacing, hitching at his breeches from time to time in an aggravated way. "Mr. Verson, Saunders is shifted out of Mr. Bowles' division, disrated to captain's servant. Saunders is to be Mrs. Blackwell's servant, berthing in the pantry. She will act as loblolly boy to the surgeon, pick oakum with the invalids, and perform whatever other duties Doctor VanArsdel or Mrs. Blackwell may assign. Dismissed, all of you."

"Some days is more exciting in the Service than others," Captain Blackwell said to Mercedes late that evening. She lay next to him in his cot. Besides the revelation of Saunders, and the spider, *L'Unite* had been mustered to man the yards and fire an eleven gun salute to Admiral Sir Home Popham, arrived in *Ganges*, 98. "I should be unhappy if I thought I offended you with all that bluster and bellowing out earlier."

"You didn't, James. Thank you for allowing Saunders to remain aboard. If you'd put her ashore, Brazil would have been the death of her."

"I've known captains put their mistresses ashore wherever they happened to be in the world, once they tired of them."

"*Canallas*. But it is easier for a white woman to find a protector. I fear you will not like what Saunders told me today of how she came to be on the defaulters list."

Mercedes recounted her conversation with Saunders, trying to keep to the words actually spoken in the way she'd observed of the Navy. Captain Blackwell emitted an agitated grunt, swung his legs out of the cot and sat up.

"You tell me this now, Mercedes, after I have committed to Saunders remaining aboard. Mr. Strong a pederast. I cannot have them both aboard after what you tell me. I do not like to be managed, Miss."

He jumped up and began to stride like Adam back and forth in the confined space. It was late, Mercedes was tired and she felt tears rising in her eyes. She pushed them down, unwilling to shed any except under the direst circumstance. There was real anguish on Captain Blackwell's face, so much did he value Mr. Strong and his excellent store of maps, but she could not have done differently. It would have been a greater sin to hold back information from her husband and the ship's commander.

She rose and put on her dressing gown.

"Where are you going?"

"To my cabin to sleep. Pray do the same, and leave off flogging yourself. You would not have put Saunders ashore to be made a whore of any more than you would have put me on the lower deck." Mercedes stood in front of him, reaching up to stroke his beard shadowed face. "You wanted me to believe that would happen if I did not lie with you, but I never did. You are a gentleman, darling. Not one of the London swell variety, a true gentleman. One who suffers when he does what he must."

He took her hand and kissed it. "You will come to me in the morning?"

"Of course, Captain, if you wish it." She smiled at him. So often did Captain Blackwell want to lie with her in the early morning, Mercedes associated with the erotic the sound of holystones grinding over her head and the flogging dry of the decks.

"I do wish it. Goodnight to you, Mercy, sweetheart."

The vibrant emerald green of Brazil with her dramatic mountain peaks and lush over exuberance of life and sensuality receded in *L'Unite's* wake. Mr. Montelongo sat with Mr. St. James in the sick berth, foregoing a last sight of the tropical shore. Mr. St. James had in fact been bit. But as the war-like spider had delivered its venom through both the material of Saunders' cap and Mr. St. James's trouser leg, the full payload had not been dropped. The flesh around the bite was red, swollen, and wretchedly tender. Along with this, the chaplain experienced a swelling in his member — his virile member — that caused Doctor VanArsdel to tell Mercedes, "You must not visit the sick berth patients at present. Mr. St. James has reacted to the poison, in a way that would satisfy even the seventy celestial virgins of the Mahometans."

Older men must be allowed their poetical flights. Though his condition was at once painful and humiliating; he'd supplanted Saunders as the talk of the ship; Mr. St. James tried to bear up.

"She disappears, Brazil," he murmured to Mr. Montelongo. "And only one full day ashore to explore the tenth, the thousandth part of her wonders."

"You have one great spider and a collection of curious butterflies and beetles. And any number of monkeys and tropical birds."

The crew had taken on various pets in Rio, in spite of the captain's and the lieutenants' attempts to dissuade them from spending their meager wages, or trading their slops.

"They will not do where we are bound, I fear." Mr. St. James sighed, but he was not beaten. "How I should have loved a fortnight in the Brazilian forest."

Mr. Montelongo eyed the chaplain as though doubting he could survive two days in the Brazilian jungle. "I should think we must be grateful to get away."

Aside from Mr. St. James's unfortunate condition, Mr. Montelongo referred to the affair with the sailing master. Mr. Strong had gone across to visit the Admiral in Ganges and requested to be invalided out. He did look unwell, gray of face, having apprehended that Captain Blackwell, and indeed L'Unite's entire crew, had smoked him. Mr. Strong was a respected man and Admiral Popham, after consulting Captain Blackwell, had no hesitation and at once put Mr. Strong on a ship for England. Mr. Strong, the experienced man in the Pacific, sailed off, taking his prodigious store of maps back to England with him.

"This does not change our orders, gentlemen," Captain Blackwell said to his lieutenants and master's mates. "We are ordered to improve the Admiralty's maps by surveying anchorages and channels favorable to the Navy and British commerce. We shall do just that. Improve the maps we have, and make them where we don't." He was almost as sanguine as he sounded, for the business with Mr. Strong had been managed without discredit to him or the ship. But it was not a favorable start to the mission, and what damage the lack of the sailing master might do them he could not tell.

CHAPTER EIGHT

The ship was hove to in Desolation Bay with two of her boats away, the gig with Captain Blackwell, two midshipmen and his boat's crew, had gone to the East and Mr. Bransford and his party in the red cutter to the West. Mr. Verson presently had the deck, but after the making of noon he was to lead a party in the launch to a beach due North of *L'Unite's* present position for fuel. Mercedes and Mr. Montelongo walked the deck in the forenoon watch, hoping for warmth from the feeble sunshine, but in fact both were chilled to the bone in spite of layers of clothing.

All the ship's people originally from warmer climates suffered more from the cold than the Englishmen. Though the mariners must feel the biting air as they worked the ship, knocking ice from her rigging, yards and sails, they contrived to ignore the weather and endured it without comment.

"It should be called Desolation or Extremadura." Mercedes looked over at the miles of brown hillocks interspersed near and far with towering glacial ice. "Should it not, Mr. Montelongo?"

In the forenoon and afternoon watches Mercedes walked the deck alternately with all eight midshipmen. She was an object of worship in the midshipmen's berth: lovely, good natured, and completely unobtainable. She tried to show no preference for the company of one young gentleman over another, but Mr. Montelongo, with whom she could converse in Spanish, was a favorite. They were the oldest of shipmates from the time of sailing together in *La Trinidad*.

"The birds seem to delight in it." Mr. Montelongo smiled at the varieties of comic penguins hurtling themselves in and out of the surf. The birds were a constant source of amusement not just for the chaplain, who was in raptures, but for the crew in their idle moments.

"You knew then, about the sailing master?" Mercedes revisited an earlier conversation; they could not have spoken of it except there were no other Spanish speakers by.

"I suspected," Mr. Montelongo said. "Shall I tell you how?"

"Please do."

Mr. Montelongo was silent a moment, pacing at her side, trouble clouding his youthful face.

"In the same way you might recognize when a man takes an interest in you for more than your acquaintance. Desire. Do you understand, Doña Mercedes?"

"He was attracted to you."

"Yes, if I do not mistake. He wanted to know me in the way of the Greeks. I did not return the sentiment, but my issue was with him. It may not be so with any right feeling man." Mr. Montelongo turned and looked at her with real concern.

Mercedes took his arm. "I'm sure you are aware there is a vast deal of difference between being compelled and doing something from personal choice." She felt a fraud uttering those words. Her experience of compulsion and choice were what were vastly different from Mr. Montelongo's: she'd been courted aboard *Inconstant*, he had been raped.

"Naturally I am, ma'am. I am fifteen. What happened aboard *Inconstant*...confirmed me in what I'd previously felt. No one can like being forced, Doña Mercedes. But I know what I prefer."

Mercedes could find nothing to say. She pressed his arm. Mr. Montelongo, betraying his great apprehension, ventured, "Would Captain Blackwell put me off the ship if he knew?"

"He might if you did anything about it while aboard his command. But as to what you do ashore, who you choose to love, I don't believe either of us is so great a hypocrite we'd hold what a man loves against him."

"You greatly relieve my mind, Miss Mercedes." Mr. Montelongo spoke in English, for young Jack Verson came running up from the direction of the quarterdeck.

"Mr. Verson's respects and duty, ma'am, Mr. Montelongo, and they are about to shoot the sun."

Mr. Verson and the party in the launch were two hours past the time appointed for returning to *L'Unite*. Captain Blackwell was in the maintop, scanning the bay with his telescope in the fading light, concern written on every feature. Besides Mr. Verson and young Jack, who'd begged to go ashore with the working party, the launch's crew was composed of twenty men and two midshipmen, Mr. Montelongo and little Mr. Allen. It was a source of comfort to Captain Blackwell that his very capable coxswain, Narhilla, formed one of the party.

Captain Blackwell climbed to the stunning height of the main topgallant mast crosstrees and studied the surrounding bay once more, nothing but a few patches of flotsam and ice. Visibility was becoming poor as the pale sun set, and a mist rose up from the surface of the sea. He slid down a backstay, his hands burning with the effort.

"Mr. Bransford, course due North," Captain Blackwell said. "We will retrieve the launch."

There was no more than half an hour of daylight left and it might take *L'Unite* twice that time to work to Mr. Verson's position to windward.

"God send they are able to light a signal."

"Amen, sir," Mr. Bransford said.

The launch's crew did have a signal fire lit where the boat was drawn up onto the shingle beach, their mission having been to collect wood. They surrounded Captain Blackwell on the strand, when he climbed out of the gig run up on the beach.

"Oh sir!" cried Mr. Allen. "How glad we are to see you."

"Well, Mr. Allen, and what's this about? Not making the rendezvous and hanging about freezing on a beach like a pack of goddamn...Mr. Morrow, get this youngster into the boat and give him one of those blankets."

Mr. Allen's teeth were chattering so hard he was incapable of answering.

"Narhilla, what's this about?"

"It was me as convinced Mr. Allen to remain ashore, sir. Mr. Verson, young Goodman Jack, and Mr. Montelongo went off to climb yon summit, which you can't see, sir, over my shoulder bearing northwest. To take sightings, sir. They left about three bells in the afternoon watch by my reckoning and when they weren't back by the end of the watch, well ..."

"I see. Thank you, Narhilla. Mr. Allen," Captain Blackwell called to the boy shivering in the gig. "You did the right thing, not leaving your first officer stranded. Mr. Hoffinger." Captain Blackwell turned to the lieutenant of marines. "We shall unload the provisions and your men are to make camp on the beach. You are to light the blue lantern if Mr. Verson and his party return and a boat will be sent directly, otherwise we shall bring a boat ashore in the morning."

Captain Blackwell divided up the men to put some of the fresh hands in the launch and those of the launch's crew like Mr. Allen who were suffering most into the gig. The avarice of native peoples for ship's boats was well known. Who could forget Captain Cook? Captain Blackwell did not intend leaving one of his boats on the beach all night.

He retired to his cabin after seeing the launch's crew either brought to the sick berth or returned to their messmates and a double ration of grog. Mercedes jumped to her feet when he walked in.

"We retrieved the launch and all her people, except Mr. Verson, young Jack, and Mr. Montelongo. One of them must have been injured in their climb up a summit. It is already below freezing and only the middle of the first watch. I left a party of marines on the beach in case they appear."

He threw himself into the armchair and then grasped her hand and pulled her onto his lap.

"How I hope...and what of the marines, James? Do they not feel the cold?"

"They are only soldiers, sweetheart, bred for shore duty. And though I have nothing against them personally, a sailor has no love for a soldier you know. An Army officer is trusty and well-beloved of the King, while we sea-officers may not fail as we will answer the contrary at our peril. But I take your point. They shall be well enough with their tent and a fire, and had damn well better assist Mr. Verson if he returns."

"When he returns."

He squeezed her as his only reply, savoring the warmth of her in his arms.

Mr. Montelongo and Jack emerged from a marsh and struggled up the hillock in front of them. Both expected to see the wood they'd spotted when they'd reached the summit with Mr. Verson of the first great hill, overlooking one of the many inlets of Desolation Bay with *L'Unite's* working party below. When they gained the top of the hillock, the first pangs of dread seized Mr. Montelongo. Before them was another great stretch of marsh, and beyond it, not the wooded forest they'd expected to find, but more low hillocks choked with reeds and brush in the depressions. Mr. Montelongo looked back across the marsh through which they'd just struggled. A low mist was gathering over it, the sun was a cold ball one could look directly at. It appeared quite near the horizon, shielded by the densely clouded sky.

"Stop! Hold hard," Mr. Montelongo called.

Young Jack, assuming they were to go on, had plunged forward downhill. At Mr. Montelongo's hail he turned, looking over his shoulder, and promptly fell sprawled. He slid a ways downhill over the broken shingle and rock before Mr. Montelongo caught him up.

"I'm sorry, Jack," Mr. Montelongo said, wiping the blood from Jack's skinned palms.

"And Miss Mercedes made them." Jack shook his head over the holes in his mittens.

Mr. Montelongo tied his handkerchief round a deep cut on Jack's knee, over a tear in the trouser leg.

"We must turn back and find Mr. Verson," Mr. Montelongo said. "It grows late and we are no closer to that wood."

Jack made no objection, having been trained to obedience. He was limping when they set off in the direction they'd come.

"I shall take you in tow, just for the first stretch," Mr. Montelongo said.

He knelt and took the boy on his back. Mr. Montelongo found the mud in the marsh caking upon his half boots. He went along slowly with his head down, lifting his feet carefully at each step in order not to lose a boot. A half hour after they'd entered the marsh, Jack said, "Are you sure this is how we come in?"

Mr. Montelongo looked round. The sun was two fingers width from the horizon, and as long as he had its pale glow Mr. Montelongo felt he could find the strand and *L'Unite*. Yet the lowering mist over the marsh, and the cold; Jack already shivered against his back; and the coming darkness made him uneasy. What if he were to become confused and walk in circles, unable to find the other side of the marsh.

"As soon as we are clear of these reeds, we shall begin hailing your father." He set his teeth, shifted Jack higher on his back, and moved on.

They emerged from the marsh as the last light left the sky. Mr. Montelongo set Jack on his feet. He leaned over, fatigued, his hands planted on his knees.

"Can you walk?"

"Oh, yes sir." Jack took a few more or less unimpeded steps.

"Why don't you call me Juan, since we are ashore. This way." Mr. Montelongo endeavored to sound decided, like the British Navy men he so much admired.

But he could not be certain of their direction until the stars were well up, and only then if it were a clear night. Mr. Montelongo consequently walked slowly, and if any excuse were required Jack's lameness might be pointed to.

"Is it time to send up the minute gun, Juan?"

"By all means."

"Ahoy there! Ahoy!" They cried together, after the count of three.

Full dark and they stumbled along, holding hands after having nearly lost one another when only a few feet apart. A half hour since a light snowfall had begun and they were brittle with cold.

Mr. Montelongo was wretchedly sleepy, all he wished for in life was to lie down and never be obliged to get up again. Their hails, at ragged intervals, were spiritless.

In the silence after their last cry came a faint answering hail. Though he'd never been particularly devout, Mr. Montelongo sent a private prayer of thanks to the Virgin. He and Jack shouted back through parched lips and chilled throats.

Jack slipped his hand from Mr. Montelongo's grasp and ran forward, calling out "Pa! Pa!" Several moments later Mr. Montelongo nearly stumbled over Mr. Verson, kneeling down beside Jack, and examining the rent in his trousers.

"And Juan carried me part of the way, though I daresay I can do this last board to the ship on my own."

Mr. Verson looked up at Mr. Montelongo, who managed a stiff salute. Mr. Montelongo could not trust his voice. So great was his relief he was afraid he would cry, like young Jack was doing now, resting his head on his father's shoulder. Taciturn by nature, Mr. Verson patted Jack's back in silence. The look on his face, however, spoke volumes. It told Mr. Montelongo they were far from the safety and comfort of their berths aboard *L'Unite*.

"I believe you must have executed a circle in returning, Mr. Montelongo, rather than proceeding in a straight line, but I congratulate you. I will say nothing for the present of your dashing off without leave." Mr. Verson eyed his son as he said this last. "Thank you for keeping company with Jack."

Mr. Montelongo noticed, as they went along, Mr. Verson kept his head up, frequently scanning the sky. Consequently, the first lieutenant repeatedly barked his shins against unseen boulders, once taking a nasty tumble and landing a sprawl the way Jack had done earlier. They were obliged to join hands again, the night being so dark.

At last, in a depression between two hills filled with scrub and stunted trees, the snow still falling steadily, Mr. Verson halted. "Let us see if we can gather enough dry tinder to make a fire." Mr. Verson and Jack were both limping while casting about for dry branches amid the undergrowth. Given the state of his companions, Mr. Montelongo brought in the most fuel. Though he was mortally cold, he took off his gloves and began plying his flint and steel. Mr. Verson took it from him, and struck a spark on his third attempt.

They built the fire in the lee of one of the low hills, up against its shale side. Deep drowsiness was once more overtaking Mr. Montelongo, he nodded where he sat with his arms clasped round his legs, close in to the fire. Mr. Verson was across from him in much the same posture, except that he held Jack on his lap, huddled against his chest.

"Mr. Montelongo, if you please." Mr. Verson motioned to him.

Mr. Montelongo rose hesitantly, swaying on his feet, and came round to Mr. Verson's side of the fire. He sat down next to the first lieutenant, who beckoned him closer, putting his arm round Mr. Montelongo's shoulders.

When they were thus huddled together under Mr. Verson's Magellan jacket, Jack said, "You might call him Juan, since we are ashore."

"We must stay awake, Juan, watch and watch. Do you hear me, Jack? We shall rise every half glass and walk about. Dance the hornpipe if we have to. And in the morning we shall proceed to the ship." He gave both youngsters an encouraging squeeze.

In spite of the piercing cold, his growing thirst and hunger, the strain of fatigue and fear, Mr. Montelongo had never felt quite so tenderly cared for, and such a sweet sense of belonging.

Captain Blackwell kept the deck all night and before the light of dawn had fully illuminated the sky the blue lantern was lit on shore. The gig went into the water in double quick time and Mr. Bowles pulled across, returning with the marines, and Mr. Verson, Mr. Montelongo and Jack huddled together in the stern. Captain Blackwell was so relieved his legs felt weak beneath him; quite apart from the real affection and esteem he bore Mr. Verson and Jack, he would not be condemned for having lost his premier. The crew cheered their first lieutenant as he was helped aboard.

Doctor VanArsdel and Mercedes hurried the two youngsters below, and Captain Blackwell, after Mr. Verson saluted the quarterdeck, took the first lieutenant to his cabin.

"McMurtry, grog and vittles for Mr. Verson." He had the first lieutenant by the arm and assisted him, hobbling, to a seat at table.

Mr. Verson took grateful swallows of the rum and water. "I'm very sorry, sir, I allowed the young men to wander away botanizing. They were eager to bring back a few beetles and rocks for Mr. St. James and they became lost. When I finally came upon them it was full dark. We tried to make our way back to the beach, but the evening being so black, and after several nasty spills, I decided we had to wait until morning to return. I apologize, sir, I shall not let my party out of my sight in future."

Saunders rushed in and dove beneath the table where they sat.

"Saunders, what are you about?" Captain Blackwell cried.

"Doctor says Mr. Verson's feet are to be attended at once, sir," Saunders' voice came from below.

"Well, Mr. Verson." Captain Blackwell pulled his own legs back against his seat, glancing down. "*L'Unite* is relieved to have her premier back aboard. See you take more care in future."

"Aye, aye, sir."

Captain Blackwell jumped up from the table as Mr. Verson put his head in his hands.

Saunders' ministrations caused Mr. Verson as much pain as relief. The sensations were akin to what was taking place in Mr. Verson's heart. Last night he'd discovered those feelings of tenderness and desire he'd thought had fled along with Jack's mother were not dead in him. His pain came from the realization that a fifteen year old foreign boy had awakened that ache and longing in his breast.

Captain Blackwell quit the great cabin to check on the youngsters in the sick berth. He walked in as Doctor VanArsdel was amputating two toes of Mr. Montelongo's right foot. Mercedes abruptly turned young Jack Verson around to face her, and yanked down his trousers.

"Not my trousers, Miss Mercedes. What are you about?" The indignant boy clutched at his waistband in an attempt to get the trousers back up.

79

"She's examining your appendages for damage, yonker, so you had best submit." Doctor VanArsdel snipped the second toe. "There, Mr. Montelongo, I am sorry for your loss but it is only two inferior toes. You shall be able to walk after a time without difficulty."

"I am obliged...Oh, sir!" Mr. Montelongo said, as Captain Blackwell stepped around the canvas partition. "How fares Mr. Verson?"

"Well you should ask, Mr. Montelongo, since it was you got him into this confounded mess. You are fortunate not to have lost more than your toes, sir. And as for how many Mr. Verson may lose, I could not say. The doctor, no doubt, will attend to him now." Captain Blackwell and the doctor exchanged bows. Doctor VanArsdel collected a few instruments and departed.

"Ma'am, how is the boy?"

"No mortification to toes, fingers, or other vital parts." She hugged young Jack, who resisted her embrace for the sake of his dignity.

"Mr. Montelongo, you are a midshipman, a sea-officer. And whereas I might expect shatter-brained behavior from a — " Captain Blackwell paused, catching Mercedes' disapproving look. "Whereas I might expect unthinking behavior from a boy of six, you are an officer in training. You are never to wander away from your commanding officer unless under orders. You are to think of your duty at all times and how your actions will affect your shipmates."

"Aye, aye, sir. No more botanizing unless under orders, and I am to think of my duty and my shipmates. No more shatter-brained capers, sir."

"Very well, Mr. Montelongo." Captain Blackwell cleared his throat. "*L'Unite* is glad to have you back aboard, and you Jack. I shall send word how Mr. Verson does."

As soon as Captain Blackwell had moved around the canvas curtain Jack vaulted over to Mercedes' side, where she was tucking the bandage in around Mr. Montelongo's remaining toes. "Oh, Miss Mercedes, we were mortal cold. Pa held me all night, and Mr. Montelongo too. And Pa put my hands in his shirt and my feet down his breeches — "

"Jack, *chico*, we must help Juan Luis into a cot. He needs to lie down, he's had a very great ordeal. Since your cut does not bother you, run up to the great cabin and McMurtry will give you breakfast, and desire him to send a broth for Mr. Montelongo, if you please."

L'Unite was another three weeks surveying anchorages in Tierra del Fuego. The ship traded with the native peoples, but always over her side. The miserable raft like craft were brought beside the ship, from which the Indians bartered fish, cockles and mussels, and the occasional wild celery. Captain Blackwell would not allow his boats ashore to trade, or for any reason other than wood and water.

"That is not our business," Captain Blackwell replied to Mr. St. James's request to go ashore to bring the word of God to the savages. "This is a surveying mission, Mr. St. James. The Admiralty permits you to study natural philosophy subject to the demands of the Service, and you are to decide for yourself whether you will replace the missionary in the Sandwich Islands or remain with the ship when the time comes. That sums it up, does it not, sir?"

Mr. St. James had to assent, aside from his duties as chaplain and schoolmaster, those were the terms of his service aboard *L'Unite*. Yet it could not be wondered at if he found it difficult to believe *L'Unite's* captain was the son of a clergyman.

There were those aboard *L'Unite* who credited the unlucky young chaplain with the ship's ill fortune over the next six weeks, when contrary winds kept *L'Unite* from proceeding west round Cape Horn. Seamen are a hardy but also a superstitious breed, very willing to assign blame for the disasters of the sea to their fellows. Besides a parson, many right man-of-war's men mistrusted a woman aboard. No one dared point at the captain's lovely young wife. And the only other woman aboard was Saunders, considered too insignificant to move the power of the gods.

L'Unite sailed south, southwest, and the decks were covered in snow day after day. The surrounding ocean was a seascape of heaving gray waves and floating ice. Magellan jackets and woolen trousers were served out to all hands. And in these southern latitudes the next misfortune befell.

Captain Blackwell was not sleeping more than four hours at a stretch. From the setting of the first watch, he was on deck at midnight and again near four o'clock in the morning. He and Mr. Morrow, the bosun, a stocky bulldog of a man, went over the ship knocking ice from her rigging, yards, and canvas with belaying pins and their gloved fists. As a consequence of this schedule Captain Blackwell retired earlier, shortly after hammocks were piped down. The keeping of town hours was a custom of the distant past.

He expected to find Mercedes in his cot when he retired, for warmth. The galley stoves were not lit except for cooking. The men on the berth deck were kept from freezing by the enclosed atmosphere, the body heat of close packed humans. Captain Blackwell had to make do with just one tiny woman. But such a woman: soft, warm, and willing. How much pleasanter to lie down next to a sweet smelling woman than in the fug of men crowded onto the deck below.

"Oh, you're so cold." He'd stripped off his clothes and lain down in back of her. "I did not mean you should go away." Mercedes put her arm back to bring him against her. "You smell so nice."

Blackwell chucked. "There's something I thought I should never hear."

"Like fresh air and salt spray."

"We've plenty of that."

"Still snowing?"

"Yes. What is this?" He grasped a handful of Mercedes' nightgown.

"I was cold, Jim."

"I was cold, Jim." Blackwell imitated her in a high voice, making her laugh. "Orders are orders, sweetheart, however much we may not like them."

"You may take it off me now you are here to keep me warm." She raised her arms obediently over her head.

"You best believe I'll take it off you, Miss," Blackwell murmured, flinging the garment over his shoulder. "I suppose my bulk is good for something." He molded his body back around hers.

"I can think of a thing or two your bulk is good for." She trailed a hand up his thigh.

"Saucy, is it? What we must think of is punishment for disobedience to orders."

"Perhaps a dozen strokes." Mercedes pushed her bottom suggestively against his loins.

"I should make it a round two dozen." Blackwell raised himself beside her, gently pushing her forward on her belly.

Blackwell tented the bedclothes over them. He lifted Mercedes' hair and kissed the back of her neck, her shoulders, her back, and her bottom. Pressing his arm between the mattress and her body, he fondled and caressed, making sure she was ready. He had no notion of causing Mercedes pain, knowing his was a considerable bulk to bear.

He pushed her thighs apart and settled between them. "Hold hard, sweetheart," he whispered, to stop Mercedes' squirming. "Be still. Oh!"

Blackwell clamped his jaws shut so that only muffled groans escaped him, and Mercedes turned her face into the bolster. They were obliged to be quiet in their love making with the cabin walls made of nothing more than deal board, and with Saunders slinging a hammock in the great cabin itself. Panting with the exertion Blackwell lowered himself over her, after they'd both suppressed cries of pleasure.

Mercedes squeezed his fingers interlaced with hers. "You always fuck me so well."

Blackwell had never heard her use coarse language; he was frankly shocked. "Do not use vulgarities, ma'am, it ain't fitting." The absurdity of such a statement struck him, in his present position, joined to her as one flesh, and he laughed. "Or I shall have to punish you again." He gave her a feeble imitation of what moments before he'd been doing in earnest, and they both laughed. "You've taken the vitality right out of me."

After saying this, his weight came down on Mercedes, knocking the breath out of her, just as on the night of the wreck. In the first seconds Mercedes thought it might be part of his jest, in the next she knew he would never do such a thing. "Jim, Jim!" She clawed and heaved herself out from under him.

Her heart beat hard as she knelt beside him on the cot. "James, darling." She pushed his long hair away from slack features. Captain Blackwell's eyes stared, open and unseeing.

Mercedes jumped out of the cot and pulled on her dressing gown. She felt Captain Blackwell's pulse; slow and irregular. *"Dios mio!"* She flung open the sleeping cabin door.

Half way to the great cabin door, intending to send for the doctor, she stopped and began to turn round in confusion. Had not Captain Blackwell told her, directly and by countless actions, that the commander of a King's ship could not show weakness? Illness, incapacity, were not these the gravest kinds of weakness. "My God," Mercedes repeated under her breath. She racked her mind for the name of the sentry at the door.

"Mr. Hickman, pass the word for the doctor," Mercedes said, opening the great cabin door and standing in the doorway in a relaxed attitude. "The Captain has eaten something, he has an attack of the bile, so quietly, if you please. I should not like to put him even more out of temper."

Mercedes shut the cabin door and raced back to Captain Blackwell. She shook his shoulders and slapped his cheeks—not very hard. He was breathing, his pulse was ragged, and he was certainly insensible.

She pounced upon Doctor VanArsdel when the sentry closed the door behind him, bringing him immediately into the sleeping space. "He is insensible, Doctor."

Doctor VanArsdel bent over Captain Blackwell's naked form, feeling his pulse, watching his respiration, much as Mercedes had already done. "What was the Captain doing before the attack?"

"What do you suppose, Doctor," Mercedes cried. The smell of sex in the small cabin was evidence enough. "Do something for him."

"Help me turn him over."

They managed to roll Captain Blackwell on his back, and the glistening wet on his thighs and loins further attested to his activities.

"Heavy men are prone to apoplexies, Miss Mercedes. You must help the Captain resist his baser appetites. He eats far too much, and though he may have the urges of a younger man, young he is no longer." As he spoke the doctor was dealing Captain Blackwell vigorous slaps.

"Doctor, please."

Doctor VanArsdel leaned over Captain Blackwell and grasping his nipples firmly between his fingers he gave them a vicious pull and twist. He then had to jump back as before the recoil of a gun, for Captain Blackwell sat bolt upright with a bellow.

"Goddamn, hell and death, Doctor!"

Mercedes, retreating out of the lantern light, was heard to sob in the silence that followed.

"What is this, ma'am?" Captain Blackwell barked out at her. "You summon the doctor because I fall asleep."

"You were not asleep, sir," Doctor VanArsdel informed him in a cold tone. "You were insensible. Would she be crying otherwise?"

"Are you crying, Mercy, sweetheart?" his voice softened at once.

He reached around Doctor VanArsdel, extending his hand to her, but the doctor was shining light into his eyes, measuring his pulse, palpating his skull, temples, and neck.

"It may have been that blow to the head just before *Inconstant* paid off, a latent injury," Doctor VanArsdel said. "Or it may be due to overindulgence, to the too frequent satiation of animal — "

"Thank you, Doctor." Captain Blackwell stood up. Mercedes immediately stepped forward when he staggered, he shook his head at her. He did not require assistance. "Thank you for your attendance, and I am sorry you were called from your cot."

Captain Blackwell marched Doctor VanArsdel to the great cabin door.

Mercedes did not rush to him once he returned to the sleeping cabin. He felt he might have mortally offended her this time, and he wondered what he could say to excuse himself.

"The Doctor told me you passed the word I had an attack of bile."

"Oh James!" She fell on his breast at last. "What should I do if you were to leave me? I could not bear it." He felt she held herself back, as though afraid to harm him.

Captain Blackwell embraced her and gathered her up, disregarding her protest, and put her in his cot to show he wasn't feeble. He ignored the tingling numbness down his left arm and over his chest, and settled beside her.

"Listen now, sweetheart. I beg your pardon if I frightened you. You may wear nightgowns and use all the vulgar language you wish, but don't treat me like a goddamn invalid. Whatever the good doctor says, I ain't going anywhere. We are after all on a ship."

CHAPTER NINE

The passage to Juan Fernandez islands took sixty-seven days, some of the most anxious ones Captain Blackwell had lived at sea in twenty-five years in the service. When the wind had finally come easterly, *L'Unite* ran before it. He'd certainly experienced weather as bad as the four day gale that came on after they got their wind. It blew so hard they could carry no sail. But what Captain Blackwell had never seen was the whirlwind that arose to windward, out of which in one of the squalls two balls of fire fell on board. One of them struck the anchor housed on the forecastle, and bursting into particles burnt bosun Morrow and Narhilla. They had ever after wounds as if made with a hot poker the size of a sixpenny piece.

The whirlwind reached within two cables length of *L'Unite* and passed ahead of the ship.

When it had gone Captain Blackwell said, "Mr. Wilson, mark the log. Whirlwind encountered in latitude 50° bearing North, of half a glass duration."

The gale carried off the greater part of the livestock and all the vegetables stored at the stern of the ship. Near one third of the crew were on the sick list with ruptures, injuries from the cold, and several cases of what could only be named scurvy. Captain Blackwell was extremely concerned for his ship and her people, and not least for his wife and child. Mercedes had become in the family way the evening of his apoplectic fit. He worked the ship's position by the sun and the stars, and checked his results against those of the master's mates, the officers and midshipmen, and Mercedes' calculations. The last days before they'd raised John Fernando, as the British seamen called the islands, Captain Blackwell would not care to live over again.

But he had the great satisfaction of looking now upon the green slopes of Juan Fernandez, at the rows of tents on shore set up to shelter the invalids and guarded by a detachment of marines. Onboard he oversaw the work of rigging ship going on round him. He had parties taking on water and other shore parties hunting seal, butchering, salting and putting the flesh into barrels. The blue tinge was leaving Mercedes' lips and fingernails, she was beginning to glow with health, and Captain Blackwell could not have adequately expressed his relief in words.

Though her child had been conceived in less than propitious circumstances, Mercedes' delight in her condition was genuine. The last thing Captain Blackwell would have wished for her was another miscarriage. At the same time what she would endure in childbirth he would not allow himself to imagine. It was like anticipating how one might behave in battle; it really did not do to over think certain matters.

Apart from his concern for her, which was considerable, Captain Blackwell found he could contemplate becoming a father with some equanimity. Nearby Mr. Montelongo and Mr. St. James were discussing the curious behavior of the birds during the whirlwind. Unlike in your strong gale, the birds didn't seem to trust in the solidity of the ship and would not land on her. The noise of their shrieking had been enormous, and many had plunged into the sea to avoid the swirling winds, while those that had not escaped in time were sucked in a spiral vortex away and out of sight in an instant. Captain Blackwell listened to the young men's discussion with a benevolent glow in his heart. He felt he should know just how to guide a son, who would of course make the sea his profession.

"Mr. Montelongo," Captain Blackwell said, turning to face the two young gentlemen.

"Sir!" Mr. Montelongo stepped forward. He'd been standing at the lee rail, hands clasped behind his back, while Mr. St. James leaned upon it at his ease.

"Now the wounded are landed, you may take Mr. St. James ashore in the jolly boat for a botanizing excursion. If Mr. St. James pleases." Captain Blackwell bowed to the chaplain.

"Oh, yes, sir. Thank you, sir," Mr. Montelongo and Mr. St. James cried in concert.

"Boat ahoy!" called out Mr. Bowles, the officer of the watch, to an approaching whaler's launch. "Watch the fucking paintwork."

There were two other ships in Cumberland Bay, a harbor well known to fur traders and whalers for its supplies of wood, water, and stores.

"Mr. Bowles, I believe there is a lady in that boat," Captain Blackwell said.

Mr. Bowles blushed to the roots of his fair hair. At that moment a bonnet framed face looked up at him from the whale boat. Its' coxswain brought her gently against *L'Unite's* side.

"Sideboys! Mr. Morrow, prepare to receive a captain aboard."

It was not the master of the whaler *John Bill* who came first up the steps, but his lady Mrs. Jennings, holding a basket in her teeth as she climbed like a Malay pirate. Jennings was right behind her, his beaming, bearded face greeting the deck. *John Bill* had been one of the convoy escorted by *L'Unite* from England to Brazil, so she could claim a connection to the war ship. Captain Jennings seemed entirely sensible of the compliment paid him when he was piped aboard with the honors of a post-captain.

"Captain Blackwell, how do you do? Thank you for your kind reception." Captain Jennings took off his hat to the quarterdeck. "Mrs. Jennings and I have come to pay our respects. I suggest we allow the ladies to have a gam while you and I discuss another matter. I have some intelligence for you, sir."

Captain Blackwell bowed Mrs. Jennings into the great cabin then ran up on deck as the men were piped to dinner. He took Captain Jennings to the starboard side of the quarterdeck, the domain of senior officers.

On the lower deck the coxswain of the *John Bill* had been invited to mess with Narhilla and his mates.

"We hear as your skipper's wife is poorly," said *John Bill's* coxswain, by way of cordial dinner conversation.

"Don't believe everything you hear, mate," Narhilla said. "Because why? Because our Missus is a rare plucked 'un, that's why. At the moment Mrs. Captain Blackwell is brave, we are obliged to you."

Mercedes was braving the onslaught of Mrs. Jennings, an American from Nantucket who'd married into the British whaling fleet much as she'd married into the Royal Navy. They'd met at suppers aboard the ships under convoy but hadn't been suffered to have much conversation, surrounded as they were by the captains and ship's officers. The distance separating the opposite coasts of their shared country of origin was as vast as the cultural divide between them. Except for a common language they shared no national heritage, as would have been the case with any other civilized nation.

They'd been born in a country barely civilized at the edges, and raw inside. Mrs. Jennings from the settled east coast of America had more the speech and manners of the frontier, whereas Mercedes' mother had done everything in her power to bring European culture to the fore in her daughter's upbringing. Her efforts had been remarkably successful; Arabella de Aragon had defied the wild Spanish settlement on the western coast and raised a gentlewoman.

"All my children were born at sea," Mrs. Jennings was saying, at ease in the captain's armchair. "Jennings attended on my last lying in, our Jemmy as just turned twelve. Fainted dead away."

Mercedes stared at Mrs. Jennings. A ship was no place for nicety and families had to care for one another, but Mrs. Jennings' story made her wish Captain Blackwell might not be forced into such a situation. "We have a fine surgeon in Doctor VanArsdel, ma'am, I trust he will attend my confinement. How many children have you?"

"Five."

"Five born at sea! I congratulate you, and I wish I may be so fortunate. How many boys and girls?"

"Five boys, Mrs. Blackwell, and all away in other ships except young Jemmy. I had a girl child, died."

"I'm sorry for it." Mercedes thought of the child she'd lost. Was there such a thing as gender at that earliest stage of development?

"It is like another lifetime, so long ago. I'm past all that now so I've taken the liberty to bring you a few things I found useful. I hear you're in the family way." Mrs. Jennings nodded at her as she leaned over the basket she'd brought aboard.

She extracted from her basket a most peculiar arrangement of ropes and canvas. Mercedes eyed the object askance. It might be a restraint for her, her husband, or the child.

"It's a little harness, you see, to put the child in when you need to use the head," Mrs. Jennings said. "Because believe me, dear, you will not be able to so much as piss without the child by you. You dare not for they may stab themselves on a harpoon or throw themselves out the stern windows soon as you turn your back."

"I see, and I am obliged to you. This end is the — "

"Aye, that end you clew up. T'other end with the canvas short pantaloons you put the child in."

"It is ingenious, Mrs. Jennings, thank you. Did you design it yourself?" Mercedes turned the contraption in her hands, wondering how easy it would be for the child to hang itself.

"Who else? Jennings might have I suppose, were he not so hellfire busy much of the time."

"But Captain Jennings must be pleased with so many boys."

"Naturally. All of them want their own squadrons."

Mercedes recalled Captain Blackwell telling Saunders women were of no use in the Navy.

As though Mrs. Jennings read her thoughts, she said, "What shall you do if it's a girl? Man-of-war, and all."

"Love her extra, I suppose, to compensate her for it."

Captain Blackwell threw himself on his cot exhausted after driving his men hard throughout the afternoon and evening watches to bring the sick and wounded back on board. They completed their water, wood, and the preserving in barrels of the seal meat. Some of the carcasses, indeed, they'd turned over to the *John Bill* and the other ship in the bay. But *L'Unite* was now under way carrying all the sail she could bear, crossing the one hundred fifty leagues separating the Juan Fernandes islands from the Main. The intelligence Captain Jennings communicated was of an English packet ship having been denied entrance to the port of Valparaiso. As one of *L'Unite's* missions in the Pacific was protection of trade, she was flying down with a press of sail to investigate the matter.

He held his hand out to Mercedes, she'd just finished telling him of some contraption Mrs. Captain Jennings had given her. Captain Blackwell was sorry to hurry her and the ship's company away from Juan Fernandez. He'd meant to rest and recruit for a week longer, but duty and the demands of the service came before every other consideration. He shifted in the cot to make room for her.

"Did anyone ever call you Jemmy when you were a boy of twelve?"

"Why, sweetheart, you know when I was twelve I was called Mr. Midshipman Blackwell. And commanded a gun division aboard the old *Etrusco*." He yawned and passed his hand tenderly over the small bump of Mercedes' belly. "Have you thought what you will call your child?"

"I should like to call him Edward James. Then we shall honor both grandfathers and you." Mercedes squeezed him. "And Emma, if we have a girl."

After his mother; he'd married a kind and considerate woman. But what he said was, "We shall see what she has to say to a 44 gun frigate." In his weariness he'd repeated his earlier remark to his officers and Captain Jennings when speaking of the vessel blockading the port of Valparaiso. He was asleep, his enclosing arms falling slack from Mercedes' body, the first loud snores escaping him.

L'Unite was reconnoitering the vessel lying two sea miles under her lee, beating back and forth in the road outside the harbor of Valparaiso. Captain Blackwell was in no particular hurry, he could afford to wait until conditions were right to fall down upon her and accept her challenge. The foreigner was a 50 gun Spanish built frigate of the same class and age as *La Trinidad*, if he did not mistake, and he had taken *La Trinidad* with a 28 gun ship. *L'Unite* had long since been cleared for action, but the wait had been instructive. Captain Blackwell watched the other ship tack and set sail. She was by no means a crack ship, but not an ill handled one either. The view of her quarterdeck was the most puzzling part about her. Captain Blackwell studied it from the maintop through his telescope.

The commanding officer wore the uniform of Spain. He was a giant of a man, for even at this distance and through a glass he appeared much bigger than his fellows. The crew was composed of diminutive brown natives, mostly naked; he'd taken many such prisoners out of *La Trinidad*. It was the absence of the ship's officers that confounded Captain Blackwell. Where were the lieutenants, the mids, the master? Saving the one big man apparently in command, there were no other uniforms on deck.

Captain Blackwell returned to the deck the way he'd gone up, not sliding down a backstay, but making his slow descent through the shrouds. He felt no especial need for caution, nor any severe trepidation in facing the enemy to leeward. Though the foreign ship was competently handled, whether she could fight her guns at the same time, particularly without officers leading the gun crews, was another matter. What inspired caution, even in gaining the deck now, was his desire to cause the least possible perturbation to the Spanish authorities in Valparaiso.

Francis's advice in a diplomatic capacity would have been most welcome. And his brother spoke Spanish. Captain Blackwell wished he were aboard once more. He had two Spanish speakers in Mr. Montelongo and Mercedes, more among the crew, but he would not allow Mercedes on deck during an action. And as to Mr. Montelongo, Captain Blackwell could not avoid his English bred prejudice against a foreigner. A suspicion lurked that his words might not be translated as he meant them.

Captain Blackwell strode onto the quarterdeck. "Mr. Wilson, close with the foreigner, if you please." In a louder voice he called out, "Mr. Verson, run out the starboard battery. Mr. Montelongo." Captain Blackwell looked around for the young man. "We are going to speak her. You will translate exactly what I say, if you please."

"Ship ahoy! What ship is that?" Mr. Montelongo called through a speaking trumpet. *L'Unite* had approached within two cables length of the 50 gun frigate. "His Britannic Majesty's ship *L'Unite*,

Captain Blackwell commanding, desires entrance to the port of Valparaiso!"

"Heave to, or we shall sink you." In a tremulous voice Mr. Montelongo translated the foreign captain's reply from across the sea.

"Thank you, Mr. Montelongo. Go to your station."

"Aye, aye, sir." Mr. Montelongo saluted and hurried down the companion ladder to the gun deck.

Captain Blackwell stepped to the break of the quarterdeck. "Men of *L'Unite*, we are going to close the foreigner, but we will not fire the first shot. Do you hear me there? We will stand her fire. She must fire first. And then we shall make them smell hell!"

Three huzzahs followed Captain Blackwell's speech. Then the men stared across the water at their adversary with sanguine expectation.

There was nothing of elegance in the action that followed. *L'Unite* had the weather gage and edged down on the foreigner. The lion and castle of Spain did not fly from her masthead, the signal midshipman was at a loss to identify her colours. When *L'Unite* was within 50 yards of her, at a range where her guns could not miss, the foreigner opened fire. In rapid succession *L'Unite* answered with three rolling broadsides.

"Run her out, lads, run her out," Mr. Bransford shouted to the crew of the number two gun, starboard division.

"If he thinks he'll win a yard arm to yard arm smasher with the skipper he may kiss my arse!" Narhilla cried, captain of the number four gun. He hauled with the others to bring the gun inboard.

A 32 pound round shot came shrieking in and dismounted the number two gun, scattering her crew in the path of a cannon of fifteen hundred weight. The gun carriage shot back and knocked Mr. Bransford off his feet and into the larboard bulkhead.

"Number four gun crew, secure that gun," Mr. Montelongo called out as loudly as he could, raising his voice above the tremendous din of *L'Unite's* and the enemy's cannon fire. "Davies, McMurtry, carry Mr. Bransford below. Number six, fire!"

The order was roared out at the main deck gun crews, "Vast firing. Hold your fire." It seemed to Mr. Montelongo, Mr. Bowles, and the other midshipmen and seamen that they'd been living in that hell of smoke and din and blood and death forever. The hot part of the battle, the cannonading, had lasted fifteen minutes. Captain Blackwell's ceaseless gunnery practice had paid off. The gun crews ran their guns in and clapped on and held them inboard, loaded and fired like automatons, in spite of the enemy's fire, the cries of the wounded, the loss of their shipmates and officers. They had subdued the enemy by rate of fire, the foreigner having managed only three broadsides to *L'Unite's* seven.

Mr. Bowles came aft down the main deck, giving orders for the housing of the guns and the removal of the wounded as he came. He patted the shoulder of each of the shaking midshipmen he met, much as the captain might have done. When he arrived at the aftermost guns, Mr. Bowles said, "Narhilla, double lash the number two gun and pass the word for the carpenter's crew. Mr. Montelongo," Mr. Bowles extended his hand. "Shall we send to see how Mr. Bransford does?"

Mr. Montelongo took Mr. Bowles's hand in an unsteady grip. "By all means, sir."

Mr. Allen practically fell down the after companion ladder in his haste, his eyes wide and his cherub face stained with gunpowder. "Captain's compliments, Mr. Montelongo, and you are required on the quarterdeck."

The battle had indeed been a yard arm to yard arm slugfest, and *L'Unite's* upper deck was in a state the uninformed might have described as disarray. *L'Unite's* mizzen had been struck down upon the caps, and much of her rigging appeared shattered and hung useless. Men were still being carried below to the cockpit. But all was well with *L'Unite* for Captain Blackwell was on his quarterdeck, shouting orders.

As he was going aft Mr. Montelongo met Mr. Bransford with his head wrapped in a bandage and one arm in a sling. "I am relieved to see you, sir."

"My sentiments are much the same, Mr. Montelongo. I'm obliged to you both for your kind wishes and your good actions." Mr. Bransford bowed and moved away forward.

"Mr. Montelongo, I am rejoiced to see you. In a moment Mr. Verson's party will return with the officer in command of that ship

and I shall require your translation. Step below and wash, son."
Captain Blackwell eyed the blackened, blood splattered form of the
midshipman. "You are perfectly presentable in my opinion as you
are, a fighting man, but I understand your countrymen have nicer
feelings. I should not wish to offend by presenting them an officer
covered in blood."

"Yes, sir. I mean...aye, aye, sir."

Mr. Montelongo need not have hurried and trembled so as he
washed and dressed in a clean uniform, for no officer came aboard
L'Unite from the enemy vessel. Mr. Verson sent word by
midshipman Mr. Byron, returning in the gig to *L'Unite*, that not
one of the men left alive on the foreigner would admit of being an
officer. None wore uniforms except the big captain, found dead
near the mainmast with his papers stuffed in his mouth. Officers
could not be distinguished from men, and Mr. Verson was taking
possession of the foreign ship.

"Thank you, Mr. Byron. Mr. Bell?" Captain Blackwell turned to
his carpenter.

"Three foot of water in the well, sir, and holding. No shot below
the waterline, and repairs under way for six above, sir."

"Your mate Mr. Bohan and three of your crew are to go in the
gig under Mr. Byron to assist Mr. Verson. Mr. Morrow, run out a
cable and prepare to take the foreigner in tow. Mr. Bowles, you
have the deck. Mr. Bransford, Mr. Bell, if you please. We shall
conclude the inspection in the cockpit, where you must stop, Mr.
Bransford."

Three hours of intense labor were needed to patch up *L'Unite's*
damage and pass a cable to *Argonauta* — such was the fanciful
name of the ship Mr. Verson now commanded. The efforts of the
carpenter's crew in plugging the shot holes below *Argonauta's*
waterline prevented her from going down on the spot, but the 50
gun ship was certainly in a sinking condition. The worst damage
had been done when an 18-pounder exploded on her lower gun
deck, killing and maiming the gun crews and causing the
abandonment of the entire deck. "Like working in a knacker's
yard," Mr. Bohan grumbled to his mates aboard *Argonauta*.

L'Unite, with her shattered prize in tow, stood into the Bay of
Valparaiso at two-thirty in the afternoon. All hands were at their
stations as *L'Unite* came slowly into the harbor with her gun ports

open. The two ships had just lumbered past the shore batteries, every officer and man on deck holding his breath. Captain Blackwell had his glass trained on two third rates and a frigate at the bottom of the bay when the cannonade roared out. He'd just remarked that only the frigate had her yards crossed, and he jerked round toward the shore battery at the roar of 42-pound cannon.

"They are saluting, sir," Mr. Bowles and Mr. Montelongo piped in unison.

No cannonballs ended their shrieking progress in the bay round them.

In eight fathom water toward the bottom of the bay *L'Unite* cast off the tow line, tacked gracefully round in spite of her jury rigging, and fired a thirteen gun salute in return to the shore's compliment.

"This is surpassing strange," Captain Blackwell muttered.

A great deal of activity was going forward on the decks of the two ships of the line across the way and though he would have liked to, Captain Blackwell considered it impolite to use his glass to study the movements of the Dons. Instead he stood with his hands clasped behind his back, feet planted apart, turning his beam to the Spaniards. Mr. Allen, who'd already had a thrill packed day, had no such reservations.

"There they go, they are launching the barge from the three decker. And what a cock they're making of it. Lord, some poor sod has got a ducking. Oh, they fished him. That must be their admiral, it all that finery."

"Is it an admiral in that barge, Mr. Montelongo?" Captain Blackwell asked.

Mr. Montelongo strained his gaze across the distance. "A Vice-admiral, I believe, sir."

"Mr. Morrow, prepare to receive an admiral aboard. Sideboys! Mr. Hoffinger, your men on the quarterdeck if you please. Mr. Boyne, run below to the cockpit and give my compliments to Mrs. Blackwell. She may wish to return to the cabin and prepare to receive a visitor."

"Oh, may I go, if you please sir?" Mr. Allen cried out in his over-excited state.

The ferocious look Captain Blackwell gave him by way of answer sent Mr. Allen scurrying to the taffrail and Mr. Boyne running below.

"Look alive, there, Mr. Montelongo," Captain Blackwell said.

After Mr. Montelongo returned the obligatory "Aye, aye, sir", Captain Blackwell glanced at the young man beside him and was sorry he'd spoken. The handsome midshipman, his uniform quite smart and correct, and his person shining clean, was swaying slightly on his feet, and not with the send of the sea. Mr. Montelongo's experiences on the main gun deck during the action, Captain Blackwell gathered, had been the opposite of a boy's imaginings of thrilling battle. He regretted having to put an additional strain upon him, though it was of an entirely different nature. And then, as the Vice-admiral's barge approached and Captain Blackwell caught sight of the resplendently clad, fine, sturdy, gray mustached officer in the stern, he hardened his heart to the young man's distress. The demands of the service were physical, emotional, and intellectual.

The Spanish Vice-admiral came aboard *L'Unite* to the wailing of the bosun's pipes, the stamp and clash of the marines, and the salutes of the quarterdeck. The Vice-admiral's flag lieutenant stepped between the Spanish and British officers and commenced his introduction in a declamatory voice. Mr. Montelongo immediately began to strain to translate the many titles possessed by the Spanish grandee before them.

"Never mind, Mr. Montelongo," Captain Blackwell murmured. "Just tell me when there is anything said of our mauling their ship."

The flag lieutenant stopped, coming at last to the end of the Vice-admiral's titles. It was Mr. Montelongo's turn.

"Captain James Blackwell, His Britannic Majesty's ship *L'Unite*." Mr. Montelongo moved to one side.

Captain Blackwell stepped forward extending his hand, and Vice-admiral Ávala did a thing that made the officers, the marines, and the watch on deck give a decided start. He took Captain Blackwell's hand then yanked him to his breast in a close embrace, thumping him upon the back.

Vice-admiral Ávala had last met Captain and Mrs. Blackwell at a subscription ball in Gibraltar marking the Peace. He claimed an acquaintance with Mercedes' mother, Ávala having been one of Arabella de Aragon's most ardent admirers. This was the relish on the dish of victory Captain Blackwell had served up to Valparaiso, and it was no less savory to the Vice-admiral for having come about with so little effort on his part. Ávala was delighted, for what had transpired was one of his captains, a giant of a man full of martial promise, had gone mad. "Crack-headed, violent, and money-getting," was how the Vice-admiral described the *Argonauta's* captain, Don Cosme Gastón.

He had seized his command and subverted his officers and then proceeded to blockade the port of Valparaiso in His Most Catholic Majesty's ship. During the preceding four weeks Don Cosme had held the port hostage, turning back ships desiring to enter the port and preventing any save fishermen from getting out of the harbor. Always standing well clear of the shore batteries, Don Cosme sent his demands into the bay through those same fishermen. His outrageous calls for titles, lands, honors and promotion seemed to prove the *Argonauta's* captain had come undone.

This was the tale Vice-admiral Ávala told to Captain Blackwell through Mercedes' translation in the great cabin of *L'Unite*. Ávala had a small store of English, enough to act the hale, hearty fellow, and the delight in his face spoke his feelings more. After all, the Vice-admiral had not had to cross his yards and sail out to deal with his problem, as the governor, the port authorities, and the merchants had been crying out he should do.

No corresponding pleasure was anywhere in evidence in Captain Blackwell's countenance. From extreme preoccupation over what the Dons would make of his shattering their frigate, Captain Blackwell was moved to control his temper. He would have liked to give Vice-admiral Ávala a good thumping for allowing him to sail in and risk his ship and his men — his wife and child! — to clean up his mess. An image of the captain of *Argonauta* dead against the mainmast, his orders, which he'd either tried to consume or his officers had stuffed in his mouth, rose in Captain Blackwell's mind. Pity and a desire to make Ávala feel his displeasure roiled in his breast. His trouble was in having to deal out this verbal thrashing through Mercedes, a thing he was most unwilling to do.

Consequently Captain Blackwell sat mum while Vice-admiral Ávala expended his gallantries on Mercedes. She continually threw him concerned glances as the Vice-admiral pratted. How far foreign they would have to go not to encounter admirers of Mercedes' mother, he could not tell. Vice-admiral Ávala made the third of Captain Blackwell's personal acquaintance.

It was not discretion or wisdom kept Captain Blackwell silent, but a desire not to discompose his wife. He called it weakness, but as with most decisions he'd taken with her welfare in mind Captain Blackwell found this one turned out to the good. Vice-admiral Ávala was a well-bred man and after a ten-minute visit in *L'Unite's* great cabin, and a glass of Madeira, he allowed the conversation to turn to matters maritime. The disposition of the shattered *Argonauta* and her people were discussed. Captain Blackwell concluded the meeting with Vice-admiral Ávala without having made an ugly situation worse. He'd even begun to frame in his mind the letter he would write to the Admiralty.

Mercedes rose to meet him when Captain Blackwell returned to the great cabin after seeing Vice-admiral Ávala over the side. "I am so sorry. Twenty-five men wounded for no affair of the Crown's."

"It's a rum go," Captain Blackwell said. "But as the *Argonauta* was obstructing trade, and the Dons are pleased about it, I suppose I was within the confines of duty. I shall puff it up as zeal in my official letter, but how I should have liked to avoid it. Not only for the butcher's bill, but for the rigging and yards. We are very much cut up. Mercy, sweetheart, what was that Ávala said to you when he took his leave made you turn pale?"

Mercedes wanted to protest that she had not lost her color, but perhaps she had, for she'd been angry enough. She gave Captain Blackwell a steady look. "He told me the Governor and some of the merchants are already planning a ball and supper in your honor, and that I would be well advised to give you a hint. While your officers will be most welcome, Mr. Montelongo might wish to remain on board *L'Unite*."

"Threats, is it? Damn his insolence!"

Captain Blackwell jumped to his feet and began to pace the cabin, obviously suppressing worse oaths. Since the episode of apoplexy Mercedes dreaded seeing him in a passion. Many wives would have withheld the warning, and Mercedes wondered if that might not have been the better course. She considered it only for a moment. After a battle, a day of loss and grief, she could not be artful and managing, nor would she be at any time.

"Why would he say such an inappropriate goddamn thing?" Captain Blackwell stood still to look at her. "That young man behaved very well today, very well indeed."

"There is your reason, I believe. Spain has the devil of a time manning her ships and attracting promising men for officers. Mr. Montelongo, you are aware, is a Spanish gentleman serving in the British Royal Navy. They despise him, and perhaps in their secret hearts they envy him."

Mercedes was relieved when Captain Blackwell stopped pacing and threw himself into the armchair. She sat beside him on the small sofa.

"I suppose I understand. I should not like to see an English officer in their corps. But I shall not deny Mr. Montelongo the shore. He must have his turn for liberty. If he may not go to this grand ball, then I shall send him ashore with a party of seaman. Narhilla will see he don't get his throat cut."

The two lieutenants, Mr. Bowles and Mr. Bransford, were glowingly happy and amused amid the chattering throng at the ball in the Gran Teatro. Their faces shone so with vigor and pleasure, that it was hard to imagine these same young men had done their share of execution. Both being golden-haired they were quite what the young ladies of the port imagined British gentlemen ought to be, and consequently the two sea-officers received more than their share of the ladies' attentions. The only allay in their great good fortune was Mr. Bowles considered Mr. Bransford possessed of an unfair advantage with his arm in a sling.

"Captain Blackwell's officers enjoy themselves immensely," Vice-admiral Ávala commented to Mercedes. At a slight remove Captain Blackwell stood in conversation with a group of military and civilian gentlemen. "They are the belles of the ball."

"That would be beaux, I believe, sir," Mercedes said. "Beaux of the ball."

"You are quite right, I'm sure. You understand these English. What I cannot conceive is what the ladies see in those pale faced, beef fed young men."

"Have a care, sir, if you please. You touch very close to home."

"I beg your pardon, *Señora* Blackwell. I cannot help but think of you as one of our own. Assist me to make no further blunders, and tell me how Captain Blackwell would receive a gift of plate. The tradesmen of the town contemplate bestowing a complete service of silver plate upon him."

"Why, I'm sure he would be gratified to receive such a mark of their regard, and count himself most fortunate. But what he should value above all things is naval stores, if such a gift were within the gentlemen's power."

Vice-admiral Ávala regarded her in silence a moment. "You truly are a sea-officer's wife. Who would have thought it, the daughter of *La Costeña*."

"I must tell you, Don Ignacio," Vice-admiral Ávala had invited Mercedes to call him by his Christian name, "I do not care to hear my mother called so."

"I blunder again and most sincerely beg your pardon. I would not offend the daughter of Doña Arabella for the world. How she would have delighted in a grandchild. It is the pity of the world she did not live to meet him, or her."

"Now I am obliged to you, sir, for those kind words. You are able to perceive I'm in the way all ladies wish to be who love their lords?" She'd saved up the phrase flung out by the Reverend Blackwell; Captain Blackwell had apparently come by his loud voice both by training and by nature.

"It is a talent some old duffers have. May I?" Vice-admiral Ávala held out his arms to embrace Mercedes.

Captain Blackwell glanced over as gray mustaches brushed his wife's glowing cheeks. "Gentlemen, you will excuse me. My wife looks fatigued." Bowing to the merchants and officers, Captain Blackwell felt he'd spent quite sufficient time with them, he hastened over to Mercedes and the Vice-admiral.

"Captain Blackwell, Vice-admiral de Ávala was just offering me his kind felicitations. He was saying how pleased my mother would have been."

"My heartfelt congratulations to you too, Captain Blackwell." Vice-admiral Ávala bowed. "May you have an English son to raise for your King's navy."

The Vice-admiral took his leave and walked away with a nonchalant swagger.

"Damn his insolence," Mercedes said.

"My thoughts exactly, sweetheart. Are you tired, should you like to leave?" It was well on in the evening. There had been a supper, then the ball that was presently underway. Another collation would be served in the early hours of the morning.

"Not tired, no. But I would like to retire, if you please." She turned to him, stretching up to speak in his ear. Captain Blackwell leaned down to hear her. "I should very much like you to stroke me, on the inside."

Captain Blackwell looked at her briefly, surprised, and then he turned away, an eager, almost boyish expression on his face. Mercedes took the arm Captain Blackwell offered her. He clapped his hand firmly over hers. "We shall break the line just aft of the Governor." He nodded toward their host and led her forward.

CHAPTER TEN

L'Unite sailed away from the coast of Chile well found in canvas, spars, cordage, even spare masts had been turned over by the grateful merchant community. Captain Blackwell was able to send his carefully worded dispatch to the Admiralty by way of the packet ship *Fleance*. The packet had nearly dismasted herself in her haste to beat back into the port of Valparaiso so that the master's screaming wife could be delivered of her child on land. Had he found the port closed to him on this second attempt, the master told Captain Blackwell, he might have been obliged to resort to self-murder. Matters having turned out happy, Captain Blackwell was fairly certain *Fleance's* master would reinforce his having called the action a victory in Valparaiso.

Vice-admiral Ávala managed one last sally, inviting Captain Blackwell to return for Mercedes' lying in, so that her child might be born in a civilized locality. Captain Blackwell considered Ávala heedless and insolent from clew to earring, yet he expected no better from a Spaniard. On the other hand Valparaiso had been a most welcoming place and the gift of naval stores raised the port very high in his esteem. He did consider Valparaiso an eminently civil town, and in his heart Captain Blackwell wished they might be near such a place when Mercedes' time came. It was thanks to the good citizens of Valparaiso Captain Blackwell would not have to husband his stores during the next phase of the cruise.

He was still a husband to the ship and to Mercedes, and he went through the phases of her condition with her as the ship pursued her course. In the early weeks her ardor for him was such that he dared not enter the great cabin, unless he was prepared to be set upon and made to bull her until she gave him leave to go. This time could not have lasted long enough to satisfy Captain Blackwell, but as Mercedes' body ripened, her skin stretching to an extent that amazed him, she naturally became less fond of tumbling about with him.

In latitude 16° South Captain Blackwell watched a large body of spermaceti whales churning the seas; calls of "She blows!" from the ex-whalemen of the ship ringing out. In route to the Isle Cocas, it had been one squall after another bringing incessant heavy rains, with intervals of thunder and lightening. They hoped for a few fair days to dry out the men's clothes, sodden with moisture and perspiration.

In the five wet days spent surveying at Isle Cocas they found an abundance of good water, mullet and dog-fish, though their catch was precious hard to retain, the sharks being so numerous and voracious. Around noon, during the brief periods when the sun shone, the men working on shore doffed their woolen jackets and spread them on bushes to dry. Back aboard ship the garments turned up completely fly blown, the insects attracted by the sweat permeating the cloth; later the jackets became covered in maggots.

Two days after *L'Unite* quit the Isle Cocas the first cases of yellow fever appeared. Doctor VanArsdel shaved the heads of the patients, and sponged their temples and poles with vinegar and water. He bathed them in warm water, and administered ten grains of James's powders every four hours. Soon there were too many sick for such rigorous care and too few available to administer it. Mercedes was forbidden to attend in the sick berth, and for once Doctor VanArsdel and Captain Blackwell agreed. Who knew what exposure to yellow jack might do to her child.

The entire midshipman's berth was struck down, and when young Jack Verson was reported on the sick list, Mercedes could restrain herself no longer. She went to the first lieutenant's cabin to care for the boy.

There were no midshipmen healthy enough to escort her, and Saunders had been returned to her former duties as foretopman in Mr. Bowles' watch. "I cannot spare her to nurse the sick, Doctor,"

Captain Blackwell had said. "With so many on the list I must have her in the tops."

Saunders was delighted, not that her reinstatement should have come because of the terrible illness sweeping *L'Unite*, but she told McMurtry; "I owe the Missus a debt, but I ain't no nursemaid. I'll leave that to you, mate."

No one was aware Mercedes was with young Jack. She'd dismissed Mr. Verson's servant, taking over his seat beside Jack's cot. The boy alternately shivered, his teeth chattering, and threw the bedclothes from his little naked body as he sweated in delirium. A basin was by her stool and Mercedes mopped Jack's face and neck with a wetted towel when he burned with fever. Jack emitted low growls and bared his teeth like a dog. Mercedes recalled Captain Blackwell describing Jack's abandonment by his mother, the landlady allowing him to stay in the house like one of the establishment's dogs.

Jack came out of one of these shivering, growling fits. Mercedes leaned over and tucked his blankets in around him, now he'd become calmer.

"You would never say to a fellow he might lay down with the dogs if he were cold." Jack hiccuped. "Would you, Miss Mercedes?"

"Certainly not." Mercedes was surprised by Jack's suddenly piping up, and to find herself fighting back tears. "Nor shall anyone ever say so to you again. All that is over. You are with us now. A valuable member of *L'Unite's* crew, the gentleman son of her first officer. Dear Jack."

Jack sighed happily under her caressing hand, but a flush rose to his face, and he began to pant slightly. "The Captain's son will always have your breast to lean upon, that much is certain. Still I don't see ..." Jack tugged at the blankets covering him and tossed them off. "I don't see how the child is to survive in this world."

Mr. Verson and Captain Blackwell came into the lieutenant's cabin at the end of the first watch.

Mr. Verson lent over Mercedes. "I shall take over now, ma'am. You are so very good, Mrs. Blackwell," he took the towel from her hand, "here is the Captain to take you to your quarters, ma'am."

Mercedes rose from the stool where she'd been seated. They regarded the pale little form in the hanging cot: young Goodman Jack was sleeping as though insensible.

"He's more peaceful now, he was suffering before. Good night, Mr. Verson." Mercedes turned away and took Captain Blackwell's arm, tears shining in her eyes.

No words of chastisement for disobeying his order not to attend the sick were uttered as Captain Blackwell led her to the great cabin. He glanced surreptitiously at her and saw the state she was in, on the verge of breaking down into full blubber and he did not blame her. All hands well enough to work were exhausted with the extra watches and the care of the sick, and Mercedes was in a delicate condition.

Captain Blackwell was relieved, once they'd settled in his cot, when Mercedes reminded him seamen were not the only beings made of resistant material. "We shall give the invalids what remains of the sweetmeats sent aboard in Valparaiso," she said. "And those turtles the hands caught on Isla Cocas will make an excellent restorative broth."

In fact they lost none of the sick. The young gentlemen recovered, and their schoolmaster too, for Mr. St. James had taken ill with the rest. They were once more at their lessons in the great cabin; Mercedes and young Jack sitting to one side; looking at first like so many monks at vespers with their bald heads. *L'Unite* proceeded to the Gulf of Panama, then the winds being favorable she dropped down to cruise the cost of Peru, putting into Callao in blessedly fine weather. Spring air and gentle breezes aside, Captain Blackwell found Callao a filthy disreputable port. He took on stores as fast as ever he could and bore away for the Galapagos, returning to the Main after having added to their knowledge of Las Islas Encantadas. Captain Blackwell and his ship were off the coast of Mexico, near a place the Indians called Mazatlan, when Mercedes' time came.

She'd retired to her sleeping cabin early in the evening, declaring she felt a little unwell.

Captain Blackwell had stood up from his desk where he was working on coastal elevations. "Good night, sweetheart. I wish I had thought to request the Admiralty send an artist on this cruise.

How we have missed one, with only mine and my officers' ham-fisted efforts."

"One cannot plan for every circumstance, James, darling. Goodnight."

As a sea-officer Blackwell certainly knew the justice of Mercedes' statement. He was also accustomed to being roused in the middle of the night and becoming instantly and fully awake to any emergency. Even so Mercedes had to shake him violently to wake him.

Blackwell bolted up in his cot. "What is it, sweetheart? Oh, that. Lie down here, Mercedes. Let me help you."

She insisted they first remove the linen Blackwell had been asleep in and replace it with sheets she had set aside, a heavy, much used set she did not mind discarding. Blackwell grumbled, assisting her to change the bedclothes, but his seaman's sense of order admired her preparations for the coming gale. He helped her into the berth and leaned over her, squeezing her hand. Mercedes' body stiffened with pain, she returned the pressure of his hand and turned her face away to the bulkhead, gasping. It was horrible to see her suffer. Blackwell could think of nothing to say when the spasm passed, his heart was so full; of dread for the pain she must endure, of hope for the child, and of his love and need for her, his wish that she should not leave him. He pressed his lips to her forehead.

"I love you too, James. Send Saunders to me on your way to pass the word for the doctor, if you please, darling."

There was relief in his posture as he went out of the sleeping cabin, and in his voice when he called out, "Saunders! Look alive there, your mistress wants you."

Captain Blackwell spent the rest of the middle watch on deck. The watch changed, and changed again. By breakfast time the entire ship's company was aware the doctor had been sent for, and *L'Unite's* missus was being brought to bed of the captain's child. No sounds came from the great cabin reaching farther than the sentry at the door, their captain's lady was not one to put up a fearful shriek and try the nerves of the crew. She was a gentlewoman, was their missus, but the silence was a trial in its own right. At the beginning of the forenoon watch the gunner stepped over to Captain Blackwell and took off his hat.

"Yes, Master Gunner, what is it?"

"Number one starboard carronade ready, sir. In case Mrs. Blackwell needs the assistance, like." The gunner knuckled his forehead. It was a widely held belief among seamen the report of a great gun would assist a woman to bring forth her child.

Captain Blackwell received the suggestion as it was kindly meant. "Thank you, Mr. King, I am obliged to you. Stand by, if you please. Pass the word for McMurtry."

"McMurtry," Captain Blackwell said, when his steward presented himself on the quarterdeck. "Go below and send in to the doctor with my compliments, and how does Mrs. Blackwell do?"

McMurtry was only too ready to run below and find out what they were all eager to know, but he reappeared again on deck in a very short time. "The doctor's duty, sir, and it...the blessed event ain't happened yet, sir. He will send should you be wanted."

Captain Blackwell gritted his teeth over Doctor VanArsdel's impudence, he was not a man of particularly fine feelings yet he did understand when he was considered a heedless brute. And this had long been the doctor's assessment. He was contemplating the nearly universal opinion that found Mercedes too intelligent and fine a woman for him. His hands were behind his back, and he was making it his study to control his distress and concern for her, when there was a cry of "Sail ho!"

"Where away?"

"Fine on the starboard beam, sir."

"Mr. Bransford, shorten sail, she is closing to speak us. Mr. Morrow, hands to their stations, no shouts no calls. Mr. Allen, what do you make of her?" Captain Blackwell stared severely at the midshipman of the watch. In his heart he was relieved to have a professional distraction at this particular juncture.

Below in the captain's sleeping cabin Mercedes was covered in sweat and staring at Doctor VanArsdel in a dull, dispassionate way. The naval surgeon was obviously discomposed, he'd had little occasion to attend upon parturitions. He was better versed in seamen's complaints: ruptures, dislocated limbs, splinter and shot wounds, venereal disease. Doctor VanArsdel's affection and esteem for her were no doubt genuine, but at the moment she felt a certain resentment towards him. He'd early on declared to her that he appreciated her 'importance to *L'Unite's* commander, and indeed, to all her people'. Yet all he was good for was to watch her struggle and declare she bore her pain as stoically as he'd ever seen a foremast jack endure an amputation. At least in the other case the horrible event was over at a stroke, for Mercedes the experience went on and on. Saunders had the good sense to keep silent, and lifted her shoulders and supported Mercedes when she needed it.

When at last the baby's head was visible, and Mercedes, lying back against the bolsters, looked as though she were reaching her limit of endurance, Doctor VanArsdel rose from his position between her spread knees and flung out of the sleeping cabin. "Pass the word for the Captain," Doctor VanArsdel told the sentry at the door. "Give Captain Blackwell my duty, and tell him Mrs. Blackwell needs him. Quietly, if you please, none of your bawling out."

Captain Blackwell received the summons just after the lieutenant commanding the Spanish sloop of war had come up *L'Unite's* side and been presented on the quarterdeck. They had exchanged bows and handshakes when the midshipman came panting up. Captain Blackwell turned to his officers lined up behind him. "Mr. Verson, you will take over communicating with the lieutenant. Mr. Montelongo, make the situation known to commander Ochoa." Captain Blackwell bowed again to the lieutenant and ran for the companion ladder.

The Spanish lieutenant wore a reserved, displeased expression but as soon as Mr. Montelongo informed him Captain Blackwell's wife was in childbed below, a knowing smile came over the lieutenant's face. Then there were smiles and nods all round, and when Mr. Verson made his opening inquiries it was amid a feeling of good will by no means present at the outset.

Captain Blackwell rushed into his sleeping cabin and was immediately brought up by the sight of Doctor VanArsdel sitting between his wife's spread legs. And between Mercedes' thighs, bulging from that most tender part of her, stretched unbelievably, was a large, bloody, monstrous thing. He staggered. Saunders became aware of his presence, she turned and knuckled her forehead and yielded her position holding Mercedes.

He collected himself and stepped forward. "You sent for me, sweetheart?"

"Oh James, no. No I didn't." Mercedes shook her head. Sweat from her dripping hair wet the bedclothes. "Oh! Oh, no."

"Once more, Miss Mercedes," Doctor VanArsdel said. "Captain, help her up. Support her."

Mercedes sat up, clutching him around the shoulder and chest, straining against him. "You knew I did not wish him to see me like this, Doctor!" Mercedes raised her voice in an unaccustomed way, she screamed at Doctor VanArsdel. The baby rushed out of her body. She sank back into the cot as though all the life were gone out of her. Captain Blackwell turned from her, to the slimed, blood splotched creature in the doctor's hands, with a pulsing cord still attaching it to Mercedes' body.

The next moments were a blur. He heard Mercedes' voice, "Saunders, see to your Captain," and his arm was taken in a firm grip. As Saunders led him out of the sleeping cabin and dropped him into his armchair, Mercedes said, "You had no right, John. Why does the baby not cry?"

Captain Blackwell sprawled in his chair, his mouth agape. He had seen many, many horrible sights in his service career, but giving birth, and to live through such an ordeal, surpassed all. He was shaken, severely so, but he did become aware that Saunders, and McMurtry too, were in the cabin with him. A weak baby's cry came from the sleeping cabin, and Captain Blackwell's two attendants breathed again.

"Give you joy, sir, give you joy of your first born!" McMurtry said. "Do we have a young Mr. Blackwell or a Miss?"

"Saunders!" Doctor VanArsdel called from the sleeping cabin.

Saunders hurried away, and Captain Blackwell rubbed his hands over his face. "Thank you, McMurtry, but I couldn't say. I didn't notice I was so...so — "

"Right, sir. Would a glass of brandy be in order?"

"Bless me, it would be welcome of all things."

Doctor VanArsdel came out to him shortly after and took a seat at Captain Blackwell's invitation on the sofa beside him. McMurtry left to fetch another glass, and the ship's surgeon and captain regarded one another.

"Is it a boy or a girl, Doctor?"

"You have a son, sir, I wish you joy of him. A great, strapping boy, he must weigh ten pound at least, and cost your good lady a deal of suffering to bring into this world. You will no doubt wish to go to your family in a moment, after we have a word, sir."

The doctor's view that most men took their sexual lives far too lightly was well known in the ship. To them it was a pleasant much sought after diversion, for their ladies it could be life and death. McMurtry came in and poured Doctor VanArsdel a glass of brandy and refreshed Captain Blackwell's glass, and when the door shut behind the steward, the doctor warmed to his subject. "A very adult experience, child birth, would not you say, sir? One would suspect it is the female of the species that is the stronger. Contrary to conventional notions."

Captain Blackwell merely nodded, his brandy glass held in slack fingers. "I should like to see Mercedes as you say, Doctor." They watched Saunders pass through the great cabin with a pile of bloody linen in her arms. "Pray let me know what is in your mind. Her well being is everything to me."

Doctor VanArsdel sighed. "Your son's birth was normal in every way except for the baby's size. I had to cut her at the end or her flesh would have torn. Now it will make a neat wound and heal well, I hope and trust." Doctor VanArsdel paused, as Captain Blackwell palmed his forehead rather forcefully before he could stop himself. "The end of it is Miss Mercedes has wounds both external and internal. She will require a minimum of six weeks to recover. During this time marital relations would be dangerous to her health, she might take a fever from the introduction of — "

"I take your meaning, Doctor, I am obliged to you." Captain Blackwell felt the opposite of obliged. He resented the assumption he should force Mercedes to do anything dangerous to her health or contrary to her feelings, but he couldn't indulge in a fit of temper and confirm the doctor in his beliefs. "She once told me a child must take precedence in her affections. I have been warned, you see, that I am to be disrated."

"She is the soul of honesty, to be sure. With your leave, I will look in on Miss Mercedes and the child once more and then you may go in to her." Doctor VanArsdel stood up, and then turned to Captain Blackwell. "Or should you prefer to accompany me during the examination, sir?"

There was nothing of impudence in the doctor's question.

"Thank you, no, Doctor."

He heaved himself out of the armchair when Doctor VanArsdel emerged later, and listened to the doctor's admonitions. The last thing the medical man said in taking his leave was, "She is prodigious proud of her boy, sir." Captain Blackwell nodded, saying to the sentry at the door; "Pass the word for Mr. Verson, and he is to report in the great cabin in half a glass."

The life of a ship did not stop because a son was born to her commander. Blackwell felt the waters of duty almost closing over his head. He turned to his sleeping cabin, trying to compose his features, and walked in to find a Madonna in his cot. Such was his first impression when he looked on Mercedes cradling her child. He instantly knew this was the picture Mercedes had planned he should see of motherhood, not the other horrific one of pain and struggle. He remembered her words of the evening before; certainly one could not plan for every contingency, the queer nature of the ship's surgeon for one.

She turned to him with a beautiful smile on her face, and though she didn't remove a hand from her child to extend to him, Mercedes moved over on the cot so that Blackwell could get one leg up on it.

"What do you think of him, your son Edward James?"

She raised the sleeping baby so Blackwell could view him better. He pursed his lips at the red skinned creature with his outsized, misshapen bald head. The child slept peacefully, wet lashes on fat cheeks. Blackwell had a bad moment, a shameful moment, when he imagined the eyes opening and being yellow colored, like Queenie's.

"Why, he is a fine, big fellow ain't he," he managed. "What color are his eyes?"

"They are blue, but that may change. He is so little, so new." Mercedes caressed the baby's cheek with the fingers of one hand.

"Little? Little, indeed! The doctor says his size caused you much pain, and additional wounds — "

"Oh, the doctor!" Mercedes looked earnestly at Blackwell and then at the baby in her arms. "Why do we not try the cradle Mr. Bell fashioned, and then you can lie beside me."

The ship's carpenter, Mr. Bell, had constructed two cradles; one for each of the sleeping cabins, using the space of a locker beneath the fixed berths. The cradle was in the form of a drawer that slid out from beneath the cot, in which cushioning and small blankets had already been laid. There were holes round the rim of the cradle through which lines could be passed in case of a heavy sea. Captain Blackwell hauled the cradle out and fixed it in place with pins. He reached for the child. Mercedes gave the baby a tender kiss, and handed him his son.

Blackwell was surprised at the heft of the child. He looked into the wrinkled face as he placed him in the bed, willing the child to stay asleep so he might have a few moments with his mother. The baby's eyes fluttered open when he was transferred from warm hands to lifeless blankets; he regarded his father for a moment then closed his eyes, as though shutting them against a disagreeable sight.

"You are right, sweetheart, his eyes are blue." She'd moved far over on the cot to make room for him. He put his arms carefully round her. "Tell me how you do, Mercedes."

"I'm a bit shattered. A perfect wreck after the battle."

Blackwell squeezed her gently, kissed the top of her head and murmured, "No, never."

"I heard what you said to the doctor. What is disrated?"

"It means lowered in rank. Midshipmen are sometimes disrated for topping it the brute, and turned before the mast. Disrated to the rank of seaman so they may learn what life is for the hands. It don't happen often."

"James, darling, I've always been happy with you, on this ship and in your other commands. I am doubly so now, with your son." Mercedes raised herself and leaned over Blackwell in order to see her sleeping boy. Then she turned her frank gaze on him, and he saw that pride the doctor had spoken of in her expression. She reached up and touched his face. "I shall be your lover again. If you still want me, after what you've seen."

"If I still want you! Hell and death, woman." Blackwell clasped her tightly to him. He recollected her condition, his arms loosened about her, and he said, "Forgive me, sweetheart."

"I wish you would not treat me like a goddamn invalid, sir."

She stretched up on the cot and kissed him, a short tender kiss that pacified them both, for afterwards she and Blackwell lay together without speaking. Mercedes started in his arms, she must have fallen asleep, when McMurtry called in, "Mr. Verson to report on the Dons, your honor," in what for the Navy was a hushed, sickroom voice.

The child began to put up a poor weak mewling, surprising for his size, and given the lung capacity of his parent, who could make his voice heard from stem to forepeak of a second rate.

Mercedes was instantly awake. "Let me have him, James, if you please."

Blackwell grimaced lifting the boy from his cradle. He was a load, and though it was nothing to him, he did not wish Mercedes to be bending and hefting the boy out.

"You are to call McMurtry or Saunders or I to put him in and out. It is too much for you in your present condition."

Mercedes took the baby and settled him in her arms. Blackwell backed toward the door, watching her kiss and caress the child. When she opened her dressing gown and encouraged the melon head toward her breast, he bolted out.

CHAPTER ELEVEN

Edward James Blackwell was baptized on a Sunday in longitude 110° West before the entire ship's company. *L'Unite*, having sailed from the coast of Mexico, was prepared for the passage to the Sandwich Islands. The Spanish sloop of war they'd spoken the day of Edward's birth had informed them it was war between Britain and France, handing over newspapers in French and Spanish. From the lieutenant's manner it was suspected Spain had declared as well. Nevertheless, commander Ochoa, after Mr. Montelongo let slip the captain's lady had once been Doña Mercedes de Aragon, sent aboard *L'Unite* two sheep, six fowls, twelve tongues, several pumpkins and two bags of bread. *L'Unite* responded with a gift of rum, porter, and cheese, which she could ill afford to give away. Yet the occasion and the honor of the ship demanded the sacrifice. The Spaniard was eager to part company after the exchange, bearing away for Acapulco, after delivering the further intelligence of a French privateer following the merchant fleet into the Central Pacific.

Mr. St. James officiated at the baptism following Sunday service. The gathered company were all polished and correct, the seamen ranged up as the congregation, with their officers to one side and the marines on the quarterdeck. Captain Blackwell stood beside Mr. St. James, Mercedes holding the baby before the makeshift font. Edward had not grown into his head as yet but he was become much handsomer, his skin having lost the disagreeable red of the newborn. His eyes continued blue, large and luminous. The crew would have made a pet of him, but from the start it was clear Mercedes would not have it. She allowed no one to be alone with the boy besides his father, McMurtry, Saunders, and the doctor for short intervals. But when she walked on deck, the child a fixture in her arms, the lieutenants and midshipmen were seen to relieve her of the baby, even members of the crew from time to time. It diverted the men to catch sight of bosun Morrow or Narhilla with the skipper's son in their meaty paws. The Christian portion of *L'Unite* was deeply taken up in the ceremony to bring the child into their community.

Captain Blackwell held Edward over the font when it came time for the blessing, the awning stretched over the quarterdeck flapping and cracking over their heads. Discomfited away from his mother, Edward flailed his limbs and cried in his odd, strangled way. Smiles were hid behind hats and hands when Captain Blackwell hurriedly gave his son back into Mercedes' arms. She put the boy against her shoulder, and with this comfort and the faces the midshipmen made at him behind the captain's back, Edward was quiet and proper right through the benediction.

The baptism concluded, the men were dismissed and went below or stood about the deck to await the pipe to dinner. Captain Blackwell turned to Mercedes. It was four weeks since Edward's birth and Mercedes looked just as she had before becoming with child, more slender in fact. The additional stress accounted for it.

He felt a particular tenderness toward her. That morning when he had come back into the great cabin following his dawn appearance on deck, she'd met him in her dressing gown, silently taken his hand and led him into his sleeping cabin. She'd done things to him that did not compromise her recovery but that most definitely relieved his tension and pleased him, pleased him very much. He had reason to bless the fact he'd married a woman who so exactly understood the physicality of a man. Still, he wondered whether what they'd done that morning had given her any pleasure. He didn't like to think of her doing what she'd done out of duty, or because of the talk of the licentiousness of the women of the South Sea islands.

"Come, sweetheart," he said. "Allow me to take you below to rest before our guests come in."

Mr. St. James, Mr. Verson and Jack, Mr. Hoffinger of the marines, and three of the midshipmen were invited to Edward's baptismal dinner. In this company, before the commander's wife and son, the talk was decorous. Conversation turned on the curious flora and fauna to be found in the Sandwich Islands, the advance of the Word in the larger settlements, and the reputed cleanliness and attractiveness — according to the esteemed Captain Cook — of the people.

Much the same discussion was going forward in the gunroom, the midshipman's berth, and in the lower deck messes. But the emphasis was more upon those feminine flowers of the islands than on other natural phenomena.

"Captain Cook writes that the women of Hawaii make less difficulty of granting personal favours than those of any other country in the world," Mr. Bowles informed the gunroom.

"It was the Spanish Main, Nathan, if you please," Mr. Bransford said. "Cook said it is universally allowed that the women, both of the Spanish and Portuguese settlements in South America, make less difficulty of granting personal favours than those of any other civilized country in the world."

Mr. Bowles looked only slightly put about, his opinion coincided with young Mr. Bourne — Cripplegate, to his particular friends — that he should like to be learned but for the necessity of reading books.

"Not a sentiment Captain Blackwell should be pleased to hear expressed, I daresay." Doctor VanArsdel handed the decanter to Mr. Bowles.

"No, indeed." Mr. Bowles grinned, pouring himself a bumper. "How diverting to see the Captain holding young Edward this morning. First time I've ever seen him do it."

His table companions smiled and nodded.

"Gentlemen, I give you Mr. Edward Blackwell." Mr. Bransford raised his glass.

"Mr. Edward Blackwell," chimed the gunroom officers.

"And to the women of the Sandwich Isles," Mr. Bowles declared. "May they make less difficulty granting their favours than any other *uncivilized* country in the world!"

In the first days of the passage, *L'Unite* proceeded west barely touching a sail except to make it draw better, over a blue and tranquil Pacific. The ship ran off one hundred eighty nautical miles in twenty-four hours for five consecutive days. Captain Blackwell gloried in the speed, the fine sailing qualities of *L'Unite*, the ever increasing longitude at each days' noon observation.

Then they lost their wind and the ship drifted, her head turning to all points of the compass. The boats were hoisted out and towed ship, intense physical labor that gained them little, though it did serve to move them away from their own collected filth. Drawn by the rubbish and commotion the sharks found them. Six, seven, and eight foot aggressive tiger sharks and oceanic white-tips, that leapt from the water and bit the oars of the struggling boats.

After ten long days without a puff of air, light and variable winds set in. Captain Blackwell and his officers made the most westing they could from the changeable breezes, while faint lightning sparked on the horizon all round them. At midnight on the fifteen day after sinking the coast of South America a heavy squall of wind hit *L'Unite* from the north northeast, bringing with it a torrent of rain. Captain Blackwell had been hoping they should find rain, he'd begun to worry about their water. His wishes were answered on that score, the watch on deck nearly suffocated in the downpour. They were soon engulfed in tremendous thunder and lightning, and all hands recalled the St. Elmo's fire that'd struck *L'Unite's* anchor rounding the Horn.

Captain Blackwell believed it was the forerunner of the equinoctial gale and for three days they battled a heavy sea, so heavy they could carry little or no canvas. At eight o'clock in the morning of the fourth day the weather moderated and the ship found herself in the midst of a great boiling sea, completely surrounded by spermaceti whales: The important fish on whose account *L'Unite* was in the Pacific. The great eyes of the whales looked at the ship when they surfaced. They rolled to one side as if to get a better view of her and her people. A frail wooden ship they could easily knock to sticks individually, let alone were they to act in concert. There were no cries of "She blows!" from the whalers aboard, so stunned were all hands by the size of the creatures and their multitude. One of the ex-whalemen, a massive Brava man from the Cape Verdes, said to Narhilla, "Reckon it could've been a whale we hit off Cape Clear, mate."

"Land ho!" cried the lookout in the crosstrees, snatching everyone's attention from the leviathans in the sea. "Five points off the larboard bow, sir. Land bearing south southeast."

"Mr. Montelongo, take a glass up and report." Captain Blackwell turned to his other officers. "Mr. Allen, fetch my best telescope from the great cabin. Mr. Bransford, course south southeast to close, but we will stand well off, there are bound to be reefs."

Mr. Montelongo called down that the land appeared to be a small island, or series of islands. When his glass was brought on deck, Captain Blackwell followed the midshipman into the maintop.

"Sir!" Mr. Montelongo saluted, when he came puffing up on to the platform. The lookout had already moved up to the main topgallant mast crosstrees.

"We call them atolls," Captain Blackwell said, after studying the islets lying in line running southeast to northwest. "This is our mission, Mr. Montelongo, we have found the whale, now we are to seek anchorages for the whalers. There may be a prime one on our lee, but we shall have to watch ourselves. Nothing worse than a coral reef for a lee shore." Captain Blackwell grinned at the young man. But as he had a three days' beard and his eyes were red rimmed from keeping the deck, his smile looked more savage than those uncharted islands.

Whatever good humor Captain Blackwell had felt at sighting the islands had dissipated like the low haze over the sea by the time the noon observation was taken. His calculations put the ship in longitude 156° West 2° South, they'd been pushed south and east of their course by the storm, and he was very unwilling to be caught in the doldrums. At this season of the year it could be difficult to near impossible to beat against the northeast trades, and *L'Unite* now needed to sail as close to a northerly course as she could manage to make the Sandwich Islands.

"Mr. Verson, launch the gig and the red cutter," Captain Blackwell said. "I shall take the gig ashore and parlay with the natives."

He and his first lieutenant looked leeward at the scattering of huts on a crescent beach facing the lagoon; canoes were drawn up on a strand, but the village was deserted. Outside the lagoon *L'Unite* stood off and on. "Mr. Bowles will command the red cutter and take soundings on the southeastern end of the lagoon, working his way back to the ship. He will come in support of the gig if needed. Mr. Hoffinger, I want five privates and a corporal in each of the boats. Mr. Montelongo and Mr. St. James are to attend in the gig. Mr. Allen, run below to the great cabin and give my...belay that, Mr. Allen."

"Aye, aye, sir," was heard from all sides as Captain Blackwell strode below to his cabin.

He found Mercedes sitting on the lockers with Edward propped against her. She sat next to the open stern windows, trying to catch whatever breeze might waft in. A towel was near to hand, with which she wiped Edward's drool, and the child's sweating face and her own.

"I go ashore to trade for vegetables and fuel." Captain Blackwell seated himself the other side of Edward. "I should return this watch."

"Shall we stay long? It is so much pleasanter when we are under way."

"It is a deuced sweat bath, ain't it? But the requirements of the Service you know, survey, water and wood. We shall be away soon, beating up as hard as ever we can for the Sandwich Isles." Captain Blackwell considered his son, who would have fallen forward mouth agape but for Mercedes' sustaining hand on his midsection. "You must be proud of your boy, he is very good. Hardly ever cries."

Captain Blackwell stood up and took his leave; he didn't notice Mercedes looked the opposite of pleased with his praise of their son's disposition.

Though Edward was so young Mercedes had yet begun to feel all was not right with her baby boy. He seldom cried, and when he did it was a weak, strained sound. She would find him awake in his cradle looking vaguely about, his arms and legs flailing uncontrollably in the way of babies.

It troubled her Edward did not react when he caught sight of her peering down at him with the excited jerks of his limbs signalizing a baby's recognition of his mother. Mercedes spoke to him in English and Spanish, sang to him, cuddled and kissed him. There was no maid to attend him and it was she who changed his nappies, bathed, and fed him. She played games with him, naming his eyes, nose and ears, and other body parts; yet Edward showed no particular attachment to her. He did not cry when she left him, as comfortable in McMurtry's arms as hers, nor take particular notice or pleasure when she returned.

Mercedes held her son up facing her and gazed into Edward's large blue eyes, which wandered everywhere without looking into her own. *"Ven, mi amor, vamos a esperar a tu padre arriba."* She pointed to the deck over their heads and rose. *"Donde podemos respirar."*

The natives had run off into the bush. Captain Blackwell was attended by the gig's crew, and Mr. Montelongo and Mr. St. James, who'd been brought for their knowledge of the Spanish and Polynesian languages. The party could feel the eyes of many upon them. Marine sentries were posted with half the gig's crew to guard the boat. Captain Blackwell, trailing his midshipman, chaplain, and escort of marines and seamen, walked across the beach to examine the native canoes.

"What do you think, gentlemen?" Captain Blackwell said, standing beside a sailing canoe. "Expertly crafted, is it not, and she would lie very close to the wind."

Captain Blackwell received somewhat disinterested looks from his shipmates, but the faces of the crew lit up when a native party was seen to approach, carrying someone upon a litter.

The people, brown, muscular, and handsome, came down to the canoe house with their burden and halted before the British. They did not set the litter down. From atop it an ancient, white-haired man with skin like the aged leather of a smith's apron addressed them, in a mixture of Spanish and the native language.

"Are you Spaniards?" the old man asked.

At a nod from his captain, Mr. Montelongo said in his beautiful formal Spanish, "We are from His Britannic Majesty's ship *L'Unite*, your excellency."

"Yes, Spanish." The old man shook his head. "Last come, they called our land La Isla Disafortunada. Have you any tobacco?"

After a further interchange Mr. Montelongo bowed to the old man and turned to Captain Blackwell. "He says they will trade fish, coconuts, and breadfruit for nails and anything of iron, sir, but they rely upon rain water and have only the poorest copra for fuel. The chief offers women, sir, he calls them *nikiranroro*. Women of easy virtue I take it, sir. The cost is one stick of tobacco for...a—"

"I understand, Mr. Montelongo," Captain Blackwell said, amid the smiles and self-conscious looks of the men.

"He believes we are Spanish, sir. I could not make him understand the difference between Spain and England."

This went a way toward explaining the chief's attitude in Captain Blackwell's opinion. "Tell him we shall trade for provisions."

They were being rowed back to *L'Unite* after dining on fish and coconut milk at the chief's invitation in his hut. Bare breasted women young and old had served them, bringing to Captain Blackwell's mind Mercedes' remark about her breasts sagging to her waist if unsupported. He said to Mr. Montelongo, "I believe traders have been here before us. That head man was a deep old file."

Just how knowing the chief of the Unfortunate Isle was became apparent next morning when Captain Blackwell made his first appearance on deck. He emerged from below decks to a crowd round the entry port. Several native women already stood about among the crew lining the larboard rail, and there was Mr. Bowles, the officer of the watch, leaning down to give his hand to the next female to come aboard.

He quickened his stride and was among them in a moment, casting a glance over the side, where two native canoes were unloading twenty women. "Belay that!" Captain Blackwell called out sharply to Mr. Bowles. So absorbed were the men around him they positively jumped to find him in their midst. "Ladies, back in the boats, if you please."

Captain Blackwell stepped forward alongside Mr. Bowles and hurried the confused women back over the side into the waiting canoes.

"What is the matter with the fat man?" called one of the canoe paddlers to his mate. "He is sending them back. You there! We want tobacco. Te baa kee, understand?"

"It is no use," the man in the second canoe said despondently. "The *I-Matang* is probably a castrate."

"Mr. Morrow," Captain Blackwell addressed the bosun in an undertone, "serve those warriors out ten quid of tobacco each. Call our best Polynesian speaker and make them understand they are to leave and not approach the ship again." Captain Blackwell raised his voice. "Mr. Bowles, in my cabin."

Pitying looks from the men on deck followed Mr. Bowles as he went below in the captain's wake.

In the great cabin Captain Blackwell was happy to find Mercedes and the boy not yet up and about. He could count on her, when she heard him speaking to one of his officers in the great cabin, not to emerge inopportunely and interrupt ship's business. Captain Blackwell turned to face his third lieutenant, a sturdy, capable young man of nineteen, who had sailed under his command ever since he was a reefer. Mr. Bowles stood before him all attention, his hat under his arm, reminding him of his younger self. He too had desired women and pleasure just as ardently as Mr. Bowles, and been willing to risk punishment in the pursuit.

"Did you have the first lieutenant's leave before you allowed those women aboard?"

"No, sir. I did not."

"This will not do, Mr. Bowles. There were but twenty women in those canoes. Twenty frightened women, and we are two hundred ninety men. The old chief over there is used to fur traders and sealers coming into his lagoon with a crew of thirty hands. He has no concept of the numbers of men aboard a man-of-war. At least I hope he don't." Captain Blackwell grimaced, and exchanged an uncomfortable glance with Mr. Bowles. "No, it will not do. When we make the Sandwich Islands the men shall go ashore by watches to rest and recruit."

"Aye, aye, sir."

The lieutenant was looking at him expectantly. Captain Blackwell wondered what more there was to say, and then he recalled he had to play the great man. "I'll have no more neglect of the standing orders, allowing civilians aboard without leave. Dismissed, goddammit!"

Captain Blackwell did not relish the name of hypocrite, turning away women who would have brought comfort to the officers and men in the way his own wife did to him. He was no moralist, yet he must do what was best for the ship.

There was not a soul aboard *L'Unite*, or outside of it, who was not grateful for the gale that strengthened the southeast trade wind. The officers, men, and boys, the supernumeraries like Mercedes and young Jack Verson, were relieved to have the wind at their backs. *L'Unite* was pushed through the doldrums with thunder and lightning chasing her, the equatorial heat easing as they beat up for the Sandwich Islands. As for the old chief, the *nikiranroro* who'd barely escaped the white beings, the warriors and all the people of the Unfortunate Isle, they believed their god of thunder had not failed them. *Tabuariki*, when called upon, had sent a great storm to blow the ship away.

L'Unite had been on rationed water for a week, so long was her passage, when the island of Hawaii was at last raised several hours before sunset. Its splendid mountain peaks had been visible from two hundred nautical miles out at sea, with the appearance to the crew of the promised land. All hands were on deck as the southern tip of the island was approached, a wild coastline with white capped waves breaking against the shore. In one spot, molten lava flowed into the sea in a spectacular meeting of fire and water. A cry of "Sail ho!" turned attention from nature's fury.

"Two points off the starboard bow, sir," the masthead called down moments after the first hail.

"She's spotted us, sir," Mr. Verson said, his glass clapped to his eye. "And she's making from us with a press of sail."

"What do you make of her Mr. Bowles?" Captain Blackwell said.

The officers and midshipmen were clustered together on the forecastle. Mr. Bransford had the watch and remained on the quarterdeck.

"Ship rigged, sir, smartly handled and very fast. She appears to be pierced for thirty guns." After a prolonged study through his glass, Mr. Bowles lowered his telescope and faced Captain Blackwell. "She could be our Frenchie, sir."

"She might, indeed."

Though they longed for a snug anchorage and the comforts of shore, the men wished for a prize even more. Barely concealed smug and knowing looks lit the seamen's faces as they knuckled their foreheads to Captain Blackwell, striding past them to the quarterdeck.

"Alter course in pursuit, Mr. Bransford. And pipe the hands to supper, if you please."

They might be up with the chase in an hour or two, and Captain Blackwell wanted the men well fed and ready to clear for action well before then. But the officers' supper hour came and went, and as the last light left the evening sky neither ship had gained. Most of the hands kept the deck at nightfall, the talk turned from the women of the Sandwich Isles to the prize, and what the ship they hoped to capture might contain; barrels of spermaceti oil, even more valuable ambergris. After the setting of the first watch Captain Blackwell went below to his cabin, to warn Mercedes they might have to beat to quarters in the night.

Mercedes had done a rare thing; she'd left Edward alone in the great cabin. The baby was lying inside the canvas and rope contraption given Mercedes by Mrs. Jennings all that time ago on Juan Fernandez. He went down on one knee beside the boy. "Where's your mother, son?" Edward didn't look at him, he had a considering look on his infant face as though examining the canvas and lines that held him. Captain Blackwell guessed Mercedes was in the quarter gallery. Off and on she'd been seized by the flux since their passage through the doldrums and their visit to that Unfortunate Isle. He rose and went into his sleeping cabin and changed his uniform coat for a round jacket to pass the evening on deck.

L'Unite's motion had become lively, not unlike a bucking horse, and when Captain Blackwell emerged into the great cabin there was Edward rolling loose upon the deck. The boy was laughing as he tumbled, but Captain Blackwell felt a sick dread for Mercedes' darling when Edward struck so hard against the base of the stern lockers he was thrown into the air. He ran forward and caught Edward as though he were a rugby ball.

The frigate gave a great lee lurch, meeting the current running out of a channel between islands, and Captain Blackwell fell on to the stern lockers, his head toward the unlatched windows. As he slid headlong Captain Blackwell tossed Edward between his legs back into the great cabin; he heard a thump and cry as he flailed for a hold. It all happened so rapidly that he did not think to cry out. He had been at sea, man and boy, for twenty-five years, but this time he hadn't a hand for the ship. When his considerable weight hit the partially opened window it flew wide; he tumbled headlong into the sea.

Mercedes hastened out of the quarter gallery to attend to Edward, who was howling in a most unusual way. She found him on the deck, a great lump already rising on his forehead, turning red with the effort of his cries. "*Pobrecito, pobre de Edward. Sana, sana.*" She rocked him guiltily, trying to soothe him, but Edward continued to bawl, gulping for air between shrieks. He stared with tear filled eyes toward the stern windows, which were wide open. Supposing this might somehow frighten him, Mercedes eased to her feet. Still with Edward clutching her, she took a boat hook from one of the racks on the bulkhead. She was preparing to lean out and catch the window latch when McMurtry entered the great cabin.

"Ho there, Missus, don't be a leaning out the barky that way. I'll tend to it." McMurtry came and took the boat hook from her. "What ails young master? Anxious to catch the Frenchie too, is it?"

Blackwell began hailing the ship as soon as his head cleared the surface of the sea, but aboard *L'Unite* every man's attention was focused on the chase ahead. He might have been saved by getting aboard one of *L'Unite's* boats usually towing behind, but he'd ordered the boats in when the chase began. With the ship traveling at six knots she was a quarter of a mile away within five minutes. He roared and hailed anyway, until his ship was no more than a small speck of light, a white flash of sails against the dark background of the islands.

His voice was hoarse, he choked and spat sea water, and when Blackwell finally ceased his hailing the silence, the solitude, and the desperation of his case almost overwhelmed him. Blackwell tried to take his bearings, he was a strong swimmer and he could hold out some time, the temperature of the water being moderate. He was aware the current was carrying him northwestward, away from the large island where they'd observed lava flowing to the sea. Blackwell fixed Arcturas and several other stars in the night sky by which he would be able to judge the passage of time. His rescue depended upon his being missed, and he was much absorbed with when this might occur. How long before Mr. Verson put the ship about and came in search of him, launching the boats to fan out over a greater expanse of sea.

Hours passed and Blackwell rested floating on his back or hanging in the water face down. Yet whenever he ceased moving he rapidly grew cold, so he swam in a diagonal direction toward shore, until the struggle against the current exhausted him and he stopped to tread water and rest again.

After a time, swimming or resting, Blackwell could not control his chattering teeth or the trembling of his limbs. He began to doubt he would survive until dawn. It was hard to credit just that morning; or the morning of the day previous, for it was early morning again; he'd lain in his cot between smooth sheets caressing Mercedes. She'd returned to his bed, to his arms, to his ardent attentions. Blackwell made her dominate him, to make sure she did not bear more than she was able. This was the way they'd started their intimate life together, when Mercedes had expressed concern over his bulk. He felt something close to self-pity, contemplating all he had to lose; a woman he loved fiercely, a career he'd suffered for his entire adult life and most of his youth, and a little son he hardly knew.

His heart was in confusion. He was infinitely glad he'd given Mercedes his Power of Attorney, and written his letter to Francis. Francis was a sensible good fellow and he would support Mercedes. Yet Blackwell was angry anyone besides he should have to do so. Knowing Mercedes would likely not need any man's support was small comfort. Their son needed his father to guide him, his brother Francis wouldn't know which captains to place the boy with when the time came for Edward to learn his profession.

Blackwell had grown accustomed to think of Edward as he would be in future, of his older self. His present emotions toward the child were less easy to face; the ignoble jealousy he felt watching Mercedes pet and love the boy, it was the reason he fled the cabin whenever she suckled their child. In his afflicted state he felt a terrible resentment, toward God or fate, or the powers that had sent him out with an admonition he must not fail. It might be his father was right, and he understood neither God nor man.

During what Blackwell judged must be the fore part of the morning watch, when he'd been in the water some ten hours, his vision became so hazy he couldn't distinguish the stars. He fought against panic when he realized he was unsure of the direction of the land, or of the tack the ship had been on when she'd sailed away from him. He decided he must float and tread water and conserve his strength, and strike out for land when dawn came.

Daybreak seemed a distant much longed for country whose shores he felt he'd never reach. Despair warred with the strong animal spirit, the will to fight that had kept him alive through countless battles. Exhaustion overtook him and Blackwell must even have slept, for he came awake in a rush of adrenaline when something solid bumped his shoulder. Shark, was Blackwell's first thought, and he struggled against fear and the urge to thrash that might stimulate the beast's ferocity. He was bumped again, in the back, not from below where a shark could be expected to attack. Blackwell flung out his arm and encountered a blessed thing: the floating trunk of a tree.

The holy stoning of the deck over her head woke Mercedes at four o'clock in the morning. She rose, and though she could not see Edward in the dark cabin she knew he slept there, cradled in a locker beside her own cot, with the sweet respiration and face of an angel. Mercedes put on her dressing gown and crept into the captain's sleeping cabin. His cot was empty; it had not been slept in. Captain Blackwell must have passed the night in a hammock chair on deck because of the chase. She settled in his cot and didn't wake until the ship was alive with the sounds of hammocks being piped up and the smells of breakfast cooking in the galley.

"Never tell me his honor is still in his cot?" McMurtry said, bringing in the first dishes and setting them on the table before Mercedes.

"He is not. Nor has he been this night. Did not Captain Blackwell keep the deck?"

"I'll go ask Mr. Wilson. He had the morning watch."

McMurtry came back to the cabin ten minutes later, a frown darkening his ill favored countenance. At sight of him Mercedes leapt to her feet.

"Which the Captain wasn't on deck all night, Missus. The starbowlines did think it odd, there being a chase."

"Pass the word for Mr. Verson."

The chase was still in sight, with the last in the chain of the Sandwich Islands lying on *L'Unite's* larboard beam, when Mr. Verson ordered the ship to heave to while a search was conducted for the captain.

A little more than half a glass later the first lieutenant was knocking on the great cabin door. "Captain Blackwell is not aboard, Ma'am. I'll put the ship about and order the boats in the water. We can cover two sea miles with the boats spread out, and we shall beat back along last night's course." Mr. Verson's face was full of anxiety and a deep concern. Once before he'd had to deliver such wretched news of loss, on that occasion to Captain Blackwell.

"Thank you, Mr. Verson." Mercedes was very pale. "We...we believe, McMurtry and I, he went in the water about nine or ten last evening."

"That's right, sir. After hammocks was piped down. The stern windows was open."

"Saunders, you are relieved of duty until further notice." It was clearly a gesture meant to assist his captain's wife. "McMurtry, you will be required in the gig. Mrs. Blackwell, ma'am." Mr. Verson bowed to Mercedes and hastened from the great cabin.

Edward began to cry, as though sensible of his mother's distress. Mercedes heaved him up and hurried into her sleeping cabin where, trembling, she gave him her breast. She couldn't think of her beautiful boy as she looked down at him, caressing his smooth cheek. All that was in her mind was the scarred face of his father, of how desperately she wished to hear Captain Blackwell's heavy tread and his loud voice calling out, "Mercy, sweetheart!"

Why had she not attended to the open stern window the evening before when Captain Blackwell must have been in the water calling out to them, nor raised the alarm when he was not in his cot four hours since. Four precious hours; she shuddered, her heart ached; and she groaned aloud. As soon as Edward was sated Mercedes changed her gown for a volunteer's costume. She'd purchased the shirt, waistcoat, breeches and jacket, the entire ensemble when Mr. Montelongo had bought his kit, to wear in the event the ship saw action. With a length of linen bandaging Mercedes bound her breasts tightly, before putting on her shirt and jacket. She slung the captain's second best telescope over her shoulder and took up Edward.

Saunders jumped when Mercedes rushed from her sleeping cabin in men's clothing, she was more confounded still when Mercedes plopped Edward into her arms.

"I go to the masthead to look out for the Captain. If Edward becomes too much for you, take him to the Doctor. If you please, Saunders."

No one dared say a word to her when Mercedes appeared on deck, the seamen giving way before her, knuckling their foreheads as she passed. She went to the foremast shrouds and began the climb to the masthead. The lookout moved respectfully up to the crosstrees after assisting her through the lubber's hole, to allow Mercedes privacy on the platform.

She scanned the sea forward and around the ship. Every man and boy in *L'Unite*, and in the ship's boats, strained to discover a form in the water. The watch changed, the hands went to dinner, and Mercedes remained in the tops. She could feel no hunger, her anguish was too great; but during the afternoon watch she did suffer from the fullness of her bladder and breasts. Yet she could not bear to leave her post, afraid if she descended she might miss spotting Captain Blackwell.

The hands were piped to supper, and then the first dog watch was over. Narhilla came up to relieve the lookout at the foremast, nodding to his mate as he took up his position. The man finishing his trick shook his head sadly and cast a meaning look at Mercedes clinging to the mast below them. The sun sets promptly in the tropics, and at three bells in the last dog watch Mr. Verson called in the boats.

Darkness fell and Mercedes sank to her knees on the foretopmast platform. Her cries reached Narhilla and he came down from his perch and knelt beside her.

"On deck, there!" Narhilla called. "Mr. Verson, sir, Mrs. Blackwell needs assistance."

Mr. Verson ordered a block and a line for a whip, and the seamen swiftly had Mercedes on the deck. Even the officers and men who had been with Captain Blackwell during the taking of the Spanish ship *La Trinidad* had never seen Mercedes in such a state. They did not know quite where to look as she passed them, led between the first and second lieutenants. Ever before the captain's wife had appeared to them the picture of controlled, demure, obedient womanhood. The woman who passed them sobbing was the opposite of all that, her only coherent utterance a passionate cry of "Oh, James! Oh, Jim!" The men pitied her with their whole hearts, and not a few were amazed Captain Blackwell could have inspired such affection and devotion.

When he'd encountered the floating trunk in the hours before dawn Captain Blackwell's hopes had risen. He prayed Mercedes would raise the alarm when she came into his cabin to lie with him in the early hours. But his mind had cleared with the rush of fear, followed by the enormous relief of finding the floating tree. It was a relief tinged with hope of salvation, and practically speaking he felt he must certainly be missed by breakfast time. Mr. Verson would put the ship about, and Captain Blackwell now felt he could hold out another day and longer, and he should make a bigger target in the sea clinging to a log. He was wretchedly thirsty, and hungry of course, and he turned over in his mind whether he had better not abandon the blessed tree if he saw an opportunity to swim ashore.

Dawn found Captain Blackwell closer in to land than he'd credited, flotsam in the sea does tend to shore. The decision of whether he should attempt to get ashore was taken from him, for in the full light of day he found himself surrounded by war canoes.

They boxed him in and he had no choice in the matter when strong arms were extended and plucked him from his log.

CHAPTER TWELVE

The warriors tossed Captain Blackwell to the bottom of the canoe. He found himself toward the stern, unable to see over the gunwales of the craft, which rose four feet high. When he'd recovered warmth in his limbs after the twelve hour soaking, and drank a gourd of water he found mercifully at hand, Captain Blackwell tried to take stock of his situation. The warriors sat two to a thwart, moving the canoe rapidly, seamlessly through the water. He counted twenty pair of paddlers, and behind him was a steersman in the stern of the canoe, which rose in a graceful curve twelve feet over the man's head. Separating him from the canoe's coxswain, Captain Blackwell became gradually aware, blinking away the crusted salt from his eyes, were a number of decapitated, disemboweled bodies tied wrists and ankles to wooden spars.

The realization he was captured by a head-hunting expedition served to concentrate Captain Blackwell's faculties remarkably. The warriors he observed in the after part of the canoe were young, powerful men. Naked except for a short skirt like covering of the loins, copper skinned, with strong muscular arms and chests. These men must surely see in him a portly, middle-aged white man. The warriors began a frightful bawling and crying out and Captain Blackwell supposed from this, and from the changed rhythm of their stroke, they must be nearing a landing place.

The canoe ground in the shallows and Captain Blackwell half rose with the warriors to bring her ashore. Only then did they take notice of him, none having looked in his direction since tossing him into the canoe. The nearest of the paddlers in the stern turned to Captain Blackwell and waved a three foot long wooden club at him with a fierce scowl, his mate on the larboard side meanwhile delivering a well aimed kick. Captain Blackwell sank down again in the canoe's bottom while the paddlers jumped out and ran the craft up the beach.

He tried to remember how many war canoes had been in the water around him; each would contain forty warriors, but he was not long in discovering the enemy's number. The paddlers leaned in when they had the canoe well up on the beach, each grasping his killing club. Some took up skin sacks that Captain Blackwell guessed, by their shape, contained heads. A half dozen came to the stern and shouldered the wooden stakes from which hung the corpses. Captain Blackwell supposed he had near the same status as the dead men, for he was motioned out of the canoe at the same time.

There was but one other canoe drawn up on the beach. This still put him among eighty fighting men, who were at present eagerly awaiting a sailing canoe coming up last to the landing place. In it were the chief, the principal officers of the party, and a small crew to paddle and sail. The warriors on the beach stood well back as the chief's party came ashore, the spearmen held their eight foot long bone and hard wood weapons like sentinels' pikes. The chief wore a long striking red colored waist-cloth, contrasting with the warriors' simple garb. On his head was a wickerwork helmet covered in red and a scant few yellow feathers.

The warrior who led Captain Blackwell forward positioned him correctly when the chief was ready to receive him. Captain Blackwell would have doffed his hat, the chief being a man of obvious dignity, but he'd no hat, shoes, or stockings. He'd kept his shirt and breeches and even a belt at his waist with a knife, and a flint and steel stuffed deep in one pocket. Fortunately neither clothing, nor his bedraggled appearance from the long soaking could disguise his natural authority. Captain Blackwell executed a bow before the chief.

"Captain James Blackwell, sir, of His Britannic Majesty's Ship *L'Unite*. At your service."

The chief responded with his own name, Ata Gege. But to Captain Blackwell this was indistinguishable in the chief's discourse; so was the question that seemed to be put to him at the end. They were at a stand. By word and gesture Captain Blackwell was given to understand the chief might like a present of his shirt. He pulled the fine lawn garment made by Mercedes' own hand over his head. He had the sense to hand it to one of the lieutenants, who gave it over to the great man. Captain Blackwell thought the chief to be of his own age by the firm, muscled trunk, and the stern lined face. Ata Gege was a dark skinned man, darker than most of his tribe, which somehow added to his forbidding almost sinister presence. In spite of this he looked quite fine when he'd donned Captain Blackwell's shirt, though it fell almost to his knees.

But the chief was more pleased, far more so, when Captain Blackwell was relieved of his belt and knife. Ata Gege girded the billowing shirt with them. Captain Blackwell was allowed to keep his breeches to cover his modesty; they had not discovered the flint in his pocket.

The interview was abruptly at an end. The same warrior who'd led Blackwell forward, coxswain of the canoe he'd been in, came and took charge of him. As he was led away one of the lieutenants called an order, acknowledged by the coxswain with a raising and lowering of his club. The warriors shouldered the canoes, an honored detachment carrying the corpses, and the party moved inland off the beach. Blackwell hoped their encampment might not be far, he must stay in sight of the landing place if he'd a hope of signaling, or of the war party being sighted by his ship.

By mid-day his illusions of remaining near shore had vanished. The warriors marched across a valley opening to the beach, leaving the canoes in a shrine like house. Blackwell tried to fix the position of this shelter in his mind. If he could steal away from his captors he might be able to handle the sailing canoe on his own. Speculations of this sort occupied his thoughts until they started to climb out of the valley.

The terrain rose so steeply Blackwell found himself fighting his way up, grasping tree limbs and roots in what felt like a vertical assent. Warriors pushed at his broad backside in the most difficult spots, as if he were some species of pack-ass. His feet suffered much; they were bare, and not hardened like the feet of the foremast jacks. In the first hours of the march Blackwell glanced repeatedly over his shoulder to the sea, scanning the ocean for a flash of white sail. But as the day wore on, and they descended into the next valley and began an equally precipitous climb up its farther slope, weariness and a sense of despair overtook him. Blackwell went along with his head down.

At last the march halted when the sun was no more than an hour from the horizon. There seemed nothing distinctive about the site Ata Gege had chosen. Blackwell sat down in the enemy's camp, but shortly after he'd cast himself to the ground on the spot indicated by the coxswain, there were suddenly more people among them. Blackwell didn't know from where the people emerged, he was simply astounded to see women moving about the camp, and youngsters of the age of midshipmen.

The women immediately set about building shelters, making poles of saplings and using the broad leafed forest plants to thatch the roofs. The young men and warriors uncovered a pit dug in the earth, a pit that Blackwell guessed might have been constructed when Captain Cook was an infant. The men lit fires where they warmed large stones that were then layered in the oven with banana leaves.

A young man near Blackwell, about the age of Mr. Allen, struggled to strike a spark with his stone implements. Blackwell heaved himself up and knelt beside the boy. He withdrew the flint and steel from his pocket and rapidly produced a spark. The boy fed the flame with tinder. Bearing a load of stones, the coxswain of Blackwell's canoe came over to them. The natives exchanged a few words and Blackwell was obliged to show his flint and steel. The coxswain suffered him to replace them in his pocket, after a smile and a wondering shake of the head.

Blackwell remarked that smile and shake of the head at what the white man might do next in the people's behavior toward him from that moment on. One of the women brought him a leaf serving bowl containing some sort of tasteless vegetable puree and bits of fish, and a welcome gourd of water. He would not be obliged to refuse the cannibal dish: no man's meat was offered him. His own supper having restored his wits somewhat, Blackwell observed the ceremony with which the warriors distributed the choice parts of their uncooked enemy to particular friends.

Having carefully set those parts in the prepared ovens they turned to Blackwell with what he felt was particular attention, a knowing light in their eyes as though already picturing his own parts a simmer there. The entire company moved off to a stream not far distant. The men led Blackwell to their bathing spot, and respected his wish to take himself a little way apart. Back at the campsite one of the women brought a coconut shell containing ointment. She rubbed a decoction of herbs mixed with hog's lard on Blackwell's injured feet.

"I am very much obliged to you, ma'am," Blackwell managed to choke out.

The woman, a comely bare breasted lady, smiled at him as one might at a favorite family dog, though the dog was to be eaten at some later time. She signaled to Blackwell to rub the ointment on his chest and shoulders by mimicking the rubbing of her own shoulders and breasts. He did not at first take her meaning, being distracted by the sight of her uncommonly well-formed breasts, but eventually it dawned on him and with a blush he dipped his hand in the shell.

The young woman did not remark his discomfiture. She moved behind him and spread more of the oil on his back. His skin had burned raw since he had no shirt to shield him. Blackwell tried to harden his heart to the young woman, who sang while rubbing soothing ointment on his back. Her voice was a gentle counterpoint to the chanting and stamping of the men. But she was after all the enemy, one of his captors, who seemed to be preparing for a night of celebration.

The coxswain approached them from out of the revelers and jerked his head at the young woman attending Blackwell. She led Blackwell to a mat in a shelter apart from the *maneaba* where the ritual feasting, and singing and dance took place. He lay down on the mat, his expressions of gratitude to the handsome young woman still on his lips as he fell into a deep sleep. His arms and legs were flung out, he hadn't truly slept for a day and a half, during which his fatigue and suffering had been considerable. It was not long before Blackwell was emitting the loudest and most raucous of snores.

The young woman Tiaba and her companions, women of the serving class and boys equivalent to soldier's pages, were at first shocked by the white man's vulgar snorts. Though they knew he was to be kept with the pigs until next season's sacrifice, they had not expected him to fit in quite so well. The youth Blackwell had helped in starting a fire could not contain a titter, and when they found he did not wake, the whole company burst out laughing. Then they proceeded to imitate him in turn. The people generally were excellent mimics, skilled at the faithful reproduction of birdsong and a range of natural sounds, imitating even posture and expression. Tiaba and her friends succeeded amazingly well. With the laughter, snorts, and grunts, it seemed as though a whole tribe of Englishmen were carrying on a drunken revel.

Blackwell came suddenly awake near midnight. He felt a sensation of pressure on his chest, as of a strong hand or a weight of water pressing him down. He turned his head and met the eyes of the young woman who'd attended him earlier. She was several feet away supporting herself on her elbows, while from behind her the coxswain took his pleasure of her. She met Blackwell's gaze with the same patient smile. Clearly here was a woman who did her duty. Blackwell turned away; the sight reminding him of his youth aboard men-of-war.

He forced himself to be calm, to slow the painful, unaccountable beating of his heart. His reflections naturally turned to the woman who'd granted him the last favor, to Mercedes. She'd given him love and comfort during the entirety of their married life, and for sometime before when they were mere *enamorados*. But thoughts of his dear, gentle wife would not do. They brought a flood of other feelings; a yearning for home, for his ship, for his life of honor.

He'd been a prisoner of the Spanish in his youth and of the French as third of the old *Etrusco* when she went to pieces on the coast of Brittany. He'd survived captivity then, he hoped and trusted to survive it now. He would not dwell on the fact that he'd been exchanged by both European nations, and then he'd been a sprightly youth rather than an oldster with a pain in his chest.

Yet fatigue claimed him. He came awake again at four o'clock from a profound sleep for the changing of the morning watch. He was instantly and completely awake. Men were moving through the encampment, war clubs and spears in hand. A man in the vanguard crept into their shelter and raised his club over the sleeping form of the coxswain. Blackwell leapt up with a great bellow and hurled himself at the legs of the assailant. He managed to knock the man off his feet, and jumping up Blackwell put his right hand to his side for his sword.

With no weapon he fell bodily upon his opponent as he attempted to rise, casting his full sixteen stone atop him. He heard the breath whoosh out of the man. He grasped the hand clutching the killing club, twisting the weapon out of the man's grip. Long, intimate experience with sword, cutlass, boarding axe and tomahawk was on his side. As soon as Blackwell had control of the club he dealt his enemy a lethal blow.

In the dark of the early morning hour, with the war whoops and grunts and cries of the combatants drowning out even the background screech of insects, tree frogs and other night creatures, Blackwell could not tell one native from the next. He couldn't make out which were his natives, his original captors, and which the attacking party. The idea he might make his escape in the melee occurred to him at the same instant Blackwell spotted the coxswain a few paces away. The young woman was behind him, a shell knife used for skinning animals clutched in her hand. The coxswain stood off two attackers while pushing her behind him toward the surrounding forest.

Blackwell roared out "*L'Unite!*" — the only battle cry he knew — and rushed upon the group. Together he and the coxswain beat the other men back. The coxswain led and they fought their way to the *maneaba*, Tiaba fleeing into the forest. They found Ata Gege in the midst of the heaviest fighting, inside the sacred house itself, and Blackwell did what he'd been trained to do. Having identified the captain and the ground to be defended, Blackwell made Ata Gege's enemies his own. He was no stranger to a close fight, and the conflict was much as it would have been on a packed quarterdeck. There was no room for elegant swordplay, it was blows and kicks and hammering the other man with whatever was to hand.

The attackers had fallen on Ata Gege's encampment with killing clubs, spears, and shields. But the advantage shifted in Ata Gege's favor when Blackwell entered the fight, roaring like a madman. Everyone knew white men had powerful *mana*. Nothing else could explain their blessed existence, and the gods favoring them with so much cargo.

Blackwell came out of that furious state of mind necessary in a close action. The aftermath of battle had always been more trying for him than the close hand to hand fighting. The hosing of the decks, the butcher's bill: learning of the loss of officers he esteemed, young gentlemen, old shipmates. Ata Gege's men had carried the day, his enemies lay either dead around them or were fleeing into the forest. In true martial fashion Ata Gege, as soon as he had an initial report of damages from his surviving lieutenants, dispatched men into the forest to run down and kill any survivors they could capture.

The coxswain was not one of the men sent on this duty and he sought Blackwell out, finding him on the edge of the crowd gathered in the *maneaba*. Clasping him by the forearm the coxswain looked earnestly into Blackwell's face and delivered a speech in a slow, deliberate tone, almost as though speaking to a small child. Blackwell stared at the coxswain; he'd always had translators under his command. He determined to learn the native tongue, and studying the man's posture and expression, Blackwell felt sure he'd been congratulated on the action just fought.

"Captain Blackwell, sir, at your service." A feeble rejoinder, yet Blackwell hoped it would do.

He had no particular linguistic talent, unlike his diplomat brother Francis. Blackwell found the native language distressingly loaded with vowel sounds conjoined in ways that made him despair of ever distinguishing a word. He was further confounded by the wretched sense he should have fled rather than fought alongside these people. Yet would they not have run him down, a heavy white man, just as they were now doing the attacking tribesmen?

The coxswain gave Blackwell a cheerful look, and made a last attempt to communicate. Motioning to his own chest, he said, "*Kanaka maoli* Mahin," and raising a respectful hand to Blackwell, "Captain James Blackwell, His Britannic Majesty's ship *L'Unite, aikāne. Aikāne.*"

Blackwell bowed again. He was surprised at the perfect repetition of his name, the inflection of voice was a copy of his own. There was nothing savage about the look of the man either.

Blackwell had lived too long in the company of men to be mistaken; Mahin's expression was friendly and open, even brotherly. It gave Blackwell pause.

So did the scene unfolding before him. Blackwell looked on in barely concealed astonishment and distaste as the warriors directed the women and boys in the decapitations.

The sight made Blackwell's gorge rise, and he hoped when he turned away the natives would not take offense. None was meant; he recognized the respect of the women, the warriors, and the boy pages toward their slain enemy; their treatment was better than he'd witnessed in some Englishmen toward the foreign dead.

Silence had fallen in the *maneaba* and Blackwell, looking round, found all eyes upon him. The grisly work had been done, some of the warriors clasped new filled hide sacks, and the women and boys were clustered together. There were bodies yet intact and Blackwell experienced a terrible dread when he met expectation in the eyes of the crowd. The great man stepped over to Blackwell, followed by his lieutenants and the coxswain Mahin, who'd apparently earned his step. Ata Gege offered Blackwell his own knife.

Did they believe he only lacked the proper tool with which to take the heads of the men he'd killed? Blackwell hid his fear, uncertainty, revulsion, and distress behind the set expression he wore on his quarterdeck. He grasped the knife Ata Gege offered, he could hardly do otherwise, and backed out of the presence of the chief.

Blackwell was not a particularly learned or cultured man, but he did have a highly attuned instinct for survival. It had seen him through fleet actions and single ship encounters, innumerable boarding, cutting out, and shore expeditions. His ability to make a vital decision quickly, unaided, did not desert him. Once out of the *maneaba* he scanned the camp, and followed by Ata Gege, his officers, and all the surviving people, Blackwell returned to the shelter where he'd slept.

He bent over the man that had first attacked Mahin and knocked out the incisor tooth from the lower jaw with the handle of the knife. Collectively the people gasped. He straightened from where he'd leaned over the body, a scowl masking his distaste, and met universal approval on the faces of the people. Blackwell wiped the blade on his breeches and returned it to Ata Gege.

"*Kanaka kō,*" Ata Gege said, sheathing the knife.

Murmurs of agreement met the chief's pronouncing Blackwell a real man. Ata Gege walked off and the excitement was done. The people disbursed to attend to their dead and wounded, and prepare for the day's journey. Mahin brought Blackwell to march with the officers, and though the terrain was no less challenging, the hands and shoulders that pushed his backside up the steeper slopes were more respectful than on the previous day.

The people were in good humor, like sailors on the homeward passage, and Blackwell thought they must be approaching the home village. Their attitude toward him was considerably changed, as though they had already accepted him as one of their own. The women and boys were deferential to him, and once or twice Ata Gege himself fell into step with Blackwell. When this happened, all other company melted away.

Europeans would have considered Ata Gege a savage no doubt, and Blackwell was alive to the man's very real power and ferocity. Yet the sidelong glances Ata Gege cast at him as they went along were intelligent, even hopeful Blackwell perceived with some surprise. Was the wild bushman a true man of war not unlike himself, hoping to learn the secret to gaining the white man's cargo: steel weapons and tools, iron nails, muskets and gunpowder.

CHAPTER THIRTEEN

The crew of *L'Unite* was still adjusting to the loss of their skipper and the sight of his grieving widow walking the gangway and forecastle, her face shielded behind a veil. McMurtry and the men serving the great cabin could not become accustomed to Mercedes' hollow eyed look, and they still sent in a tremendous breakfast, dinner and supper as though Captain Blackwell were there to partake of it. "She'd cast herself overboard after the skipper, I'd warrant," McMurtry told his mates, "were it not for the little 'un." *L'Unite* had been anchored in forty feet of water three quarters of a mile from the largest international settlement in the Sandwich Isles, during the three weeks following her commander's loss at sea.

Mr. Verson had sent all the boats saving the jolly boat away to different points around the islands. He could prosecute the duty of surveying at the same time they searched for Captain Blackwell. While the boats were away Mercedes hoped. And when they returned without the captain seated in the stern, the lieutenant or midshipman in command studiously avoided her eye. Mercedes' grief opened like a fresh wound each time.

She couldn't help torturing herself with visions of Captain Blackwell treading water hour after hour, becoming exhausted, and giving up his struggle in those precious hours when she'd not raised the alarm, but slept comfortably in his cot. She was forced to wean Edward, she'd feared feeding him her bitter regret along with her milk when it simply dried up.

Naturally, the ship's officers and her people were affected by his loss. Gone was the cheer in the seamen's voices as they went about their duties, the capers of the midshipmen, and the jests and raillery of the officers. The ship was in mourning and the small parties of liberty men Mr. Verson was allowing ashore were as subdued in leaving *L'Unite*, even with the delights of shore awaiting them, as they were in returning to her.

Mercedes felt Captain Blackwell's absence with all her senses. She'd lived with him amicably in the cramped quarters of a fifth rate, indeed they'd been happy. Mercedes never knew him do a cruel or unkind thing. There'd been sharp words and certainly loud ones, but she also received his gentle tones, his voice like a caress during their intimacy. She longed for him, for the contradiction of the man, his hands and voice tender while his cock was hard and insistent inside her. She listened for his voice and foot fall, she woke early in the morning to go to his bed. She could still smell him on his uniforms and linen.

The day following the return of the last boat from its' search and survey mission, when she felt she could command herself, Mercedes sent word to Mr. Verson by one of the midshipmen, that she should like to see him when he was at leisure. She did not pass the word for the first lieutenant. Mercedes had not sailed in men-of-war for the last year and longer without absorbing their strictures, both the explicitly stated and the undeclared rules. She comprehended a ship's business to some degree, and knew *L'Unite* had completed her water, wood and stores, and done her duty in the Sandwich Islands. When Mr. Verson was announced and walked into the great cabin Mercedes stood up.

They halted with Edward between them, playing on the checkered canvas covered deck, and Mercedes curtsied in response to Mr. Verson's bow and gave him her hand. Mr. Verson took it for a moment. "I'm happy you sent for me, ma'am, I was just going to request a word with you. I wished to inform you, we shall sail in three days' time." Mr. Verson appeared uneasy, perhaps anxious lest it look as though he gave up the search for Captain Blackwell prematurely. "Forgive me, ma'am, but nothing can withstand the seduction of these islanders. Women, and a life of ease, overcome patriotism in the minds of our seamen."

Mr. Verson fell abruptly silent. The strain the lieutenant had been under was written on his face.

"Indeed, Mr. Verson, I know you have completed your refreshment. It is the reason I sent for you, sir. I wished to first say Edward and I are prepared to exchange quarters with you and young Jack whenever it is convenient to you." Mercedes went and collected Edward from the floor. Much as she might need his support, Edward didn't seem to want her and showed it by trying to pull down her hair.

Mr. Verson stared at her. "No, ma'am, if you please. As long as you are on this ship you shall occupy the captain's quarters."

"There is the other reason I wanted to speak to you, Captain Verson. I wish to be put ashore, with Edward."

Mr. Verson looked frankly shocked. She had only ever called him Mr. Verson and of all the things she could have said to him, it appeared this most unsettled him. "No, ma'am, that I cannot do. He would want...you must allow me to see you home to England."

"I have no home except where he is!"

She'd stunned Mr. Verson with her outburst. Mercedes instantly regretted it. "Forgive me, sir. Do please sit down and allow me to offer you a glass of wine."

They each drank a glass of Valparaiso claret. Tears leaked from Mercedes eyes, and she neither wiped away nor heeded them, they were so constant in her life now. Presently she said, "I wish to be put ashore because I cannot believe he is dead. I know you will say it is against all reason, but this is where he was last and so I must stay."

Mr. Verson set down his glass and leaned forward in the captain's armchair. Mercedes was the opposite of an unreasonable, hysterical being, and she'd shown a perfect understanding of her altered circumstances in her recognition the ship must sail, with Mr. Verson as her commander. She and Mr. Verson were much of an age, but in looking on him now Mercedes was convinced he'd no clue what Captain Blackwell would have wanted on this emotional side of his affairs.

"You must permit me to give this matter some thought, Mrs. Blackwell."

"Of course, Captain, but I should like you to consider that I am not under naval orders." Mercedes feared sounding harsh and froward. "Neither would I do anything to prejudice your command."

"Would you attend a memorial service for Captain Blackwell?"

Mercedes apprehended immediately a burial service would be the proper thing for the sake of the men of *L'Unite*, and an orderly transition of command according to the custom of the service. But the idea struck at her heart and she very much doubted she should take part in such a ceremony, standing as the widow of Captain Blackwell before his men and officers. Her relationship to the Royal Navy had never been an easy one.

"I will do it for your sake and for the good of the ship, but I should like your permission to leave before the end, if you please. Before you commit his body, his empty coffin, to the deep." Mercedes could not hold back a sob. Mr. Verson reached out a hand and took hers, no longer a commander but a friend who felt some fraction of her loss and pain.

Mercedes had been taken on a tour of the settlement days after *L'Unite* first anchored; king Kanakoa of Oahu's compound with its well built shelters, canoe houses and *heiau*, the fish ponds, the numerous village residences and several *maneaba*. That first tour had ended, as it did on the day Mr. Verson was having his audience with Kamehameha, at the Mission house. Mrs. Bing received Mercedes, Edward, and Saunders. The severe evangelical matron's face instantly softened at sight of the little boy.

Mrs. Bing — who stirred out of doors only for Sunday service and Bible classes — would not give up the long dress and petticoats of Europe and must have expired in the tropical heat. She was delighted with Blackwell's fair haired blue eyed son, perhaps as a reminder of the native sons of other climes. "His paternal grandmother is said to have had blue eyes," Mercedes told Mrs. Bing on their first meeting, by way of explanation as to why her son should so far not resemble her. "I never met her, alas." Mercedes left her son momentarily with the enchanted Mrs. Bing while she spoke to Saunders outside the house.

"You are at liberty, Saunders. Meet at the landing place at sunset, if you please."

Saunders knuckled her forehead, "Aye, aye, Missus."

Mercedes watched her walk out of the clearing where the Mission house stood. Dressed in seamen's duck trousers, loose blue tunic, and the ever present cap she wore over her braids, Saunders looked like any other liberty man from *L'Unite*.

Mr. Verson had made it clear he expected Saunders to remain with Mercedes if the local chiefs granted her permission to reside in Honolulu. But the first officer's orders did not change the fact Saunders was a seaman not a servant. In truth, Mercedes was half frightened by the enterprise she'd set in motion, though she would not alter it. Her heart knew only her love for Captain Blackwell and a deep need to stay by him. Yet *L'Unite* had been her home for over a year and Captain Blackwell was certainly present there too, in every part of the ship. Mercedes went in to Mrs. Bing to tell her of her decision to make her home, temporarily, in Honolulu.

Mrs. Bing had sewn shapes in different colored fabrics and stuffed them with odd bits of cloth and yarn for Edward. The boy was on the bare wood floor of the Mission parlour fascinated with these toys. Edward could sit up and crawl and he was beginning to pull his sturdy frame up to stand clinging to the furniture.

"That's a fool notion, if ever I heard one," Mrs. Bing's said, when Mercedes explained her intention to wait for Captain Blackwell in Honolulu. "But grief makes folk do queer things."

Mercedes wondered at her tactlessness, but Mrs. Bing was obviously a woman of strong moral fibre, to have come at her age to the islands. Mrs. Bing, who'd meant no offense by speaking her mind, and little did she care if anyone took it, in the next moment assured Mercedes of her support and that of Mr. Bing. She would be delighted to watch dear Edward whenever the need arose. Mercedes expressed her gratitude in a way that made Mrs. Bing's face pucker in disapproval, no doubt considering her overly effusive, and altogether too Spanish.

Mr. Verson and Mr. Bing returned at last, and over tea discussed their meeting with the great king Kamehameha.

"It is most fortunate, sir, and for Miss Mercedes' case, the great chief is in residence on Oahu. He is making preparations to attack the island of Kauai, the northern half of Kauai is the last holdout to his dominance of the entire island chain."

Mr. Verson bowed slightly and said in a low tone, "I should not think the residents of Kauai would agree with you, sir."

"Why, no, I suppose they may not. Our own local king Kanakoa is a decent enough sort, though a godless savage. But it is Kamehameha that has put a stop to the reprehensible acts of human sacrifice, even cannibalism, in these islands. Forgive me, ladies, for speaking indelicate."

Mrs. Bing sniffed and turned up her several chins. Mr. Verson looked searchingly at Mercedes.

"The king is a great man in many ways, ma'am. Kamahameha is the tallest, largest man I have ever met. A most imposing figure, but he does seem to appreciate the usefulness of foreigners," Mr Verson glanced significantly at the missionaries, "and he has pledged you his protection during your stay here in the Islands. Should you choose to stay."

Mercedes felt her heart thumping before the reality of remaining in the Sandwich Islands with her infant son and a black sailor, while *L'Unite* sailed away. She could hardly trust herself to speak and struggled to keep a composed expression.

Mr. Bing intervened. "Yes, and all the great man wanted in return was —"

"As to that, sir," Mr. Verson said. "It is a matter that can hardly interest the ladies."

When she and Mr. Verson took their leave of the Bings to return to the ship, Edward set up a most uncharacteristic howl at being parted from his colored shapes. Mercedes tried to reason with him, allowing he would play with them again when next they visited Mrs. Bing. She was eventually worn down by Edward's ill-conditioned bawling and Mrs. Bing's outcry, and let Edward keep the red circle. The poor child clung to it with a look of such happiness that Mercedes nearly began blubbering too. She was obliged to hand Edward to McMurtry, so she could lean on Mr. Verson's arm on the walk back to the gig.

Mercedes came under further obligation to Mr. Verson and the men of *L'Unite*, and King Kamehameha and his subjects. *Kauila* trunks and branches and heaps of grass were cut and appeared on the site of Mercedes' new house. Wood and thatch, by rights the property of the king, were granted by the Hawaiian sovereign. Mr. Verson organized the men in their off watches to construct the house. This was not an enforced duty, the men had to volunteer for the building project, but they nearly all did so. It was an opportunity to get ashore even if there was work to be done, and the late skipper had been popular. If the foremast jacks had often named Captain Blackwell a hard old horse, they also respected a commander who was a thoroughgoing seaman and never shy in a fight.

Their pigtails, ear-rings, and rough appearance notwithstanding, seamen are in general kindly, even tender hearted, and many of them were rather in love with Mercedes and with Captain Blackwell's little son. They built her cottage double quick, and made it snug and tidy. It was only of two rooms, a bedroom for Mercedes, and an all purpose room with a table and chairs and the sofa from the captain's cabin. A cot and hammock could easily be slung in the main room, one for Saunders and the other for young Mr. Blackwell when he was breeched. Instead of a floor of flat stones covered over with mats in the local way, the cottage had a raised wood floor and a deep, covered porch ran around the perimeter of the entire dwelling in the style of the Mission house. An outdoor cooking shelter of the type used by the natives was set behind the little residence. Locating the privy and the well caused the most controversy among the seamen, some claiming particular knowledge of homesteading while others knew the niceties due to a lady.

With the volunteers working watch and watch during the daylight hours, the crew completed the cottage and its out buildings by the end of the afternoon watch on the second day. They furnished the house with a fine large bedstead for Mercedes, the few pieces from the captain's cabin, and brought down hammocks, an officer's cot, Mercedes' and the Captain's sea chests, and all her linen and sewing accoutrement. The men made the house, complete with dead lights for shutters over the window openings, a comfortable dwelling place for their commander's wife.

Mr. Verson, after much agonized consideration, ordered a strong storage built beneath the floorboards of the cottage where he hid an arsenal of weapons. Cutlasses, an officer's sword and rapier, tomahawks, muskets, balls and powder; as well as axes, adze and other tools valued by the native population. Mercedes and Saunders could both handle a sword, cutlass, and pistol, and Mr. Verson would not leave them unable to defend themselves if it came to a fight. They could use the weapons and tools to trade in the case of extreme exigency.

"It's up to you to make sure our Missus and the little 'un don't go hungry. Do you hear me there?" McMurtry said to Saunders. Her willingness to stay in Honolulu when *L'Unite* sailed had surprised them all.

"What do you take me for, mate?" was all the reply Saunders made him.

She and McMurtry were in the yard facing Mercedes and Mr. Verson, who stood together on the porch of the new cottage ready to address the men, just as on the quarterdeck.

Mercedes and Saunders were to spend their first night in the house, returning to *L'Unite* in the morning for the burial service. The sun was setting, casting the clouds overhead in brilliant hues. Mercedes stepped to the end of the porch, holding Edward in her arms. All but the anchor watch were gathered in the yard. McMurtry and Narhilla, the captain's followers, were near at hand, standing with Mr. St. James. *L'Unite's* officers, petty and commissioned, lined up at the side of the gathering.

"Men of *L'Unite*," Mercedes began, "I am deeply in your debt for the fine house you have built me. I am obliged to Mr. Bell and his mates for the furnishings, and to all of you for your many kindnesses now and in the past to Captain Blackwell's son and to me. I shall...I am sure the Captain would be grateful for your generosity." She turned toward the officers and curtsied to them, and then back to the men, but her voice failed her and she could not go on. Instead Mercedes did something that made even the most hardened cases pipe their eye. She raised Edward's chubby hand to his forehead in salute to them.

"She is like Penelope awaiting the return of Odysseus." Mr. St. James sighed.

"Oh, aye?" McMurtry glowered in the chaplain's face. "Did this Penelope lass have an idiot son too?"

Mr. St. James's mouth fell open in shock. McMurtry would have knocked the man down who dared say such a thing of Captain Blackwell's son. Only that morning, in telling Mercedes of his decision to leave *L'Unite* and proceed to the island of Hawaii in the king's entourage, Mr. St. James had said; "To convert a man-of-war's crew into Christians is an impossible task." The trouble was Mr. St. James didn't quite comprehend the men, and failed to see how McMurtry's unhappiness found vent in his bitter expressions. McMurtry knew of what he spoke, he was Edward's primary caretaker next to the boy's own mother.

However much truth might be in the remark it was not meant to be vicious, McMurtry's feelings were anything but toward Mercedes and Edward. He'd looked after Captain Blackwell from the time he was master and commander appointed to his first sloop. He'd been there when they'd fucked the Spanish galleon and taken the Miss, as McMurtry still thought of Mercedes, a prize along with a fortune in gold.

"Losing the skipper were cruel hard," McMurtry said to Narhilla as the assembly broke up. "But now the Missus and the bairn." McMurtry shook his head. Like Mercedes he was at a loss to go any further. For him there would be nothing special about the barky without Captain Blackwell and his little family in it.

Captain Blackwell's family rested poorly that first night ashore. Mr. Bell and his mates had made Mercedes a grand bedstead, their nod to her refusal to believe in Captain Blackwell's death. They'd made the bed uncommon big to contain him. It was quite large enough to hold herself and a man of Captain Blackwell's girth, so Mercedes put Edward to sleep next to her. She'd lined the opposite edge of the bed with rolled blankets to prevent him spilling out. Edward cried from the moment she put out the candle.

At first she let him scream, reasoning he was disturbed by the change of environment and must accustom himself to it. Then she patted and shushed him, to no avail. Edward became more inconsolable, gasping for breath as he bawled. Mercedes rose and struggled to light the candle.

Saunders must have heard her blundering about in the dark for she called in, "What ails the little man?"

"I think he misses the motion of the sea. Will you come strike a light?"

Saunders came in and had a candle flickering in a moment. Mercedes collected Edward from the bed and walked the room rocking him in her arms. He was a sturdy fellow and his weight strained her back.

"Why not lash him in my hammock, then he can swing next to you. You give him a shove now and again, like at sea."

"But where shall you sleep?"

"I'll sling the officer's cot, with your leave. Always wished to sleep in one."

"Let's do this thing." Mercedes put Edward down on the bed.

He immediately began to howl, flailing his arms and legs in anger. Mercedes and Saunders marched into the other room, took down the hammock and hung the cot in its place. In Mercedes' bedroom, too, the carpenters had set hooks in the walls. In no time Saunders had the hammock slung and Edward lashed into it, wrapped in his small blankets and holding his red circle. She gave him an exploratory push, the hammock swayed, and Edward fell silent with a last hiccuping gasp.

Mercedes wished Saunders good night and crawled back into the wide empty bed, a smile and traces of tears on her face.

Captain Blackwell arrived at Ata Gege's principal *ahupua`a* or landholding with his feet severely cut up, the skin of his back, shoulders, face and chest burned red, and so insect bitten he took a fever. It was fortunate he'd had an opportunity to demonstrate his mettle in the raid, if fortunate is a word that can be linked with such desperate killing. He was not led to live among the pigs, instead Ata Gege ordered a hut built for Captain Blackwell on the salubrious lagoon, and Mahin organized his meals and care.

The serving woman Tiaba and her companions brought food to him, and they, the boy pages, Mahin and his mates, took it in turns to keep him clean. He was delirious, lying on a mat in his hut at the outset. Once or twice Captain Blackwell reached out and fondled one of the serving women, murmuring "Mercy, sweetheart," when they'd leaned near, their hair falling across his face or chest. Never did the women or men attending him take offense at his odd manners and language. Captain Blackwell recovered from the worst of the fever, still weak as a kitten, and it was he who was humiliated by their intimate attendance. In seamen's vulgar parlance, he needed help pumping ship.

By the second month of his captivity Captain Blackwell had recovered sufficiently to sit outside his hut, and walk to the bathing places with the men. The women still brought his meals, and they came to visit him in what he thought of as the off watches. In the evenings one or more would show up at his hut with shells to shave and pluck the hair from his chest. He supposed they only waited his recovery of full health before they peeled him entirely. Body hair seemed to offend them, and though the removal was a painful procedure he bore it without complaint, like a great patient dog.

He was learning the customs of the people and their *kapu* system along with their language. Captain Blackwell had at first invited the women who served his meals to eat with him, until the extreme disapproval on their faces and the shrill objection in their voices taught him differently. He could now speak a few words of the native tongue, and supplementing this with signs and gestures he communicated in a rudimentary way. He watched Tiaba approach with her implements of torture. Everyone had their assigned duties in the community, he was learning, and Captain Blackwell thought it would not be long before he would be given to understand his.

"Good evening to you, Captain James Blackwell."

"Good evening, Tiaba. Won't you come in?" He had already mastered the civilities.

Within half a glass another of her companions arrived and the women were sitting about on mats while he reclined on his elbows to give them easier access. It was in this way, listening carefully to the women's gossip, that Captain Blackwell received important information about his captors. He came to understand the community was in mourning for the son of Ata Gege, who had died in what had otherwise been a successful raiding season.

The water of the lagoon lapped gently at the coconut trunk pilings set in blocks of coral rock that supported the hut. The ladies' fingers probed his chest, and the sun set in a blaze of glory. He might have felt like a prince of Araby, albeit one with a perverted taste for pain, but he didn't so far forget himself or his precarious existence among the people. Captain Blackwell studied the long, narrow approach to the lagoon through which no ship could pass, nor even a ship's boat or canoe in certain seasons. The light left the sky, and as he could no longer look out toward the blue Pacific; he longed for that life of freedom on the open ocean; Captain Blackwell stood to let the ladies know the evening was at an end.

He had lost that other life, when he had felt himself important in the affairs of the world. He was reduced to hard concentration on the chatter of the women as they took leave of one another. He managed only to distinguish Mahin's name, Tiaba's, and his own conjoined in some serious matter. A vague apprehensive filled him when Tiaba took his hand and led him into the hut. She let down the sides of the hut and made them fast for privacy, indicating he was to kneel on a mat in the manner of a supplicant.

Mahin walked in, unarmed, though not wearing his habitual cheerful expression. The two natives knelt opposite him. Captain Blackwell wondered if Tiaba hid a weapon beneath her bark cloth skirt. On top, of course, she was quite bare. Very solemnly Mahin took an object from Tiaba that she must have had hidden about her person. He placed a braided collar round Captain Blackwell's neck. Tied to the necklace was a plaited sack. Captain Blackwell opened it and found an incisor tooth inside.

He jerked his head back and then recollected his manners. "*Mahalo nui loa*, Mahin, Tiaba." Pulling the mouth of the sack closed he let it fall against his chest.

They had anticipated more than a polite thank you very much, judging by their astonished faces. In an admonishing tone Mahin said, "You must always wear it, it will protect you from your enemies. The ghost of the man you killed will warn you when they are near."

They looked at one another with incomprehension on one side and perplexity on the other. Mahin rose, but when Captain Blackwell and Tiaba moved to follow, he made a negative gesture. He said a few sharp words to Tiaba, and stalked out of the hut.

Tiaba seemed to decide to get on immediately with her orders. Tossing aside her skirt she came up close to Captain Blackwell and rubbed her body against his, in a way that made his heart thud. Then she turned and knelt on her hands and knees in front of him, assuming the position. Blackwell recalled Mercedes' gentle voice when she was with child, and he'd been afraid to hurt her; "We shall do it like the natives, Jim, if it eases your mind."

His mind was anything but easy. It was full of Mercedes, and a life she was very much a part of, his old world and view of himself as a sea-officer and an English gentleman. He had an Englishman's dread of blundering, and in his present circumstances Blackwell knew a strong desire not to offend Tiaba, and more particularly Mahin. Even confronted with Tiaba's open willingness, he understood she was Mahin's woman and it went against his personal code to mount another man's mare.

Blackwell was not an idiot, incapable of seeing what was in front of him; he understood the people were not monogamous. They formed bigamous groups, with multiple husbands and wives. He'd read of it in Mr. Banks' account before ever sailing for the Pacific. He felt it was not quite the thing; and Blackwell would admit of being shocked the first time he came across one such group initiating a girl of twelve or thirteen into their number. They'd watched her perform the act of Venus with a broad shouldered, muscular man in his twenties.

At least he had not been sent a child to take to bed. He might get away with pleading his recent illness, if his body did not betray him.

"Come, Tiaba," Blackwell said, casting himself down on his sleeping mat at some little distance. "I don't need that. Not strong enough."

Tiaba got up, casting a doubtful glance at Blackwell's breeches, his only garment. She came and stretched out beside him and put her hand on the cloth over his cock as though to say, "What about this then?" Blackwell took her hand away, brought it to his lips and kissed it. Tiaba's face crinkled up, her expression one of mild revulsion.

She was positively lovely even frowning, and he was afraid he'd offended her. He would certainly have liked to sink into her creamy brown flesh, for the sheer refuge and comfort.

In desperation Blackwell started the child's game he'd seen Mercedes play with Edward of naming body parts, he in English and Tiaba in her language. Like any youngster Tiaba loved a bit of fun. Before long she was laughing at Blackwell's pronunciation of nose, eyes, and lips in the native; her pronunciation of English words being far superior. She subsided with a sigh onto his chest, and Blackwell put his arm round her shoulders in fatherly fashion.

This didn't please Tiaba in the least. She jumped up, gave Blackwell her patient smile, and bid him goodnight. After her departure Blackwell lay on the mat thinking he had most certainly grown old. There was a time he would not have hesitated when invited to board a beautiful woman. That time was from before he was a married man, and he began to brood on whether the wiser course might not have been to lie with the girl. He didn't like to think of Tiaba skipping off to report to Mahin her failure to do her duty, he'd always been irritated by midshipmen who made excuses. He could only hope they would put it down to his age, the peculiarities of a white man, and his recent illness.

Blackwell's sleep was disturbed by vague apprehensions Mahin might punish Tiaba, some native version of laying her across the cannon in the captain's cabin. He was relieved next morning when they arrived and treated him with their usual easy manners. A smiling Tiaba accompanied Mahin, but she carried no breakfast.

"Come, Captain James Blackwell. You will eat with the men."

Mahin brought Blackwell to the men's shelter where he was to mess. Ata Gege had ordered Blackwell's education to begin, in all the employments of men in his *ahupua`a*.

The memorial service Mercedes had feared attending did not pain her quite as she'd anticipated. She was not required to say a word but only to sit under an awning stretched over the quarterdeck with the officers, facing Mr. St. James. What was far more difficult was the leave taking of *L'Unite's* officers and her people. The service halted at the point Mercedes and Mr. Verson had agreed upon. The gig, already in the water, waited fully manned. Mr. St. James, who was to go ashore with Mercedes, handed the Bible to Mr. Verson. Captain Verson would read the final words over a coffin set up on a plank, draped in the Union Jack.

Mercedes shook hands with the master's mate, the petty officers, and the midshipmen, from little Mr. Allen to Mr. Montelongo. After shaking Mr. Montelongo's hand, Mercedes kissed him on both cheeks, in the manner of their country.

"God bless you, Juan Luis," she said in Spanish. "You are among good honorable men."

"I know it, Doña Mercedes. God bless and keep you and the dear boy."

And then it was time to shake hands with Mr. Bransford and Mr. Bowles, the lieutenants who'd welcomed her into their homes in London. Their faces looked older from worry and the strain of the search for Captain Blackwell. She would have kissed them too but for a notion Captain Blackwell would not like it. In taking leave of Doctor VanArsdel and young Jack, Mercedes could show no such restraint, and embraced and kissed them both.

She turned and curtsied to the men with tears in her eyes and Mr. Verson took her arm and led her to the entry port. Before handing her down into the gig, he clasped her hands. "We shall return for you, Mrs. Blackwell, you have my word."

Mercedes swallowed hard and nodded. "The demands of the service permitting, Captain Verson."

She climbed down into the gig and Narhilla took her elbow until she found her seat. McMurtry was in the boat too, holding Edward. Captain Blackwell's followers didn't care to be present either when he was committed to the deep. Captain Verson had ordered them into the gig.

The officers and men of *L'Unite* lined the port side as the gig pulled away, their hats in their hands. They'd done all they could for her and being right man-of-war's men in a short time they turned back to burying Captain Blackwell, so that *L'Unite* could unmoor and stand out under Captain Verson's orders. When the gig had pulled half way to the shore Mr. Montelongo, commanding the boat, unbent naval discipline so far as to address Mr. St. James. The chaplain had been somewhat set aside in the ship's farewell to her late captain and his wife.

The talk of the young gentlemen loosened the men's tongues too. The gig's crew was made up today of Muslims and lascars who could not be impressed by the Anglican ceremony aboard *L'Unite*. Under cover of their chatter McMurtry took the liberty of muttering, as though to himself, "Black his half boots every fortnight or they will rot in this swelter," and other homely advice.

The boat ground ashore and the officers and men jumped out. Narhilla turned to Mercedes. "You are to be set dry foot ashore, Missus, Captain Verson's orders. Are you ready?"

"Yes, if you please, Narhilla." Mercedes allowed herself to be carried ashore, like Edward in McMurtry's tender arms, though she had splashed ashore through the warm surf many a time before.

Narhilla set her on her feet just as *L'Unite's* cannons boomed out a salute; the coffin had gone into the sea. Mercedes caught her breath and held out her arms for Captain Blackwell's son. Moments before in the gig, looking at McMurtry with Edward, she'd wondered how she was ever going to take the boy from him. McMurtry put Edward into her arms immediately, with a manful set to his face. Seamen prided themselves on being able to withstand anything.

Mercedes whispered to Edward, "*Un beso para McMurtry, mi cielo,*" and held the boy out. Edward rarely chose to obey her, but he slapped his small hands on McMurtry's ill looking mug and kissed him. Mr. Montelongo ordered the gig away, looking apprehensively at the two sturdy British tars. Mercedes, Saunders, Edward, and Mr. St. James were left upon the shore.

Mr. St. James was for marching immediately to the Mission house where he was staying, but Mercedes and Saunders wanted to watch *L'Unite* win her anchors. Mercedes let Edward down, he'd been squirming to be set loose, but she kept a careful eye on her son lest he eat sand or tumble into the surf. She and Saunders could not be moved until L'Unite had sailed over the horizon.

Mercedes remembered such a feeling of desolation at the departure of a ship, when she'd looked out the window of the Dey of Oran's palace and not seen Captain Blackwell's ship *Inconstant* in the harbor. She collected Edward, sandy, wet, and happy, from where he was sitting, fascinated, watching the surf lick his toes. She'd not had the consolation of Captain Blackwell's child on that last unhappy occasion, though she'd wished for it at the time. Edward gave her the strength to walk up the beach with her two companions, to begin life on an island in the immensity of the Pacific.

Once King Kamehameha was convinced the British ship had departed, and the captain's widow quit the beach, he sent canoes with his best divers to bring up Blackwell's coffin. The burial service had taken place where Mr. Verson had had *L'Unite* careened, and the same *kanakas* who'd helped scrape the weed from her bottom were sent down for Blackwell's coffin. King Kamehameha would not miss the chance to salvage the wood, nails, and more especially the eighteen-pound cannon shot with which the coffin had been weighted.

CHAPTER FOURTEEN

Mercedes was anxious over what she should do with herself on the island. Saunders' reason for agreeing to stay when *L'Unite* sailed became apparent after enough time had passed for the ship to be a hundred leagues away. Then the community of shipwrights, carpenters, sail-makers, caulkers, coopers, and seamen from every nation returned to Honolulu, and Saunders joined them. Nothing exceeded their courtesy and good nature to Mercedes if they met her in the village. They would doff their caps, some even knuckled their foreheads, though they would have been at daggers drawn with her husband or any sea-officer. Kamehameha lured the craftsmen with the promise of an easier life, multiple wives, and a climate and land of unsurpassed beauty. The seamen took to Saunders, and it was she who brought food into Mercedes' little household. But that was all before the cholera struck.

She told herself it was only shite, but cholera is an ugly, wasting, debilitating illness. While the epidemic raged she went into the natives' houses; learning their language and their family arrangements; from the huts normally meant only to shelter stores while the occupants sleep under the over arcing stars to the airy and spacious palaces of the *ali'i*. It was only excrement, the body's leavings, but there was so much of it. As the mother of a child in nappies she was no stranger to it, but she was often oppressed and almost overwhelmed. What kept her going was having survived cholera herself in Africa, through the dedicated nursing of a

Persian woman and an African guard. She hoped to do the same by some of those stricken now.

Mercedes disliked leaving Edward in anyone else's care for the length of time she was obliged to do. She didn't doubt Mrs. Bing's piety or goodness — her personal belief was the big woman could do with less piety and more bathing — but she had been Edward's constant caretaker and could not like giving that up. Yet worse would have been to expose Blackwell's son to the sick, and all the horrors of this illness.

The young and the old seemed particularly vulnerable, but there were warriors too succumbing. The cholera drove Kamehameha back to his base in Hawaii, his plan to fall upon Kauai postponed. Mercedes was called early into the home of Kanakoa, to attend the local king's old father and his youngest child, a girl of two. In the *ali'i's* house, and in the huts of the humblest, Mercedes witnessed the tenderness and open-heartedness of the Hawaiians in their domestic lives.

She was present when the king's daughter died, with Kanakoa holding one little hand, and his third wife holding the other. They had nursed the toddler and the king's father together; Kanakoa taking as great a share in the bathing and cleaning as any of his wives or serving women; but the little girl breathed her last while the old man was improving. The mother's shrieks brought Mercedes out of a reverie, dazedly wondering why some were taken and others not, where she stood at one side of the room. The poor woman was striking her own forehead with a coral and shell bracelet she wore in a gesture of grief. Kanakoa reached a hand out to stay her. Mercedes left the chamber and went to look in on the king's father.

The old man was sitting up on his mats, looking attentively toward the chamber entrance when Mercedes appeared. He must have heard the mother's cry.

"The little one has gone over the rainbow?"

"Oh, sir, yes."

She reached out and took the old king's wrinkled hand, and tears ran down both their faces for the small child.

"I wish it had been me, than one so young." There was bitter disappointment in the old man's voice. Then he said, in a tone of resolution, "Wishing cannot make it so, and we are not granted to choose our time."

Mercedes thought on the wisdom of those words. She helped the old king to the close stool and was settling him on his mats when Kanakoa came in. Mercedes immediately moved to leave the chamber.

"No, Mercedes Blackwell, do not go. Come with us to the burial place."

Kanakoa sent for bearers for his old father, and the entire household proceeded to the burial ground where a pyre had already been made. The Hawaiian way was to take more time in preparing the body; the bones of important chiefs saved and housed in special burial places; but during this time of sickness and with so many deaths spirits were hastened on their journey. Mercedes followed near the end of the procession.

She'd seen many funeral pyres, laden with the bodies of children, the corpses of the elderly, and handsome men and women sent in flames to the native gods. But she'd never before been invited to attend, and Mercedes' heart ached to see the little bundle catch fire, to hear and smell the disintegration of the flesh. Her tears fell with those of the mother and father, and grandparents, and everyone who had known the sweet, happy child. Mercedes thought of her own dear boy and the tears came faster.

She was combating the disease with what had saved her: a constant serving out of fresh drinking water and keeping the sufferer clean. Both labors required the ceaseless hauling of water. Mercedes heart and her back ached. Evening was coming on and she wanted to go collect Edward, hold his comforting little bulk in her arms, and take him to the bathing place and wash away the smells and the grief.

She was some way down the footpath when Kanakoa caught up to her. Mercedes was startled and at first a little frightened by his coming after her; she had slipped away from the funeral and feared she might have broken some *taboo*. Kanakoa was a fine figure of a man; tall, bronze colored, a dark eyed handsome man; but he'd never played the brute before Mercedes. She curtsied to him.

"White men do not approve of the way we honor our dead. Thank you for defying them, and coming with us today. Are you a believer in the missionaries' god?"

The answer was a complicated one, yet since Mercedes had been raised in a Christian country, and married in an Anglican ceremony, she said simply, "Yes."

"So is Minni's mother." The king spoke the diminutive of the dead child's name with renewed tears in his eyes. "May it give her comfort. The missionaries speak of their god's love for us, but they do not love us. Only you have come among us when we needed a father and a mother."

Mrs. Bing did not stir out of doors, but Mercedes knew Mr. Bing had made efforts, among his own converts, to give comfort and relief.

"Mr. Bing visits the sick," she said. "He shall be as sorry as I for the death of your dear little girl."

Kanakoa gave her a long considering look, as though there was much he would say. "You were secure in the protection of Kamehameha, you are doubly so with mine, and that of the people. We don't forget, we who recount the deeds of our ancestors back to the first canoes to reach these shores."

Though she could not criticize Mercedes for visiting the sick, Mrs. Bing did not approve of her industry. Mercedes directed the community of seamen in bringing water from upstream to be stored in casks, and stationed throughout the village to make access easier for those tending the sick. The seamen, led by Colonel Frasier the master shipwright, could not refuse Mercedes' gracious requests; somehow from her they carried the weight of orders. Mrs. Bing would never have been seen in the company of seamen, they were fornicators and drunkards to a man. She wondered Mercedes could daily have contact with them, with only a black servant to loan her countenance.

But Mrs. Bing said nothing against Mercedes' conduct. Not when she walked back and forth to the bathing places, nor when she began to leave aside shoes and make her blouses and Edward's little shirts from the fawn colored native *tapa* cloth. Mrs. Bing even managed to hold her tongue when Saunders took up with Colonel Frasier, moving into the shipwright's ramshackle house instead of sleeping under her mistress' roof where she belonged. She kept her temper under all these provocations because Mrs. Bing knew the epidemic would run its course. When that happened she did not wish to give Mercedes cause to take Edward from her.

Despite Mrs. Bing's forbearance, that day came anyway. Mr. Bing had buried ten natives, the cream of his Christian converts, and two Europeans, though one man died from venereal disease and another from a knife wound inflicted by his mate. The natives had sent scores more in flames to meet their ancestors. The epidemic passed and Mercedes came to the Mission house one morning without Edward.

"It has been a blessing, your care of Edward these last days. I am very grateful, but I cannot have him so much indoors. Captain Blackwell would not like it. I can even hear the Captain say, 'Do not take too much care of the boy, nothing tends more to health than air and exercise.'"

"You would have Edward run about like one of the savages? Excuse me Mr. Bing, like a native?"

"Yes, to some degree. I want Edward to swim and run and fish, and do all the things boys love to do. I shall bring him to visit, you may depend upon it."

"Is that your notion of how a gentleman's son should be raised?"

Mr. Bing's head jerked up at his wife's ungracious remark.

"Captain Blackwell wished his son to become a sea-officer. I have seen what their life is, Mrs. Bing, and how young they are expected to learn their duty. When I think of what they must undergo before they even reach manhood, I am sure you will agree that it is not wise to treat boys too tenderly."

"Do you not worry he does not talk?" Mr. Bing said.

"I do, sir. He does say a word now and again, so I know he can speak. But for all that I speak to him in English and in Spanish, he — "

"Perhaps that's part of the problem," Mrs. Bing said, "and now the poor child must contend with the native babble."

Mercedes' face for the first time took on a look of ill-temper, and Mr. Bing said quickly, "Should Captain Blackwell object to

Edward's beginning private instruction? I know he is very young, but I mean to start a school. Edward might be my first pupil. I have many useful books, you may borrow any you wish, and I think Edward may particularly enjoy a book of illustrated birds. It is just here." Mr. Bing leaned forward and handed Mercedes a fine folio volume.

Mercedes opened the book and carefully turned the pages. "You must take care he treats your books with respect. I am very much obliged to you, Mr. Bing. Would an hour and a half in the morning be quite enough at his age?"

"Four hours," Mrs. Bing said. "An hour and a half of lessons and then you must allow him to stay to a visit afterward. We are such good friends."

"I know you are, Mrs. Bing. Shall we say until midday? I will collect Edward before dinner time."

Now the negotiation was concluded, Mrs. Bing asked, "Who is with Edward now? Can you not bring him?"

"He is with Saunders." Mercedes rose from her chair. "And I think it best we start the lessons tomorrow. Today he shall have a holiday. Good day to you, Mrs. Bing. Mr. Bing, I am sure Captain Blackwell would wish me to express his obligation to you, especially were you to begin the mathematics with Edward."

Mr. Bing bowed Mercedes out and returned to sit in his favorite chair. "She is a most decided woman, Captain Blackwell must have been a specimen of a man to catch her fancy."

Mrs. Bing harrumphed. "Leaving dear Edward with that Jezebel Negress."

Mr. Bing sighed, he'd long ago learned Mrs. Bing was more care than help.

The Jezebel Negress was watching Edward's attempt to join in a game of tag with two island boys. Edward was brought up by tufts of grass, fell into scrub brush, and tumbled over his own feet, much more than he actually played the game. "He goes on like that," Saunders said to Colonel Frasier, "and he'll end scarred like the Captain before his voice breaks."

"Oh, aye, before he's out o' short pants," Colonel Frasier said. "What's wrong with the wee laddie?"

"I think his head oversets him," Saunders said.

Saunders and Colonel Frasier had out their laugh, and when Mercedes walked up to them on the beach they were quite composed. She went immediately to Edward, a half coconut in her hand, and stripped him of his shirt and breeches. Mercedes rubbed him over with oil, then she kissed him. "Go play, sweetheart." Edward took off at a fast waddle, fell, recovered, and sitting up found a cluster of minute conical shells at his feet. He spent the rest of the afternoon sitting in the sand naked, shaded by Mercedes and perfectly happy, sorting shells by size and degree of pinkness.

Mercedes had been brought up in Monterey, a coastal settlement in California consisting of a collection of adobe houses, a presidio or military installation, and the Jesuit mission. A provincial, even savage place by European standards, yet Mercedes was aware that even in such villages there was society.

Honolulu was just such a town, upon which nearly all the European nations were converging for trade and profit. Merchants in the Canton and fur trade, and whalers came in to rest and recruit, and Mercedes visited with two British ships from Captain Blackwell's Atlantic convoy. She was proud to serve refreshments to the masters on the porch of the house the *L'Unites* had built her. Yet along with the gentle breezes from the sea she could feel their disapproval wafting toward her.

The merchant captains and their wives would look at Edward, playing quietly on the floor, dressed in shirt and short pants for these occasions, and shake their heads. They saw a tremendous big boy, brown as a nut, endlessly amused with putting shells, or stones, or nuts into a woven bowl one by one, dumping them on the floor, and then starting again. "Are you counting, young man?" they'd ask. Edward would cock his head and look away from them, even when Mercedes made him greet visitors and shake their hands when they took their leave. Part of the trouble was Edward's size caused people to believe Blackwell's son older than he was.

Mercedes found she was easier among the permanent residents of Honolulu. The seamen, shipwrights, and artisans had a reflexive respect for an officer's wife, and the natives, since the epidemic, could not have treated her with greater kindness and attention.

Fish, taro, coconut, yams, fruits, pork and chicken in their season were brought to Mercedes; it was this in part that allowed Saunders to move to the shipwright's house. Mercedes traded finished sewing work for cloth, woven mats and bowls, candles made of *kukui* nuts strung together, all the necessities of life.

The natives she'd attended all visited her, and they were more respectful of her privacy than the Europeans. They would stand outside her yard and call in, not entering until they'd been recognized: Just as in the captain's cabin aboard a man-of-war. She could not think of the great comfort the natives gave her without emotion. Now Mercedes understood enough of their language, she gathered they did not think it unreasonable she should wish to be where she might communicate with Blackwell's ghost. In fact the natives thought well of her for it; of her comprehending, in spite of being white, that no one dies and absolutely disappears.

The other very great solace to Mercedes was the natives' love for Edward. They doted upon all children; Mercedes had never been among a people where the entire community brought up the young, until living in Honolulu. Neither had she witnessed elsewhere the degree of devotion and care shown not just by women, but also by the men. Most of the Europeans could not tell which children belonged to which adults. Mercedes had a grasp of the men and women paired as husbands and wives, having gone into their homes. But even she could not quite keep up with the natives' tendency to adopt children from other families and give away their own in return.

Edward was not of an age that he might wander about on his own, but Mercedes knew he could find a meal at any house in the village if he were hungry, and be given a mat in a shaded corner if he were tired or unwell. In unguarded moments Mercedes' heart ached, not only for Blackwell but also for how the world would receive his son once he came to manhood, when his differences would be more remarked.

Except for these inward misgivings Mercedes lived a peaceful life in Honolulu, if a lonely one. *Makahiki*, the year end festival came and went once, then twice, and her life continued in a quiet vein. Until the morning Edward nearly drowned.

She was in the water with the surf breaking gently at her back, giving Edward a swimming lesson. She'd shown him how to put his face in the water, and move his head to breath. After supporting him for a time Mercedes would release Edward, back off a few paces, and let him swim to her. All was well until the boy gained a little confidence and dared to open his eyes. The underwater life he saw made him scream.

It was a scream of delight, not fear, nevertheless Edward took in a great mouthful of sea water. He reared out of the water choking, and in his distress flung himself at Mercedes. His momentum, and a wave striking her at the same instant had Mercedes off her feet, and they both went underwater. Edward managed to both clutch at her and flail at once, and Mercedes struggled for the surface. She got her face above water, took a gulp of air, and was dragged down by Edward reaching up and gripping her round her neck.

Mercedes' heart began to pound. What had begun almost comically had turned ugly. If Edward could not calm down she would have to strike at him to save herself, the child she loved above all others and had always treated with such tender care. She no longer had a footing below, the bottom had shelved and she was out of her depth. Mercedes was treading water, grappling with Edward, trying to keep both their heads above the surface, when a strong arm came round her and lifted her up.

There was now a large, brown, muscled body between her and Edward. Mercedes found herself beneath Kanakoa's arm, while he had Edward clasped in the other, like so much baggage. The native king hauled them through the surf and deposited the two of them beneath one of Waikiki's many coconut trees. Mercedes immediately crawled over to Edward, dragged him onto her lap and put him head down over her knees to cough the water out.

When he was better and sitting upright in her lap, she and Edward clung together at peace this time, beneath the coconut tree and the eye of Kanakoa.

"I see you know what to do," Kanakoa said mildly.

"Thank you, sir, thank you for coming to our aid. He has had these little bouts before, gulping in water rather than air, but never so serious." She kissed the top of Edward's head.

Kanakoa knelt down on one knee beside them. "I shall carry you both home."

He was reaching out to pick them up as one bundle, but Mercedes jumped to her feet.

"I can walk, but I would be obliged if you would take up Edward."

Edward was subdued on the walk home, done in by the misadventure. He leaned his face against Kanakoa's shoulder, and only hung on tighter when the king led them through a stream so that Mercedes could wash the salt from her skin. On the footpath outside her cottage, in view of the Mission house, Mercedes turned to Kanakoa.

Kanakoa set Edward on his feet, rather than put the boy into her arms. "I will say nothing of his being too great a burden for you. No, do not thank me again," Kanakoa said as Mercedes opened her mouth to speak, "come and meet me, beneath the trees."

Tears leapt into her eyes, and she recalled the feel of those strong arms around her. Mercedes turned away with the slightest of nods, and pushed Edward before her into the house.

She did not wait to arrange her assignation; she sent immediately to Saunders to come sit with Edward. After Saunders arrived she left the house without a word of explanation, and with a thudding heart. She would not allow herself time to stop and think of the risk, the dishonor, the disloyalty, and marched straight upcountry into the forests that were the king's property. Mercedes had been accustomed to receive Blackwell's attentions almost daily and she yearned for a man's caress, for the oblivion of pleasure. She could not be mistaken in the jolt of desire she'd felt being shared by Kanakoa.

Even so, when she was a distance from the settlement and he joined her in the forest, Mercedes gave a start and her heart began to hammer. He took her kindly by the hand and led her to an area of caves formed of lava rock. Near the entrance of a cavern Kanakoa stopped.

"This is a place of refuge and shelter in battle." With a stone bladed knife Kanakoa cut broad leaves and laid them just inside the mouth of one cave. "A place for women and children to shelter, the men being at war." He laid his *tapa* mantel over the bed of leaves and held his hand out to Mercedes.

He had understood much; that she could not lie with him in the cottage built by her husband's men, nor go to him in his palace with his many wives and children about; she took his hand. She allowed him to lay her down, but gripped the cloth and leaves beneath her rather than him, and at the critical moment she would have withdrawn if she could have. His lean muscular body, his smell, were so unfamiliar; she thought *Oh James, oh Jim.* Kanakoa did not try to kiss her, there were no tender words. Perhaps his emotions were as hard as his body. There is a certain point in intimacy with a man after which you cannot cry off, and Mercedes knew she was well past that point.

She surrendered to the experience, but not to the native chief, she took as well as let herself be taken. Kanakoa was a young and vigorous man, and her body was eased if a little bruised on the walk home. He left her before they reached the edge of the forest, still kindly disposed toward her, but without any discussion of meeting again or words of attachment. Mercedes had, before this time, wondered if she was fit only to herd with the beasts.

Beast or no, she was a sensible being. Mercedes put up her chin and reflected if Kanakoa could take the act lightly, as though they'd merely sat down to dine together, then she would not let it affect her at her core. And when she came closer to the heart of Honolulu there was a distraction in the unusual number of people, natives and Europeans, buzzing about the streets.

"Have you seen the war ship, Aunty?" the boy Keiko from the Mission house called to her as he ran past. "A great war ship has come in."

She quickened her step, but not toward the waterfront, much as she longed to know if the ship was *L'Unite*. Mercedes ran home, her breast in a turmoil of emotion over her present and her future, because there was a practical matter needed attending without loss of a moment.

Saunders was anxiously awaiting her return, with Edward napping inside, and jumped up from her seat on the porch. They agreed that Saunders should go down to the landing place and bring back the particulars.

Darkness had fallen before Saunders returned and Mercedes learned of the Russian vessel.

"Everything ahoo on the deck, Missus, even the hawser uncoiled, the rigging served and parceled in all directions. The topmasts, topgallant masts, and studding-sail booms nearly black from want of scrapping. Makes you sick to look at it." Saunders sniffed, she considered herself a right man-of-war's man.

"How many guns does she mount, Saunders? What of her mission and her captain." Mercedes had thought she would be indifferent if the ship were not *L'Unite*, but she found she was still an officer's wife.

"She's pierced for twenty-four and mounts twenty long guns on the main deck and six twenty-four pound smashers on the upper. Heavy guns for a mission of exploration. Their excuse being, they come from Russian America where the natives aren't half so agreeable as here. Ungodly cold it is there, Missus."

"You know so much of them."

"Near the whole crew flushed into town at once. They have six officers with the commander, and ninety men. Couldn't have left aboard more than half a dozen to tend the barky. We could cut her out with a boat and a dozen *kanakas* if we chose."

Mercedes and Saunders exchanged a conspiratorial glance. "Her captain, her crew?"

"A stupider, greasier set of ruffians I never met with. The captain of the *Vostok*, as she is called, I saw at a distance. A flash cove—ah, gentleman—Missus, by his fancy dress."

Count Nikolai Andreyevich Dermidov, captain of the Russian frigate Vostok, was used to cutting an elegant figure. In Paris he kept the showiest coach and four in the town, his rents from extensive landholdings worked by serfs in mother Russia were rumored to bring him two million *livre* a year. Count Dermidov, Captain Dermidov, could well afford the carriages, the townhouses in London, Paris, and St. Petersburg, the gigantic estate in the country and the villa beside the Black Sea. He need not have gone into the Czar's service to suffer the hardships of a mariner's life. But he was a man who enjoyed control, dominance, and possession: It was what he was accustomed to.

Within an hour of coming ashore Dermidov heard of the British woman living on the island. He was not particularly interested; Anglo women were pale, prudish, freakish creatures to his mind. Then he learned the woman was a Spaniard, and she lived alone since her husband's loss at sea, accepting neither native nor European lover in his place, and Count Dermidov's attention was fixed. He set his first lieutenant to discover how an introduction to the widow could be arranged. Next day Count Dermidov called on Mr. Bing.

"Aunty Mercedes, Aunty Mercedes!" called Keiko, from Mercedes' front yard.

Mercedes and Saunders were in the cook house at the back. It was not a good time for visitors, Mercedes was preparing the evening meal of fish and breadfruit. But at a nod from Mercedes, in a strong voice Saunders called out, "Come back here, child."

The boy came through at a run. "Aunty Mercedes, Mr. Bing sends to know if you will receive the Russian ship captain. They come this way."

"Hell and death!" Mercedes said, and turned to Saunders. "Can you stay?"

"Nor I wouldn't miss it."

"Thank you." Mercedes hardly had time to run into the house and put on slippers before Mr. Bing was calling in from the front porch.

"Gentlemen, please walk in."

The door was already standing open, and passing through it, Mr. Bing and Dermidov became entangled as they pressed in together.

The introductions were made, Mercedes curtsied and offered her hand and Count Dermidov bowed over it. He wore his country's military outfit, a uniform jacket, waistcoat, shirt, breeches, stockings and boots. Mercedes wondered if Captain Blackwell would have worn boots in this climate. They were in the cooler half of the year, but even so Mercedes, in order not to be enclosed with the Russian count, immediately suggested they sit on the porch.

Saunders came with a tray containing glasses of cold tea. She brought Edward forward, who'd been hastened into his visiting clothes.

"Count Dermidov, may I present Edward James Blackwell. Edward," Mercedes said, "give your hand to Count Dermidov, Captain of *Vostok.*"

Edward held out his hand like a little man, his head cocked to one side. Count Dermidov rose and shook Edward's hand. Afterwards the Russian eyed the boy sharply while conversing with Mercedes and Mr. Bing. He told them of his last call on the coast of California, before proceeding to the Sandwich Islands.

"You are from a blessed land, Mademoiselle," Dermidov said. It had already been established she was from the Spanish Main and spoke French, the language preferred by the Russian nobility. "The Bay of San Francisco will be an important harbor one day, if the country prospers. It has the best anchoring grounds in the whole coast of America, an abundance of wood and water, and the game! Red deer in such numbers, capital shooting."

"I've never been so far north, I've not seen San Francisco. May I ask if you spoke any other men-of-war?" Mercedes now felt eager for tidings of *L'Unite* and her people.

"No, I am desolated to say, for I see you hoped for word of a British ship," Count Dermidov said. "Perhaps you wish to be taken away from these islands."

Mercedes considered his tone and his words over familiar. She glanced at Mr. Bing. He feigned to know more French than either she or Dermidov would credit. In French she replied, "Not at all, sir," and in English, "I understand you have an artist aboard the *Vostok*, Captain Dermidov. Mr. Bing has a handsome illustrated volume of birds. What a fine addition the birds of the Sandwich Islands would make to it."

"His name is Alexandre Ivanovich Selyenin. I shall send him to you directly." Count Dermidov bowed to Mr. Bing.

Alexandre Ivanovich Selyenin turned out to be the bright spark among the otherwise dismal Russian crew. Like his countrymen, Sacha, as the young man immediately requested the English name him, had a temperament much given to melancholy. Yet such a state of mind is hard to maintain in the tropics, even by men who insisted on going about in woolen trousers and flannel waistcoats. Unlike the common run of his fellows Sacha was a well-educated and well-groomed young man, possessed of a great deal of tact. After his introduction to the missionary, Sacha could be seen wandering the settlement in company with Mr. Bing and Edward.

On one of those days when Mercedes had given leave for Edward to spend the better part of the day with Mr. Bing, so that the three could go on an extended ramble, the boy Keiko appeared in her yard in late afternoon. "Aunty Mercedes! Aunty Mercedes! Mr. Bing says come at once." Mercedes cast aside her book and ran, frightened, after the boy across to the Mission house, bounding up the porch steps in unladylike fashion. She was imagining what accident could have befallen Edward to cause such a summons. He was steadier on his feet now, but he still tended to run into anything upright — trees and posts — from always looking at his feet wherever he went.

Mercedes found Edward rocking back and forth on the parlour floor. Mrs. Bing sat in her usual chair, a puckered, disapproving look on her face. Mr. Bing and Sacha were standing about grinning like boys, passing a sheet of parchment back and forth between them. Mercedes dropped to her knees in relief beside Edward, put her arms around his shoulders and squeezed him. Edward paid her no heed, and tried to continue his rocking.

"Look, my dear lady, look at this."

Mr. Bing turned the drawing he was holding round for Mercedes to see; she'd been staring up at him, a touch of accusation in her gaze. Mercedes stood up and took the drawing. It was a detailed sketch of the Oahu honeyeater. The curved beak, the long fanning tail, the fine head and sharp eye were captured on paper to the life.

"A very fine rendering, Sacha. I congratulate you," she said.

"It is not mine, Madame Blackwell, that is your son's drawing. Dear Edward is the genius drew it. Give you joy, ma'am. Your son is a prodigy."

Standing in the parlour of the Mission house staring at Edward, Mercedes began to cry. She was so overcome she had to walk out onto the porch, where her tears fell as she looked out on the waving palms, comforted by the click and clack of their fronds and the beat of the surf. At last she went in to retrieve Edward, and take a proper leave of Mrs. Bing. The old lady harrumphed and mumbled, "Do you still think he belongs naked on the beach with the natives?" Mercedes leaned down to kiss her cheek, wetting her with her tears, and Mrs. Bing shook her head. She disliked an emotional display.

Sacha and Mr. Bing followed her and Edward out onto the porch.

Mercedes turned to them. "From the bottom of my heart, gentlemen, thank you for discovering what it is he can do. This blessed talent."

"We observed the honeyeater perhaps ten minutes, no more," Sacha cried. "And look what he produced! Think what he could become with training. It will be curious to see what he will make of the constructs of man. I must have him draw the ship. May I take Edward to sketch *Vostok*?"

"We shall see, tomorrow, perhaps the day after." Mercedes was concerned, she knew his rocking signified upset and discomfort. Edward was a creature of habit. "I need to bring him home and give him supper. He becomes peckish if he isn't fed on time, just like his father. Dear Mr. Bing, Sacha, many, many thanks, and good evening to you."

Three days later Mercedes accompanied Sacha and Edward to the harbor. They watched, fascinated, as Edward took the pencil in his chubby fist. Sacha began to draw the *Vostok* on his parchment. Edward glanced at the young man's sheet and turned his gaze, which never seemed to focus on anything in particular, on the 20-gun frigate at anchor. Edward began to draw lines, almost without looking at his parchment, with his blue, half somnolent stare directed on the ship. Her contours, her masts, rigging, hull and railings took shape beneath his hand.

Edward produced the image uncommon fast, but he hadn't done with the complicated standing and running rigging before a little crowd was pressing round him. The natives, who were fine sailors, as well as the Europeans exclaimed over the accuracy of Edward's rendering.

"I shall make a comparison of Edward's drawing to the ship's dimensions, ma'am," Sacha said. "And I do believe we shall find he has scaled it exactly. How very remarkable!"

Remarkable was the word on everybody's lips. The natives who knew Edward, a child they might have knocked on the head as being unfit, acknowledged that here was evidence of the boy's powerful *mana*. Count Dermidov had ordered his gig hastily into the water after one of his lieutenants pointed Mercedes out amid the crowd on the quay. He came upon the scene as Edward was sketching in the ship's boats, and he was the reason Edward's mother left his side.

The sun had become bright upon the water and Edward shifted his gaze between the ship, amid the brilliant reflections of the morning sun, and the white parchment under his hand. He didn't like people pressing so near, nor when his mother and his familiar friend Sacha stepped away. But Edward maintained his concentration. He had a feeling when he was creating, a feeling he could not yet name joy. His head moved up and down, the light winked on the water, and the paper flashed white with the beautiful dark symmetry of lines under his hand. Edward felt ecstatic, as though lifted up and away from the confusing world where he knew he did not belong. He let himself slip into the embrace of this other realm, and fell over shaking and convulsing. The pencil rolled out of his grasp onto the planks of the quay.

Mercedes thought Count Dermidov would never leave; he'd visited her every day, each time finding excuse to stay longer. At present all she wanted to do was go and lay down beside Edward. He was tucked into the big bed in the next room, pale of face, but breathing normally and trying to sleep. Mercedes, the seamen on the quay, and the *kanakas*, had carried him home. Saunders and Colonel Frasier met them, running down the footpath from the village, and Mr. Bing and even Mrs. Bing came out when the procession arrived bearing Edward. Mercedes and Saunders had maneuvered everyone out of the house except Count Dermidov, whose sense of entitlement kept him there long after decency dictated he go.

"I have a brother who is afflicted by fits, Mademoiselle," Dermidov said. "He has grown to manhood, there is hope for your poor son. My brother lives in Paris under the care of the renowned Swiss Doctor Constant. Dear Mademoiselle. Allow me to carry you to France where your son may receive the care he needs. And you, my dear, shall order your gowns from the Rue Cambon."

Mercedes apprehended Count Dermidov was throwing down his strongest card. He believed she would be desperate to get off the island and return to civilized Europe. What had given the Count the idea she was the sort of woman to be lured with beautiful clothes, she did not know. But Paris gowns and society, and the best doctors in Europe for Edward, were what he was holding out to tempt her. In the last days, with the revelation of Edward's unique ability, the question of whether Captain Blackwell's son would do better in Europe or by remaining in the islands had become of the utmost importance to her.

She could not be grateful for the Count's insinuating offer, she despised the way he called her Mademoiselle rather than the proper Madame due a married woman. His behavior brought the Reverend Blackwell to mind; selfish men who could admit of no greater duty than what was due them. Mercedes was angry, glad the weapons in the house were hidden away, she'd seldom felt such a strong desire to deal with a problem at the point of a sword.

She stood and took up a position by the door. "I am sensible of the generosity of your offer, Captain Dermidov, and of your great condescension. But I must decline for the same reason I have not accepted your invitations to dine aboard *Vostok*. While I do not know the state of relations between our two countries I cannot board a Russian man-of-war. How would it look if our countries were at war, a British captain's wife accepting aid of the enemy."

"It would look as though you cared more for your son's welfare than matters of state."

"And irreparably damage Edward's prospects in the Royal Navy. Captain Blackwell's fondest wish was his son should become a sea-officer."

"That boy will never make a sea-officer, Mademoiselle." Dermidov clapped his hat on his head on his way out. "You will be fortunate if he learns to do up his own laces."

Saunders came into the main room from the bedroom where she'd been sitting with Edward, listening.

"I should prefer one of the natives to a man like that...Count."

She was immediately sorry to have spoken, and ashamed.

Saunders said only, "Damn the man's cheek, Missus."

"Yes, three times three." Mercedes shot her a grateful look. She went and checked on Edward, and came back. "Can you stay?"

"Aye, aye, Missus. Just you give the word and we'll break out the arms chest. We can send to the Colonel to set a watch outside the house, or to Kanakoa if you wish."

Mercedes felt that at least where Saunders was concerned, she had not been very discreet.

"No, I do not think we need raise the hue and cry."

They talked about Edward while hanging the officer's cot, and Mercedes wished Saunders good night. In the bedroom Mercedes took off her light muslin skirt, her corset and blouse made of *tapa* cloth, putting a shift over her head as a nightdress. She stretched out carefully next to Edward. He lay with one arm behind his head staring at the ceiling. Although Edward bore little physical resemblance to his father, his attitude was unmistakably Blackwell's.

"Mama?"

"Yes, my darling?" Mercedes had wrung out a cool cloth and was placing it over his brow.

Edward put his hand over hers on his forehead. "Don't leave me."

Mercedes watched Edward lying beneath the white plumeria bordering the footpath in her front yard, the fragrant blossoms drifting down and settling on him. How was she ever to let the boy out of her sight again? She'd kept him home from lessons and they'd spent the morning lying quietly in bed together. Saunders put off the morning callers with the latest on Edward's recovery; he had awakened refreshed though he was weak and pale. Mercedes rose and dressed at dinnertime and brought Edward to the bathing place. Afterward she prepared a broth for him and the usual fish and poi for herself and Saunders. Near sunset she sat on her porch reading, or trying to, while Edward gazed upwards through the wide spaced branches over his head.

Count Dermidov's steward approached from the direction of the landing place, bearing a box before him. Mercedes walked out and met him near the plumeria tree.

On top of the box was a sheet inscribed, 'For Edward Blackwell'.

This was the first contact she'd had today with the people of the Russian ship; if she'd offended *Vostok's* captain, she'd apparently offended them all. Mercedes took the old humidor the steward held out and opened the lid. Inside amid the fragrant smell of cigars were parchment paper, charcoal, and pencils, both black and colored.

"Did Mr. Selyenin send these?" Mercedes asked.

The steward shook his head. "No English." He backed away from Mercedes, with a nervous glance at Edward.

"Look, my dear, what Sacha has sent you."

Mercedes knelt down next to Edward. They both peered into the box, Mercedes wondering about the wisdom of allowing Edward to draw again so soon after his fit. It puzzled her too, that the usually thoughtful Sacha should send such a gift at this time. Voices raised down the footpath caught their attention. Count Dermidov had met his steward and was shouting in Russian, gesturing toward Mercedes and Edward. Hearing the commotion Saunders appeared on the porch from the back of the house. All of them watched Count Dermidov draw back his fist and knock his steward down.

The steward did not get up, he remained in the dust on his backside. Count Dermidov stalked into the yard. Mercedes jumped to her feet. She'd never seen a like display in the Royal Navy, for Captain Blackwell to have done such a thing was unthinkable. She was equally shocked and frightened, and she turned to Saunders standing on the porch and said the single word "Sword". She could smell Count Dermidov as he came closer, a mixture of sweat and damp woolen clothing, and an overriding reek of spirits. She tried to place herself between Edward and the Russian captain, but Count Dermidov, though his movements were clumsy, was in a passion.

He grabbed Edward by the upper arm. "I see you have accepted of my gift."

"We thought it was from Edward's friend Mr. Selyenin. Let go of him, if you please sir."

"Selyenin hasn't a *sou*. It is my gift and I should like to hear from the boy." Count Dermidov shook Edward so hard the contents of the box rattled. "Should you like to keep that box Master Blackwell, and come aboard my ship?"

"Take your hands off my son this moment, sir!" Mercedes glanced over her shoulder. Saunders was easing up behind her, with her arms held behind her back.

"I should like to hear from the boy," Count Dermidov repeated.

He jerked Edward off his feet. The box fell from Edward's hands, the contents spilling. Edward cried "No I shouldn't!" He was released and plopped down on his bottom. Mercedes stepped round Edward toward Count Dermidov. The sword Saunders had put into her hand when she reached back for it was already raised. She swung it in a two-handed blow that caught the side of the Count's head with the flat of the sword. Saunders rushed forward as Count Dermidov attempted to rise and knocked him flat with a blow from a war club. She let out a whoop of triumph and the Russian captain lay unmoving in the yard.

Saunders and Mercedes leaped up from crouching beside Count Dermidov when his steward advanced upon them. They met the steward, Mercedes holding the cavalry sword with Edward clutching her skirt, and Saunders wielding the war club.

"No farther," Mercedes said to the man.

The steward held up his hands, palms outward, and gazed with melancholy resignation past them at the prostrate form of his captain.

"He ain't dead, though shouldn't you like to be rid of the evil brute," Saunders said. "I always wanted to use one of these." She struck the thick end of the club into her open palm with a resounding smack, and a significant look at the steward. "Trick is, not cracking the skull when you don't mean to."

Mercedes put a restraining hand on Saunders' club arm. "Time to send for Colonel Frasier."

The altercation had not gone unnoticed, not by Keiko, the boy who attended at the Mission house. He was already running down the footpath with Colonel Frasier, two seamen, and several *kanakas* following behind. All of the men came to bend over Count Dermidov and make admiring comments on their handiwork. Held in Mercedes' arms, Edward tried to hide his face against her neck and shoulder.

"There now, little man." Colonel Frasier patted Edward's back. "Naught to worry from this one here, your good Ma and Saunders served him out."

"I am extremely concerned, Colonel," Mercedes said, shifting Edward and nodding toward the *kanakas* surrounding the Russian steward. "How are we to pass this off without the Russians retaliating against us, or against the people."

"Nay, Missus, we shall send for a barrow and cart him back to his ship. Tell his first we found him dead drunk outside the village. Do you hear that cully?" Colonel Frasier spoke in the steward's direction. "Your captain fell down drunk and we were kind enough to give you a hand bringing him back to his ship. Ten to one his pride won't allow Captain Cossack here to tell the true tale when he wakes, if he can remember it through his aching head." Colonel Frasier snorted and went over and nudged the prone Count Dermidov with his foot.

Mercedes urged the men not to handle Count Dermidov too roughly as they picked him up and tossed him into the barrow. She imagined the Count would be used with even less delicacy as they moved him from barrow to boat, to row him to his ship. Mercedes stayed behind at her house under guard of a seaman and one of her neighbors, big Mo. Colonel Frasier, Saunders, and the rest carried the captain and his steward across to *Vostok*.

"You can tell them aboard whatever you wish, mate," Saunders said to the steward on the pull across. "But was I you, I wouldn't stand behind a man who knocks you down like a dog."

"You don't know these aristocrats. He ordered me to steal the boy," the steward said in good English, shielded by the dark tropical night. "I wouldn't."

"Damn good thing you didn't, mate. Because why, because if you'd snatched away Captain Blackwell's son the natives would have massacred you all. They believe the boy marked by the gods."

CHAPTER FIFTEEN

Blackwell broke the surface of the crystal clear water of the lagoon in unison with Mahin and several others, kicking down five fathoms to move the stones holding the net, slowly closing the trap on the gleaming swirling reef fish. He swam well and strong, wonderfully alive to the rush of the tepid water, the sunlight filtering through from above, to the beauty and challenge in the underwater landscape. He felt as much a part of this natural world, and the life of the village, as he'd ever been aboard a man-of-war. Several more passes and the great net would be hauled in with its threshing cargo of bright colored bodies.

The time when he'd been weak and dependent was long since past, and he'd learned much about Ata Gege's *ahupua`a* and his place in it. He enjoyed all the pursuits of men in the community, among them fishing collectively as they were now doing. The men on the beach and in canoes took over hauling in the great net, and then the work fell to the servant women, waiting on the beach to clean and dress the catch.

An immature white-tipped reef shark had the misfortune to cross paths with Mahin as they swam ashore. Mahin caught it by the tail and dragging it through the surf, he heaved the four foot long fish upon the beach.

"Brother!" Mahin waved.

Blackwell hustled through the surf to block the shark's retreat. It had flopped into a foot of water when he reached it, grinning like a boy. He grabbed upwards of its pointed tail and gave an almighty heave. He maintained no kind of dignity before Mahin, they truly were like brothers. But they indulged in only a few more tosses of the wretched creature before they allowed it to escape, and turned to the important business of the day.

They walked to the boathouse, a great structure sixty feet long by eleven wide, sheltering three new built canoes. The two war canoes were complete except for the fancy work. Artisans were laying in cowry shells in intricate patterns atop a layer of gum paste in grooves cut into the gunwales of the craft. Figureheads waited to be affixed at the bows; the carvings depicted a warrior holding in his hand a severed head. Blackwell's particular concern, the occupation that had absorbed him heart and mind for months was the third craft, Ata Gege's sailing canoe.

The expertly built sailing canoe with its stabilizing outrigger was not near so massive as the fifty-one foot long war canoes, but Blackwell had been involved in her construction from the start. He'd helped fell and haul the *koa* trees that formed the canoes' hulls, becoming as deeply involved in the building as he'd once been with the running of a ship. Much of his hope rested on what Blackwell knew, with a keen professional eye, would prove to be a sweet sailing craft.

Word had reached Ata Gege, remarkably over the rugged terrain and through neighboring tribes mostly hostile to his own, that Kamehameha of Oahu and Hawaii was readying an army of invasion. Everyone understood new war canoes must be made, and Blackwell experienced the sense of urgency as much as any of the men and women, who were all driven by a singular purpose.

He took part in shaping the bow and stern end and hollowing the great logs. After the wood was seasoned the expert craftsmen shaved the sides with sharp stone adze, until a thin walled craft emerged from the *koa* logs. At last the boys and women ground the canoes' frames with volcanic rock until they were remarkably smooth. Blackwell used carpentry skills learned early as a midshipman, showing the natives different methods of joining the planks and trim to the vessels' hulls. Today he and Mahin were stepping the sailing canoe's mast. They would fit the flexible mast into the cap and lash it to with strong line twisted of coconut fibre, run the adjustable shrouds that supported the mast, and the sheets attaching to the single woven mat sail. All of this was work he liked and to which he was well suited, and eager to perform as leading to his ultimate goal of sailing the neat craft in open water, a possibility just within his grasp. Though he'd adjusted to life among the people, learning to live as they did, he hadn't succumbed to their siege mentality and forgot the wide world outside.

Mahin turned to him with an expression that reminded Blackwell of the head-holding warriors of the figureheads, a sort of gleeful leer. Together they pushed and carried the sailing canoe out of the boathouse. Much of the time, as now in the final stages of work on the sailing canoe, he was happy and well satisfied. This did not signify he'd forgot Mercedes or his duty as a Naval officer. Blackwell still had an Englishman's heart beating in his deeply tanned breast.

There had been a painful period when he studied and thought on escape and of his former life and habits daily. Yet months after he'd ceased to think where *L'Unite* might be on the vast oceans, of the Admiralty and the Royal Navy, of his life of command, Blackwell still pictured Mercedes. Not in England with his father, certainly not in London; but in Gibraltar with his brother and Francis's new wife. He wanted her to be among friends. She might send to her uncle Severino Martinez in Ceuta, a reliable man who would take as great an interest in her welfare as Francis. These daydreams gave him comfort and he would not think of her, with her lively spirit, shut up in the rectory with his father. He liked the notion even less of Mercedes residing in London or Bath, fast towns to his mind, where a woman of her qualities would attract many suitors. The possibility Mercedes might start another family was intolerable to him.

Just when he and Mahin had begun glancing up the path toward the village for their midday meal, a little naked boy came pelting up. Mahin jumped from the sailing canoe and caught the child.

"Look who's here!"

He tossed the boy in the air with as much energy and good spirit as when he'd heaved the shark. The artisans working in the canoe house sauntered out in anticipation of dinner and joined Blackwell watching the pair. Mahin set the shrieking child on his feet, let him take a few steps away, and then grabbed him by one arm and leg and began lifting him up and down and twirling him round.

Aloka screamed in happiness and mock protest, and when he was released, dizzy and delighted he staggered over and grasped Blackwell round one leg.

"Easy there, son." He patted the boy's dark head.

Blackwell would not have liked to admit he often felt uneasy for the boy, old womanish, he wanted to intercede at times, like during Mahin's rough play. Aloka was a toddler but the name didn't suit, at nearly two he could swim as well as he could walk, in fact preferring to go everywhere at a run. The people had their own way of bringing up the young, and it wasn't as though Aloka was an unimportant being in the village. He was the spare rather than Ata Gege's heir, but he was still Princess Kalani's child. Blackwell's memories of his son Edward had grown vague, he'd known him so short a time, but he did not recollect Edward being half so nimble as Aloka.

The adolescent boys bearing food arrived, the meal brought to the canoe fashioners in order not to lose a moment. The men amused themselves while they ate calling out animals for Aloka to imitate. He was already an accomplished mimic, and when someone called out 'Captain James Blackwell', his bow legged rolling stride was a perfect imitation, particularly as the boy resembled him to an astonishing degree.

Aloka's minder, one of Princess Kalani's ladies in waiting, came for him at the end of the meal. Tiaba trailed in the noble woman's wake, and she and Mahin moved off together. The women Blackwell considered beautiful, and sexually desirable, were generally of the lower classes. He was attracted to young women like Tiaba with her slender well-formed arms and legs, her incomparable breasts, and her body as yet untouched by excessive child bearing. That first faltering decision of his not to bed her had been taken as a signal he considered himself above lying with a servant girl. The lady in waiting, Momo, she was called, gave him a coquettish smile as she lumbered away leading Aloka by the hand.

Ata Gege had sent Momo and other ladies of the minor nobility to him, substantial women one and all, and it would have been foolish to hang fire. At last he was summoned by Princess Kalani to her palace, a spacious dwelling divided into several apartments on the side of the lagoon where the breezes seldom failed.

Princess Kalani's servants had unwound the yards of yellow and red *tapa* cloth she wore until she stood naked before Blackwell. She'd looked at him that first time with a sad gaze, her eyes obscured behind large puffy cheeks. Kalani had lost the man she loved — brother and husband — and Blackwell read only resignation in her look as he approached her. Kalani might not answer his idea of beauty, with her enormous breasts, each the size of a large melon, and her massive trunk like thighs. Yet she was a young woman, like Mercedes, who'd no doubt experienced as many hopes and hardships.

He'd lost several stone from his first illness, and with the rigorous life he'd been leading he'd never gained back the weight. Kalani was as tall as him, and she weighed more. Still she was a woman, and Blackwell had known how to please women since he was a sixteen year old midshipman on the Mediterranean station.

He was not in love with Kalani, nor she with him. The foremost duty of a princess was to produce heirs. Kalani had borne one child before Aloka, fathered by her brother who'd been killed in the raids the season he was taken. This child would inherit Ata Gege's place, the future chief, the *ali'i kāne*. He had powerful *mana* as the offspring of a royal brother and sister, but the people had high expectations of their leaders. For his part, Blackwell could not call the princess or any of her ladies tender names. There was only one woman he would ever call sweetheart.

"Stop thinking, brother." Mahin slapped him heartily on the shoulder, and tapped his own temple. "Too much thinking. Come, I'll protect your wide flank."

One of Ata Gege's lieutenants came to fetch them to a makeshift parade ground. Mock combat was just another part of the day, and Mahin walked off imitating Blackwell's gait, which to him meant something of a fat arsed waddle. He'd become famous in the village for certain qualities. Introspection, for Blackwell found it expedient not to speak too much and to maintain an officer's reserve; and he could not live down having arrived a portly white man. In the field of battle he'd been teaching the warriors basic field signaling, taking a hand in working them up, the way he'd done many a boat's crew in preparation for a cutting out expedition.

Blackwell was summoned to the cliffs used as a lookout post before the exercises ended. He found Ata Gege there, gazing out to sea, performing the ritual necessary when the white man's ship was sighted. Blackwell stepped up and joined Ata Gege in the ceremony, which consisted in part in their standing side by side, circling an arm with clenched fist out from their bodies toward the ship. This would urge the foreign vessel away from the lands of Ata Gege of Kauai.

From their high vantage point, he watched intently while the foreign ship missed stays and slid to leeward. At the outset of his captivity even this lubberly mishandled vessel, so obviously not one of the Royal Navy's, would have raised turmoil in Blackwell's breast. But he no longer thought of the people as his captors, and he could barely remember why the good opinion of men in Whitehall and the Admiralty had been of such importance to him. The desires of his heart had changed, so much so he hardly recognized some of them as his own.

Ata Gege had been praying at his personal *heiau*, there at the top of the cliff, for success in the coming raid.

"We have done all we can," the chief said. "And when our canoes are consecrated you shall bring the muskets and gunpowder to fight Kamehameha. The men of Kauai will resist, we shall never be ruled by the king of another land."

He and the chief were bound together by honor and by hope. After the successful raid and the launching of the canoes, he was to take the specially built sailing canoe to Oahu and bring back arms. None of Ata Gege's tribe could do this, but a white man buying munitions was above notice and suspicion. It was the culmination of Ata Gege's ambitions, and his own. Blackwell suspected the chief of having formed this plan upon the day he fished him out of the Pacific.

There were lieutenants among Ata Gege's warriors who were far more experienced than Blackwell at the type of raid they would launch before dawn next day, and it was one of these men who would lead the attack. He was in charge of conducting the war party out to the raiding ground and back. The canoe was a craft that now felt to him like a living being, almost an extension of himself, and he was a powerful oarsman. He could sail a single masted craft alone, and in Ata Gege's sailing canoe Blackwell led his men through the long channel out of the lagoon. Blackwell could feel his way along the passage to the sea as well as any man born there.

Behind them on the shore of the lagoon burned a sacred pyre tended by the tribe's priest. Each warrior had cast an offering in the flames, receiving in return a sort of benediction that gave the men the greatest comfort, making them feel protected by the gods from wounds and death. Kalani handed Blackwell the hind quarters of a baby pig, dried and wrapped in *ti* leaves to cast upon the great fire. Sixty warriors paddled away from the beach, with he and Mahin leading in the sailing canoe. On shore Ata Gege stood, he would not attend in the canoes until they'd been properly consecrated, while the eerie phosphorescent wake of the craft seemed to connect the warriors to their chief.

The canoes made the first long dog leg turn of the channel and were lost to Ata Gege's sight. They paddled for just under an hour, Blackwell calling out directions that changed the chant of the stroke-maker in each of the war canoes. At last the sound of the surf beating upon the rugged shore was heard, and he felt his heart leap to the call of his natural element. He began the chant, taken up by the men in the war canoes, that would spur the paddlers through the fierce north setting current hugging the Nā Pali coast, to the calmer waters of the open sea.

Once they reached the true Pacific, with the wind at their backs, each canoe raised its single sail. A half hour's sailing brought Ata Gege's men parallel to the valley and the settlement chosen for the raid. The fierce paddle on the return voyage would be the last test of their strength, but he and all the warriors had trained for that as well.

In a long board Blackwell brought the three canoes to the headland bordering the curving arc of the beach, beyond which lay clustered grass huts, the village they meant to raid. The canoes were brought safely through the surf and beached in a cove one side of the headland, and left under guard of a dozen boys. The experienced fighters, Blackwell and the lieutenants and their men, fanned out in a wide arc after marching across the headland. A detachment was sent to drag the villagers' canoes into the surf and set them adrift, while the remaining men moved a quarter mile inland. Ata Gege's warriors took up positions behind the village.

He and Mahin were beside one another when the signal was given for the attack. Blackwell rushed forward with the rest. He carried a war club in one hand and a spear and four foot shield of his own making in the other. Ata Gege's warriors performed a *haka*, a war dance, ending in whoops as they reached the village, and Blackwell met the first men running out from the huts, and felt the crack of their skulls underneath his war club. He followed Mahin as he ran into one of the huts and hurled his spear into the back of a man too occupied to heed the war cries. A woman screamed, and Blackwell saw the spear pierce through the joined bodies of a couple in the act of love.

He turned round and staggered outside. Some of the villagers were fleeing for the shore, with Ata Gege's men pursuing, jumping in the air and slapping their thighs, and hurling spears at their backs. Blackwell ran for a hut larger than the rest where the shouts of battle resounded. As he rushed into the dwelling a shrieking naked woman ran past him, the glimpse he had of her showed she was with child. Blackwell entered with his heart in his throat, in time to see a big man clubbed down by Ata Gege's first lieutenant Manu. He must have been the village headman, larger than his men making a last stand round him, and when the big man fell he landed atop a little boy he'd pushed behind him.

Blackwell cried out and at the same moment was struck from behind. He lost his feet for a moment, sank down on his knees still looking toward where the headman's body was crushing the child underneath. He sprang up with a roar and attacked the man who'd clubbed him.

"Peace!" roared Manu.

Blackwell realized his opponent was on the ground, and fighting had ceased round him. Ata Gege's men had taken the village by complete surprise and they'd already exterminated every man of fighting age. He staggered over and heaved the headman off the child, who lay suffocated, dead under his father's body. He wanted to weep.

Outside an old man and woman were kneeling in the dirt imploring Ata Gege's men for pity.

"Leave them!" He barked at the warriors looming round the old couple.

They immediately obeyed, backing away from him and the old people. Manu reinforced the order when he emerged from the hut a moment later. The lieutenant gave leave for the taking of heads, not a moment was lost, they trussed up two bodies as well. The men were ordered back to the canoes. The loud wails of the survivors pierced Blackwell's heart.

Ata Gege's party returned to the landing place at a dog trot shouting with exhilaration, not yet conscious of fatigue or wounds. Blackwell, in the van of the company, did not become aware of the group of women and children under guard in the rear until they'd arrived at the cove where the canoes waited.

He hurried to take possession of the sailing canoe from the adolescent boys guarding it, calling out to Mahin to run her into the surf. He was desperate to avoid the shameful scene on shore, the women and children huddled together crying. One of the lieutenants shouted to him, and he had no choice but to halt with the canoe still ashore.

Manu made a rapid distribution of the captives between the two war canoes. The men stowed the enemy heads, and the two corpses went into the stern. Blackwell remembered sitting among them once. Manu led a slim boy of seven or eight and the boy's mother to Blackwell's canoe and shoved them into it.

"Now you may lead us, Captain James Blackwell," he said.

As they ran the canoe out into the surf, Blackwell called out to Mahin, "Is this necessary?"

Mahin glanced at him. They both leapt into the canoe and began paddling. Blackwell jerked his head at the captives.

"Each canoe must bear the weight of the captives," Mahin said in a conciliatory tone.

The same man who was so open hearted, playing with his son, seemed to have no pity and thought him merely over nice, unwilling to carry captives in his canoe. No discussion could take place as they concentrated on maneuvering the canoe through the breakwater. In any case how could he explain the tangle of emotions in his breast. He hadn't the words in the native; even in English it would have been difficult. After an action he'd always experienced a depression of spirit, as he tried to put the waste of human life out of his mind. The closest he'd ever come to speaking of the complex feelings war engendered had been with Mercedes.

The sight of the woman and boy cowering forward would not allow him to forget the bloody raid. The type of warfare he'd been accustomed to; ship against ship, cannons fired yard arm to yard arm or in a running sea battle; he wondered if there was less of honor in it and more of reserve. A separation from the enemy that allowed a man to believe he was not committing inhuman acts. Fighting toe to toe with clubs and spears, falling upon a sleeping village: was this the life soldiers led? Blackwell felt contempt for them, the old disdain of the sailor for the soldier, but in his heart the feeling turned inward now. He was ashamed. Naturally there would be women and children in a village, why had he not realized the raid wouldn't be only against fighting men.

Mahin spoke to the woman and boy, crouched in the bows of the canoe, in the same tone he'd used with Blackwell during the short time his status was the same as the corpses riding in the war canoes. He directed the pair to bail water or distribute their weight in the craft. Looking at them, man, woman, and child, Blackwell was astonished. The people, even Mahin, at once so kind and generous, could turn bloody and ruthless in the pursuit and defense of their way of life.

The royal family, Ata Gege, Kalani and her son Kaumuarii, were lined up to one side of the three canoes. Blackwell was grateful at least little Aloka was not there. Behind them ranged the minor nobles of the village, and he stood among this group. Ata Gege's lieutenants, and the people fanned out over the beach. A little apart were the captives of the raid, who had to look on the severed heads of their leaders, fixed to the prows of the war canoes.

The heads of the men with highest rank from the raided village were chosen to adorn the canoes; sanctifying with their great *mana* the raids to be carried out in them. One of the heads belonged to the bulky man who'd crushed his son to death. Looking on this sight, Blackwell cursed himself for his deliberate ignorance of the ways of the people. He'd been so intent on his own purposes he hadn't allowed himself to see them fully.

Led by the village priest they chanted and made a lane to the sea for the launching of the two great war canoes, with their grisly heads staring toward the sea. The chant and drums reached a fever pitch and the canoe was rolled forward, gaining speed over *koa* log runners. Before each canoe gained the surf, first the body of a slain enemy was thrown underneath it, and then an adolescent boy dragged shrieking from the group of captives.

Blackwell had seen men, deserters and criminals, hung at the mainmast yard arm, he'd seen the terrible punishment of flogging round the fleet, but the screams of those boys as they were crushed beneath the heavy canoes almost brought him to his knees. The only thing kept him upright was a wretched self-interest.

When his companions, the other *ali'i*, looked at him and saw his pallor, his stricken face, he hoped they might think it due to consciousness this would have been his fate but for his skills as a fighter. He would have been housed with the pigs, fed, and kept alive for this ceremony: to bring his *mana* as a white man to the launching of the canoes. He was aware of what fate might yet hand him if he did not play his part to Ata Gege's satisfaction.

He watched the priest stride into the crowd of captives and drag out by the wrist the boy who'd come there in his canoe. The boy's mother made a futile effort to hold her child back, but the look in her eyes spoke her despair. The priest slung the boy up on his back, and Blackwell saw why a younger child had been selected for the consecration of the sailing canoe. The priest began to run round the small vessel with the boy clinging to him.

On the eve of returning to men of his own kind, the much planned for object of the last years of his life, he stood by and watched in horror. Was there any going back to civilized life after this?

The people's chanting and the beat of the drums heightened, until the exhausted priest with the child hanging upside down now on his back, stopped at the prow of the canoe. The crowd made a lane to the sea, the drum beat rolled out, and the priest grasped the boy by his ankles. He swung the boy in a wide arc for the prow of the canoe. Blackwell stepped forward and with the sound of smacking flesh, caught the child before he struck.

A gasp went up from the crowd. No one dared look at Ata Gege.

Blackwell, clasping the child to his breast, turned and faced the native chief. "*Ali'i Nui* Ata Gege, this canoe sails to bring back the cargo of the white man. For such a voyage to succeed we must not offend the white man's god." He set the trembling boy down, pushing him in the direction of his mother. "I am one of them, as well as the husband of the great Kalani, and I say the white man's god would not like the sacrifice of a boy child."

He met consternation on the faces of the people, and the vexation of the old priest at having the ancient ceremony disrupted by a godless interloper. The reaction of Ata Gege was the only one of significance, the chief stared, his face as stern, set, and unreadable as his own had ever been in a crisis on the quarterdeck.

After a tense and considerable pause Ata Gege said coolly, "If the white man's god is offended by the sacrifice of a pure, young spirit, what does he want? Is the boy not pure enough, does the white god require an infant? Or is he a god of lust, does the white man's god prefer a woman."

A brief, anxious chuckle rose from the people.

He'd come to know them to some small degree, and as individuals he valued them much. They cherished their familiar life, ruled by rituals and the seasons, and they would do whatever the gods required to sustain it.

He would not call what he felt toward them Christian duty, a desire to leave them better off than when he found them. He was deeply sensible of the brotherhood Mahin and many others had shown him from earliest days. He bowed his head for a moment before answering Ata Gege. He said his own private prayer that the God of his father, the Reverend Blackwell, would not condemn him for what he was about to tell the people of Kauai.

"The god of the white man is a god of cargo, he wants many things. He wants baskets of sennit twine and nut paste for caulking, dried poi and sweet potato and salted fish for the journey, and water in calabashes and bamboo reeds. This is what the white man's god requires for a successful journey, not the sacrifice of his people. Who would bring him all the things he must have if the people were killed?"

Blackwell looked Ata Gege in the face as he finished his speech, and not for the first time caught a cunning glimmer pass over the older man's features. Ata Gege's implacable gaze rested on him, while he stood with long practice in the attitude of a captain before an admiral. The fifty-seven year old Ata Gege, fiercest of head-hunters in his day, and present leader of the people of the Nā Pali coast of Kauai, turned to his subjects and said; "Well, what are you waiting for? Bring those things named by Captain James Blackwell. And when the god of cargo is satisfied we will feast and launch the sailing canoe. To the white man's settlement!"

There were shadows moving on the shore. He could not at first make them out and he stroked cautiously nearer, fearful his journey might be hindered at the last hour. When he was within musket shot of the shore he recognized the two figures moving about there, just as they plunged together into the water. He maneuvered the canoe to meet Kalani and her son.

Kalani was more graceful in water. Like all her people she was a powerful swimmer, and she and Aloka reached Blackwell's canoe in a dozen strokes. Once alongside he extended his arm to help her aboard but Kalani would not take it. She grasped Aloka and heaved him into the canoe instead, and then she kicked away, floating backward.

"Take your son, Captain James Blackwell," Kalani said, in her breathless gasping way. "If he stays the *Ali'i Kāne* may kill him. There can be only one king. Aloka is a good strong boy. Make him a chief of the white men. Like his father."

Blackwell looked at the little boy kneeling in the bows, returning his gaze out of an innocent copy of his own face, and at the boy's mother. Kalani believed he would never return, he was deeply touched she would give up her child to him. He managed to put a stern quality in his voice. "Great *ali'i* Kalani, I will take the boy." He would make no further promises to ease her mother's heart. "*Aloha* Kalani." He paddled away from the princess, tears standing in his eyes.

To Aloka he said in a voice emotion made gruff, "Keep your head down, son, do you hear me there."

At the outset, as he was paddling like fury to put the canoe through the strong current, Blackwell believed his decision to bring Aloka one of the most ill-judged ones of his life. It was roughly a two hundred mile voyage. A negligible distance both in his experience of sea faring, and certainly in the history of Aloka's people. His ancestors had crossed three thousand miles of ocean at a time when the Vikings were raping Blackwell's own forbearers. Fear for the boy was what it amounted to, he was unable to watch him properly while managing the canoe.

But Aloka proved to be a hand after his father's own mariner's heart. He stayed low in the bows when Blackwell tacked, he bailed the canoe when told, and he crept aft and sat between his father's knees to eat his day's ration and drink his cups of water. Blackwell was amazed at the boy's maturity, which confirmed him in his belief that gentlemen's children were brought up entirely too tenderly.

On that first day of sailing, they lost their wind at noon and floated on a calm sea. Blackwell paddled for a space, stopping to throw loops of sennit lashing round Aloka when he needed to relieve himself over the side. Blackwell, fastening a sennit cord to his wrist that bound him to the canoe, spilled over the side in his turn. The west wind came up in the afternoon and increased throughout the night, and Blackwell hoped between sailing and paddling to run off close to ninety miles each day.

His strategy was to do much as he had done when commanding a sloop in the Mediterranean. Stand out from the islands by day and creep in toward them by night, when fires would reveal the locations of tribes along the coast. He had the advantage of a keen memory and having studied charts of the Sandwich Islands. In addition Ata Gege had taken him to an ancient and sacred place where the people's ancestors set up a great rock tablet with stones pointing the way to the inner islands, and to distant Oteheite, Bora Bora, and Raiatea.

But he had not counted upon the variable currents and airs between the islands, and when they hit the channel separating Kauai and Oahu it required all his strength, energy, and training to keep the little vessel from being overwhelmed. As he battled through the rough seas, the back of his mind worked on the possibility of missing the port of Honolulu, their provisions running low, and being forced to put ashore.

Aloka had not been conditioned, as he had, to subsist on a meager ration of water. He had no desire to hear his son cry for hunger and thirst. His weakness in bringing the boy was one of many discontents by the end of the fourth day of sailing, when they'd crossed the difficult channel. He raised the canoe's sail to a steady following breeze, and steered a course as near south and east along Oahu's coastline as the vessel would lie.

By nightfall a gale of wind had arisen and he decided he had to stand in for the shore.

"Prepare to come about," he called forward.

Aloka crouched low in the bows, and he swung the canoe's head off the wind. It was a hard paddle to shore, with the rain driven horizontally and heading him. Blackwell opened the mouth of a bay at a point when he felt his strength was going. He could not see much beyond a cable's length in any one direction, and he had no idea of the size of the bay. He directed the canoe by the send of the sea and his mariner's instinct for a lee shore, and stopped paddling when the little craft slide into a still pocket of air. Blackwell threw out his sea anchor, a tightly woven basket weighted with stones, to maintain the canoe's position.

"The calabashes, son, the empty ones." His voice was an exhausted croak. "Get them out."

They filled their empty water vessels then sat in the tropical downpour. Blackwell peered around them, but there was nothing to be seen, no fires possible in the deluge. He was unwilling to set up the sail as an awning to protect them from the rain; it would make them instantly more visible from shore. They shared a supper of mealy fish and sodden poi, Blackwell holding Aloka on his lap and attempting to shield him. Afterwards he put the boy to sleep on top of their netted provisions in the bottom of the canoe, and covered him with the sail.

Blackwell sat in the stern of the native craft with rain washing over him. He was cold with no covering saving his *tapa* breechclout, his muscles twitched from the constant pelting and from exhaustion. Once or twice in his career he'd spent as many as the four days just past on the deck of a man-of-war, fighting a running battle or a strong gale. Then he'd been one of a team of professionals, each with his specific duties. In battle they'd known the enemy; there were no moral judgments to be made, only tactical and strategic ones. Blackwell considered the craggy shore on the canoe's lee, a wild scrubby place. He'd gained the coast of

Oahu where the largest European settlement in the islands was to be found. Yet he felt distanced from that world far more than the actual score of miles separating him from it.

The next day would mark the fifth of their voyage, and perhaps that day or the following one he would find the port of Honolulu. There would be merchant ships in harbor, possibly even men-of-war. And he would speak English again. The idea was hard to credit as he bailed water from the canoe with a calabash, and vigilantly watched the shore. He'd seen what might become of a young captive, another tribe would not take him now. He was prepared to haul his kedge and paddle for the open sea. Yet he hadn't slept more than two hours at a stretch since the start of the journey. Wretchedly tired, he still roused every few hours and bailed the canoe, touched Aloka's foot under the sail, and scanned the water and shore round them.

Blackwell awoke with a start in the early hours of morning, having dreamt his father was swinging Aloka by the heels and dashing him against the simpering figurehead of his old command *Inconstant*. The rain had moved on and he bailed the canoe one last time, pouring some of the calabashes of fresh water over his head by way of bathing. He shook himself and gathered his hair back and tied it with a braided vine cord. By the fading starlight Blackwell judged it to be about four o'clock in the morning, and with the cessation of the rain he could see a fair distance. Away on the other side of the horseshoe shaped bay was a sight that shocked him.

A square rigged ship was hove to against the sheltering cliffs directly opposite. Blackwell leaned forward and gathered up the leaves in which their food had been wrapped and twisted the greenery round his paddle, lashing it to with sennit cords. Once he had completed this trick to deaden the sound of the paddle, he hauled in the sea anchor and shook Aloka awake. He motioned for the boy to be silent and pointed across the water.

Aloka's eyes widened at sight of the grand ship, a three masted vessel lying at single anchor. Even with all her sails furled and her topgallant masts struck down on deck Blackwell knew she appeared of monstrous proportions to Kalani's son, who had hitherto viewed the war canoes as surpassing fine. He recognized her as a whaler, and a rather knocked about one, but in Aloka's view she would be the noble vessel of the world.

Hugging the shoreline, Blackwell paddled the canoe quietly out of the bay. He stopped to rest a moment at its mouth, and to remove the leaves from his paddle. In the bow Aloka was performing the ritual required when the white man's ship was sighted.

Blackwell joined him. "We shall see many such ships from this time on, Aloka. That must do for all."

"You sailed a great war canoe once, Father?"

"Once. An even bigger one."

Kalani or one of her ladies must have told the boy of his previous life. Blackwell didn't stop to consider why he hadn't approached the whaler, and called out to them in English for assistance. Instead he threw himself into a six hour paddle, and brought Ata Gege's sailing canoe past the great dome of rock guarding one side of the bay, and onto the palm lined beach of Waikiki on a Sunday morning.

He hauled the canoe well up on the shore near a group of adolescent native boys who were lounging about the landing place. Aloka had already jumped out and Blackwell leaned into the canoe, retrieving his war club and his staff with two yellow feathers symbolizing his status as an *ali'i*. The boys stepped back respectfully, especially when the braided necklace of teeth round his neck came into view. When Blackwell said in the native language as he passed them, "This is the canoe of Captain James Blackwell, don't molest it," they seemed very willing to obey.

Aloka trotted ahead of him on the footpath leading up the slope of the hill. The naked little boy veered off the path, attracted by an unfamiliar chanting and ran up the coral steps of a stone and wood structure tucked back amongst the trees. He followed, putting Aloka aside as he mounted the steps of the church and stood in the doorway. The congregation was just being seated after a hymn and the elderly minister was moving to the lectern to preach his sermon. The people worshipping noticed him standing there with his killing club and staff, which he knew were held at the appropriate angle for being in the company of friends. A dead silence fell over them, and they gaped at him. One of the last to turn and stare, in the pew nearest the alter, was the most beautiful woman in the world. At first her look was fearful and care ridden, and then joy suffused her face.

CHAPTER SIXTEEN

Mercedes' mind, as ever, was revolving on the problem of what would be best for Edward. She barely heeded the Sunday service. Edward was beside her, and next to him, Minni's mama, Kanakoa's third wife. He had offered that she should be his fourth, to make an honest woman of her. Mercedes had given no answer; she felt sure *L'Unite* must return to Honolulu soon. Her heart was not engaged with Kanakoa; it was much more her loins, if she were honest with herself; yet if she decided to stay in the islands it might be best for her and Edward to be under his direct protection. When *L'Unite* returned she would decide.

Mr. Bing had shuffled to the lectern and was standing there mouth agape. The people round her were craning in their seats and staring in the same direction. Though she thought it rude Mercedes at last turned round and was arrested by the sight of the wild bushman filling the doorway of the church. The man was nearly naked and certainly a stranger. Mr. Bing's parishioners knew they must wear proper clothing to Sunday services. More unforgivably the man carried his weapons.

Her heart gave a great lurch, she sprang suddenly from her seat, making Edward jump beside her. She stared, all thoughts and cares fled, and she ran to him. A gasp went up, and one or two people called warnings, frightened he would eat her. At the last second she brought herself up, stopping short in front of him. Only those seated in the back heard her whisper, "Oh James, oh Jim."

She marched back up the aisle, squeezed into the pew past the shocked *ali'i*, who all stared at her, and came out again leading Edward by the hand.

She passed Mr. Bing. "Forgive me, Reverend Bing, it is Captain Blackwell."

The people stirred and whispered.

"Will you go home with us?" she asked.

Captain Blackwell, clad in a *tapa* breechclout, with his hair done in a topknot, warrior fashion, silently turned and left the church, pushing a little native boy in front of him.

Outside in the bright morning sunlight she stared at him, disbelieving. He was a deep tanned brown everywhere, and he smelled like the natives, of the outdoors. "This way, it's not far." She felt giddy, relief and happiness flooded her heart. She wanted to embrace him and hold him to make sure he was of this world. But there was something in his manner prevented her, as though her touch would break him, and he would fall to pieces like glass. She hurried him to her house, glancing behind to make sure Edward was following, and curiously ahead at the little island boy attending them.

It was not until they were in her house and Captain Blackwell staggered and nearly fell, catching himself on the sturdy table that Mercedes realized he was collapsing with fatigue. She immediately gave him her shoulder to lean on and led him into her bedroom. He put his arm round her. His was a grateful weight pressing against her.

"In here, James darling."

Captain Blackwell let go of her as soon as they were in the bedroom, and sat heavily on the soft mats on the floor rather than settling on the enormous bed.

"Leave me now, if you please." His voice was no more than a croak.

Mercedes yearned to be with him, to nurse and tend him, to hear what had become of him, but she moved obediently toward the door.

He stopped her before she went out, raising her hopes just for a moment. "Mercedes, I know I ask a lot. Would you take the boy?"

Mercedes looked from the strained face of her husband to the toddler standing with his hand on Captain Blackwell's shoulder. It was like looking at a portrait of Captain Blackwell in pure brown tones. Tears rose to her eyes. "Come *chico*," she held out her hand to the boy. "What's your name?"

The boy answered Mercedes when she asked him again in the native language in the next room. "Aloka, son of the *Ali'i* Kalani and the princess' fourth husband Captain James Blackwell."

They all stared at one another.

She said, in the same formal Hawaiian, "I am Mercedes, first wife of Captain James Blackwell, and this is Edward James Blackwell. Edward, your brother, Aloka." Just like that. Edward bowed to Aloka, and she felt proud of her son, the English gentleman. The two little boys then clasped forearms in the native manner, and Aloka even pulled Edward to him and rubbed noses with him. Mercedes sent Aloka back in to his father with two calabashes of water and several hard biscuits.

Aloka came out of the bedroom again almost immediately without the victuals. "*Mahalo*, ma'am," was all the little boy remembered to say to her from his father.

Mercedes never had more need of patience, a virtue not particularly known among Spaniards or Englishmen. She longed to speak to Captain Blackwell, to look on him, to touch him most of all. Had not they much to say to one another after so long a separation?

"This must be how other Navy wives live," she said, as she prepared their dinner. She spoke in English and to herself, while the little boys played outside the cooking shelter. She could not help staring at Aloka, so remarkably like Captain Blackwell, and wondering if the *Ali'i* Kalani had taken her place in his heart.

The idea and the possibility it was what she deserved were almost more than she could bear, but she hadn't long to be alone with her mortifying thoughts. Saunders came from the front of the house into the cooking shelter.

"Is it true, Missus, the Captain returns? Did he really pop up naked in church?"

"Yes, it's him. He was not naked, he had this covering." Mercedes shaped her hands around her own loins. "The native breeches. He's not well, Saunders. He's thin and very much exhausted, and desired me to leave him alone."

"But, give you joy, Missus. Naturally his honor must be fair done up. Who knows what he's been through? Didn't you always know it though, as the Captain weren't dead. Here now, who is this?" Saunders looked down at Aloka. The boy had barreled into her legs, fleeing an imaginary pursuer. Edward, not understanding the game was chase, just stared after him.

"This is Captain Blackwell's son, Aloka. Aloka, may I present my friend Saunders."

"Well, I'll be goddamned."

Saunders' reaction summed matters up for the entire community. Mercedes had barely given Edward and Aloka their dinner on mats on the floor of the main room when Reverend Bing was seen approaching through their adjoining yards.

"How do you do, Mr. Bing?" She met him in her open doorway. "I am sorry but we shall have to speak outside. Captain Blackwell is not at home to visitors, he is trying to rest."

"Of course, of course," the Reverend said, stopping on the porch. From here, their voices just as readily reached the adjacent bedroom. "How is the Captain? And forgive me for asking, Mercedes dear, but are you quite sure that is him?"

Saunders came and joined them, and Reverend Bing appealed to her. "Have you seen your former Captain, Saunders? Is that naked heathen indeed he?"

"No, Reverend, I haven't. Because he ain't home to visitors, like the Missus said. But she's seen him, and she ought to know Captain Blackwell when she sees him. Naked heathen or not." Saunders had settled the affair to her own satisfaction, and she went to join the boys.

"Your servant has a saucy tongue."

"Which she doesn't guard because she is not my servant. Dear Mr. Bing, I will give your kind regards to Captain Blackwell, and I am sure he shall return your call as soon as ever he can." The old gentleman was looking eagerly over her shoulder into the room. She could not produce Captain Blackwell to satisfy his curiosity, but she liked and respected old Reverend Bing or she would not have bothered. "Edward, Aloka, come here and pay your respects to Mr. Bing."

Edward rose, and at a gesture from him Aloka sprang up as well. "Good day, Mr. Bing," Edward said.

"Good day, my boy. And who is your friend?"

Edward stared at him uncomprehending. Mercedes experienced a painful few moments, she had set the introduction in motion yet she hadn't meant to throw Edward into an awkward circumstance. But then Edward brightened. "He is not my friend, sir. Aloka is my brother."

Aloka favored Reverend Bing with a handsome smile and both boys skipped back in to finish their dinners. Reverend Bing stared more than ever at the little island boy seated next to his favorite pupil. The contrast between them must have struck him, the one large and fair and ungainly, the other compact, agile, with a quick, dark gaze. Reverend Bing recollected himself and said his farewell, and beat a hasty retreat. Mercedes supposed he had more than enough news to impart to Mrs. Bing.

But Reverend Bing was merely the herald before the main force, and throughout the afternoon there was a parade of the *ali'i*, the resident seamen, the whole neighborhood in short came through Mercedes' front yard. The *ali'i* who had witnessed the return of Captain Blackwell in church recounted his appearance in glowing detail, and a regular gathering of the local nobles sat for a time under the plumeria and frangipani trees between her yard and that of the Mission house. Kanakoa was not among them but his wives were, and he would hear the chiefs' conclusion directly; which was that the great spirit of the white child had summoned the foreign *ali'i*, who made Mercedes believe he was her dead husband.

She attended upon the *ali'i* while Saunders intercepted the king's dockyard mateys, who laid a claim to Mercedes as one of their own. The British seamen among them were especially urgent to discover if Captain Blackwell had indeed returned.

"Missus Blackwell says it's he," Saunders told one and all, "and he ain't so stout after his escape from the wild. But the skipper always was a hard old horse, and I expect he'll come round in a day or two. It's into the mountains for the likes of you, was you wise."

This was unwelcome news and some of the sailors were so uncivil as to point out to Saunders; "Which you would be going with us, mate, was you not a woman. Speaking of which, let's us press one or two of the native dollies to take along of us." By late afternoon the seamen had dispersed in these pursuits, and the *ali'i* retired to their cool palaces. Mercedes decided to creep into her bedroom and collect clean clothes, and take the boys to the bathing place. But up the footpath, marching toward her came Captain and Mrs. Jennings of the whaling ship *John Bill*.

"Hell and death," Mercedes murmured, but she walked out to meet them, extending her hand.

"We're not staying, we know you've had every Jack tar and *kanaka* in port through here today," Mrs. Jennings said in her blunt way. "But Tom and I thought Captain Blackwell could use a few ship's provisions. Nothing like the mess a man's used to, to set him up." Mrs. Jennings pressed a large basket on Mercedes.

Mercedes glanced in at a small sack of coffee beans and a hand grinder and a large sack of biscuits, a ham and a half dozen eggs, kippers in tins. Americans might be abrupt, but they were also the best and most practical people. She set the basket down on the grass and threw her arms round Mrs. Jennings.

"Thank you, thank you, dear Mrs. Jennings. Thank you, Captain Jennings, sir. It's what he needs of all things."

Mrs. Jennings' pursed her lips, disapproving of her warmth and enthusiasm. But Mercedes was doubly grateful to her: For her generous gift, and for her belief in Captain Blackwell's resurrection.

Blackwell lay, for the greater part of that day, in a limbo between consciousness and sleep. He was unable to relax and give himself over completely to restorative rest for the turmoil in his breast. He was prepared that returning to the civilized world should be a shock, but never had he supposed Mercedes would be there in the islands waiting for him. Somehow her gentle, sweet presence undid him. He was perfectly wretched hearing her making excuses for him to her neighbors. He'd returned to her a naked savage, body and soul worn thin, not at all the man she'd married. Not the commander of a Royal Navy ship. He listened as her voice came to him from outside. She deserved better than a man who'd done the things he'd done.

Mercedes sent him in a supper of pork and poi and more hard biscuit, and water. After supper he heard her calling to Edward and Aloka and she left the house. He was stretched out again on the mat after finishing a fraction of the food she'd made him, when he heard a man's dignified voice calling, "Stranger *ali'i*, come with us to the bathing place." Blackwell heaved himself up almost without thought and put on his *malo*. He carried out the remainder of his meal and joined the men of his own class, waiting for him on the footpath with curiosity on their faces.

Blackwell exerted himself only once more that evening, in spite of fatigue and confusion of spirit, when he heard Mercedes and Saunders stirring about in the next room. He gathered they were hanging a cot.

He forced himself up and opened the door between the rooms. "You will sleep in your own bed, ma'am."

Saunders and Mercedes and the little boys stared at him. He nodded to Saunders, and she knuckled her forehead in return.

"Certainly, Captain," Mercedes said. "Allow me first to settle the boys."

He went back in the bedroom and struck a light for the candle next to her bed, calling "Goodnight, son," in English to Edward, and "Rest now, son," to his native boy. It was not until the candle was lit he noticed he was naked, displaying the native tattooing of his loins and backside. No wonder Mercedes and Saunders had stared so. Blackwell lay back with a groan on the mat where he meant to confine himself to sleep, and listened to Mercedes' dear voice.

Mercedes thought she did a creditable job keeping her voice steady as she read aloud from 'The Arabian Nights'. It was not easy with her heart thumping so, with the anticipation of being alone with Blackwell.

Edward surprised her by wanting to sleep on the mats beside Aloka rather than in his hammock. He'd always been much attached to what was familiar. But he'd never had a friend before, and the two boys had been playmates throughout the day.

"Good night, sweetheart. I love you." Mercedes kissed Edward on the forehead.

She moved around to Aloka and kissed him too. "Good night, Aloka. We are so glad you're here."

"Good night, Ma'am." Aloka was under the impression ma'am was Mercedes' name, since it was what his father called her.

Mercedes blew out the lantern and left the room.

Edward lay on his back, his large blue eyes open, staring at the ceiling. "He will not eat her?" he said in Hawaiian. He'd heard things throughout the day about wild bushmen, and he did not remember the native man in his mother's room was his father.

"Oh, no," Aloka said. "He only eats his enemies."

Mercedes moved about her room, taking off her clothes and putting on her dressing gown. As soon as she'd entered she'd encountered Captain Blackwell lying with his face to the wall, on the mats at the foot of the big bed. His position displayed the solid black bands tattooed across his buttocks. The design was interrupted in places the dye would not take, where the scars from a grenade wound puckered the skin. She'd seen his loins were decorated with the arching native stripes when he'd faced them earlier. He was otherwise deeply tanned, and thinner than she'd ever known him. He shuddered while she gazed at him. That pained her deeply, to see him so reduced, when before he'd been such a specimen of a pork and beef fed Englishman.

She took a blanket out of her sea chest and laid it beside him, touching his arm. "Here is a blanket, it grows cold sometimes at night." She gripped his arm a moment longer. "I don't want anything from you, Jim, except you should know I love you. I'm so glad you are back."

Mercedes felt his body tense beneath her hand and she rose quickly and snuffed out the candle. She climbed into bed alone. There was to be no relief from the long vigil she'd kept for him, though he was close enough to touch. She listened for his snores, but though he turned after a time upon his back, with the loss of weight he seemed no longer to suffer the problem. She heard his regular breathing, and as Mercedes' eyes adjusted in the dark she could at least watch him sleep. His stern, care-lined face was relaxed, and she was able to gaze on the man she loved, so near. Tears of happiness filled her eyes.

Her happiness would have been complete had he come to bed, and taken her in his arms. She needed that comfort and reassurance from him. There was anguish in her breast, over her disloyalty and the beauty and allure of the islanders. She imagined princess Kalani like the young nobles of her acquaintance; youthful and lithe. Did he find her aged from the climate, and the epidemic, and the strain of missing him and raising their son alone. Not knowing whether his affections were changed made more tears come, her familiar companions.

Mercedes did not wake when he left the house at four o'clock in the morning to go down to the landing place, and check over the canoe and its provisions. The remaining foodstuffs he threw out and then emptied the water calabashes so they would dry completely before the next voyage. He furled the mat sail and stowed it, and the baskets of sennit cord and caulking more securely in the bottom of the canoe. After he'd been over the little craft making all secure, Blackwell tossed aside his breechclout and ran into the surf. Diving into the waves, his powerful strokes took him past the breakers, where he floated on his back, staring at the lightening sky. He'd rested profoundly after what Mercedes had said the evening before. He regretted in his stupefied state having made her no return.

Her tender words and her gentle presence had at once shattered and then sheltered him. It was absurd; one small woman between him and life, particularly life with Ata Gege. Yet after a blessed night of rest, Blackwell felt much restored — physically.

He was able to think, floating there with the wide world round him, about what must be his next steps in this mission. His mind was equally occupied with his wife and family. Mercedes might be offended by his having been with another woman, but Blackwell had lived the native life so intensely he could not quite remember why that should be. Mercedes was Spanish as well as English, and hadn't she shown by her kind behavior a willingness to accept him, and his bastard son. Yet Blackwell did not want her to have to be kind, to make exceptions and excuse him. He wanted it to be between them as it had been before, for her to see him as a man of powerful *mana*, her man. At once decided, he swam hard and rode the waves back into Waikiki beach.

Mrs. Bing eyed the native man striding naked across Mercedes' back yard as she returned from the privy early that morning. She bustled into Mr. Bing's bedchamber and woke him. "She's taken up with a native at last. I saw him naked as God made him, going in her bedroom door."

"That is Captain Blackwell," Mr. Bing said, sitting up with his nightcap askew. "Did I not tell you he looks just like one of our own native chiefs?"

"No, Mr. Bing, that cannot be Edward's father. This man had the dark, sinister look of the savage. And his...his nether regions were blackened. Never in life would a British sea captain permit such a thing!"

Mercedes heard Blackwell's heavy tread outside her door. She threw off the sheet covering her so that her backside and legs would be exposed to his view. She knew what her husband liked, and she heard his sharp intake of breath after he'd closed the door and come into the room. Yet he moved around the foot of the bed, instead of climbing in behind her as she'd hoped.

"Won't you lie down with me?"

How pitiful she must sound, for Blackwell looked at her sharply. But then he gave her an odd half smile and eased himself down on the bed opposite her.

"It's been so long since I've lain in a bed or a cot, I was afraid I would not sleep, and disturb you. This is an uncommon grand bed."

"Your men made it, they built the entire house."

She saw confusion pass over his features. "Mr. Verson did not want to leave me here in the islands, but I persuaded him I needed to...to wait for you." She put out her hand and laid it on Blackwell's muscled arm.

This time he did not tense at her touch. He put his hand gently over hers. "Forgive me, Mercedes, for not being a better husband to you, I — "

A pounding sounded at the door and Blackwell jumped up from the bed, reaching for his war club.

"James, it's only Edward." Mercedes got up and surprised him with a kiss, at the same time she grasped his fist holding the war club.

The rapping continued. She was standing behind Blackwell when he yanked open the door, and there was Edward knocking his head against the wood instead of striking it with his fist like a Christian.

Edward veered into the room, avoiding Blackwell, careened past both of them and threw himself on the big bed.

Mercedes sighed and returned to the bed to stretch out beside her boy. She'd hoped Blackwell was ready to be intimate. She was sorry Edward should have interrupted them, but she put her arm protectively over her son.

"Aloka's awake too," Blackwell said from the open doorway, glancing round at her.

"He may come in then."

"Come on in, son."

Aloka sprinted in, leaped onto the foot of the bed, and catapulted over Mercedes and Edward, landing prettily on the opposite side. They all laughed and began to feel easier together.

After a time, Mercedes rose and took her clothes into the main room to dress. She was not unaware Blackwell propped himself up in bed, and was straining for glimpses of her through the open door and past the bouncing forms of his sons. She hurried out to the cooking shelter to prepare the traditional English breakfast she'd planned for him.

She came back into the house loaded with plates of ham, eggs, kippers, soft tack and marmalade. Blackwell emerged from the bedroom, dressed in a white shirt and breeches he'd found perfectly well preserved in his sea chest. He stopped and gazed on the large English breakfast, tears springing to his eyes. His expression was confounded, the breeches he wore fit him awkwardly, hanging loose and low over his hips, unbuttoned at the knees above bare, rough tanned feet.

Painful conflict was evident in his whole bearing. He looked what he was, a man adrift between two worlds. Torn by the demands of each, with their wars and obligations. She was not altogether unprepared, having seen the ways of men under stress of strong emotion, when Blackwell lashed out.

"Son." Blackwell grasped Edward roughly by the shoulder as the boy stood beside the table, scuffling his feet and awaiting his breakfast. "Don't just stand there gawping, help your mother."

"No, James, its — "

She didn't finish because Edward turned his back on his father. Fury rose in Blackwell's eyes. Mercedes banged the plates down on the table and tried to get between her son and husband.

"Don't turn away when I'm talking to you. Do you hear me there?"

Aloka jumped up from the mat where he'd been watching and rushed over. He tried to put a hand on Mercedes' arm, in a protective gesture. Further infuriated, Blackwell pushed Aloka away from her.

"You've been too tender with the boy, and you see the result." He loomed over her.

"Mama, get the sword," Edward cried.

Blackwell froze, staring at his white son and then at her.

"Go to Aunty Mele's. *Anda!*"

She regretted the boys would not be eating the fine breakfast she'd prepared, as she watched them leave, hand in hand, but she knew the first thing the big native woman next door would do was feed them.

"James, please."

"What did the boy mean, Mercedes, have you weapons in the house? Answer me!"

She grew angry, her cheeks flushing. Did Blackwell not care she should have had to defend herself, only that she was possessed of arms? She ran into the bedroom and flung aside the mats he'd slept on, and with a strong heave she brought up the section of floor concealing the armament.

"Here, sir! Here is what you are after. And now may you leave my son and I in peace."

Blackwell stood rooted before the treasure concealed below the floor; tomahawks, cutlasses, his own cavalry sword, clean and well-oiled, muskets, and a lead box containing gunpowder. He let the trap door down over the strong room and caught her, marching past the congealing eggs and ham, before she was out the door.

"Don't, don't leave me." His voice was soft in her ear.

Mercedes allowed him to lead her back to the table. They sat down and she poured coffee for him into a pewter cup.

"Coffee, my god."

Then he really did begin to weep.

She kept silent while he sniffled and ate and drank his first cups of coffee in years. Mercedes let him recover, and she joined him in the meal, remembering Blackwell always had been savage until he was fed. He began to look very complaisantly and tenderly at her, as he finished the grand breakfast she'd given him.

"I wanted Edward to play with the other boys," Mercedes said, needing to share the burden she'd been carrying alone. "I wanted him to swim and fish and tumble about with the island children, but he isn't like other boys. Edward isn't like you and I." She held his eye. "He is never going to be a sea officer, he suffers from fits and his mind...just isn't...I'm sorry, Jim, truly I am."

Confusion and hurt passed over his features, his expression settling in one of deep concern. Blackwell reached over and pulled her onto his lap. He embraced her at long last, and Mercedes said, into his shoulder, "We know the fault lies with me now. You have a healthy, bright son in Aloka. It is his name must be carried on your friends' books." She sniffed. He'd told her in the Navy, commanders considered the near relations of brother officers as legacies to the Service.

Blackwell tightened his embrace and gave her a gentle shake. "Don't talk to me of faults, ma'am, you haven't got any." There was a pause and Blackwell said, his voice slightly atremble, "God made Edward what he is, and we must accept that."

She jumped off his lap of a sudden and ran into her bedroom, returning waving sheets of parchment at him.

"God gave Edward a certain genius. He can read and do sums, and he plays chess with Mr. Bing. And he drew these. Look!"

She laid in front of Blackwell a small stack of parchment, which he slowly turned over. Most were detailed depictions of birds, finely wrought and realistic renderings of island birds.

"I've hunted these," Blackwell said, separating out several wildfowl and forest birds. "I know their names only in the native." There were two drawings he examined at some length; one was of a brig, and the other depicted a coastline with a dome shaped hill in the background and a strand or landing place in the fore.

"This is Honolulu. Waikiki beach," he said, standing up.

"It is. From just past the church."

"Show me, Mercedes. Come." Blackwell held his hand out to her.

Mercedes hurried Blackwell up the footpath past the residence of Mr. and Mrs. Bing, past the church and through the grove of trees standing between it and the beach. On a promontory of rock the other side of the grove Blackwell stopped and gazed from Edward's drawing to the panorama before him.

"It is rendered exactly," he said. "There is the great hill — ah, Diamond Head — every tree, and the ships in harbor, and the mountains. How we should have benefited by such skill aboard *L'Unite* during the outward passage."

Mercedes clasped her hands together over her breast, a bright smile on her face. But then Blackwell lowered the drawings with a tightening of his jaw, as though he recollected something painful. He moved the drawing of the brig uppermost.

"What ship is that?"

"She is *Vostok*, twenty guns, a Russian ship of war on a mission of exploration in the Pacific."

Blackwell stood, legs apart, studying the drawing. At last he shook his head. "Every yard, backstay, and shroud exactly where it should be. The ship's boats, even the wretched little poop."

"The *Vostok* had an artist aboard who said he imagined Edward had scaled the drawing exactly to the brig's dimensions. We never had a chance to find out." Something in her tone made Blackwell turn to her. She hastened on, "The natives think Edward touched by the gods."

"So do I."

"I need to bring him to school, James, if you please. Mr. Bing has a school for boys. All of his students are older than Edward, of course."

Blackwell gave her his arm; he appeared to be recollecting the civilities one at a time. "I shall go with you and make Reverend Bing's acquaintance, and beg his pardon for yesterday. Would you tell me more of these fits Edward suffers from, and exactly why you had need of my sword."

Mercedes had not unburdened half of her concerns over Edward's seizures and odd behavior, when they arrived at the grass hut of her neighbor, Mele.

"Come in, come in, Wahine Blackwell," the high-pitched voice of Mele called out, after Mercedes announced herself from the path.

Inside the hut sat a two hundred fifty pound Hawaiian woman, ladling poi with her fingers alternately into her own mouth and those of the two boys seated in front of her. She rolled to her feet when Mercedes entered, with Captain Blackwell following, ducking under the low doorway.

"Mo, wake up!" Mele kicked an even heftier man sprawled in one corner of the hut. "The foreign *ali'i* is here."

Mele waited with a placid expression while Mercedes made the introductions. When Captain Blackwell expressed his gratitude for their care of his wife and child, brilliant smiles lit the natives' faces.

"How could we not feed this one, she is so skinny," Mele said, hugging Mercedes to her copious bosom as though she were a child.

"And the *akua*," big Mo said, referring to Edward in a low, respectful tone.

Captain Blackwell formally presented Aloka, though Mele had already gotten out of the boy his full family history. Neither Mele nor Mo would have dreamed Mercedes should object to her husband bringing her another woman's child to raise. The native couple's curiosity tended in another direction entirely, and when Captain Blackwell took his leave, big Mo made so bold as to ask, "*Ali'i* Blackwell, why do you wear the white man's clothes?"

Blackwell straightened to his full height outside the cramped hut. "I go to see Reverend Bing."

Satisfied with this answer, Mele and Mo stood in their yard watching Mercedes hustle her family back to her house. Mercedes' activity once she arrived home soon exhausted the Hawaiians, and shaking their great heads they retired once more into the hut.

Mercedes ran between cooking shelter and dining table with the breakfast dishes. She should not have left them unattended in the house: her battle with insect life was never ending. Once she had the dishes cleared she found Edward's shoes, sat him in one of the chairs and put them on for him. From her position on the floor Mercedes could see Captain Blackwell pulling up his silk stockings, buttoning the breeches at the knees, and jamming his feet into his buckled shoes.

"How ever did I use to wear these?" he said, lurching out of the bedroom. "Might you have a pair of drawers for Aloka, ma'am?"

Mercedes was relieved Captain Blackwell brought up covering Aloka's nakedness. She had not wanted to broach the subject and give offense. Just the day previous he'd lain shivering in her bedroom from his native adventures, yet she sensed his heart was tied to that world in the same way it had been to the Royal Navy. She brought out Edward's smallest pair of short pants. They hung low on Aloka's hips when Mercedes helped him into them, much as did his father's white breeches. She couldn't find an old shirt of Edward's that did not all but swallow the boy up. Aloka waved his arms about inside the long sleeves, laughing.

"Never mind it, ma'am," Captain Blackwell said. "The short pants will have to do."

He led them over to the Mission house with the boy Keiko running in front, calling out to Mr. and Mrs. Bing.

Mrs. Bing heaved her bulk out of her chair and shook hands with Captain Blackwell, standing with pursed lips as Mercedes presented "Aloka Blackwell, ma'am, Captain Blackwell's son." The boy was so obviously a half-caste, dark skinned and darker haired with his European features, that Mrs. Bing gave Aloka only two fingers to shake. Captain Blackwell grasped the little boy's hand and led him to take the old lady's fingers. After a rather forced exchange of civilities, Captain Blackwell requested a private word with Reverend Bing.

"I would prefer the porch, if you have no objection, sir," Blackwell said. Mr. Bing had opened his study door to show him into the small cramped closet beyond, not unlike the cabin of a sloop.

Mr. Bing bowed and led the way outside. He was sorry for his particularity, though Mr. Bing did not seem to mind it, but he had conceived a dislike for close quarters. After a life lived nearly always out of doors being in a shuttered room made him uneasy and brought to his mind a village unaware, about to be fallen upon by savages. He hoped with all his heart he might overcome this weakness, before he had to live again in a ship's cabin at sea. Yet that might be different, with the wide ocean surrounding him.

His mind revolved on his recent mode of life, standing with Mr. Bing on the porch, thinking of what the people in his village would be about this time of morning. He had to force himself to recollect his business with the European community.

"I must thank you again, Mr. Bing, for the attentions Mrs. Blackwell says you have paid her, and more especially for your kindness to Edward."

Mr. Bing bowed. "Edward is a special child. One doesn't get the chance to instruct such a mind more than once in a lifetime. It is I who should be thanking you, Captain, and I hope you will place your other son in my school when the time comes."

"I am obliged to you, sir, but I shouldn't think we shall be here quite that long." He noted Mr. Bing's sudden, unhappy change of expression, and while the older man was distracted he asked, "I would like to know about the ship *Vostok*, Mr. Bing. Mercedes tells me Edward's first seizure occurred during the Russian ship's visit, and I gather my wife has had to defend herself."

"Ah, yes. Let us sit down," Mr. Bing said. "That was a most distressing time. The *Vostok* had an artist aboard, an estimable young man named Alexandre Selyenin. Together we discovered this talent Edward has for illustration. When the captain of the *Vostok*, a Count Dermidov, cousin to the Czar, he gave us to understand—"

"Are not they all?"

"Indeed, sir. When Count Dermidov apprehended how talented your son is, he became particularly urgent with Mercedes to allow him to carry them both back to Europe in his ship." Mr. Bing paused, while Blackwell stared at him with clenched jaw. "Recollect the Count believed Mercedes a widow woman, sir, and Edward quite unprotected in the world. But he did not reckon with Mercedes. She refused to set foot on the *Vostok* for any reason, and she told Count Dermidov she never could as the wife of a British sea officer, without she knew the state of the world."

"Was it this Dermidov caused her to draw my sword?" Admiration for Mercedes warred in his breast with ire toward the Russian nobleman, who had dared to interfere with his wife and son.

"Count Dermidov overindulged in ardent spirits one evening, the Russians are much given to drink, you understand, sir, and made the unhappy decision to attempt a kidnap. Mercedes knocked the Count down with your sword to make him let go dear Edward. Her servant, Saunders, finished the man off with a blow from a war club." Mr. Bing shook his fist as he finished, unable to conceal a most unchristian glee.

Blackwell liked the old minister better and better. "Killed him?"

"Oh, no, merely knocked him senseless. Colonel Fraser and his men, and the *kanakas*, returned the captain to his ship in a barrow."

"May he feel it still, the goddamn scrub! Forgive me, Mr. Bing. And thank you for the account. Mercedes felt some hesitation in telling it me, so I thought myself justified in asking you what occurred."

"Never was it more truly said of a woman, 'Strength and honor are her clothing,' than of your good wife, Captain Blackwell. They are indeed our better halves, are they not? The civilizing influence in our lives."

Mr. Bing had hardly done rhapsodizing when shrill feminine voices raised in anger reached them. Blackwell and Mr. Bing stared at one another in surprise, and then Mercedes burst out onto the porch holding Edward by one hand and leading Aloka by the other.

"Pardon me, Mr. Bing. I have decided Edward should have a holiday from school since his father is but just arrived. He shall be back in school tomorrow. Good day to you, sir. Captain Blackwell, with your leave."

Mercedes yanked the boys down the Mission house steps and was striding out of the yard as Mr. Bing's first pupils came into it. He exchanged a bewildered glance with Mr. Bing. "I see your students are arriving, so I must not keep you. Give my respects to Mrs. Bing, if you please, and desire her to know I cannot sufficiently express my obligation to you both." Blackwell bowed and hurried after Mercedes.

He caught up to her where she'd stopped a short way down the footpath, Aloka's short pants having fallen off. He came upon them as Mercedes was helping Aloka undress. She straightened with the little trousers in one hand.

"I thought you should like to see the village," she said.

"What's amiss?" Blackwell asked. "Eh?"

Mercedes stood with her cheeks burning, but she would not answer. Edward shifted uneasily, and then piped up. "Mrs. Bing called Aloka a black heathen, and Mama told her to bugger off."

"I didn't." Mercedes protested.

He barked out a laugh. Aloka could not understood any of it, from the white woman in the wood hut with the puckered face to the tension he and Mercedes were enduring. But he understood well enough when they started smiling and laughing and he cried out, "Bugger off!"

"That's not nice language, son." His words were gentle in the native tongue. "And you must now learn the King's English." Drawing Mercedes' hand to rest on his arm, he said, "I should like to see the village."

Saunders was leaning in the doorway of Colonel Fraser's ramshackle house, built of chips salvaged from the dockyard, when Captain Blackwell's island boy trotted by on the main street. "There's the Captain's natural son gone by," she called over her shoulder to Colonel Fraser, who'd walked in early, anticipating dinner. "Oh, and now the Missus and the Captain. Didn't I tell you he would be up and about in a day? Always was a rare old brute, the skipper."

"Doesn't look so out of the common way, to my eye." Colonel Fraser joined Saunders in the doorway, putting a hand on her shoulder, and together they gazed at the retreating backs of Mercedes and Captain Blackwell.

"Captain's a shadow of his former self." Saunders sniffed. "Must've dropped three stone running savage in the bush."

"As much as that? There's Edward. Hark ye little man!" Colonel Fraser called out, then smiled at Saunders. "We must invite them to dine."

"Must we?" Saunders said evenly.

"There's something powerfully odd about that Colonel," Captain Blackwell said as they came away from dining with the shipwright and Saunders.

Mercedes did not wish to talk of the couple. He had announced his intention to spend the afternoon fishing with his sons, and so they were first going home. Saunders, and assuming she shared all with her lover, then Colonel Fraser too, knew of her relations with Kanakoa. There had not been any discussion between them, and Saunders had never let slip by word or deed that she was at all aware. But it was Saunders who always stayed with Edward when Mercedes had her liaisons, and Saunders was no fool.

"Because of his attachment to Saunders?"

There was a note of challenge in her tone, but Captain Blackwell only shook his head and mumbled, "Just something odd. Those side whiskers..."

At home he cast off his clothes almost before he reached the bedroom, and put on the native breechclout with evident relief and satisfaction. Mercedes pulled Edward's shirt over his head and surreptitiously rubbed coconut oil on his shoulders, back, and ears. If there had ever been a moment to say no to Captain Blackwell, this must be it. But she'd never done so, how could she; she'd been first his prisoner, then his mistress, and now an undeserving and disloyal wife.

Edward sensed her confusion. "Must I go in the canoe, Mama?" He had never cared for sun exposure.

Captain Blackwell loomed in the doorway. "Boy ready to go?"

"Yes, you must go," she said in an undertone to Edward. "It will be fun. And you must remember to call your father, Sir." Louder, she said, "Edward, wait outside with Aloka a moment, please."

Aloka tumbled out into the yard and Edward ambled after him, making it only as far as the porch before he sat down.

"James, I'm extremely concerned. Edward cannot swim."

"How is that?"

"I tried to teach him, but he would breathe in water. I think he was astonished at the beauty of the fishes, once he opened his eyes. He panicked so badly the last time I attempted it he nearly drowned us both. Would have done had not the ki...ah, one of the *kanakas* pulled us out."

"You astonish me. But now I am aware of it I shall take extra care of your boy. I shall lash him to me, if it eases your mind. And Aloka, you know, is a regular porpoise."

She was powerless and had to be content with his assurances. She'd imagined Captain Blackwell's other son must be a capital swimmer and sailor, or he would not have survived the voyage in the open canoe. As for Edward, his father could do with him whatever he wished; she had no rights over her son under English law.

She did not accompany them to the landing place to watch the launch of the canoe. Mercedes was intimately familiar with the notion of staying off the quarterdeck, and out of men's affairs; and Kanakoa often had business about the quay. She spent an anxious afternoon at home on her porch, moving the hooks on Captain Blackwell's breeches, and altering Edward's smallest short pants so they would not slip over Aloka's narrow backside. Her thoughts lingered on the idea of another baby. She secretly wished for a girl child, for a companion no one should be interested in taking from her. She tried not to dwell on whether she might already be with child, and the fact that everything she held dearest in life had just left in a native canoe.

A small crowd watched the launch of Ata Gege's sailing canoe. Blackwell put Edward amidships and ran the canoe into the surf, with Aloka hanging on at the bow, pretending to help run her out as he rode the waves. The fierce happiness on his face as he leaped into the canoe was hidden from those on the beach. He took up his paddle, and stroked past the breakers. Aloka, as he'd hoped, was helping Edward anticipate when to duck down and move from one side of the craft to the other as he set the single sail. The boys were soon laughing, pointing out flying fish leaping from the water. Blackwell could think of only one other experience that could give him greater joy.

His intention was to do a little sedate fishing with sennit line and carved shell hooks, and he steered into the first bay that opened to him. He found a protected spot in five fathoms water and threw out the sea anchor. They spent some time baiting the hooks with bits of pork fat, and he helped his sons cast out their lines. He was ready to cast his own, when looking over the side of the canoe Blackwell spotted the man fish swimming below them.

"It's the *ulua*," he said.

Aloka turned an excited face round to him, and Blackwell leaned down and grasped a spear lying on the bottom of the canoe.

"Edward, you must stay in the boat. Do you hear me there?"

"Yes, sir."

"Aloka, watch your brother. Stay in the canoe." Blackwell slipped over the side.

He kicked hard down to where he'd seen the fish slip beneath a ledge of rock, and he began to poke and tease it. He would spear the fish when it emerged.

Edward and Aloka were crouched at the gunwale watching. A cluster of yellow tangs swam over Blackwell and Edward gasped at their bright and elegant flashing bodies. He leaned nearer the water. Aloka made a grab for the back of Edward's trousers as he went over the gunwale, but Edward was the older, heavier boy, and he fell headfirst into the sea.

Blackwell felt the commotion above him and looked up as blond hair dashed below the surface. The surface broke a second time, and a dark haired swimmer caught Edward under the arms and hauled him upward.

Aloka kept Edward afloat, instructing him not to kick and thrash, dear brother, until Blackwell surfaced and caught him up. He heaved his catch into the canoe, and then pushed Edward by the backside into it. Aloka scrambled in, and last Blackwell retrieved the abandoned fishing lines and laid them and his spear in the bottom of the canoe. Grasping both gunwales he heaved himself inboard.

"Not so bad for a first attempt." He patted Edward's shoulder. "We shall just do that a thousand times more, then I daresay you will have mastered it."

Yet he had not counted on his son's particular awkwardness. Though they took a fine catch of fish, by the third time Edward fell out of the canoe he'd taken on so much water Blackwell was obliged to paddle hastily for shore. He got out and held the boy upside down by the ankles. When he'd coughed the water out, Blackwell set Edward on his lap.

"Can we do it again, sir?" Edward gasped. His eyes fairly rolled in his head, but he'd been enchanted with the teeming life glimpsed on the reef.

He smiled at both of them. "Not today, son. We'll go home now, your mother will be anxious for you."

Keiko had accompanied Mercedes to the landing place, and while she stood well back in the trees so as not to appear the worried mother she was, the boy ran up and down the shore watching for sight of Captain Blackwell's canoe. "There he is, rounding Ala Moana," the boy cried out. Mercedes had never heard a more welcome hail.

And she had the pleasure of watching Captain Blackwell bring the canoe ashore, his hair wet and plastered back, the water glistening on his dark, muscled body. The two boys leaped ashore and ran to her, and Edward did not arrive so very tardily behind Aloka. Edward's golden hair stood straight out from his head, she did not need to ask if he'd gone in the water. He struggled to recount his exciting afternoon and the fish he'd seen, at last signalizing he would draw them for her. No sooner had he made this wish known to Aloka, than the smaller boy towed him up the footpath at double speed. They left Captain Blackwell and Keiko to manage their catch.

"You've had a prodigious successful afternoon's fishing," she said.

"These are for you, ma'am." He handed her a snapper and a mullet fish. "Keiko will help me with the rest. I shall see you at home." Captain Blackwell bowed to her and walked away with the boy and the greater part of his catch.

Keiko took several of the fish to Saunders, and the rest to the Mission house, while Blackwell distributed his portion to Mele and Mo and the other neighbors who'd been generous to Mercedes. The natives were not surprised he should do so, and they accepted his gift almost without comment. Blackwell walked home satisfied. The native culture was now as familiar to him as naval etiquette.

In the evening he brought his sons to the bathing place of the *ali'i*. He'd been invited to make use of those particular pools, though he'd not yet met the king who'd extended the courtesy to him. The few whites in town would have found him a peculiar sight, returning from bathing wearing only a breechclout, and carrying a half-sleeping child on each arm.

Mercedes read to the two boys, though they were already three quarters in dreamland. She stopped after a page and half and lay staring at the underside of the roof. She dreaded finding Blackwell laying on the mats again with his back turned to her. She realized she was undeserving but she did in fact want something from him, she wanted it rather badly. If he could not give it her, if Blackwell's affections were engaged elsewhere, she had no right to bid him do anything against his own heart.

Blackwell was sitting on his sea chest in cotton drawstring trousers, to cover his tattooed arse. The last thing Mercedes would want to look on was a reminder of her husband's savagery. He'd never felt shy of her seeing the scars on his body; he'd seen his share of active service; but the native tattoos were something different. He stared at the area of the floor hiding the arsenal that would help him discharge his obligation to Ata Gege and his people. He had now only to deliver the armament Mercedes had been safeguarding all this time. He'd decided to tell her of his plans, his experiences; and hope.

She'd never failed to support him, and he wondered if he were capable of doing the same by her. He would not have been pleased had he returned after an extended absence and found she had borne another man's child. Yet he'd half expected her to accept his natural son, and she'd done so with her usual lack of fuss or pretension. Mercedes was wonderfully compassionate; she also had an ardent temperament, it was what had drawn them together to begin. She liked the physical act of love, and who knew better than he of what some would call the licentious nature of the islanders. Why should he suppose Mercedes had remained chaste in such a place, where everyone believed him dead.

Then again, would he not have heard it from Mrs. Bing had Mercedes' behavior been anything other than virtuous. He was sure of very little, except where Mercedes was concerned. He wanted and needed her urgently, needed to sink into her tenderness and let her caresses push away all the feelings he had, of having done wrong. He wanted to rejoin her in her world, to love her exclusively, and yet he felt with some certainty Mercedes could not want a child with him now. Whether she accepted him back as a husband was the very first consideration.

When she came in he had the stacked *kukui* nut candle lit by the bedside. He did not look at her as she began to undress, staring instead at the trap door over the weapons. "Boys asleep?"

"Yes, and I wonder if you did that a-purpose, wore them out so." She gave him a little knowing smile that he just caught, looking up at her.

"No. But come to think of it, it is a happy notion."

Blackwell stood up and held his hand out to her. She immediately came and took it. What she said next made his heart thud. "I was not quite honest with you last night, James."

He forestalled her. "Can we start where we left off this morning? You were lying in bed, I believe."

He watched her strip off the last of her clothing and lie down on the bed with her back, her rounded bottom and shapely legs exposed to his view. This had ever been a sort of invitation to him. When Mercedes lifted her hair away from her shoulder, clearly it meant she expected to be kissed. He cast himself down in back of her, threw an arm over her to bring her close against him, and spilled kisses on her shoulders and neck.

She reached back to bring him nearer, fingering the cloth of his trousers. "Wouldn't you like to take these off?"

"I thought you would not like...shall I put out the candle?"

"You need not." Mercedes put her lips to his ear and whispered, "I rather like your tattoos, I confess."

A blush crept over his face. He threw himself on his back to remove the trousers. He barely had them off when Mercedes flung herself into his arms. She pressed him back against the bed and kissed him. He clasped her to him and turned her on her back, edging her body beneath his. Floating in the sea early that morning, watching the stars fade, he'd vowed he was done with weakness; he was going to be a father to his sons, a husband to his wife, and a servant to his king.

"Mercy, sweetheart, I've missed you so." He kissed her jaw, her neck, her shoulders, and her breasts. And then he licked her, running his tongue over both her nipples before he took them in his mouth to suck.

Mercedes gasped and tried to pull him against her, atop her. But Blackwell resisted her for a moment, trailing his hand over her stomach and then cupping it over her sex. He could not suppress a groan of satisfaction and desire when his fingers slipped into wet yielding flesh. Mercedes turned her face into his shoulder.

"Oh, Jim."

It seemed an eternity since he'd heard his name, spoken in such a tender voice. Mercedes' use of it halted his headlong rush to consume her flesh. He gave her a serious, considering look as he held her, continued to caress her. She reached up and stroked his face.

"Do you still love me, sweetheart?"

"Yes, James darling, with all my heart. Love me too, very intensely, the way you used to do."

"Won't I just."

He leaned over her and whispered, "I love you," and many other heartfelt things about how lovely she was and how much beloved. He meant every word. He'd had sexual congress during their separation, but he hadn't loved and been loved like this. This woman, his own dear Mercedes, had the ability to soothe his pain, assuage his desires, and his soul.

Mercedes was glad she'd allowed Blackwell to keep the candle lit. She could look on his dear face while she delighted in his words of love and his tender touch. His body was changed and hardened. Even his feet, he pressed her small ones between his own. Those broad arching tattooed bands led the eye to his manhood, and he was by no means reduced in every respect. She felt a little frisson of fright when he loomed over her, his weight atop her not what it once was, looking more virile and more savage than he'd ever done. In the next moment he covered her, and she was twining arms and legs about his still familiar body. Blackwell pressed his flesh into her and her love and longing for him overwhelmed her. She moaned and grasped him by his blackened buttocks.

Edward's blue eyes popped open in the dark room, his heart pounding. He'd never heard such sounds from his mother. Both she and the native man seemed to be in pain. Aloka was awake, by the gleam of his eyes, and stared back at him from across the mat. "Does he place her feet on the rainbow?" Edward whispered. He was by no means so attached to his mother as other boys his age, but neither could he conceive of life without her. She had always been there.

Aloka reached out and patted Edward's cheek. "No." He cocked his ear for a moment to the sounds from the next room, and fastened on the thumping of the bed. "They play the bouncing game, like this morning."

"Should we join them?"

Aloka considered. "Father's a big man. Better we don't."

Edward was satisfied and the boys lay gazing at one another. Shortly there came a savage bellow from the other room. Edward started and grasped Aloka's hand. But all was quiet and then Edward heard his parents talking in normal, low voices. His grip on Aloka's hand loosened and the two boys drifted back to sleep.

Mercedes was both hurt and disappointed. It seemed Blackwell was willing to give Princess Kalani a child, but not her. This did not prevent her from watching him, eyes filled with love and devotion, as he strode naked about her bedchamber. He had been very tender to her; tender and forceful in just the right degrees;

always attentive to her pleasure before reaching for his own. She could never fault him as a lover.

"In my sea chest, James." Mercedes knew he looked for a towel to bring her, to wipe the seed he'd spent outside her body.

Blackwell climbed back in the capacious bed and Mercedes moved to him at once. He put one arm under her, and then leaned over and extinguished the candle with his fingers.

"I fear we will have woke the boys," she said.

"You shall have to control yourself in future." Blackwell squeezed her against him.

His arms slackened from round her, and Mercedes heard the change in his voice. "I must go back."

"Yes, I know, you are still a serving officer. Mr. Verson is past his time, but he must certainly — "

"I did not mean to England. Though of course, eventually, we shall go home. I meant to the village of Ata Gege."

This was the first time she'd heard him name the place where he'd lived his native life. Ata Gege. The name itself had a primitive ring and Blackwell's fierce appearance in the doorway of the Missionary Society church came to her mind. She shuddered, she could not help it, and then she became terribly afraid she'd wounded him.

"I'm sorry, James. I'm cold."

She rose and put on a dressing gown. Blackwell wore a strange look, propped in bed with one arm behind his head, when she sat down on her sea chest and faced him.

"No blame attaches to you, sweetheart, for your reaction. They meant to make a sacrifice of me, for the launching of the war canoes, when Ata Gege first pulled me from the sea. They didn't because I supported them in a battle, a purely defensive action that took place on the way to the home village. After that Ata Gege's people tended me when I was sick, fed me, clothed me, shared their way of life with me, and married me into their royal family. I find I owe them a duty."

Mercedes sat with her head bowed. She was stunned by how rapidly happiness had come and gone. At last she said, "Your duty dictates you must return to live with Ata Gege's people?"

Blackwell was instantly up and sitting beside her. "No, Mercy, sweetheart. Not to live. I was sent to Oahu to bring arms back to the village, so that Ata Gege of Kauai can fight Kamehameha. The people should not have to live under a foreign king. Once that duty is discharged, I shall take you home to England."

Mercedes shivered, she felt cold to her very soul at thought of parting with him again. But there was hope in her heart too, now she knew what she had to contend with. Above every other consideration she loved Blackwell dearly. "Shall Ata Gege ever let you go, once he has his weapons? Will he not want you to stay and train his men?"

"It is understood between us I will go my own way." He added, softly, "You are cold. Let me take you back to bed."

He picked her up in his arms and put her into the bed, drawing the fine cotton sheet over her. He found one of the purser's blankets and tucked it round her, before sliding in beside her.

"Kamehameha is not unlike Bonaparte. Oppressing people who want nothing to do with him."

Mercedes was glad they were in bed together again, their limbs intertwined, for what she had next to tell him. "I don't know about Napoleon, but Kamehameha is rather a friend to King George than otherwise. I am here in Honolulu on his sufferance. Mr. Verson, sir," Mercedes said, beginning to make her report like a sea officer, "entered into agreement with King Kamehameha regarding my stay here in the islands. What conditions the king may have put forward I don't know, but I believe a quantity of gunpowder came ashore from *L'Unite*."

"Cannon, small arms?"

"No, sir. The only weapons brought ashore from *L'Unite* are the ones underneath this house. And poor, ah, that is, Mr. Verson was in an agony whether to put them there. He ordered the arms concealed in casks and brought directly into the house and stowed."

"No one knows you have them?"

"No one save Saunders and I. They were for my protection and for trade, to be used in the last exigency, those were Mr. Verson's words. The whole village believes I have only your cavalry sword." Mercedes paused a moment, rubbing her hand over his smooth chest. "But I beg you will consider. Were you to arm Ata Gege and Mr. Verson had made an agreement in the name of the Crown with Kamehameha, it would be discreditable to everyone. Pray wait, give Mr. Verson a little while longer. He gave me his word, and nothing short of the loss of the ship or his life would prevent him coming. When he does arrive, you shall know best how to proceed."

Blackwell was silent for a time, but he was a man of honor, and of action. "I cannot wait long. If *L'Unite* does not return I shall take a whaler's launch or a cutter, whatever I can find will bear the load, for I make sure the sailing canoe will not, and carry those arms to Ata Gege as I promised."

If it had to be done, Mercedes much preferred Blackwell deliver the weapons with *L'Unite's* lieutenants and a file of marines at his back. Her next stroke was meant to throw confusion onto Blackwell's determined plan. "Did you know Kamehameha has outlawed human sacrifice? The people here and on the other islands he rules use pigs and the *ulua* fish. Might you not try a diplomatic solution?"

He lay unmoving and brooded for so long Mercedes began to feel she had not been so clever by half. But Blackwell returned from having drifted away. His arms closed round her and he turned so they were face to face in the dark.

"You remind me of no one so much as dear Frank, ever the wise councilor."

"Do I?" Mercedes ran her hand up his thigh and pressed it over his cock.

Blackwell sucked in a breath. "Perhaps not so much. I've had enough discussion for one evening, Miss, come." Blackwell was already rubbing her breast gently with his open palm. He ran a hand down her waist and over her bottom, pulling her possessively against him. "My dearest life. I may have been a savage — I probably still am — but will you let me love you anyway?"

Mercedes molded her body against his. "Yes, James, now and forever if you please."

CHAPTER SEVENTEEN

Captain Blackwell sat at breakfast with Aloka on his lap, across from Edward, who occupied the room's only other chair. Aloka was attempting to eat burgoo with a spoon rather than using his two fingers. Mercedes came in and went out with dishes. He'd built a covered walkway from the house to the cooking shelter, so at least she did not get wet in the frequent tropical showers. He was jolted by a distant concussion. He listened for it, and some moments later he heard a second rumble, a familiar sound muffled by distance. A third blast and Blackwell was certain; he put Aloka off his lap and got to his feet.

"We go up country," he said in the native to his sons.

He emerged from the bedroom buckling his sword round his waist and slinging a retractable telescope over his shoulder, and met Mercedes coming in from the yard.

"Do you hear it? Gunfire in the distance, great guns if I am not mistaken. We must take the boys up country. This house is too close to the shore. Higher up I might get a view of the action."

Blackwell and Aloka left Mercedes and Edward far behind in their rush up the slope of Diamond Head. Mercedes' progress was hindered as the sound of the cannonade grew distinct, the natives rushing out as she followed behind Blackwell. "Wahine Blackwell, will the war ships fire on the shore?" Mercedes reassured them if those were British men-of-war, they would most certainly not fire on the shore. But the people, who'd lived through the depredations of traders and explorers alike, concluded among themselves, "*Nānā*, better we go up country with the foreign *ali'i*."

Minutes after Aloka gained the summit of Diamond Head, Blackwell arrived and scanned the sea. Two miles southeastward, and hidden from view by the great hill up which they'd climbed, were two ships. The larger was ship rigged with three masts, the smaller a beautiful sloop of the type called a Baltimore clipper. They were ranged up with the larger, heavier ship on the sloop's quarter, firing her bow chasers, nipping the smaller ship's heels like a shepherd dog.

Blackwell clapped his telescope to his eye. "The French privateer, by God."

"By God!" Aloka cried.

Through his telescope, and as they drew closer with the naked eye, Blackwell watched the chase. The handsome sloop's foremast had carried away, or the heavier ship might never have caught her. Blackwell thoroughly approved the actions of the frigate commander, firing bow chasers only in an attempt to make the other vessel heave to. It would be the pity of the world were *L'Unite* to bring her full broadside to bear and shatter the elegant clipper.

For *L'Unite* she was, Captain Verson commanding. Or so Blackwell hoped and trusted, feeling a great lump in his throat at the noble sight. The British ship had the weather gauge and was content to herd the sloop toward Honolulu bay. At last the sloop spilled her wind and ran down the tri-colored flag. Blackwell could almost hear the order that would have been shouted through the speaking trumpet; "Enemy ship, heave to for His Britannic Majesty's ship *L'Unite* or we shall sink you. " His old command *L'Unite*, familiar in every mast, yard, and backstay, was heaving to likewise and putting a boat in the water to take possession of her prize. Through his glass Blackwell could not make out individuals swarming into the boat. They were merely tiny figures in blue jackets and cocked hats or seaman's ducks and frocks.

In the space of ten minutes he'd been thrown back into the naval world. He watched with keen interest all the movements across the water. He was much concerned whether Mr. Verson continued in command of *L'Unite*, and with the fates of all the ship's people. At the same time Blackwell felt distanced from the

Royal Navy by a greater expanse than now lay between him and *L'Unite*. He became aware Aloka was standing very close to the sheer cliff face, performing the ritual to drive foreigners from the land.

"Stand back from the edge, son," he said, even as he stepped to the boy's side and accompanied him in the conclusion of the ceremony, this last time. "Where are your brother and his Mama?"

"Oh, she's a slow arse."

"Don't be disrespectful, do you hear me there?" He wondered at Aloka's ability to pick up the worst English phrases.

Blackwell remarked for the first time the considerable gathering of natives at his back on the summit of Diamond Head, and trailing down the slope of the mountain in the direction of the village. Several of the *ali'i*, powerful young men and strong women, approached Captain Blackwell. They'd run up the slope of Diamond Head with ease, leaving their enormous elders puffing up the hillside after them.

"It is all over now," he explained. "The larger ship, the English frigate, has taken the French sloop a prize. They will send an English crew aboard her and her people will become prisoners of His Majesty King George."

"The French will be King George's slaves?"

"No, they will be sent home, with the blessing." Seeing incomprehension on their handsome young faces, Blackwell added, "In a few hours time the English will come ashore and they will most certainly wish to trade for provisions. Fish, coconuts, yams, pork. I would not offer them dog — "

"Will they want girls?" asked a bold young woman.

"Of course, *ali'i* Lani, they are not castrates," he said.

The little confabulation broke up amid laughter, and the young people spread out, repeating what the foreign *ali'i*, dressed as an Englishman today, had told them about the war ships. Gay parties of girls, and middle aged men eager for profit, and all of the boys and young men hurried back to the village and the shore to await the mariners. Mercedes was standing beside Blackwell when the last *ali'i* left the hillside.

"Will the English chief wish to meet the *Ali'i Nui*?" the old chief asked.

"I believe he most certainly will."

The old man left, he was the father of the *Ali'i Nui* Kanakoa of Oahu.

"But James," Mercedes said, when they were alone before the magnificent bay and the two noble ships. "You are the English chief."

Blackwell gave her a weak smile. "No longer. Nor have I been this long while, until…until I step aboard that ship, and then it is either command or stay on the beach. Will you be so good as to take the boys home? I need to consider. That is Mr. Verson's command over there, Captain Verson, and I'm not sure I either can or want to take it from him."

"Edward, Aloka, say good bye to your father." In a low tone she said to him, "Pray remember, all that matters to me is you."

He squeezed her hand and drew her to him, and turning his back on the ships and his sons, he kissed her. "When they put a boat off for the shore, I shall see it and be with you directly." He watched Mercedes walk down the slope of Diamond Head, his sons running in front of her with their arms outstretched, pretending they were ships under sail.

He felt as though the last of a precious existence was walking away from him. For a while Blackwell's thoughts ran on a strange scenario in which he set out farther up country, came back to the shore by night, launched the sailing canoe and keeping close to the shore as he'd done on that previous occasion, paddled away out of Honolulu. But he would never willingly leave his family behind, there could be no happiness without them. He watched the operations of the British across the water and contemplated taking upon himself once more the responsibility for over three hundred men.

Other considerations weighed with him; the ease with which he could travel between the islands in that neat sloop, to Hawaii to meet with Kamehameha, and back to Kauai. The duty he owed Ata Gege's people was ever present to his mind. It had been the Royal Navy, and his service in it man and boy, that had given him his strong sense of duty, loyalty, and honor. The Service never had a notion of inspiring such loyalty to a foreign king, to a veritable savage, yet Blackwell couldn't help the way he was made.

By the time the boat pulled away from *L'Unite* heading for shore, with a blue-coated officer seated in the stern, he'd reached a conclusion fortunate for his future career. He decided all men had their worries, and there was no reason he should suppose the young man putting off in the boat did not have his share. He would be less troubled for what had happened to the man he'd known, his former captain.

Edward, Aloka — indeed the whole neighborhood — was impressed by the file of officers, seamen, and marines, making its way directly to Mercedes' door. She ran out to them in the yard. She curtsied, the officers bowed, and all hats came off to her. Mercedes gave Mr. Verson her hand and they exchanged a warm greeting.

"Is it true what we heard at the landing place, Mrs. Blackwell? The Captain lives?" Mr. Verson stood with his cocked hat under his arm. The strong sun revealed a face aged a decade.

"Yes, sir, Captain Verson. He saw your splendid action from up there." Mercedes pointed to Diamond Head. "And he will be with us directly."

A spontaneous cheer went up from the men, McMurtry and Narhilla leading the huzzah. Mercedes wished Captain Blackwell had been there to hear it, and she hoped she did not mislead them. Mr. Verson stood smiling, his head bowed. At last he managed, "Give you joy, Mrs. Blackwell."

She hoped the cheer hadn't wounded Mr. Verson. The young man's face, his now care-lined face, held a mixture of emotions. Studying it, Mercedes thought perhaps the primary one was relief. She gave her hand to the officers. Mr. Montelongo, whom she also kissed on both cheeks, handsome and lively as ever; Mr. Allen, no longer a cherubic boy, but a gangling, spotted youth; and young Mr. Verson, now in midshipman's uniform at nine. Mercedes spoke to the men and took notice of each one, calling Edward and Aloka to shake hands first with the officers. After that she stood Edward in front of McMurtry.

"How do you do, Master Edward, do you remember your old shipmate?"

Something in that ugly visage must have surfaced in Edward's memory, for he answered straight away, "I'm prime, McMurtry," in a fair imitation of his father's speech. "And how do you do? May I present my brother, Aloka Blackwell."

This caused a sensation among the seamen. They were at once delighted with Edward, his blue eyes never looking directly at them, not even upon McMurtry his old nurse, and intrigued by Aloka. The seamen's gazes traveled knowingly between the native boy and Mercedes.

"Will you and your officers step into the house, Captain Verson?" Mercedes said. "I cannot tell you how well the house you built has served me. Us, I meant to say, sir."

Mercedes and Mr. Verson made it as far as the dining table, while the midshipmen stopped on the porch and the seamen ranged themselves outside in the yard. Before she passed into the house with Mr. Verson, Mercedes said to Mr. Montelongo, "Keep an eye on my boys, if you please, Mr. Montelongo. *No se les permite ir al bordello con los marineros.*"

"*Por supuesto que no, Señora,*" replied Mr. Montelongo, making an elegant leg. "Aye, aye, Mrs. Blackwell, and the little boys are to stay in the yard."

After Mr. Verson had refused refreshment, and only grudgingly taken a chair for fear of making her stand, they sat rather awkwardly together. It was not her place to question Mr. Verson, much as she was concerned for *L'Unite's* people. Nor was it Mr. Verson's business to report to her, though she thought he might welcome a chance to unburden his mind before the arrival of his long absent commander.

"I see young Jack is made midshipman," she said at last.

"Oh, yes, ma'am." Mr. Verson blushed. "We lost two of the reefers off San Pedro, coast of California, to a fever, and nineteen hands. And in Monterey, ma'am, we found two Spanish ships of the line and a frigate. They detained us, and I very much feared another Nooktah Sound. But the governor-general arrived and I presented your letter. With your introduction, and Mr. Montelongo's assistance, the Californios came to treat us civil in the end. We confirmed it is war with France, in Callao and Valparaiso it is all the same news."

"I'm sorry for it. For the loss of your men, Captain Verson, and for the outbreak of war, not that young Jack has entered his profession."

Mr. Verson smiled on her with real affection. "I am obliged to you, ma'am. May I know what happened to the Captain?"

"I shall tell you all I know, gladly. Captain Blackwell was picked up out of the sea after he was lost overboard by a tribe of Kauai. A particularly war-like people, I gather. He survived an illness, several battles, and a plan to make him into a sacrifice. He became a man of consequence in the tribe, and came to Honolulu some weeks ago with his, ah, his son Aloka." Mercedes could see the young gentlemen through the open doorway, not even feigning to converse among themselves, straining their ears toward them.

"Captured and released, ma'am?" Mr. Verson said, unable quite to look at her.

"I believe he may have given his parole, sir. You must not expect to find him unchanged."

At this delicate juncture the boy Keiko began to call in from the footpath, "Aunty Mercedes, Aunty Mercedes!"

Mercedes stood and asked the midshipmen to let the boy come in. The word was passed down the yard, and the boy jumped up on the porch.

"The *ali'i* Blackwell sends for his coat and hat!"

"Of course, thank you, Keiko," Mercedes said in the native language. She turned to Mr. Verson. "Might I put McMurtry to work, sir?"

"I wish you would, Mrs. Blackwell." Mr. Verson bowed. "He is yours to command."

Together they went out to McMurtry and the gig's crew, who were standing about beneath the plumeria trees with Captain Blackwell's two sons.

Mercedes explained Captain Blackwell had left home that morning without his jacket and hat, and Aloka was to lead McMurtry to his father with the desired articles. Mercedes dashed inside the bedroom, inordinately pleased she'd taken Captain Blackwell's naval jackets in at the seams. Added to that was a feeling of relief, familiar from after the court martial, that Captain Blackwell should want his uniform again. She met McMurtry outside the bedroom door, telling Aloka in Hawaiian; "This man is your father's trusted man. Bring him to Captain Blackwell, your father wants his clothes."

"Aye, aye, sir," Aloka said, showing off the new phrase he'd learned.

Mercedes handed McMurtry the cocked naval hat and blue and gold-laced jacket. "I hope you can keep up with him." She nodded at Aloka, scurrying up the path.

McMurtry almost wept at sight of Captain Blackwell. The bonny little island lad he'd been chasing behind ran headlong into the Captain's legs, otherwise McMurtry might not have recognized the tall, gaunt figure. McMurtry saluted and helped Captain Blackwell into the blue broadcloth jacket. He could not restrain himself. "Lord, sir, don't the Miss feed you at all?"

Captain Blackwell smiled as he fixed his cocked hat, his number two scraper, on his head. "She wears herself thin putting meals before me. It shall be a great comfort to my mind to have you take over the duty."

"Without loss of a moment, sir."

His steward's reaction was a harbinger of those of his officers and men. Salutes were exchanged. "Give you joy of your escape, sir," was uttered on every side. They looked on him with astonished and tear filled eyes. None more so than Mr. Verson, and after the initial round of greetings Captain Blackwell found it necessary to hurry his first lieutenant into the house.

"I must beg your pardon, sir. I don't have a statement of condition prepared," Mr. Verson said.

"Of course not, Jack. Sit down. You thought you were coming ashore to collect my widow and child, and I am obliged to you for it. None of us believes in miracles."

"One of us did, sir."

"Yes. Indeed." Captain Blackwell glanced through the open door into the back yard, where Mercedes was showing McMurtry her kitchen. He smiled, thinking of his good fortune. "You can just as well tell me *L'Unite's* condition. Begin with today's neat action if you wish, and we can work our way backward to when I was so goddamn unfortunate and lubberly as to fall out the stern windows."

A long conversation of a naval character followed. Wounds to the ship and to her people, a solemn list of the dead, particularly of the young gentlemen. His two lieutenants survived. Mr. Bransford was in command of the prize at present, as a consequence of his ability to speak French, and Mr. Bowles had *L'Unite*. The discussion of the morning's battle alone, with the list of repairs needed to both ships, the number and disposition of prisoners, and all the particulars of the chase and events leading up to the capture of the French privateer, occupied them right through dinner. McMurtry and his mates, with the ingenuity peculiar to seamen, contrived a long table where he, his lady, Captain Verson, and all the young gentlemen, including the two young Misters Blackwell, could be seated.

The gig must have been returned to *L'Unite* for provisions because a regular naval dinner of pease, pork, beer, and biscuits appeared before Captain Blackwell. He realized, as he swallowed the lump of emotion in his throat with the familiar faire, if the gig had sent to *L'Unite* news of his survival would have spread aboard his old command and her prize. The thought somehow unsettled him, and he ate his dinner for a time in silence, hunched over his plate. At last he recollected if he did not speak, naval etiquette forbade everyone else from conversing.

"After dinner, Captain Verson, we will proceed to *L'Unite* and the prize for an inspection." Captain Blackwell nodded round at his table companions. "I suppose I must show them I ain't dead."

"Very well, sir," Mr. Verson said cheerfully. "We shall beat to divisions at five bells."

Before they left the house to go down to the landing place Captain Blackwell took Mr. Verson aside, and with Mercedes standing near, he said, "You must remain in command of *L'Unite* at present, Captain Verson. I will make this clear to the men at divisions. For the moment I shall sleep ashore and assist you with repairs and provisioning. I find myself in the position of emissary between these island nations, and before I come aboard *L'Unite* as her commander I must discharge a commitment to them. I can explain it further, but we had better light along if we want to see a jury foremast on the prize before the end of the day."

Word of his miraculous survival had spread to *L'Unite* and *Intrepide*, the French privateer. Seamen lined the yards and decks of both ships and watched the gig's approach. He was piped aboard *L'Unite* and the moment he set his foot on deck all hats came off and they cheered him three times three. Great, roaring, full-throated huzzahs that reached Mercedes even, on shore, and moved Captain Blackwell deeply. He was not ashamed of the tears streaming down his face when he saluted and shook hands with Mr. Bowles on the quarterdeck. Many of the men were in the same state, from hard-faced Mr. Morrow, the bosun, standing at the break of the quarterdeck, to the ship's surgeon Doctor VanArsdel at the taffrail.

Captain Blackwell spoke to each man on the quarterdeck while the marines stood rigidly at attention looking past him. Doctor VanArsdel was unique in commenting, "You look remarkably well, Captain Blackwell. I should very much like to discover your diet and activities. And how do you find Mrs. Blackwell and young Edward?"

"Very well, I thank you. And I look forward to a conversation, Doctor." Captain Blackwell wanted to add he would like a word about Edward's condition, but the quarterdeck was no place for a private discussion. He signaled to Mr. Verson he was ready to address the men.

"Men of *L'Unite*. Shipmates," Captain Blackwell began, looking out on the scores of expectant faces turned toward him. "Thank you for my splendid welcome. I am further obliged to you for the house you built that has sheltered my wife and son these many days past. I give you joy of your capture of that French privateer. She shall harry our merchant fleet through the Pacific no more. Captain Verson will remain in command of *L'Unite* until I conclude my business ashore and in these islands. But I do assure you this is the last stage of our mission and then it is home and hearth for us."

A hearty huzzah greeted the end of the short speech Captain Blackwell had agreed upon beforehand with Mr. Verson. He stepped back and nodded to Mr. Verson; and they proceeded to divisions. This took a great deal of time as Captain Blackwell stopped and spoke to many of the men individually, men like the ship's carpenter Mr. Bell, who made the bed where he laid his head at night. Eventually the inspection was gone through, concluding with a visit to the French prisoners in the hold. Captain

Blackwell and Mr. Verson addressed the prisoners, jointly and in English, for neither spoke French.

Then the procedure was gone through again in a foreshortened fashion aboard *Intrepide*, where a smiling, tactful Mr. Bransford was in command of a prize crew. He escorted them round the handsome sloop. Their inspection ended in the cabin, where the only French prisoner left aboard, her captain, resided under Marine guard. Lieutenant Hoffinger of the marines was at the cabin door, stooped over in the low between decks. He straightened as well as he could and came to attention. They returned his salute.

"How do you do, Mr. Hoffinger?" Captain Blackwell said.

"Very well, sir. Wish you joy of your survival, sir."

While they exchanged pleasantries the strains of a violin started up in the cabin and the tender notes of a Corelli *adagio* drifted out. Mr. Verson nodded to Mr. Hoffinger, who rapped sharply on the cabin door, and called in, "Captains Blackwell and Verson, and lieutenant Mr. Bransford, to see Captain de Artois." The marine held the door open and the three of them crowded into the cabin.

A small, dark man turned from facing the stern windows to attend to them, lowering the violin from under his chin. "Blackwell, as I live and breath!" the Frenchman cried.

Captain Blackwell stepped forward and shook hands. "How do you do, Captain de Artois?"

"Sadly, not well, as you see. I am a victim of your countrymen's zeal."

"I was Captain de Artois' prisoner once, gentlemen, when I was third of the old *Etrusco* and she went to pieces on the coast of Brittany." Captain Blackwell bowed to Mr. Verson and Mr. Bransford. "In another lifetime."

"It is Baron de Artois, if you please, and I will have you notice I am no longer in the glory line. I am sorry to have deceived you, Mr. Bransford, as to my knowledge of English, but it was charming to hear you speak French. Admit you enjoyed topping it the man of the world before your beef fed companions!"

This was coming it rather too strong in a French prisoner, however exalted in rank. The British mariners stared at Baron de Artois with deep disapproval. The French nobleman was quite oblivious to the dark looks, and even went on as though encouraged, "Yes, in that other lifetime you and I had an understanding, Blackwell."

"Captain Blackwell, if you please, sir." Mr. Verson leaned in toward Baron de Artois, none too politely.

"Oh, Captain Blackwell, I do beg pardon. You see when I knew him, when we were intimate, the Captain was a lieutenant, or perhaps a young gentleman. It was so long ago. We took to one another instantly, I even passed him one of my mistresses."

"Sir, with your permission," Mr. Verson cut in, facing Captain Blackwell, "Mr. Bransford and I will await your pleasure on deck."

Salutes and bows were exchanged and the two young officers withdrew.

Baron de Artois raised his brows, turning to Captain Blackwell. "I hope I did not discompose the young captain, I forget you English are such prudes. Fierce in war, timid in love, n'est-ce pas? Would you care to be seated?"

Captain Blackwell squeezed his long legs beneath the table, and accepted the glass of Rothschild Lafite de Artois's servant offered him. He contemplated the fine wine, the neat cabin with sheet music and books strewn everywhere about, and Baron de Artois's fine suit of clothes. There was captivity, and then there was captivity.

De Artois piped up, "Is it true what is said of you? You ran savage in the bush marrying local princesses and leading a tribe of head-hunters?"

"We're not well enough acquainted for you to question me in that goddamn impertinent manner. All that in France was a long time ago, as you say." Captain Blackwell sounded affronted, but he was more amazed this account of his experiences had reached even a prisoner aboard ship. "But we all must come about, and so I give you warning to hold yourself in readiness to move your quarters ashore."

The Baron's unchanged demeanor left doubt as to how the news affected him; if it were he being put ashore after having lost a beautiful, valuable vessel to the enemy, Captain Blackwell's heart would have been breaking. They conversed civilly for a space,

Baron de Artois offering Captain Blackwell the services of his *chef de cuisine*, truly an artist in the kitchen.

Captain Blackwell stood, stooped over in the low cabin to take his leave. "You are about to go ashore in one of the most gracious lands I have ever known. It is also one of the most savage. Bear that in mind, Baron de Artois. Thank you for my wine." He bowed and left the cabin.

After a few words with Mr. Hoffinger respecting the prisoner, which Baron de Artois could very well hear, Captain Blackwell went on deck. He found Mr. Verson and Mr. Bransford in their shirtsleeves directing the work on the jury foremast. The lieutenants met him in the waist.

"Baron de Artois is an adventurer, gentlemen," he told them. "We can put him ashore temporarily, for our convenience, but we cannot leave him here. A man like de Artois could cause no end of trouble."

"Nothing for it but to clap him up snug in his cabin, and away for Antigua, sir," Mr. Verson said.

Captain Blackwell was never more grateful for the plain good sense of Mr. Verson. It was burdensome but their duty was to carry Baron de Artois, and the more nefarious part of his crew, to the nearest British port in the Caribbean. He bowed to the lieutenant. "Now that is settled. Come to think of it, Baron de Artois is no seaman. It couldn't have been he commanded this ship, taking prizes and playing Old Harry with our merchantmen."

"No, indeed, sir," Mr. Verson said. "It was his premier, a relative of his, Mr. Victor Mont Blanc. He is taken into the gunroom aboard *L'Unite*."

A smile of approval lit Captain Blackwell's face. *L'Unite* knew how to treat an officer and a true seaman. "I should be happy to make his acquaintance. Carry on, gentlemen."

When the work of repair was in hand, Captain Blackwell proposed going ashore to meet with the local chiefs.

"I am prepared to be completely guided by you, sir, in our dealings with the natives," Mr. Verson said. "I...I apprehend you now speak the language."

Captain Blackwell bowed. "In that case, let us discuss the terms between you and Kamehameha before *L'Unite* sailed for the Pacific Northwest."

They repaired back aboard *L'Unite*, where Mr. Verson escorted Captain Blackwell into his cabin. Nothing had been changed in the familiar space, saving the absence of the furniture that had been left with Mercedes. He was a little dazzled by it, the noble sweep of stern windows at one end of the cabin letting in bright tropical sunlight. He had to concentrate as Mr. Verson gave his earnest account.

Finding none of the trade goods the Admiralty had seen fit to send in *L'Unite*; blankets, bolts of cloth, oil lamps, chamber pots; acceptable to Kamehameha and his people in exchange for provisions, and more importantly as a surety for Mercedes' safety ashore, Mr. Verson had traded gunpowder. Kamehameha had been interested only in arms, ammunition, and a promise of protection by the British in case of attack by foreign powers.

"I hardly knew how to act, sir," Mr. Verson said. "I didn't feel myself empowered to make any promises, nor to trade weapons to a foreign king. I traded Kamehameha gunpowder, but I made no promises of British aid, sir, then or in the future. In exchange the king provisioned the ship, granted land next to the Mission for Miss...for Mrs. Blackwell's use, and pledged his protection of her until the return of the ship."

"I am infinitely obliged to you, Jack, on a personal level. Nor do I think you did ill on the professional side under the circumstances. The Navy is a hard service."

"Amen to that, sir." Mr. Verson's posture, his whole being expressed relief in the sanction of another who understood the strains of command.

Mr. Verson repeated his desire to be guided by Captain Blackwell in all matters respecting the Sandwich Islanders. In a subdued tone, Captain Blackwell said, "I do speak the native. What manner of fool would I be had I lived among them so long without I learned."

Irrespective of his language skills, it was a confused meeting took place that afternoon in the palace of the *Ali'i Nui* Kanakoa of Oahu. Captain Blackwell was savvy enough to make a show for the

Ali'i Nui. Besides Mr. Verson they mustered every midshipman not engaged in vital ship's business, scrubbed and polished them, and with a file of marines presented themselves before the chief.

Kanakoa and the other nobles had been at the bathing places with him, they'd seen his tattooed loins and backside, and it was clear they found hard to accept the foreign *ali'i* and the lost English captain as the same man.

"The lieutenant we remember," Kanakoa said. "And it is clear he holds you his chief. What is incredible to us is an English sea captain should have survived among the primitive peoples of the Nā Pali coast of Kauai. They continue in the ways of the ancients."

Captain Blackwell was uncomfortable under Kanakoa's gaze, the king would understand the life he'd led. He made no response; such a space of time went by in silence that the white men present began to stir uneasily. Captain Blackwell willed them to be still.

"Had it been Waimea on the other side of Kauai, it would not astound us, for there rules the brother of one of our own people."

Kanakoa's tone had turned genial, conversational, and Captain Blackwell breathed again.

"Maybe the tribes are related, for I was treated with kindness. I seek the *Ali'i Nui's* support, on behalf of King George of England, provisioning the ship *L'Unite*, and leave to billet prisoners and others ashore."

Captain Blackwell observed Kanakoa as he sat considering the request. He had an intelligent, and a kind face. It was a combination he'd come to expect in the people. Here was a man who had the physical power of a warrior, but who did not lack imagination. A doubtful look settled over Kanakoa's features; Captain Blackwell was aware many of the local nobles believed Mercedes had fallen under the delusive power of a foreign *ali'i*.

The *Ali'i Nui* Kanakoa rose to his full height, his feathered cape falling over massive shoulders, and extended his hand. They shook in European fashion.

Captain Blackwell could feel his men relax round him. Kanakoa grasped him by the forearm in the native fashion, and pulled him close. "It is not for King George. In defiance of any other chief, I call you brother."

Captain Blackwell was pondering the king's odd speech, with Mr. Verson and the party of reefers and marines trailing after him. As they approached the house the delicious scent of broths and sauces reducing over an open cook top overtook them. The wonderful aromas emanated from Mercedes' outdoor kitchen. McMurtry, when he'd heard of the foreign captain's offer of his cook, had pressed the master French chef at the double and brought him ashore.

"Mr. Allen." Captain Blackwell picked out the nearest midshipman, as he and Mr. Verson were stepping inside the house. "Light along to the Mission house. My compliments to Mr. Bing and Mrs. Bing, and would they care to join us for supper." He had constantly to jump from one world view to another. "We have the better part of two hours before we must do the civil, Jack. Let's get to it."

"What's all this then?"

Saunders came upon McMurtry keeping a squinted eye on the Frenchman from the shelter of the covered walkway in Mercedes' backyard.

"Why, there you are at last, mate," McMurtry cried. "I'm surprised you have the stones to show your face round here."

"Don't be an ass, McMurtry. Though no doubt they are better off now the mother cat's tongue is here to lick them."

At that moment Aloka pelted around the side of the house. He and Edward threw themselves at Saunders, leaving no doubt they were all fast friends. McMurtry was silenced even more when Mercedes came into the shelter, and gave Saunders her hand.

"Listen, Missus," Saunders said. "Word is Kamehameha sailed from Hawaii. He will be here in two, three days time."

"Oh, Saunders, come with me. The Captain will want to hear this." Mercedes hurried Saunders before her into the house.

In those three days the men of *L'Unite* worked like fury under his, Captain Verson's, and the diligent lieutenants' constant direction. This was not to say the officers and men did not have liberty, it had been a long ocean voyage from the Spanish Main. A careful schedule had been worked out for the men's refreshment.

Mr. Bowles in particular was in love with shore life in Honolulu. But except when they were granted precious leave, every hour of the seamen's lives was taken up with ship's duties and routine. Blackwell told Mercedes privately, "If we went off watch for a single moment, the ship would be deserted." He was especially keen in guarding his skilled men, the carpenters, coopers, and sailmakers, from becoming the compatriots of Colonel Fraser.

It was a fatiguing three days, during which he saw little of his wife and less of his sons, who were asleep when he at last came home in the evenings. There was no time for fishing or hunting, and he looked back on the life he'd led with sincere regret. He made it his habit now to stop at the bathing place on his way home from seeing the last boat away to the ship. He would arrive in Mercedes' bedroom naked and dripping, holding his naval clothes away from him.

On the night before Kamehameha was due on Oahu, they warped the prize out of Honolulu Bay, and he had the satisfaction of seeing her riding the swell as a tender on *L'Unite's* lee. At no time had he sanctioned bringing the heavier frigate into the Bay, though he could have guided her through the coral reef in safety. He returned home to find Mercedes asleep on the mats with his sons. He knelt beside them and kissed the fair head and the dark one. Mercedes woke and he assisted her to her feet.

He closed the bedroom door. "Are you ready to go aboard *L'Unite*?"

"Yes, James, whenever you say. I've found quite a store of flannel and cambric and worsted wool. I had to look into every corner of Honolulu, but I believe I shall be able to make up three trousers and shirts each for Edward and Aloka, and any number of stockings."

Such were the concerns of a woman, warm clothes for her young ones for the trip round Cape Horn. Blackwell smiled, it gave him great comfort, she gave him great comfort, and he wanted just to hold her.

"I'm sorry for Mr. and Mrs. Bing, to lose Edward will be such a blow," Mercedes said. "She would take him from me if she could."

"Mrs. Bing? She should see a whole different side of you were she to try."

"I haven't the generous heart of the islanders. I couldn't happily give away a child of mine."

Blackwell was holding her then, and they were silent. He wondered if she thought of Aloka too.

"I hope we may be able to take a proper farewell of them," she said.

It was not out of disrespect to the old missionaries that Blackwell didn't answer, he'd already fallen asleep.

The invitation to dine with Kamehameha and bring 'his officer' caused Captain Blackwell some consternation. It was issued in as informal a manner as could be among the royals of the islands, presented to him by one of Kanakoa's cousins in such a way that the singular 'officer' could not be mistaken. He understood he was not to bring an entourage; one officer would be allowed, and perhaps a guard of marines.

He planned to keep to himself Kamehameha's reputation, known throughout the islands. He'd lured chiefs into meetings under the guise of a truce and knocked them on the head: his own relative in one case. Captain Blackwell was in a confusion of spirit determining which of his officers should accompany him to face the great chief. In the end he let the custom of the service decide, he took with him the most junior commissioned officer, Mr. Bowles.

They were escorted into the royal grounds. He and Mr. Bowles, and four Marine privates. Three gawky youths and their corporal, who, Captain Blackwell made no doubt, would be cut down in seconds if Kamehameha chose to give the word. Outside the principle *heiau* they waited until Kamehameha emerged, surrounded by his chiefs on either hand. The king was dressed in scarlet cloth wrapped in many folds round his torso and waist, a feathered mantle, and on his head was an elegant cocked hat with a plume after the French fashion of a previous age.

Captain Blackwell swept off his own blue and gold laced hat and bowed to Kamehameha.

"Captain James Blackwell, of King George's service, or is it Ata Gege's?"

"How do you do, *Ali'i Nui* Kamehameha. It is both. May I present my officer, Mr. Bowles."

Mr. Bowles received a quick glance of the royal eye while he made his bow, and then Kamehameha gestured for Captain Blackwell and his party to follow. Once inside the king's palace, a large wall-less space open to the breezes like all native houses, Kamehameha became less formal. He shrugged off his feathered cloak and hat, and three quarters of his followers melted away. Captain Blackwell noted the apprehensive shifting of his remaining men, while many covert glances were thrown at the king.

Part of this unease seemed to be explained by the entrance of a number of Kamehameha's wives, the king's men backing away with lowered eyes. Kamehameha brought forward Ka'ahumanu, his favored wife, and two of her sisters — also his wives —to be presented to the Europeans. The ladies smiled, displaying gleaming white teeth. They were delighted with him, upon discovering they need not speak the reprehensible pidgin English islanders used to communicate with foreigners. Ka'ahumanu in particular was a sprightly creature, both beautiful and pert. She put Captain Blackwell in mind of Enoch Bourne's spirited young wife Missy.

They did not have the company of the ladies for long as it wanted little time until the dinner hour. Mr. Bowles, who'd been basking in their smiles, was downcast when the ladies retired to their separate meal. There'd been a look of worship on Mr. Bowles' face when Ka'ahumanu was present, despite Captain Blackwell's lecture beforehand about Kamehameha's law making any congress with the fair queen a corporal offense.

Captain Blackwell was seated at Kamehameha's side, along with Kanakoa and several of the royal family. Most of the king's men, including those armed with muskets and blunderbusses, took Mr. Bowles with them to the opposite end of the room for their meal. The marine guard had been made to stop outside the king's dining house.

Few men could make him feel diminutive in size, but Kamehameha definitely did. He was tall, perhaps seven foot, powerfully built and with strong, chiseled features reminiscent of the Romans. Captain Blackwell guessed Kamehameha might be a decade older than he, but underneath his scarlet vestment the king's body was lean and hard in middle age.

From the start of the meal it was apparent the discussion was to be between them alone. "This father of you and me is urging a war between us. Two only, perhaps, you and I, will be slain."

Captain Blackwell knew the king meant Ata Gege, but he chose to be obtuse. "King George desires peace, provisioning, and secure harbor for British vessels in the islands ruled by the *Ali'i Nui* Kamehameha."

"King George, yes, good and distant King George. Are you a relative of his, Captain Blackwell? No. A relative of mine rules at Waimea, a mere boy of twelve. His guard of thirty could be overwhelmed, and the way made clear for Ata Gege to rule all of Kauai." He paused significantly. "Ata Gege must be a friend to King George. Or he would have killed you, eaten of your body. The tale of your sojourn in these islands reached me, Captain Blackwell. And I am moved to tell you both Ata Gege and King George shall reward you. All you should give in exchange is the French vessel, which costs you nothing."

Naked desire shone in Kamehameha's eyes for the prize *Intrepide*. In her he could cross the treacherous seventy-five mile channel between Oahu and Kauai, so difficult to negotiate in canoes and open craft, and fall upon Kauai the way he'd done upon Maui.

"The French vessel is not within my gift, *Ali'i Nui*. *Intrepide* belongs to His Majesty King George of England. She will be sailed three thousand miles to the nearest British port in Antigua, there to be taken into the service or sold for the benefit of the Royal Navy."

"You could command differently. Are you not an *ali'i*?"

"The men of King George would not obey such an order, it would be against their interests. Their loyalty is to England and their own purses."

Kamehameha wore a look of vexed disappointment. He stuffed the last pieces of banana into his mouth and stood up. Captain Blackwell and every other man present, including Kanakoa, immediately rose too.

"How was the crossing, Captain Blackwell? You made it in Ata Gege's sailing canoe."

"Among the worst days I've ever lived at sea, *Ali'i Nui*. I should not like to have to retreat across that channel in case of disappointment and disaster." He knew he was bold in saying so. Yet he stood composed with his hands behind his back, as though waiting to be dismissed or led away to execution.

The remark did not please Kamehameha. He began to stamp up and down the long room, his men backing out of his path. Plainly they feared rather than loved him. The ladies, Kamehameha's wives, chose this inauspicious moment to reappear. Several would have run away again, but for the master's eye falling on them and freezing their retreat.

At last Kamehameha halted, glaring at Captain Blackwell. "You are authorized to propose to the windward chiefs a general peace, allowing things to remain as they are."

His relief was great; he had feared the king's reaction to having his wishes thwarted; and he bowed to Kamehameha. He was about to express his obligation and take a hasty leave, Mr. Bowles having come up behind him, when Ka'ahumanu was heard to whisper, "Such a handsome young man."

Kamehameha whipped round upon Ka'ahumanu and cuffed her so hard she almost lost her feet. Captain Blackwell's heart began to throb. He threw a glance at Mr. Bowles, who was white-faced and stricken. Kamehameha's guard, the royals, and all the other wives present wore similar expressions of grief, for Kamehameha did not stop with the one blow. He grasped Ka'ahumanu to steady her and then struck her another pair of sharp raps.

Kanakoa, holding his old father by the arm, stopped before Captain Blackwell on his way out of the dining house; "Leave now, *ali'i* Blackwell. This moment."

Captain Blackwell paced the main room of the house, hitching at his breeches in the old furious way, while Mr. Bowles stood by with his head bowed and his hat under his arm. They were discussing the embarkation and distribution of the French prisoners when Mercedes came up. She hesitated in the doorway, shooing Edward and Aloka back into the yard with the marines.

"Come in, ma'am, come in," he cried. "We are to go on board *L'Unite* at once, without loss of a minute."

"Yes, sir." Mercedes looked a little doubtful and she made to move past him to her bedroom. He caught her by the arm as she passed, with an urgency that made both Mercedes and Mr. Bowles jump.

"With your leave, sir, I'll send for the gig's crew to take away the dunnage." Mr. Bowles touched his forehead and bolted out.

Captain Blackwell slid his hand to Mercedes' elbow and steered her into her bedroom. "Should you like to know what happened?"

She sat down and folded her hands in her lap, and he thought he saw them shaking. He told her of Kamehameha's lust for *Intrepide*, the king's disappointment when he could not command her, and his offer of a general peace. "In a square rigged vessel Kamehameha could sail from here to Kauai as easy as kiss my hand. There is nothing for it but to put to sea with both ships, proceed to Ata Gege and deliver the arms. I will tell him of the proposed peace, and perhaps he may maintain it with an armed defense."

Mercedes had risen and he watched her collecting items from around the room and packing them into her sea chest.

"And I have not told you of a terrible thing Kamehameha did after giving us a good dinner, when the ladies came back into the dining room. His favorite wife Ka'ahumanu is with him, and she happened to refer to Mr. Bowles as handsome. He struck her, more than once. In front of all of us he beat her, and there wasn't a goddamn thing any of us could do."

Mercedes was frozen with one of her chemises clutched to her breast.

He was on his feet. "Ka'ahumanu is only nineteen, she deserves every kindness and indulgence from the one she calls husband." He leaned down and kissed Mercedes. His urge to protect, to show the tender attention wives deserved overwhelmed him. His blood was up and he must either fight or do the other thing. He pushed her toward the bed, deliberately unmindful of the duty owed to the three hundred men outside his door.

One of those men recalled him to his duty. McMurtry knocked on the door, calling in, "Gig's crew for the dunnage, your honor."

"Hell and death." He stepped away from Mercedes, wiping his mouth.

"Wait, Jim, just a moment."

"Hold hard!" He called, in the direction of the closed door.

"Might you not allow me a farewell supper for my island friends? Barrels and casks would then have to come ashore for the party and they might be returned to *L'Unite* without remark. No one knows I have the arms. No one need know, save your trusted men, they are taken away again. We can make a fair noise and cover the nailing down of the floor, and you might make it known you wish to take the bed to give reason for the workmen and the fuss."

He came near her. "You and those boys are my country now. I would forsake all others for you."

Captain Blackwell flung open the door and strode out into the main room. He sent for his officers; McMurtry and Narhilla from his gig's crew were already by. When they were assembled in the main room he explained what o'clock the evening party was to take place, and elaborated all the events that were to transpire before, during, and after the festivities. He watched the sense of purpose, the determination creep into the faces of Mr. Bowles and the other officers, as they apprehended they were to wipe Kamehameha's eye. Even the bringing arms to a heathen chief did not concern them now, so powerfully had they been set against this man — the huge intimidating scrub — who would beat a woman. He had not sought the moral high ground, it had been handed to him by the jealous, evil temper of the King of Oahu and Hawaii and Maui.

The neighborhood round Mercedes' house could smell a party, and Mele and Mo led the charge, appearing with four great bundles of poi. Other natives arrived with their catch or produce, and a regular field kitchen was set in motion under the direction of the master chef. The chef called orders to the natives he'd recruited for his *sous-chefs*—he would have nothing whatever to do with the English—and cursed them in French. This rather amused the big men and women, and they laughed and called him 'little madman'. By the time the sun went down, and the velvety warm night was closing in, there was a considerable gathering in Mercedes' yard.

Many of the minor nobles and all Mercedes' neighbors were there, Mr. and Mrs. Bing, and the European community represented by Colonel Fraser and the few dockyard men who were not deserters. It would have much resembled the gathering the day of Captain Blackwell's return from the wild but for the presence of the British officers and French prisoners. Four French musicians, the artist of the kitchen, and all *Intrepide's* officers were attending. Captain Blackwell hoped their presence would account for the detachment of marines he meant to maintain ashore, until he had his people safely aboard ship.

Supper was a strange affair with the men and women eating separately in order not to outrage the native sensibility, while the French quartet played music from the Continent. They dined on poi and island fish, shellfish, and vegetables prepared in a bouillabaisse. The dessert consisted of several great quivering figgy dowdies. In the front yard where the men supped, the French chef could be heard from the back loudly disclaiming the puddings.

After supper the party came together again, and before the entertainment started Mercedes brought Edward to Mr. and Mrs. Bing to present them a portrait. No parting gift could have been sweeter to Mrs. Bing. Mercedes had encouraged Edward to draw while studying his reflection in her looking glass. He held the charcoal portrait beside his face and gazed at the missionary couple, both old people exclaiming how remarkably like it was.

"Only look, Mrs. Bing, he has writ very pretty on the back, 'To My Esteemed Friends Mr. and Mrs. Bing, From Your Humble Obedient Servant, Edward James Blackwell'." Mr. Bing beamed proudly at his best pupil.

Edward had been mouthing the words of the inscription his Mama had told him to write as Mr. Bing read them out. He allowed Mrs. Bing to hug and squeeze him, and to cry over him with a good grace. The entertainment began and spared Edward a further mugging.

The carpenter Mr. Bell, two of his mates, and a collection of a dozen or more petty officers and foremast hands formed themselves up as a choir. Without accompaniment or preamble they launched into 'Farewell and adieu to you Fine Spanish Ladies'. All the seamen present roared out the chorus, and inside the house McMurtry and Narhilla pulled up the trap door and began bringing up the arms.

The seamen honored them with three more songs. Their hearty voices produced a pleasant booming effect, which was followed by loud cheers as each song ended. The Englishmen would not venture on those ballads commemorating battles, like the one between *HMS Nymphe* and the French *Cleopatre*, for fear of giving offense to their prisoners with lines like 'We'll take this haughty Frenchman, or force her for to run!' After the fourth ballad the choir bowed and retired. As more torches were lit for the next entertainment the singers melted away into the night. Some went to assist in the removal of the arms, or the disassembly of the captain's grand bed, and others carried away the provisions still remaining ashore.

Into the light cast by the flames of the torches stepped two figures identically dressed in Spanish costumes of pantaloons, doublet, and cape. The two swordsmen bowed to the onlookers and removed their hats. A little gasp went up from the gathering of seated natives, and the Spaniards boldly threw back their cloaks. Each pulled a rapier with a sibilant whoosh from its scabbard. The combatants turned to face one another, bowed, and took up their stances.

"Une, deux, riposte!" an enthusiastic Baron de Artois cried.

"Alto!" A female voice.

Mercedes, one of the *espadachins*, stepped toward her opponent Mr. Montelongo with her palm outstretched. Mr. Montelongo took from her the proffered guard and each fixed ball to sword point. They bowed theatrically to roars of laughter from the audience, and like actors on stage took up their positions.

"Now, if you please, Baron de Artois."

"Une, deux, riposte!"

Mercedes and Mr. Montelongo fought a controlled duel, they'd had just enough time to work out a few attacks and counter-attacks. The natives cheered them equally; they were proud of Mercedes' skill and dash, but they also loved the handsome, graceful young man. The enthusiasm of the crowd spurred Mercedes and Mr. Montelongo to fight with invention and spirit.

But at last Mercedes cried out *"Paz!"* and Mr. Montelongo's sword immediately came down. He stepped over to Mercedes and together they bowed to the audience, to shouted and uproarious approval.

Mr. Montelongo took Mercedes gallantly on his arm, his eyes still blazing, and led her to Captain Blackwell's side. Mercedes met Mrs. Bing's disapproving gaze, and the astonished ones of the two little boys. For his part, Captain Blackwell merely glanced at her as he drew her hand through his arm and then looked away. The sight of her heaving bosom and flushed cheeks could awaken an inconvenient ardor.

The next entertainment quickly assembled at a stern glance from him. Mr. Allen, young Mr. Verson, and two other sturdy young gentlemen, lined up in front of the audience, looking conscious to be following swordplay with dancing. Yet when the hornpipe struck up they began to leap and caper. Huge smiles broke out on the bronzed faces of the natives, and when Colonel Fraser sprang into the dance a roar of approval went up from the crowd. Soon the dancers were joined by British seamen released from their duty, the dockyard mateys, and even one of the French musicians, a seaman from Biscay.

Amid the shouts arising when one of the *kanakas* jumped into the dance, Captain Blackwell slipped away into the house. He found Mr. Verson in the bedroom with a working party, sealing barrels.

"That's the last of it, sir. It gives me the greatest satisfaction, how happy this turned out." Mr. Verson blushed, it being somewhat un-navy like to speak of success.

"Very good, Jack. Give the signal when we are ready to proceed to the boats." He looked around the emptied room; the soft woven mats remained on the floor where he'd once passed a fitful night. Captain Blackwell collected his war club and his staff of office from where they leaned in a corner. "Give the word, Captain Verson." He raised and lowered the two symbols of his native existence in half-conscious salute and returned to the celebration.

Aloka had joined the dance and was leaping up and down in a fair imitation of his Saxon forbearers. Mercedes turned to him, her face lit with a brilliant smile, clapping her hands to the tune. She'd never looked more beautiful, more desirable, a woman whose lively charm irradiated his life.

Mr. Verson signaled and the fiddlers stopped their playing. The dancers collapsed to the ground laughing and holding their sides. Captain Blackwell stepped forward, his staff inclined to call attention.

"Alas, ladies and gentlemen," he spoke the rounded syllables of the native language in his strong quarterdeck voice, "though we would like to stay and dance with you all night, we must be away on the king's business. We go on board our ships tonight, and in the morning we will salute you and proceed to sea. For my part I will never forget the kindness and attention of the people of Honolulu and Oahu to my beloved wife and son. I shall always think of you with gratitude and esteem. And when I return to England I shall make King George aware of the valuable friends he has in the people of Oahu."

Captain Blackwell stepped back and found his officers ranged behind him, looking astonished at his long speech in the native. He did not see Mercedes, and supposed she'd wanted a private moment in her old island home.

"Son, go fetch your Mama," he said to Edward. "Tell her if we do not depart the people will involve us in any number of *hula*."

Mercedes walked through the house one last time, turning round in her bedroom and making sure she left nothing behind. And then he was there with her, from one moment to the next, without a sound. She wondered at it, for he was a big man.

"And so you sail with the foreign *ali'i*?"

"He is my first husband and I have a…a great passion for him."

"You must go at once. You, Mercedes Blackwell, shall always be welcome back. Kamehameha asks for men, and though it would never be by my hand, the king is greatly angered."

Those words made her weak at the knees, and there was no chair at hand to sit in, nothing but some mats upon the floor. Edward walked in and stared at her, opened his mouth to speak, but no words coming out he looked at her in confusion.

"Your father will have sent you to make me come away."

She extended her hand to Kanakoa, who took it in a firm grip. "God bless you. And thank you for being my particular friend. Edward, bid the king goodbye."

"Goodbye, sir, and thank you for being my friend."

It was what he had said to many and many that evening.

"*Aloha*, Edward James Blackwell. Take care of your mother, and your sister."

"Why, sir, you must mean m'brother."

She came out of the house leading Edward by the hand. They had to wade through an interminable crowd, while she and Edward were patted and squeezed and farewells were said. At last they emerged and Captain Blackwell had his party marching to the landing place.

Edward looked back as the outline of the house grew fainter in the diminishing torchlight. He suddenly realized he was not to sleep in his accustomed place, and bursting into tears he stopped dead on the footpath. Captain Blackwell knelt down and picked Edward up almost without breaking stride, and allowed him to blubber all over his gold laced jacket.

"I want to go home." Edward raised his golden head and looked at Captain Blackwell with swimming eyes.

"The ship's your home now, son. You were born there." He could not pat the boy's back because he held the war club and staff in his free hand.

Captain Blackwell's other son ran in the van of the company with the younger midshipmen, who'd all bonded over the hornpipe. Reaching the gig first, the young gentlemen nodded approval of the skipper's dark son for the way he jumped in and settled himself in the gig. Captain Blackwell set his great awkward boy in the stern. McMurtry held the war club and staff, while Captain Blackwell stripped off his jacket, hat, waistcoat and sword. The steward affected poses with the native weapons, causing winks and wry looks among the gig's crew. Captain Blackwell removed his shoes and stockings last and handed them to McMurtry.

"I shall be with you in half a glass," he said in a low tone, bending over to squeeze her hand. "Carry on, Captain Verson."

Captain Blackwell trotted away down the beach to the canoe house to recover the sailing canoe of Ata Gege. Mercedes felt as though something were squeezing her heart, watching him go.

"Don't worry yourself, Missus," Saunders said. "There's still a dozen lobsters ashore and there's us to watch the skipper's back."

"I know it, Saunders, I could always count on you. But still I...Stay away from Kamehameha if you can, he is a violent man. *Que Dios te bendiga.*" Mercedes embraced Saunders and tears came into her eyes. She probably would not see the other woman again this lifetime.

"I never knew a friend until I met you, Mercedes," Saunders whispered, her wild braids pressed against Mercedes' cheek. "Keep well, and if you cannot, come back."

Saunders was a mysterious person to the last and her words gave Mercedes a strange sensation. There was a deal of sniffling from the captain's Christian wife and son in the gig on the pull to *L'Unite*. The heathen half of the family would have disgraced them further had not Mercedes intervened, for when the gig came alongside *L'Unite* Aloka made to spring for her side like a cat.

"You must wait until the captain goes aboard the big ship," Mercedes called to Aloka in Hawaiian. "The men will tell you when it is your turn."

Captain Verson was piped aboard *L'Unite* with the ship's officers and marines lined up to receive him. He turned round once he'd returned the salutes of the quarterdeck to give Mercedes his hand. She managed the ascent without incident, assisted by the seamen, who knuckled their foreheads to her. And then the seamen manning the entry port and those in the gig heaved Edward up like a parcel. No one would have known what a heavy, awkward package he was from their expert handling. Aloka, when given the nod by the mariners, judged the rise perfectly, sprang and caught the manropes, and came up *L'Unite's* side like a right sailor.

"Shore detail dismissed below," Mr. Verson called, when all the ship's boats had returned.

Mercedes took the boys over to the taffrail and she was scanning the surrounding water for Captain Blackwell. Edward stood quietly beside her but Aloka was already dashing about the quarterdeck, excited by the great ship and looking into everything.

She knew she should take the boy below where he wouldn't interfere with ship's business, but she couldn't possibly leave the deck until Captain Blackwell was aboard.

Many other anxious gazes were turned shoreward. The ships were stationed three miles from the bay of Honolulu, a fair distance to paddle in a dead calm, and Captain Blackwell had given orders *L'Unite's* boats were to be taken in, in preparation for standing out to sea.

Captain Blackwell was conscious of his escort out of Honolulu, two war canoes flanking him, each would contain forty men. A mile out they began a chant and lit torches meant to ruin his night vision. The distorted flames and chant reminded Captain Blackwell of the dark side of the civilization that'd just given him a warm farewell. What little hair he had left on his chest and arms stood on end. He was pursued by chanting warriors who could capture him at will, sink his body in the deep off shore waters, never to be recovered. They ran behind him like Cerberus; he wondered what held them off. He stroked steadfastly, never breaking his rhythm, and when the two noble ships were within hail the torches went out and the chanting ended like a bad dream.

"There he is!" Mr. Verson said at last. "Mr. Hoffinger, if you please."

"Boat ahoy!" The marine called. "What boat is that?"

"*L'Unite*," came the response from Captain Blackwell.

"Prepare to receive the Captain aboard," Mr. Verson ordered.

The shrill call of the bosun's pipe made Aloka jump and Mercedes caught him and made him stand by her side. Captain Blackwell came through the entry port, barefoot and bareheaded. He returned salutes and joined Mr. Verson on the quarterdeck and command of *L'Unite* passed back to Captain Blackwell, uneventful, with a minimum of fuss just as they'd planned. Captain Blackwell put on the worn jacket and boots McMurtry brought him, and went to supervise the hoisting in and stowage of Ata Gege's canoe.

"Should you like to see the captain's cabin?" Mercedes said, leading the boys below.

Aloka was delighted with the captain's quarters, from the coach where he was to sleep in a hanging cot, to the two neat sleeping cabins — a large one for his father and a closet for his wife — to the noble great cabin with its row of stern windows which looked out onto a calm sea and a beautiful star filled night sky.

She was somewhat overwhelmed, back in this familiar space. The sleeping quarters had been turned out and cleaned, and if Mr. Verson and young Jack had ever inhabited them it did not show. Everything was Navy style, spotlessly clean and exactly ordered.

On Aloka's fifth or sixth skipping circuit of the apartments, he ran straight into Mercedes' legs. "Where is the bathing place, Ma'am?"

Mercedes was recalled to duty. "Oh, yes, it is time to bathe."

She showed the boys to the quarter gallery, not the one with the toilet, Aloka had loved that, but the one from which the Captain checked the set of the sails. Mercedes had earlier asked McMurtry to put water there for the purpose, and she led the boys into the space to bathe from a bucket. Aloka cried a little when he comprehended he would not be allowed to jump over the side of the great ship into the sea. He hid the fact by splashing water on his face. And he followed her obediently and climbed into the cot with Edward, even patting the other boy's face when Edward began to cry for his bed at home.

The seamen had hung two cots for the Captain's sons in the coach so Mercedes climbed into the unoccupied one to read to the boys. She fell asleep in that most comfortable of beds. When she woke she left two sleeping angels, the dark one and the fair one. She went quietly out into the great cabin where the lamp was lit, swinging in its accustomed place over the armchair. She fetched a book and sat down beneath the light, but she could not concentrate. Memories of the last time she'd been here in this cabin, and of her loss and grief would not allow her to feel easy. Every nerve was straining for the sound of Captain Blackwell's tread, for his loud voice calling out orders.

Blackwell entered his cabin at midnight conscious of having broken a promise to Mercedes. He'd become wholly absorbed in the business of the ship, and was only now reflecting on the rapidity with which he'd stepped back into the life of naval command. He found himself making innumerable decisions and driving matters forward in the old accustomed way. And thanks to Mr. Verson's good management, he sensed a happy ship round him. The men were healthy and willing at their duty though they'd been so long and so far foreign. He shared with them that strongest desire of men of maritime nations everywhere, to put to sea and set a course for home.

But Blackwell's home, as he'd told Edward, was the ship, and perhaps it was having returned to her that gladdened his heart so. A sight to lift it farther was Mercedes asleep in the armchair, still clad in the costume of a Spanish *caballero* of the last century. She looked so delightful in those pantaloons revealing her curves, that Blackwell felt more forcefully all she'd done for him. He knelt in front of her much moved and put his hand on her leg.

Mercedes woke with a start and looked at him, dazed, as though waking from a nightmare. She lunged forward and threw her arms over his shoulders. "Oh, Jim! You are come back."

"I suppose I'm forgiven for leaving you in that uncivil manner earlier. How are the boys? Edward still upset?" Blackwell gave her his hand, and took the lantern from its hook.

"Edward is a creature of habit, you know, he wants what he's used to. But he is much comforted by Aloka. Do you know what Aloka said?"

Blackwell grunted by way of answer. Stretching out at last in his cot he realized he was dead tired.

"'A cot is the best place in the world to sleep,' he said. Truly his father's son." Mercedes lay down beside him, her tone becoming serious. "I don't wish to add to your worries but I am concerned for your sons. The one is so awkward, and the other so eager."

There was a long pause, then he said, "And you calculate if their father, a regular sea dog, can fall overboard so much easier for little boys."

"I never thought any such thing, I — "

"Forgive me, sweetheart. I'm fagged out. It was only my own fears made me say such a deuced awkward thing. But you are not to worry, the entire ship's company will watch over those two little brutes with the greatest attention."

It seemed to him Mercedes feigned satisfaction with his declaration. She was an intelligent woman and Blackwell did not suppose she would delude herself. Here, on the far side of the world, they were a very long distance from safe and secure harbor. A thousand accidents or unforeseen circumstances might befall. He wanted to tell her he was sorry for the upheaval he'd caused yet again in her life. But all that escaped him was a whispered "I love you," before he slept.

CHAPTER EIGHTEEN

When the morning watch was called at four o'clock Captain Blackwell got up and splashed water on his face and rinsed his mouth before going on deck. He was alone in the sleeping cabin, Mercedes would have retired to her own sleeping space hours before. His cot did not really allow two to sleep comfortably. On deck Mr. Wilson, master's mate, had just come on duty. Mr. Verson had formed the same habit of rising for the changing of the watch, and he and Mr. Wilson stood together at the binnacle.

"Good morning, sir."

Captain Blackwell returned their greeting and in another few moments led Mr. Verson away to the taffrail. Mr. Verson had been a captain yesterday, he was now a lieutenant, but by mid-day he would be a captain again aboard the prize *Intrepide*.

"You will wish to take a few followers into the prize. Young Jack, I suppose, Mr. Verson?"

"Thank you, sir. I should like to take Mr. Wilson. If he might be promoted to acting third lieutenant he will do for lieutenant and master. And I would like Mr. Montelongo, if you please. Since he is one of the best of the midshipmen's berth I shall also take Mr. Bennett." Mr. Verson referred to a scrawny, malformed little runt of a midshipman, who had not improved over the course of the long commission. "I hope you will not think me too bold, sir," he said, pulling a paper from his pocket. "I've prepared a list of the men from my watch I'd like to take aboard with me. But as to Jack, he is at an age when he wants to be free of the parental eye, if you take my meaning, sir. He considers himself one of *L'Unite's* mids and I believe he would feel it a come down to transfer to a mere sloop, under his father no less. So I should consider it a great favor were you to allow Jack to remain with *L'Unite*, and a greater service to the boy were you to form him up, sir."

This was a long speech for the taciturn and shy first lieutenant, and Captain Blackwell appreciated how much Mr. Verson had matured with the weight and responsibility of command. He'd noticed a similar change in his other lieutenants. Mr. Bransford and Mr. Bowles were no longer quite the carefree youths they'd once been. Stalwart, hard-driving sea officers had taken the places of the youngsters he'd known. Captain Blackwell was heartily glad Mr. Bransford would be his first, and Mr. Bowles his second lieutenant; he had every confidence in them. He thanked Mr. Verson for his compliment respecting young Jack, and told him he would look over the list of names. "Bring Mr. Wilson to the great cabin after breakfast," he said.

Captain Blackwell checked the set of the sails; having stood off from the island by night *L'Unite* was easing her way south and westward back to Honolulu. He ran below where Mercedes was just opening the door of her sleeping cabin. In the half light she looked a vision, with her hair round her shoulders and in her flowing dressing gown. He put his arm quickly round her slender waist and steered her into his sleeping cabin, determined to show her how much he appreciated her forbearance, her kind acceptance of him and his wild native son. Truly she had loved him through better and worse.

At breakfast Captain Blackwell was the recipient of devoted glances as Mercedes handed him his coffee and the marmalade pot. He'd come very close to fulfilling his promise of making her scream with pleasure. But Mercedes was a gentlewoman, and she would never so far forget herself in a ship with three hundred men. The recollection of their intimacy made Captain Blackwell smile.

They were finishing the breakfast of toast, eggs, bacon, dolphin fish fillets, yams, marmalade and coffee from California, when the sentry at the door announced Mr. Verson and Mr. Wilson. Mercedes rose and excused herself; she would present the boys formally to Doctor VanArsdel. Captain Blackwell stood and watched her curtsy to his officers, their bows in return. He couldn't help the smug feeling that crept over him when he noted Mercedes moved a little stiff, as though she'd had a hard ride. As soon as the door closed behind his family and the midshipman he'd summoned to escort them, all semblance of pleasure left his face, and he turned to business with his officers.

Captain Blackwell invited his family and the doctor, if he were at leisure, to the quarterdeck for the twenty-one gun salute to King Kamehameha and Oahu. Excitement permeated the deck, with the slow match burning in tubs — the ship had beat to quarters — for although it was blank firing the L'Unites loved to work the great guns. Mercedes barely had time to kneel down beside Edward and Aloka and explain, "There is going to be a great noise when they salute Kamehameha."

The firing of twenty-one eighteen pounder cannons makes a tremendous impressive din. Before the last booming round Edward was attempting to hide his whole head in Mercedes' skirt, while Aloka was letting out war whoops in time with the discharges.

The reverberations and smoke had barely died away when Aloka pulled free of Mercedes and shot over to Captain Blackwell.

"That was the thunder of the gods!" he cried, in his shrill childish voice. "Father, I want to go up there." He pointed at the rigging of the mast nearest them.

"I'll take you up another time, son," Captain Blackwell said, not unkindly in the native. "Now the ship must get underway."

He turned his back on Aloka, who darted away to Mercedes' side. Just as quickly the boy dashed off again, this time springing for the mizzen shrouds. He caught hold and clung on. Captain Blackwell heard the shocked gasps behind him, and turned to see Aloka climbing up the ratlines, while the seamen stationed in the mizzen and his officers looked on with stricken faces.

Captain Blackwell ran across the deck and scrambled up the shrouds behind Aloka. For a large man he moved remarkably swift. He called to Aloka to hold hard. The little boy froze at the tone of his voice and let go his handholds when he was told. Captain Blackwell tucked Aloka under his arm like a bundle of sailcloth and descended to the deck.

"Bosun!" Captain Blackwell called. "Mr. Morrow, in my cabin, and bring your cane."

He marched across the quarterdeck with Aloka under his arm, looking neither right nor left, and plunged below directly to his sleeping cabin. The burly bosun, Mr. Morrow, fetched his rattan cane and followed, a grim expression set on his face.

"Seize him up," Captain Blackwell said, extending his hand for the cane.

Mr. Morrow lifted Aloka and laid him gently across the cannon in the captain's sleeping compartment, and held the boys two little hands. "Bear up now, youngster," Mr. Morrow advised him. Captain Blackwell caught up a length of flannel Mercedes had left atop his sea chest, and doubling it many times he draped the cloth over Aloka's legs and buttocks. Then he proceeded to lay on a half dozen hearty whacks with the cane, all the while haranguing Aloka in English and the native how he must never disobey orders. He was on a ship of the King's Navy.

On deck they heard the whistling thwacks followed by Aloka's startled, frightened cries.

At his station, McMurtry shook his head. "Poor little heathen's catching it something fierce."

The captain's other son was not faring well either. Edward at this point was sobbing into Mercedes' skirt. All became quiet below decks and they could only just hear the captain's stern voice, before he came springing back up on deck.

"Very well, Mr. Bowles," Captain Blackwell said. "Lower away the gig and Captain Verson and his crew may part company. Then we shall set a course for the island of Kauai."

Mr. Morrow, leading a tear stained Aloka by the hand, came up from below decks and released his little prisoner. Aloka shot over to Mercedes and buried his face in her skirt, on the side opposite Edward. Mercedes caressed his black hair. She was sorry he was obliged to learn so soon about the harsh environment he'd landed in, but not that he should be taught how to survive in it. She wanted to pick him up and comfort him against her bosom, but she guessed, being so much like Captain Blackwell, Aloka would make light of his hurt. In fact, he had already stopped sniffling and begun to peek round at Edward. They made a game of hiding their faces in her skirt, until Aloka lunged over and grabbed Edward by the head.

"Three cheers for Captain Verson!" Mr. Morrow called out.

The first lieutenant with his prize crew went over the side.

Edward and Aloka joined in the hearty huzzah, and when the gig was away to *Intrepide*, young Jack Verson strolled over to them.

"How do you do, Mr. Verson?" Mercedes said.

"Very well, ma'am, I thank you. It is not really parting, you know. At least not until we set a course for the Horn." With these brave words and a bow to Mercedes, Jack gave his attention to Edward and Aloka. The boys had moved to the taffrail to watch the boat ply between the ships. He won them over completely by admiring the welts on the back of Aloka's legs. "M'father, that is Captain Verson, always threatened to lay me across the gun in the captain's cabin, but I cannot recollect he ever did. And to think it is but your first day aboard, and already you've been beat by the Captain himself."

The beating endeared Aloka, and by association Edward, to the entire ship's company. It did more than a direct order to watch over them could have done. Mr. Morrow never mentioned the flannel cloth, nor the tears standing in his commander's eyes as he wielded the cane, and the incident was very much blown up by the seamen. They called Aloka a 'rare plucked 'un', and afterwards began to refer to the boys as master Al and master Ed.

In the chops of the channel between Oahu and Kauai later that day, young Mr. Verson and Mr. Allen were standing on the larboard gangway looking out at the deep blue white capped water of the channel. Then they turned and gazed below in to the waist where the native sailing canoe was secured with the ship's boats.

"To think the Captain crossed this deuced ugly stretch in an open boat." Mr. Allen shook his head.

"That's seamanship, Charles," Jack Verson replied.

Captain Blackwell felt the voyage to Kauai went uncommon fast, his mind naturally turning on the long days of paddle and sail going to Oahu. By sunset the two ships had reached the designated point off the island where they were to alter course and gain sea room for the night. Earlier, following the noon observation, Captain Blackwell had begun work on his written orders to his officers. Tomorrow he meant to take the sailing canoe into the settlement of Ata Gege.

An hour before supper Captain Blackwell, alone in the great cabin, called out, "McMurtry, pass the word for the signal midshipman. My compliments to Mrs. Blackwell, and would she return to the cabin."

Mercedes and the midshipman arrived together. Captain Blackwell dispatched the young man to create a message desiring Captain Verson to dine aboard *L'Unite*.

"I will have my officers in to supper, with your leave, and afterwards give them my orders and explain what's to take place. I desire you would write out a fair copy beforehand." His words were formal as he handed Mercedes his orders, he wanted her to know the content of them. He tried to soften what she was to read there by taking her in his arms briefly, before she sat down to write.

Supper was a somewhat constrained affair. The officers were preoccupied with the mission that lay ahead, but they found an amiable topic of conversation in Edward's remarkable skill with the signal flags. Edward had looked over Mr. Hogan's shoulder at the signal book while he was laying out the flags, and suggested a pattern before the midshipman had fairly begun. "'Captain repair aboard. Supper.'" Neat as you please," Mr. Verson said. Edward had been allowed to study the signal book, and even to sort the flags, which he took great delight in. Naturally he did so under the supervision of the signal midshipman.

Mercedes sat at one end of the table with Edward and Aloka either side of her, and Captain Blackwell presided at the head, surrounded by his officers in order of rank. The supper concluded with toasts, confusion to the enemy and the like. Until Mr. Bowles offered up, "To the incomparable women of these Great South Sea isles," following which, with a conscious look, Captain Blackwell stood and proposed the King. The party moved into the great cabin then, so that the coach could be converted from a dining room back to a bed place for Edward and Aloka. The little boys went out to the quarter gallery to wash and then Mercedes led them back through the great cabin. They made their bows and said goodnight to their father and the ship's officers.

Seamen are nothing if not efficient and the long table and chairs and every dish, platter, and speck of food had been whisked away when Mercedes returned to the coach with Edward and Aloka. Two cots were slung side by side, one lower than the other, and a lantern swayed from a hook set in the beam over their heads. Mercedes helped the boys into their cot and lying down in the lower one she began reading to them. The clink of the men's glasses in the next apartment, and the rumble of their deep voices formed a background to that night's story. Captain Blackwell raised a strong authoritative voice to address his officers, and Mercedes fell silent. She and the Captain's sons lay in the coach listening.

Captain Blackwell finished speaking and paused while glasses were refilled. "Gentlemen. What I've described is the case where everything runs according to my plan. We all know the best plans may go awry, particularly where a naturally warlike people are concerned. If I do not make the signal after the fourth day it is most likely I've been knocked on the head. You are therefore to wait seven days only, by which time if I have not signaled, you are to proceed to England by way of Antigua." He went on in a harsher tone, "Let us put aside delicacy, gentlemen. It is likely the natives will send, if things turn ugly, part of me to the ship — a thigh bone, or both thigh bones — within a very few days. They do this out of respect for me, and indeed, for you as my white tribesmen." He looked pointedly at them, each in turn. "Then you will know, and you are to follow your orders. Put to sea, return to England. Under no circumstances is anyone to be left behind here in the islands, and there will be no retaliation, no rescue of any kind attempted. I will not have one of those goddamn actions where an entire village is bombarded for the sake of one white officer."

A long, shocked silence followed his speech.

In the coach, Edward whispered, "Mama, you crying?"

Blackwell had no doubt what Mercedes saw when she emerged from the coach after his officers had taken their leave was a worn middle-aged man. Sprawled in his armchair Blackwell certainly felt old and wondered if he had the vitality for the next day's activities. Once there would have been no question, but of late he'd begun to worry over the future, and about the short, short duration of life. Mercedes came and sat on the sofa beside his chair, tucking her feet beneath her. One of her finest qualities was she never felt the need for idle chatter.

It was he broke their companionable silence. "You will have heard my orders to my officers?" Mercedes nodded. Her tear stained face tugged at his heart, for she hardly ever cried. "It's not as bad as all that, sweetheart. I had to paint a black picture for my officers, prepare them for the worst. The truth is these things rarely happen when one is prepared for them. It is far more often the random chance knocks us on the head."

"Had not you better rest, James darling?"

Blackwell heard both devotion and anguish in her voice. "I have one or two things I need to discuss with you first."

Mercedes put her hand over his on the arm of the chair. "Let's go to bed and discuss them."

Blackwell heaved himself out of his chair, convinced now he must look a true graybeard, and followed her into the sleeping cabin. She lay down with her cheek against his chest, he kissed the top of her head and felt tears moisten his skin. She must feel she was spending her last night in her husband's arms.

She sniffed. "Forgive me, Jim. What is it you needed to discuss?"

"I expect to return to you in a day or two, sweetheart, and I hope you believe I will do everything in my power to do that. But if I were to give up the number of my mess, I desire you will go to England in this ship. You need not settle there, but I should like you to go to my brother. Frank will assist you to exercise the Power of Attorney, and he can help you buy a little establishment for yourself and Edward. Between you and m'brother I'm sure you will know how to educate Edward, so I need say nothing on that head."

"You know I will do whatever you wish."

"Thank you, sweetheart, that makes me easier. When I was with the people before I used to think of you in Gibraltar with Frank, and it gave me great comfort. The other matter I wished to speak of is Aloka. I can take him with me tomorrow, return him to his people, if you wish. I never meant to foist my bastard on you."

Mercedes drew away to look him in the eye. Blackwell had not put out the dark lantern, partly so he would not fall asleep just yet, but also because he liked to look on his wife's naked body. He did not dare tell her what Kalani had said about the *Ali'i Kāne* murdering Aloka when they grew older. "There can be only one king." That would have decided Mercedes' tender heart, and Blackwell wanted to hear what her true feelings were toward his native son.

"Your father once asked me how I should like raising a brat of yours by another woman."

Blackwell grimaced. "What did you say?"

"Why, at the time, that I could not say. Now I can." She reached out and touched his face. "I would never keep a child from his mother, were such a thing to happen to me it would break my heart. But if Aloka's mother gave him you, she must have had her reasons. I should very much like...if the choice were mine I should like him to stay with us. Edward loves him, and Aloka is good for him. It's a selfish reason I know, but I love him too. He is a dear, bright boy, and you must have been very like at that age. He looks just like you."

Her voice sounded wistful, and she lay down again next to him so he could not see her face.

"Bless you, sweetheart. I want to raise the boy but I would not offend you for the world, were your ideas different. I believe I will make a seaman of him." He even began to compose in his head the letter he would leave, so in the event the next days' business went awry his wishes regarding what captains Aloka should be placed with would be known.

His son as a naval officer was agreeable to contemplate: Blackwell wished he might be there to guide Aloka's steps. Happy reflections on his child's future only deepened his sense of what was due Mercedes. After the love and devotion she'd lavished on him and his, he owed her a deal more honesty than he'd given her. It was his fear of Mercedes changing toward him that had kept him silent. He wanted a zealous reception from her, not a dutiful one.

He sighed and rubbed his hand over his face. "Kalani is fond of the boy but she is not a mother in the way you are, tending the child everyday. Aloka was looked after by her ladies in waiting. A combination of omens made Kalani the *kuhina nui*, she is considered almost sacred. Her primary duty to the people is to produce heirs. The year I was taken captive, her brother died. He was the husband she truly loved. The rest of us she views as no more than duty."

"It will not be dangerous for you to appear in the village without Aloka?"

"Oh no, for it is much as it is in England. A father has all rights and power over his children. I could strangle the boy with my own hands, if I chose." He'd contemplated whether he could do just that when they spent that first night in Oahu, rather than let Aloka fall captive to a hostile tribe. "But what I fear...I should not like you to think...do you remember our talk of prize bulls in the coach to Hampshire? I never felt so much like one until I was brought to bed Kalani, as though there would be consequences were I not to please. I hope, sweetheart, with all my heart that is not how I made you feel all that time ago."

Mercedes was silent, he felt exposed, and then she said, "I've always been happy with you, darling. As I've told you before, but perhaps you'd like to hear it again? You are the best lover a woman could wish for."

Blackwell gently shifted their positions, he propped himself on his elbow and leaned over her. He'd told her, essentially, he'd been a man-whore, and still she wanted him. "It is very ungentleman-like in me, but I want you to know. Kalani outweighs me by four stone, over my previous bulk. I'm not in love, nor is she."

"You are saying it does not signify because your heart was not engaged?"

"Wives are not like children, you cannot love them equal."

His voice had grown hoarse and he kissed her. Mercedes returned his kisses and ran her hands over him in a way that made Blackwell think, after all, he was not so tired. He was on the point of boarding when Mercedes said, "Do you think we should, you —"

"Hush, Miss," Blackwell murmured, moving his lips over hers.

The door to the sleeping cabin opened and Blackwell jerked his head round, trying to shield Mercedes with his body at the same time. Edward stood there like an apparition in his white nightshirt, an expression in his blue eyes even more vague than the usual.

"Son!" He cried, jumping up and advancing on the boy. "You better learn to knock before you enter my bedchamber."

"Jim, I think he's asleep." Mercedes sat up, clutching the bedclothes round her.

He scooped up Edward and sat down on his sea chest with a blanket thrown over his lap and his son on his knee. In another moment the boy would have seen him punishing his mother most severely, a sight Blackwell should not have liked to inflict on his already disturbed son. In the dark passage just outside the sleeping cabin Aloka was hopping from foot to foot.

"Aloka, sweetheart, come in," Mercedes called.

She rose at once, put on her dressing gown, and went out into the passage and gathered the boy in her arms. Aloka had a good view of her, but naked adults were nothing to him. He let his head fall on her shoulder as she brought him in, and clung to her for just a moment when she put him down in the cot.

"What are you doing here?" Edward said, suddenly looking up at Blackwell.

"What are you doing here, sir," Mercedes said.

"Yes, what she said."

"You wandered in your sleep, son."

Mercedes went out to use the quarter-gallery and when she returned all three of them were in the captain's cot. She squeezed in; it was not like the luxury of space in the big bed on the island.

"Ain't we cozy," Blackwell said.

"Mama cried," Edward offered.

"Yes, I know. And I've just been telling these young gentlemen, ma'am, I will be gone for a day or two and they are to mind you. Or when I return I shall know the reason why."

"And stripe our arses," Aloka cried, removing the cover from over his head for a moment.

Blackwell put his hand atop the lump beneath the bedclothes. "Yes, what he said."

Captain Blackwell was compelled to leave his family early next morning when Ata Gege's sailing canoe was hoisted out, along with the blue cutter. He had insisted the cutter's crew must be all volunteer, and that the men be made aware of the danger involved in pulling into the territory of a hostile people. There was no shortage of hands willing to accompany him, both McMurtry and Narhilla were allowed into the cutter's crew. By mid morning it had been fully provisioned and manned, and the cutter and the sailing canoe were towing behind *Intrepide*. From the prize's quarterdeck Captain Blackwell raised his hat in salute to *L'Unite*. His wife and sons waved back at him from her decks, and *Intrepide* filled away for Kauai.

"Here is where you take up your position, Mr. Bowles." Captain Blackwell maneuvered the sailing canoe effortlessly alongside the cutter. They'd reached the last dog leg but one before Ata Gege's lagoon, setting out buoys as they came. "The arms and tools, if you please."

An oiled canvas sack with several muskets, a flask of powder and a bag of balls, two cutlasses, and a valuable collection of axes, adzes, and carpenter's tools were passed across to him in the sailing canoe. He'd left his naval jacket and cocked hat aboard *Intrepide*, so that he wore only shirt and breeches — no stockings or shoes — improper dress for a naval commander entering foreign territory. Captain Blackwell was returning to Ata Gege in much the same state as when they'd first met.

"I shall look forward to seeing you soon, Mr. Bowles," he said in parting. "Remember they have lookouts on those cliffs I pointed out to you, they likely watch us now. Keep to your orders. Carry on, Mr. Bowles."

"Aye, aye, sir," Mr. Bowles said. "Good luck, sir."

"Good luck, sir," echoed the crew of the blue cutter, watching Captain Blackwell's strong stroke as he paddled away. Less than half a glass later the cutter's crew heard whooping shouts and ululations coming from the direction of the lagoon.

"Let us hope they are celebrating," Mr. Bowles said.

They strained but heard no more, and then the time came to make their way out of the channel. Mr. Bowles gave the order that turned the cutter round and she set her course for *Intrepide*; every man in her imagining, according to taste, they left behind a scene of orgy or cannibalism with their commander as the central actor.

For the last hundred and more yards he'd been accompanied by many of the men of Ata Gege's village, who had leapt into the water to meet the canoe and help Blackwell run it ashore. They were shouting and clapping Blackwell and one another on the shoulders. Among them were Mahin, grinning like a lunatic, and most of Ata Gege's lieutenants. Blackwell felt a glow of brotherhood with these men. Their whoops and cries were in celebration and welcome, and they practically carried him and his canvas sack up the beach. At the edge of a sheltering ring of trees near the landing place they halted before Ata Gege.

Having received warning from his lookouts, Ata Gege was turned out in a red skirt of *tapa* cloth, a cape of yellow feathers, and a helmet that close fit his head, adorned with a singular row of feathers running from nape to crown.

"Captain James Blackwell, fourth husband of Kalani, you are returned." Ata Gege nearly smiled at him. "Did the white man's god of cargo prosper your voyage?"

Blackwell bowed, standing the correct distance and direction away from the king, his staff with its few yellow feathers inclined at the appropriate angle of subservient salute. "*Ali'i Nui* Ata Gege, I return to you and the people with a portion of the cargo that is held for you on my ship." Blackwell stooped and opened the canvas bag and passed it to Manu. "These arms and tools are the gifts of King George of England to Ata Gege of Kauai."

"We saw the big ship. This ship is yours?" Ata Gege and his men were peering into the sack. The canoe builders among the lieutenants could hardly contain their joy over the iron tools.

"The ship belongs to King George of England," Blackwell said. "I must return to the king his property, in the same way I have brought back the sailing canoe of the *ali'i nui*. In the ship are a greater number of weapons King George intends for sovereigns who will give reception, aid, and provisioning to His Majesty's ships. I bear also a message from Kamehameha."

At mention of this name the people drew back. Kamehameha was a far more present and real force in their lives than distant King George, with all his largesse. Ata Gege's stoical, lined face betrayed no concern and his strong stance did not alter. He changed the subject. "Show us the use of the white man's weapons. Later there will be feasting, for the priest deems this night propitious for the Princess to conceive a son."

Blackwell knew then what sort of day and night lay in front of him, just as he anticipated at some point Ata Gege would send for him. When the chief was ready to discuss the tidings from those other kings.

Mercedes had lived through more miserable days, but for sustained anxiety she'd not experienced the equal of the time Captain Blackwell was out of the ship. Mr. Bransford cleared the weather side of the quarterdeck, the captain's domain, whenever Mercedes wished to take the air. She paced, just as Captain Blackwell would have done, looking out on the immensity of empty sea, on beautiful blue water and white capped waves. It gave her a strange foreboding, the limitless Pacific, though she knew it was far from empty. Away on the horizon were low purple clouds beneath which lay the Sandwich Islands.

At every turn in her circuit between the number one starboard quarterdeck carronade and the main mast, Mercedes gazed at the clouds marking where Captain Blackwell was waging war — or love. Had she been like other naval wives Mercedes would have waited at home, knowing nothing of this high pitch of strain that she and everyone else aboard *L'Unite* was enduring. Her husband would have appeared after a three or five year absence, and then she might have learned something of his travails. Or she might have been called upon by the Admiralty, and sent an official letter informing her of her grief. She felt defiant, she was not like other naval wives. Nor would she have traded her present circumstances, however uncomfortable, for those of another, waiting secure and ignorant at home.

Yet she could not deny there was a deal to be said for ignorance. She might have begged Captain Blackwell to forego duty and honor, and never return to Ata Gege and Kalani. But she'd no right to ask anything of him, and even if she had, she probably would not have been aboard with him to begin were she a conventional kind of wife. He'd made all easy if he chose to stay with Kalani, his orders were very specific in their direction not to interfere with the natives. She knew Captain Blackwell was beholden to Ata Gege's people, she sensed in the tie something akin to his patriotism for England.

She would not think too deeply on the possibility he might not return, preferring to credit her feelings, which spoke of his preference and attachment to her. She was thrilled when he'd said she was now his country, and she'd let him go. Honor, duty: Mercedes understood these were the driving principles of Captain Blackwell's life. What ruled her thoughts, as she paced in the brilliant sunshine, was how much was also due love, and family.

It had been borne in upon her in a very short time after Captain Blackwell's departure that she should not be able to keep a proper eye on Aloka. As Edward's Mama, she saw to it that he should not be left alone with any but a trusted few. She immediately arranged a schedule for her son; lessons with the midshipmen in the morning and taking the air on deck, and the afternoons to be spent assisting Mr. St. James with his botanical collections, and drawing specimens. Edward was perfectly happy and so too, in his animal way, was Aloka. He was presently larking about the tops with the off duty boys and young gentlemen. His antics had already given Mercedes more than one fearful start.

He was a little rogue and she could not contain him. Aloka ran where he would, climbing up and crawling down all round the ship, skipping about her upper decks and scooting through the lower. What Captain Blackwell would make of it she could not tell. Mercedes harbored no resentment toward the boy, she'd already grown to love him, and she would certainly not like to have to admit to Captain Blackwell she'd failed to protect him. The truth of the matter was she could not prevent Aloka dashing about, squeezing himself into odd places, and perhaps falling in with company unfit for a little boy. Captain's son or not, damage could easily be done to a young sensibility.

Far from feeling any ill will for him, Mercedes knew a mother's desire to shield Aloka. If she were to entertain jealousy, it would be directed toward the distant island princess. Fidelity was not something she set her heart upon, knowing exactly what she merited in that direction, but she had a Spaniard's pride and did not like the notion of sharing her husband. It was bad enough he belonged more to the Royal Navy than to her. There were no kind feelings in her for the woman who'd made a prince of James Blackwell.

By late afternoon, after exhaustive drill, sixteen of Ata Gege's warriors could load, aim, fire, and clean a musket without making a complete cock of it. Blackwell was satisfied, having trained twenty percent of the chief's men to some proficiency in the use of the firearms. These men could then help along their less able brothers. Four of Ata Gege's men comprehended the firearm completely, as though raised to it, and they were already decent marksmen. Blackwell would entrust to these men extra flints for the locks, and a pot of oil to keep the guns in firing order. In Kauai's damp climate it would require constant care for the firearms to be any use at all. When the flints and oil ran out, Blackwell trusted to the ingenuity he'd seen so often displayed by the natives.

At twilight he went with other men of his rank to one of the bathing places. Floating for a time on his back in the sweet water of the pool, looking up at the darkening sky, a profound sense of peace invaded his whole being. It was not reasonable he should feel so; he was by no means sure this mission would run according to his wishes; yet he had not been long among Ata Gege's people before that familiar sense of belonging returned to him. He had high social status as one of the princess's husbands, but here he was not the great man in the same way he was as captain of a Royal Navy ship. He would still be expected to share the flint in his pocket with whomsoever should ask. And many of Ata Gege's men remembered pushing his fat arse up the mountain passes during the first days of his captivity.

They were hallooing to his not quite so ample and now tattooed arse to show a leg. His companions were eager for the feast and the evening's festivities. Torches were being lit, drums were starting to beat, and the smell of roasted meat wafted their way. Blackwell walked to the village among the warriors, holding on to the remnants of tranquility he'd felt in those blessed moments in the bathing pool.

He'd lost most of that sense of peace, that ease of mind, by the time the drums had beat to a crescendo and the priest called out the final blessing. The ceremony had included a series of dances, of *hula*, in praise of Kalani's fertility and his loins. Kalani lay in the specially constructed house before them, waiting for him to conceive a son with her. The odious priest led Blackwell inside. He issued a last benediction and then retreated, lowering the *tapa* cloth door for the royal couple's privacy.

Outside the prayers and chants of the community reached a fevered pitch. After this they would be free to dance and laugh and steal away two by two into the soft night. The men and women surrounding the house were therefore naturally enthusiastic. Blackwell approached Kalani on hands and knees as the prayers ended. This was according to a strict protocol; all Kalani's husbands and sons were obliged to pay her homage. It entered Blackwell's mind how his officers might view such a thing.

"And Aloka? Does he live?"

"Aloka is alive and well on my ship, Princess."

"Shall you make him a chief among the white men?"

"I will set his feet on the path."

Princess Kalani rolled her great naked body on the mats so that she looked Blackwell in the eye. "Who cares for my son?"

"My white wife, and my men look after his well being."

Kalani pursed her lips. "You will beat her if she thwarts Aloka in any way?"

He pictured dear little Mercedes holding Aloka in her arms the evening before. "I should certainly beat her, were she ever to deserve it."

His voice trembled thinking of the woman he loved, and all he stood to lose. For the first time in his life he was having serious doubts about his amatory abilities, and just then Kalani bade him come closer.

"Closer, Captain James Blackwell." Kalani had assumed the position, her mountainous backside facing him. She looked at him over her shoulder with hands and knees planted apart on the mats.

Blackwell edged up against her until his loins, his un-tumescent loins, were pressed against her backside. She motioned him closer still and Blackwell leaned over her, so Kalani could speak in his ear.

"The priest is a fool," she said. "He has misread the signs."

Blackwell was not sure what he had expected to hear from her, but these words surprised him. He would like to have said those were his sentiments exactly, but he held his peace.

"The child will be a girl, not a boy as he foretells. You will not be here to claim her, and she shall have to be killed. I could not bear it."

He was heartily glad he hadn't spoken. "I find...I am in no condition to serve you, my Princess. We are alone, and if you will be so good as not to speak of it my failure shall remain between us alone."

He took his leave of Kalani as gracefully as he could, with many assurances respecting her son that he'd been unprepared to give her at their last parting.

One of the chief's courtiers approached him outside the conception house, and Blackwell was hopeful he would be led to a sleeping place. He heaved a great sigh, feeling his years; he was nearing forty.

The courtier opened his mouth to speak just as the first shouts reached them from the direction of shore and the dancing ground. The blowing of the conch, the warning note cut suddenly short galvanized them. The other man would have run immediately for the scene of action but Blackwell stopped him. "The Princess!"

They rounded up two others, mere adolescent boys, and found a litter on which they loaded Kalani. Blackwell and the chief's courtier stationed themselves diagonally and together with the boys they hustled Kalani up country. Sweating and puffing they set her down amid her ladies in waiting, and the other women, children, and old people that had managed to reach the comparative safety of the lower slopes of the mountain.

Blackwell leaned over gasping, and when he caught his breath he ordered the boys to stay and guard the ladies. He and the courtier headed back to the lagoon. None of the calm, contained excitement he usually experienced before battle was with him, what he felt most was dread. The buoys he and his men had left marking the passage to Ata Gege's village earlier caused him a sick, inward anguish.

Once they reached the village and could hear the war cries and screams of battle, Blackwell did not detain the chief's courtier. The man ran for his weapons and the scene of fighting. Blackwell hurried to his old hut on the lagoon, which Ata Gege had allowed no one else to occupy, where the muskets had been stowed.

Blackwell burst into the shelter and found the youngest of the four native marksmen kneeling on the floor with two of the guns before him. The young man's hands were trembling, and Blackwell went immediately to help him load.

"Who are they?" His voice at least sounded calm.

"Manu says it is the brothers of the men of Purea."

The village they'd raided for the sacrifices to launch Ata Gege's canoes. Blackwell led the way round the huts and through a grove of trees toward the dancing ground where the fighting was hot. He couldn't approach directly from shore where they might be seen. Running forward through the dark canopy of trees, Blackwell stumbled over something upon the ground. He fell awkwardly, trying to raise his musket above the sand. He rolled to a crouched position, peering at what had tripped him up, and recoiled. One spear hurled through two bodies, a couple killed in the act of copulation. Tiaba's lovely young face was turned toward him, her eyes were closed, and her mouth open in a mask of ecstasy.

He let out an anguished cry and leapt to his feet. Tiaba's partner was of course his native brother. Mahin, who'd killed this way in their raid. His heart pounding he rushed forward, raising the musket to his shoulder, entering the clearing of the dancing ground.

Men stood toe to toe flailing with clubs, short-shafted spears, and fists, countering and bludgeoning with shields. A warrior was beating the body of one of the native marksmen flat with alternating blows from his war club and the musket taken from the dead man. Blackwell took aim at the enemy warrior and fired.

"Reload for me, son." He passed his musket to the youth beside him, afraid the young warrior would kill their own amid the shifting bodies.

He clenched his jaw and discharged the freshly loaded gun. Blackwell was no marksman, but he did not confuse Ata Gege's men and the raiders. His memory for faces was remarkable, he knew every man jack in the home village, and he was outraged. He fired coldly, methodically. Mahin's laughing cheerful face swam before his mind's eye, he loved him like his own younger brother, Francis.

It was the noise of the musket that drove the raiders off more than the damage he was doing with it. The attackers gathered on the shore bordering the dancing ground and retreated for their canoes. In the melee they'd still detached men to round up the survivors among the captives. Blackwell put up the muzzle of the gun when he spotted the boy and his mother that had ridden with him as they were hurried into one of the raiding canoes. They were already out of range of musket shot.

Neither Ata Gege nor his lieutenants gave the word for pursuit, they had been taken by surprise in their celebrations and been badly mauled. It was some time before they recovered sufficiently to carry the wounded to the village and the dead to funeral pyres. Almost as soon as the fighting ceased, Blackwell handed his musket to Puno, the young warrior beside him.

He retreated into the grove of trees, back to Mahin and Tiaba. He yanked the spear from their bodies with a great heave and an averted face, and then tried to put them in some kind of order. Blackwell had seen the deaths of many and many a friend and brother officer in his service career, yet his face crumpled as he tied the breechclout around Mahin's loins. Poor little Tiaba's skirt was nowhere to be found. He cut and tore a wide strip from the bottom of his shirt and tied the cloth around her slender waist. He found he could not bear Mahin's weight alone, and went to fetch Puno to assist him.

The same courtier approached him at the funeral pyres. The soot and ash on Blackwell's face was tracked with tears. At sight of the man Blackwell was struck by an even stronger desire than earlier to be led to a sleeping place, he yearned for oblivion. Yet soon he realized, whatever his selfish wishes, there was to be no comfortable lie down for him. The courtier turned onto the steep path leading to the king's *heiau.*

He found Ata Gege in prayer to his gods and his ancestors. Blackwell could not join him and add to his sins. He became absorbed in thoughts of the recriminations that might rain down, in a sense of loss, and wondering if he was not after all to see his family again. He stood by the *heiau* as he'd often done on the quarterdeck, legs planted apart, hands clasped behind his back, with a weight of care on his shoulders. Brute nature took over, and he was asleep on his feet. Ata Gege woke him with a hand on his shoulder at dawn.

In that eerie first light Blackwell looked into Ata Gege's face. He'd known many hard cases among the foremast jacks and in the officer corps, but no features he'd ever seen matched those of Ata Gege. On his face was recorded a life of struggle and constant warfare. The chief's fierce appearance fit ill with the gentleness of his next words.

"Would you come back to the land Captain James Blackwell? There will always be *ahupua`a* waiting for Aloka and for you."

The generosity of the statement startled him, the fatherly, and grandfatherly warmth of it, when he'd been expecting something quite different. He recalled his distant quarrel with his own father, over dominance and control, and how the opinion of important men had once meant so much to him. He looked on this savage man, who was capable of schooling them all in wisdom, never judging. "It would be an honor to do so, were it the will of King George and the gods we should return."

"There is your noble ship."

Ata Gege refrained from the ritual forestalling the evil of foreigners; a great forbearance, considering the disaster of the previous night. He was sure it made him the lesser man yet Blackwell was glad Ata Gege knew nothing of the nobler ship Mr. Bransford was keeping just over the horizon, with her precious cargo. Not even a hint of *L'Unite's* topsails could be seen in the distance.

"What says Kamehameha?" Ata Gege's voice, suddenly changed, broke in on his thoughts.

"Kamehameha proposes a general peace, and will allow the windward chiefs to remain as they are."

"Do you believe in this peace?"

Blackwell looked into that scarred, lined, tattooed, and, he now realized, quite old face. "No."

"What then, Captain James Blackwell?"

Blackwell drew a breath and answered Ata Gege as truthfully as he might have done any admiral. "I believe you will have to fight Kamehameha, but not him alone. You will have to contend with them all, for they are all out there. The Americans, the French, the Russians, and the British too, other ships will come. Your men will have the same weapons if you will permit me to land the gifts of King George."

Ata Gege went straight at the matter. "Do all white men worship the god of cargo?"

"For the most part, yes. If you can meet them from a position of strength, you can play upon what it is they want." As soon as he'd said the words, Blackwell recognized Ata Gege's strategy, from the time he'd fished him out of the sea. He glanced consciously at the chief.

Ata Gege was facing west, lit from behind by the sun's advancing rays. The now ancient looking face was inscrutable. "It has been a hard battle, you lost a brother. Send the signal to your men. I accept of the English king's gifts. I will embrace King George."

Among many other signs of battle, the smell of burning flesh hung in the air from the funeral fires. Blackwell supervised an orderly transfer of the crates filled with muskets, the sacks with tools, and edged weapons. He stood between King George's men and those of Ata Gege at the landing place, remorse the strongest feeling of his heart for what had and was taking place in the meeting of his two worlds. A line of sailors stretched from the blue cutter, changing mid way along to a string of natives running in a file up the beach. Still more of the people were busy heating stones, carrying broad leaves to the oven, and preparing their enemies' bodies for cooking. Blackwell wished this were not taking place under his men's eyes, but the oven was adjacent to the dancing ground and the landing place. When the transfer was nearing completion Mr. Bowles came to him, taking up the sea officer's characteristic stance, hands behind his back.

"King Kamehameha's men, sir?" He asked as a headless body was carried past them.

Every day fighting goes on between tribes, and they cut off each other's heads. Blackwell had no desire to enlighten Mr. Bowles.

"I don't believe they could have made it here quite so fast," was all he would allow. "When the last of it reaches the end of the beach, back the men into the cutter, Mr. Bowles. No shouts, no calling out. Handsomely does it."

"Aye, aye, sir. Speaking of handsome, sir, those are uncommon fetching ladies."

Blackwell glanced at the women, and he would have liked to join in Mr. Bowles' attempt to relieve the tension, but he was obliged to inform him, "Those are slave women, Mr. Bowles. And unless you wish them to think you a low vulgar sod, you'd best turn away your glims."

Mr. Bowles hustled the crew into the boat when the last bundle of tools reached the fringes of the beach, cuffing a man himself who dared to say a word to that same group of women. The blue cutter stood out in the lagoon as specified in Captain Blackwell's orders, thrice the distance a man could throw a long spear. The men watched their commander, clad only in the native loincloth, taking part in a ceremony of departure.

Captain Blackwell stood before the native chief. Ata Gege was arrayed in a feathered cape and helmet, with a wooden staff fringed with yellow feathers. Behind the native chief stretched an impressive number of people, in spite of the night's losses; warriors, women, children, the elders. There was much bowing and loud speech, and then the appearance of an enormously fat woman seemed to signalize an end of the leave taking.

"Ain't she regal," Mr. Allen breathed.

Captain Blackwell sank down on hands and knees in the sand before her. A collective gasp went up from the cutter's crew, in spite of Kalani's royal bearing. But in the next instant Captain Blackwell was springing to his feet and striding into the water, clutching his staff of office and swimming awkwardly with it to the blue cutter.

The first evening Blackwell was back aboard ship, Mercedes hurried the boys into bed even before hammocks were piped down. She went to the captain's sleeping cabin and found him sprawled naked on his cot, enjoying a breeze from the open scuttle. He pulled a sheet over his loins, still fancying she could not like his tattoos. She lay down beside him in her dressing gown, gratitude swelling her heart.

He immediately put his arms around her and kissed the top of her head. Blackwell held her tightly, silent for a long space of time. He made no move toward intimacy; he did not open her dressing gown, or turn to her to begin the caresses and kisses. She needed him, and wanted to replace with the concentration of passion his abstracted stare into the middle distance. He seemed morbidly drawn to contemplate something unbearable.

Mercedes raised herself on his chest and Blackwell pulled his gaze back from staring into his personal abyss. Once he focused on her his expression turned tender, and he raised a hand to stroke her hair and the curve of her face.

"I should like to be a man, just for a while."

He was taken aback and then a smile transformed his face. "Should you, indeed? I always had a notion you would make a capital officer, was you a man." His face clouded. "Then again, you are ill suited to knock your fellow man on the head, for buggery, and all the evil men get up to."

"Will you not allow virtue in a man?"

"Oh, aye, we have our generous, kindly impulses, but in the main — "

"It is those impulses separate men from beasts." She was straddling him now, she'd pushed back the bedclothes and been fondling him. "I only meant I should like to know what it is to be a man sensually, to penetrate."

He would never ignore a direct challenge and he reared up and clasped her. She moved over him with a desire made fiercer by her sense of having nearly lost him. She drew him into her body wishing to counter his pain with her passion, to shield him with her tenderness and love. They had never been more united, so perfectly attuned, even as they had a lively struggle for dominance. Both had been the consorts of royalty, but it was him, only him she wanted to love, honor, and obey. At one point she said, "Shall you miss being a Prince?"

"Not when I have you to make me feel like a King, sweetheart."

The recollection of his reception back aboard *L'Unite* made Captain Blackwell smile as he looked out on the spectacle of molten lava flowing into the sea. *L'Unite* was passing the largest island with its active volcano. Most of the ship's crew was on deck viewing the eruption. How many times in life did one see such a sight? It was not to be missed. Captain Blackwell's sons were standing at the taffrail together, and Mercedes was beside him.

His sons had been on deck the afternoon he returned to *L'Unite*, they'd cheered him as he was piped aboard, along with his officers and crew. And then he'd run down to Mercedes. She'd met him with the same look of joy on her face that he'd seen in the church on Oahu, when he came back to her from the dead.

Their reunion that evening had been sweet indeed; she did not see him as soiled and worn, and that gave him strength. It was necessary he should put away memories of life among Ata Gege's people, in the same way he locked away recollections of battle. What he'd done was between him and his god. There was nothing to be gained by worry over whether he could not now call himself a gentleman. He was returning to England with news of the victory in Valparaiso preceding him, a wealth of new information, and maps his gifted son would improve on their journey homeward. In truth, the opinion of those men at the Admiralty and in Whitehall had never weighed less with him. Savage, civilized, gentleman, heathen: what mattered, Captain Blackwell chose to believe, because it gave him some peace, was what was in a man's heart.

He'd kept the staff of office, though he'd left the rest behind, as the visible sign of Aloka's birthright: his standing and rank.

"Would you ever consent to come back here to live, Mercedes?"

She looked at him, her gaze dark and frank. "Do you wish for another wife? Perhaps two, pretty and young."

"You do know today is my birth-day?" He teased her, for in fact she'd given him a capital supper to mark the occasion, from which they'd all just come up on deck to drink their coffee and view the splendid volcano. "And what an ancient I grow. You shall always be younger than me, Mercedes, and always first in my affections."

He told her of Ata Gege's offer to Aloka and himself; an offer of land was not to be taken lightly; and they spoke of the graciousness of the islands and the people.

At last Mercedes said, "If you wish to return here someday, you should know by now I would follow you to the ends of the earth. I already have."

Captain Blackwell caught her hand and squeezed it. There was a troubled anxious look in her eyes, and he wondered if he had not spoken plainly enough about that multiple wives nonsense. "What is it, sweetheart?"

"I want to ask you for something, though it is your birthday."

"Please do."

She stepped closer to him, holding his hand still, and Captain Blackwell leaned down to hear her.

"I want another child, Jim."

He was taken aback, and his head jerked up. Rather than look at one another he and Mercedes both stared at Edward and Aloka, spitting simultaneously over the taffrail into the great South Sea. He admired courage and spirit, and for Mercedes to be willing to have another child with him took a deal of both. The dangers were obvious; she must have had the same thought as they gazed together at Edward, clutching young Mr. Verson's arm for support.

He felt his heart glow with love and hope. "You should know by now I will give you anything it is in my power to give." He took both her hands in one of his. "So you thought now I'm turned forty you'd better get on with it, eh Miss?"

"When we go below, sir, what a dessert we shall have."

Captain Blackwell did something he'd never done on the quarterdeck before. He turned his back on his officers, his sons at the taffrail, his ship and her crew, and on the brilliant, savage islands, and kissed Mercedes before the limitless ocean.

ABOUT THE AUTHOR

A long time resident of California, V.E. Ulett is an avid reader as well as writer of historical fiction.

Proud to be an Old Salt Press author, V.E. is also a member of the National Books Critics Circle and an active member and reviewer for the Historical Novel Society.

Blackwell's Adventures continue in Volume III:

As the long war in Europe comes to its conclusion, so does Captain Blackwell's career in the Royal Navy in BLACKWELLS' HOMECOMING, a story of the dangers and rewards of desire.

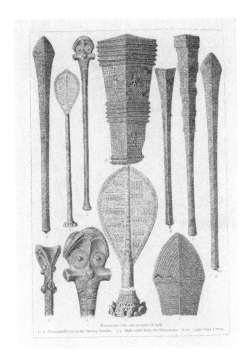

About Old Salt Press

Old Salt Press is an independent press catering to those who love books about ships and the sea. We are an association of writers working together to produce the very best of nautical and maritime fiction and non-fiction. We invite you to join us as we go down to the sea in books.

More Great Reading from Old Salt Press

A fifth Wiki Coffin mystery

"Combining historical and nautical accuracy with a fast paced mystery thriller has produced a marvelous book which is highly recommended." — David Hayes, Historic Naval Fiction

The Beckoning Ice finds the U. S. Exploring Expedition off Cape Horn, a grim outpost made still more threatening by the report of a corpse on a drifting iceberg, closely followed by a gruesome death on board. Was it suicide, or a particularly brutal murder? Wiki investigates, only to find himself fighting desperately for his own life.

ISBN 978-0-9922588-3-2

Thrilling yarn
from the last days of the square-riggers

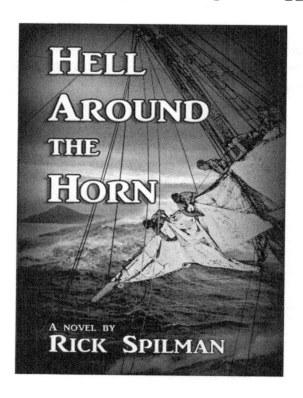

In 1905, a young ship's captain and his family set sail on the windjammer, Lady Rebecca, from Cardiff, Wales with a cargo of coal bound for Chile, by way of Cape Horn. Before they reach the Southern Ocean, the cargo catches fire, the mate threatens mutiny and one of the crew may be going mad. The greatest challenge, however, will prove to be surviving the vicious westerly winds and mountainous seas of the worst Cape Horn winter in memory. Told from the perspective of the Captain, his wife, a first year apprentice and an American sailor before the mast, *Hell Around the Horn* is a story of survival and the human spirit in the last days of the great age of sail.

ISBN 978-0-9882360-1-1

Another gripping saga from the author of the Fighting Sail series

Turn a Blind Eye

Alaric Bond

author of the Fighting Sail series

Newly appointed to the local revenue cutter, Commander Griffin is determined to make his mark, and defeat a major gang of smugglers. But the country is still at war with France and it is an unequal struggle; can he depend on support from the local community, or are they yet another enemy for him to fight? With dramatic action on land and at sea, *Turn a Blind Eye* exposes the private war against the treasury with gripping fact and fascinating detail.

ISBN 978-0-9882360-3-5

CPSIA information can be obtained at www.ICGtesting.com
Printed in the USA
LVOW05s1016150115

422947LV00022B/352/P